ALSO BY SCOTT WESTERFELD

SCOTT WESTERFELD

MARGO LANAGAN · DEBORAH BIANCOTTI

SIMON&SCHUSTER

First published in Great Britain in 2018 by Simon & Schuster UK Ltd
A CBS COMPANY

First published in the USA in 2018 by Simon Pulse, an imprint of
Simon & Schuster Children's Division, New York.

1 3 5 7 9 10 8 6 4 2

Simon & Schuster UK Ltd
1st Floor, 222 Gray's Inn Road
London WC1X 8HB

www.simonandschuster.co.uk
www.simonandschuster.com.au
www.simonandschuster.co.in

Simon & Schuster Australia, Sydney
Simon & Schuster India, New Delhi

A CIP catalogue record for this book
is available from the British Library.

PB ISBN 978-1-4711-2493-8
eBook ISBN 978-1-4711-2494-5

Printed and bound by CPI Group (UK) Ltd, Croydon, CR0 4YY

MIX
Paper from
responsible sources
FSC® C020471

Simon & Schuster UK Ltd are committed to sourcing paper
that is made from wood grown in sustainable forests and support the Forest
Stewardship Council, the leading international forest certification organisation.
Our books displaying the FSC logo are printed on FSC certified paper.

Every power tells a story.

CHAPTER 1
BELLWETHER

"DON'T GO ANYWHERE WITHOUT ME," THE GUARD said with a laugh.

The door slammed shut, and Nate was alone in the interrogation room.

He sat at the long table, staring at his shackled wrists—the handcuffs looked different today. The metal was a duller shade of gray than usual, the mechanism of the lock a little larger. A scrap of change in the dark ocean of sameness that was Dungeness Federal Prison.

Nate sighed, let his hands clank back to the table.

The worst part of interrogations was waiting for them to start.

They always brought him here an hour early and left him alone. To his right was a one-way mirror, but he felt no attention leaking through. Not yet. There was no clock, only the patterns of the prison stretching away in all directions, a shimmering grid of desperation felt through concrete walls.

This place was designed to enforce isolation. No common eating area, and the inmates were brought to the exercise yard one at a time. At first Nate was worried the Feds had learned how to starve crowd powers, until his lawyer told him that all supermax prisons were built this way.

They couldn't let Nataniel Saldana form a gang, after all. He was a terrorist as well as a murderer.

Some days it felt like his power was withering. His tendrils of charisma, hungry for obedience, attention, worship, spent the long days seeking a crowd to influence, and found nothing but stray wisps of connection. The supermax was a concrete-and-steel labyrinth, with locked doors at every junction, but in Nate's mind it was a desert dotted with broken souls.

Sometimes he thought about flipping his power inside out and disappearing completely. But the cameras would still see him. The doors would still be secured by implacable machines. Even in this locked room, Nate was shackled to the table.

Invisibility was no escape. He needed to charm his way out, in front of a judge and jury. Which meant keeping the Bellwether half of his power alive.

He waited, hoping for an audience.

At last the door opened.

"You always look so happy to see us," Special Agent Solon said.

Nate couldn't hide his relief—his interrogators had brought a crowd. Along with Agents Solon and Murphy, a new guy took up a position in the corner, a briefcase at his side. And of course Nate's defense lawyer was always here.

As a bonus, four people were filing in on the other side of the one-way mirror. Nine altogether. More than enough to hit the Curve—a rainstorm on thirsty ground.

He felt his power rejoice.

But what did all these extra people mean? Had something happened out in the real world?

Had his friends been caught?

"I'd like to start by pointing out—again—that my client is a minor, and that no parent is present." Nate's lawyer, Cynthia Rodriguez, always led with this.

Agent Solon offered his usual response, pulling a card from his wallet to read an excerpt from the Crowd Psychosis Emergency Act. "May detain such persons, regardless of age . . ."

Nate ignored the familiar words, flexing his hungry power, coaxing in the shafts of attention beaming through the one-way mirror. With his hands chained to the long metal table, he couldn't use his usual gestures. But those had all been empty bombast, he realized now, suited to the politician he could no longer be. He'd learned to adapt, guiding the crowd with twitches of his fingers, the movements of his eyes.

He drew the room's energy to himself, waiting for whatever the interrogators' questions would reveal.

Solon finally got to it. "Let's talk about the Faraday shielding in your nightclub."

"What about it?" Nate said mildly. "It's for blocking radio waves."

The new guy at the end of the table smiled at this, but didn't say anything. He was older, Asian, with a lively gray mane that made Nate think of Albert Einstein on a good-hair day.

"In a nightclub?" Solon said. "Why did you feel that was necessary?"

Nate felt a stir from the observation room. Maybe the Feds had run into another Zero like Chizara. Someone who needed protection from the stings of technology.

But then Murphy leaned forward. "Did you think that you were being watched by the government? Or some unknown force?"

Nate sighed inwardly. They were going for the paranoia angle again.

So often, his interrogators seemed to be arriving at the truth of the Zeroes. But every time they grew close to grasping crowd powers, the specifics seemed to overload their brains, and they fell back on theories about crazy kids. This blind spot kept Nate's secrets safe, but also made it hard to extract any news about the outside world.

Sometimes Nate was tempted to tell them everything, just to stir them up. Maybe that would get a few more people in here.

But it was too soon to play that card.

"We wanted people to enjoy the music," Nate said. "Instead of staring at their phones. Teenagers, you know?"

Cynthia Rodriguez looked up from her own phone and raised an eyebrow at him. The new guy didn't move, but the glittering line of his attention sharpened in the air.

He knew something about signal blocking.

"You wanted people to listen to the music," Solon said. "So was this at the request of your club's DJ, Kelsie Laszlo?"

"I can't remember." Nate smiled—they didn't even have the right Zero. "And Faraday cages aren't illegal."

"No, but killing cops is," Agent Solon said, and slid a photograph across the table. It was surveillance footage, a hospital corridor. It showed Kelsie in a hoodie, her face plain even in the grainy resolution.

"Not sure who that is," Nate said.

"Witnesses confirm it was Kelsie Laszlo," Agent Murphy said. "She was visiting one Frederick 'Fig' Larson, who was present at the crowd-psychosis killing of Officer Marcus Delgado."

It wasn't a question, so Nate didn't answer.

"Witnesses also place *this* person at that murder," Murphy said, sliding over a police composite sketch—Kelsie again, or close enough. "She was the instigator."

Nate shrugged, but his mind was racing. The interrogators

hadn't asked him much about Kelsie before, and he'd hoped they thought of her as peripheral to the group. She'd only known the rest of them since summer.

But now she was connected to the murder of a policeman.

Fig must have kept quiet about her being there the night Swarm had killed Delgado, or they wouldn't be bothering with sketches, would they? The criminal code of silence.

The question was, had they caught her yet?

Nate twitched a finger, drawing the agents' attention taut, making it brittle and anxious to please.

"I never liked Kelsie," he lied. "She wasn't really part of the group. If there's anything I can do to help you catch her, I will."

Cynthia Rodriguez spread her hands. "As always, my client is ready to cooperate."

"Do you have any information about her whereabouts?" Agent Solon asked.

Nate leaned back and said nothing, satisfied. He'd won already, and he'd hardly had to use his power at all.

"Let's talk about something else," he said.

Agent Solon frowned. "But you just—"

"He got what he wanted," the new guy cut in. When the other agents looked at him, their attention fraying with confusion, he went on, "He's not going to help you find the suspect. He just wanted to know if she'd been apprehended yet, and you just confirmed that she's still at large."

Nate didn't argue. He was happy to take credit, even if the man had figured him out.

This new guy was smart. He spoke with a relaxed assurance and an accent Nate couldn't place, a southern lilt.

Nate had to be careful here.

"It's just that I can't help you," he said. "I never knew her very well."

"Maybe I should take over," the new agent said.

Solon and Murphy glanced at each other, as if they had a choice in the matter. But the attention coming through the one-way mirror had swung to the new guy, and his dominance filled the room.

"Be my guest, Agent Phan," said Murphy, putting his pictures of Kelsie back into a folder. "Might as well try the hocus-pocus. Nothing else ever works with this kid."

"Hocus-pocus?" Nate said, looking at his lawyer.

She straightened in her chair. "If you're thinking of employing any nonstandard interrogation techniques, I will remind you again that—"

"Nothing unusual," Agent Phan said, reached into his briefcase and dropped a photocopy on the table.

When Nate saw what it was, his hands jerked in the shackles with a clink. A page from his notes on the Zeroes, the folders filled with their powers, their personalities, the results of his experiments—everything Nate had learned over the years. All in the Feds' hands now.

He'd thought keeping the notes on paper, out of his computer, was safe.

Idiot. The Feds must have pulled his entire house apart.

Phan was smiling. "Very meticulous work."

"Notes for a story," Nate said with a shrug. What a nightmare for his mother, having federal agents rummaging through her home.

His mother. The guilt of what he'd done to both his parents threatened to drag his power down. It took a force of will to draw himself back from despair.

"A story?" Phan nodded at the door, and the other agents got up and left. "We'll see about that."

Nate glanced at the one-way mirror, for a moment worried that Phan knew enough to empty the room. To rip away the Curve now, when he needed it most.

But then he felt something from the other side of the glass—a growing weight of attention on him, new bright beams pushing through.

A crowd was forming back there, a big one.

He smiled.

Maybe this new guy wasn't so smart after all. Nate's power was building again, hard and bright inside him. He was going to crush this Agent Phan.

Then the door opened, and someone else came in.

Nate could only stare. It was a white girl, pale, with dark hair, wearing ratty jeans and an FBI raid jacket over a T-shirt.

Her attention glittered at Nate, wary and contemptuous. Then she glanced at the one-way mirror, as if waiting for the growing crowd to settle. That, and the fact that she was Nate's age, could only mean one thing.

She was a Zero.

CHAPTER 2
BELLWETHER

WHO THE HELL *WAS* THIS GIRL?

She wore the same expression as Nate's parents on visiting day—discomfort in this brutal pile of steel and poured concrete. She wasn't as hardened to the supermax as the FBI agents and Nate's lawyer.

But as her attention darted around the room, taking in the coffee cup rings on the table and the shackles on his wrists, she relaxed a little. Like she was familiar with interrogation rooms.

She wasn't dressed in the standard Fed business attire. Even the raid jacket looked too big for her. So she was new to her job. Which was *what*, exactly?

What's her power?

Nate flexed his fingers, gathering the attention of the crowd in the adjoining room. He had to be ready for anything.

The girl sat down at the table.

"There's a lot I'd like to talk about," Agent Phan said, his attention dropping to a photocopied page. "But let's start with something pressing. Do you know anything about Eureka?"

Nate blinked. He didn't, but if he strung Phan along, the questions might reveal something.

"Is that the code name of a secret project?"

Agent Phan smiled. "Nothing that exciting, Nate. Eureka's a small city, about twenty miles from here. They had a blackout this morning."

Nate kept his expression under control. "In winter? That's odd."

Phan nodded. "Yeah, odd. And it was a very *considerate* blackout. Every electrical device was drained. Cars, cell towers, even people's phones went dead. Like an EMP hit the town, except the hospitals and schools were untouched. And somehow the traffic lights kept working for an extra thirty seconds, while all those cars coasted to a halt."

Nate nodded mildly as his mind turned this over. If Chizara could take down a whole town so smoothly, her skill had grown in the last month. Or was it another Zero with the same power?

No. Twenty miles from here was too close for some random Crash.

"I don't know anything about—" he began, but something swelled in his throat, choking off the words.

His friends, who he hadn't seen for weeks, and who he wondered late at night if he'd ever see again, were so near.

"What's that again?" Phan asked.

"Crash," Nate said.

He swallowed, unsure how the word had slipped from his mouth.

His friends were planning something, probably something stupidly risky. This wasn't the time to give anything away.

"The same Crash as in your notes?" the girl asked.

Nate stared at her. Her attention was a bright lance of unblinking fire. The kind of focus that had been honed with deliberate practice.

But it shimmered with nerves—fear, even.

Why was this girl afraid of him?

"Sounds like the whole town crashed," he said. "That's all I—"

But that *wasn't* all he'd meant, and that made it hard to say, even to think.

"You think it was Chizara Okeke," the girl said.

And finally Nate felt it in her stare, the weight of the crowd. It poured in from the next room, the gnawing demand that he spill his guts.

Forcing out the truth—*that* was her power.

"She's my friend," he said. Yes, that was true, and for a moment the burden of answering her lifted. Relief flooded him.

Until she spoke again.

"Not Kelsie? Riley? Or Ethan?"

Trying to distract himself, Nate noticed that her accent was like Phan's, a lilting southern drawl.

"I'm not sure this line of questioning is—" Cynthia Rodriguez began.

"It was Chizara," Nate blurted out. *Something* had to fill the yawning gap of the girl's questions.

"Whose bedroom was full of wiring diagrams of the Petri Dish," Agent Phan added. "And who purchased five thousand dollars' worth of electronics last year."

Nate almost swore. He'd been fighting so hard, and they'd already known. They were only testing him, calibrating the girl's power.

Well, it was time to push back. But to marshal himself, he needed a moment of relief.

Maybe if they thought they'd won . . .

"It's all in my notes. Chizara is Crash. It must have been her in Eureka. That's what she does."

As he said the words, relief hit Nate, the hunger for the truth lifting from him. And in the moment's respite he stretched out his fingers to pull at those glittering beams from next door.

He bound them, focused them back on the girl.

"You don't want to do this to me," he said, putting all his certainty into it.

Her stare didn't falter. "Yes, I do."

"But I'm like you," Nate said.

She smiled. "People like us are assholes. Especially people like *you*."

Nate opened his mouth to argue, to persuade, to dominate—but the words wouldn't come.

She'd met a Bellwether before.

"We were trying to help people" was all he could manage.

"You actually believe that," Agent Phan said softly. "Remind me. Isn't your crew the one that blew up a police station, hijacked a mall opening and a funeral, and killed a cop?"

"Only the police station was us," Nate said, sweet relief still sweeping through him. Being honest felt so *good*.

As his interrogators exchanged a glance, he realized something—if they *knew* he was telling the truth, he could clear the Zeroes' record.

"There were other powers at the mall," Nate said quickly. "We intervened. We *saved* people. We're the good guys!"

"Seriously?" Phan asked.

The girl nodded. "He's not even breaking a sweat."

Phan didn't look convinced. "You'd be amazed what people believe about themselves. But one thing's true, Nate. Your crew isn't the biggest threat out there. Not anymore."

"We never were," Nate said. Since meeting Glitch, Coin, and Swarm, he knew all about bad people with powers. And if the FBI was recruiting Zeroes, the problem had to be growing every day.

And here he was, stuck in prison, unable even to follow it on the news.

But this was his chance to find out something about the outside world. He focused himself on both of them, pushing the full force of the crowd into his words.

"I can help you better if you tell me what's happening out there. Just give me a clue, and I'll give you everything I can."

When Phan didn't answer, Nate focused the force of his persuasion on the girl. "Please. Talk to me."

She resisted, but the force of Nate's will drew an answer from her lips.

"Something's going to happen soon, in New Orleans. Something big. Have you ever heard of Piper?"

Nate wanted to lie, to keep her talking, but all he could do was tell the truth. "No."

Phan leaned forward. "Did they hit Eureka because they're coming for you?"

This was the question Nate had been dreading. He pulled the chain on his wrist shackles taut, hoping the pain would cut through his need to tell them.

But then the lights started to flicker overhead, the fluorescent buzzing sputtering, and he couldn't stop himself.

"It must have been Crash, filling herself with the power of a city!" he cried out. "Of *course* they're coming to rescue me!"

CHAPTER 3
CRASH

"ARE YOU OKAY?" FLICKER'S GRIP TIGHTENED ON Chizara's elbow. "I've got lights going crazy all over this place!"

"No, I got it!" Chizara said, and the bulbs overhead steadied. But yes, she'd almost lost control there for a moment—and not just of the lights.

All around her, Dungeness State Prison was a sprawl of live tech. This pile of concrete and steel was wired up good, every junction guarded and multilocked, every cell and corridor surveilled.

It was killing Chizara to keep it all from spinning down into darkness. Only the buzz from crashing the town of Eureka, the awesome feeling of doing so much bad, stopped her from collapsing under the complications. But how long could she keep all these plates in the air?

The stolen schematics didn't do this place justice. Scam's heart-to-hearts in the local bars had been helpful, but the prison guards' knowledge was patchy and nontechnical. Dungeness was a glowing maze, a seething theme park of interlocked temptations.

"The guards are confused about the lockdown," Kelsie said. "But not getting twitchy yet."

Her voice was loud and nervous. She had headphones on, trance music pumping. With her new dyed-black hair, she looked like an angry goth kid.

"But the prisoners know it's not a drill," she went on. "The excitement's turning them into a crowd."

Chizara reached out and squeezed her shoulder. Bringing Kelsie inside had always been the shakiest part of the plan. If Chizara lost control and opened all the locks, a Mob feedback loop could start a deadly riot.

"Focus on calming the guards," Flicker said. "You ready for this next gate, Scam?"

Ethan nodded, nervously retucking his overlarge tan shirt into his forest-green pants. Between the uniform and his dyed-blond hair, he looked ridiculous. But so far the prison staff had found him convincing.

The voice made a pretty intimidating prison guard. Or maybe with all the doors locked down and the comms malfunctioning, the guards were happy for someone to come along and give them orders.

Getting inside had been a piece of cake—electronic doors were easy. They'd had to lock a couple of guards in the gatehouse, along with the woman in the front office who'd pressed every alarm button on her desk. That had taken some speedy intervention, balking circuits and killing phones and cameras.

But Chizara had run through the plan a thousand times, all its pinch points and contingencies. She'd skulked in the woods nearby, watching the guards' handsets to trace the layout of the place. Memorized the routines, even studied helicopter schematics in case they needed to take one down during the escape.

After all her prep, it was thrilling to walk in the bright grid now, moving the Zeroes through this awful place in a bubble of precision malfunctions and repairs.

She hardly felt human, her head was so full of glowing, intricate circuits. Her bones free of ache after crashing the city of Eureka, her whole mind wrapped around this maze. She felt so *powerful*. This felt so *right*.

"I can see Nate," Flicker said. "He's in some kind of interrogation room. Just two more gates to bluff our way through."

Ethan went ahead, Flicker just behind him, her fingers brushing the concrete wall for guidance. Mob bounced along, her trance mood spreading out to the other Zeroes and hopefully the whole prison.

Chizara cleared their way ahead and closed it off behind. There was so much to do.

Like downing all cameras along these halls, all the sirens trying to wail.

Like opening select doors to guide the wardens off the Zeroes' route.

Like locking the control booth they were passing, ignoring the man pounding on the glass. Countering all the button pushing inside. Crashing that walkie-talkie so he couldn't report what he was seeing: four unarmed kids passing unchallenged through the halls of the state's most notorious penitentiary. One of them dancing along in headphones, the others various degrees of crazy-looking.

She checked her work as she went, like her old boss, Bob, always told her to. The prisoners here were murderers, the worst of the worst. What would they do if all the cell doors suddenly sprang open?

If she left even *one* door unlocked . . .

Chizara veered her mind away from that horror, from her memories of the police station in Cambria, where she'd lost control.

Just concentrate on the here and now.

She focused on the layout of the prison, letting the guilty part of her enjoy being so juiced up. The stolen power of Eureka gave her such great range, such intoxicating detail of Dungeness's electronic symphony of light and sensation. Her usual pain dissolved into exquisite pleasures, even as she coldly, rationally, woke or shut down one door after another.

She was Crash, and she'd been put on earth to play this music.

She reached into the next gate's electronic lock and uncinched it. Scam followed up with the bulky manual key. That had been fun, watching the voice talk the guard into handing it over.

Ethan dragged the heavy door aside.

Mob pulled off one headphone. "Mini crowd ahead. Twitchy."

Flicker nodded. "I see them. Four guards."

Chizara reached her mind in, feeling to see if they'd been issued weapons. The fizzy buzz of stun guns was absent. The guards didn't carry real guns at Dungeness, except for the perimeter patrols.

She felt Mob's tranced mood spilling toward the guards— she had to fight it to stay sharp herself.

"Ready to do your thing, Scam?" Flicker asked.

"You betcha, boss," he said.

That wasn't his real voice, of course. Ethan never sounded that confident, that determined.

Scam went forward to the mesh-surrounded steel door.

"Coming in!" he shouted.

"Finally!" a woman's voice came through. "No one's updated us! What the hell's going on?"

Scam snapped an order into his dead radio, as if talking to the control booth. Crash threw the electronic lock on cue, and Scam slid in the stolen key.

The door beeped like a reversing truck as it slid aside.

Straight-backed and ready to bellow orders, Scam went through.

CHAPTER 4
MOB

KELSIE FLIPPED HER HEADPHONES OFF HER EARS, trying to relax.

Four guards. Four Zeroes. What could go wrong?

"Winters, Young!" Ethan shouted in the next room. "Captain Rogers wants you over in Cell Block B."

The voice sure *sounded* like Ethan was in charge. Which was good. If the guards were unconvinced by his bluster, it was a short walk to the nearest cell for all of them.

As an insurance policy, Kelsie spoon-fed the guards some of her tranced-out bliss. Hooked them straight into the certainty that seemed to flow out of Ethan's throat.

It was working. There was a flood of relief from the next room, cutting through their confusion and fear. They craved order, someone to make sense of the alarms and locked doors.

Even if Ethan did look like a nervous blond toothpick wearing a prison guard uniform.

"And you two," Ethan's voice shouted. "Secure the weapons lockers. Pronto! Don't let *anyone* touch them!"

Okay, bad move—the mention of weapons, like maybe this wasn't a drill. She felt their panic kick in, razor sharp. Tried to shove it down, to get back to their relief and trust.

No dice. She felt like the walls were closing in.

Kelsie hoisted the headphones back onto her ears. Let herself bliss out, eyes closed, rocking to the beat.

The prison had been almost silent from outside, all those souls in isolated cells, dots of rage and despair. But the moment the first alarm had sounded, the prisoners had unified into a crowd. Here in its corridors, smelling the bleach and damp, the cold steel and cement all around her, Kelsie was becoming part of it.

So many trapped men. So many wasted lives.

But she couldn't let the stink of desperation stop her. She had a job to do. Make the staff willing to obey Ethan's voice. Keep the other Zeroes focused on their jobs: Flicker on leadership. Scam on controlling his desires, so the voice didn't screw this up. Crash on not opening all the electronic doors and letting the prisoners run riot.

They had to rescue Bellwether. It was Nate who'd shot Swarm, saving all their lives. Saving her from turning into something angry and murderous.

For him, Kelsie could take the heat of a thousand prisoners' hopelessness.

After a minute of music flowing through her head, Chizara pulled her forward. Kelsie opened her eyes to find that the guards had followed Scam's orders, moving away down the passages Chizara had opened for them.

The Zeroes headed along an empty corridor.

"How much longer?" Kelsie said, barely able to hear her own voice over the beats.

Ahead of her, Flicker held up a hand. Five fingers—five minutes till they reached Nate.

Kelsie smiled. She could handle five more minutes. The big, noise-canceling headphones were a reassuring weight on her ears. Her rose sunglasses put halos around the harsh fluorescent lights. The walls jiggled with the motion of her bopping chin. She had three hours of upbeat trance ready on her phone.

She could pretend this was a dance party in some old abandoned factory. With a surly crowd that just needed another song and a few more beers to wake them up . . .

How strange, comparing this inhuman place to a party. But for Kelsie, the isolated cabins the Zeroes had been hiding in were almost as bad. Like living in a coffin. At least there were people here. Angry, broken people, but human beings.

She breathed in more of the antiseptic air.

Chizara was a reassuring presence to her right. She was so in control, lit up like a goddess from crashing the city of

24

Eureka. Kelsie kept dipping into that ecstatic energy to keep herself steady.

Ethan was *not* so reassuring. But he was holding it together so far. She'd never seen him look so determined. Though for him it was probably less about rescuing Nate and more about getting out alive.

We grab Bellwether and go—that was Flicker's promise.

So far, Flicker had delivered on her promises. She was a good leader, but this was way harder than stealing food and staying hidden. It was one thing to meticulously plan a prison breakout with three superpowered friends. It was another thing to actually *do* it.

Dad had been to prison a dozen times, but Kelsie had never visited him there. It scared her how he always came back more shrunken. And this supermax was much worse than any local lockup. A place like this would've destroyed him. The rage and alienation was as hard as the cement floor.

And it wasn't one mob. It was dozens, separated by faith and race and hatred. If Chizara opened the wrong door, the Zeroes could forget making a run for freedom. The prisoners would set to killing each other, and the Zeroes would be collateral damage.

Except her. Kelsie would be something else.

In the angry tempest of a prison riot, she would become Swarm. A pure vessel of frustration, rage, and murder, every prisoner a puppet in her greedy hands.

The thought shook her, made her breath catch. Sometimes she still tasted what it would've felt like to join Quinton Wallace, to become a predator of other Zeroes. All that perfect abandon and uninhibited greed.

She felt the *hunger* of the prison around her, the rage, all the emotions that Swarm had used to dominate a crowd. She felt herself tempted. She felt the prisoners forming a crowd beast from their isolated cells.

It called for her.

Kelsie hunted for another emotion. Anything else that might outweigh the thirst for blood and vengeance.

And there it was. A feeling she'd never expected in this place. Pride.

Life on the inside gave you status, but life in a supermax made you the elite of the underworld. Same for the guards. They were paid more, told better tales about the hard prisoners they'd broken. And this lockdown only piqued that pride, further proof of what *total badasses* they all were.

She fed the prison its own pride, and it settled around her.

Chizara mouthed, *You okay?*

Kelsie tried to smile like everything was fine.

The music eased into another track. Less synth, more bass. It unwound the knot in Kelsie's chest. She clutched at the relaxing vibe and propelled it outward, hitting the Zeroes first.

Flicker signaled her to take the headphones off.

Kelsie did. "What's up?"

"We're almost there." Flicker pointed at another closed gate. "Bellwether's not alone—he's in an interrogation room."

"How many people?" Chizara said.

"A big group," Flicker said. "Do you feel them?"

Kelsie nodded. A real crowd was close. Not a bunch of inmates in isolation, but people shoved together into a couple of small rooms.

They were nervous, but also professionally detached.

"One room is crowded with civilians," Flicker said. "Nate's in the other one, with his lawyer, some guy in a suit, and a girl our age. Her eyes are looking down at something . . . holy crap, that's Nate's handwriting. All those notes he took on us!"

"So they know about our powers?" Ethan squeaked. "What if they're waiting for us? I *told* you that crashing a whole city was too freakin' obvious!"

His panic hit Kelsie like a stomach punch. She stumbled, but Zara grabbed her, and Kelsie felt her crashed-up certainty again.

"Scam, *relax*," Flicker ordered. "They look just as freaked out as everybody else."

"We can't back off now," Chizara said, that maniacal-goddess glow in her eyes.

"But how do we get him out of there?" Ethan asked. "A roomful of suits isn't going to take orders from me!"

"You'll think of something, Scam," Flicker said. "Or the voice will."

They were depending on the voice again.

Kelsie slipped her headphones back on.

In the storm of anger and impending violence and sick pride, she needed music to remind herself who she was. Otherwise she'd get washed away. She recited Cambria club names to ground herself, moving along Ivy Street.

The Boom Room, Starlite, Fuse, Nightowl . . .

Being in this prison had stoked her ever-present homesickness. Dungeness was a nowhere place. All the walls were the same glossy gray, and it felt like she was a million miles from daylight. She couldn't tell north from south.

Chizara waved open the last gate, revealing a single guard on a stool by a normal-looking door.

Ethan stepped forward.

"We're with Phan," he said smoothly.

The guard gestured them through, like three teenagers and a pimply guard were not an unusual sight.

Flicker went first, then Chizara, then Kelsie, slipping off her headphones.

Three strangers sat around the table, but Kelsie's eyes skated right off them onto the guy in the orange jumpsuit, handcuffed to the table and glaring up at them.

Nate. They were halfway home.

All they had to do now was get him out of here.

CHAPTER 5
SCAM

ETHAN SCANNED THE FACES AROUND THE INTERRO-gation table. This wasn't the crowd Flicker had promised—just an old guy in a suit, the woman who spoke for Nate's family on TV, and a girl Ethan's age in an FBI raid jacket.

Oh yeah, and Glorious Leader, wearing a prison buzz cut and handcuffed to the table. He looked annoyed. Like he didn't *want* to be rescued.

"Listen to me, Nate," his lawyer was saying. "There's no way out of here. If you get your friends to surrender now, we can—"

"It's okay, Cynthia," he cut in. "I'm sure they have an exit plan. Right, guys?"

"Duh," Ethan said. "Bust in. Save the day. Make a run for it."

It was maybe the stupidest plan the Zeroes had ever made. Not that *any* of their plans ever worked out like they were supposed to. But this one involved breaking into a place it was impossible to get back out of.

"It's all under control," Flicker said.

The girl in the FBI jacket gave her a hard stare. "I doubt that, Riley. Did you bring the usual suspects?"

A frown creased Flicker's face, and she started babbling: "Crash to take control of the prison. Mob to—"

"Zip it," Nate snapped.

Everyone in the room turned to him. He hadn't even used his power, but all eyes were on Glorious Freaking Leader.

"Crash, keep everything locked down." Nate nodded at the girl in the FBI jacket. "I need to talk to her."

Ethan stared at the girl. She was pale and kind of skinny—and cute, he noticed now. She was also the right age to be a Zero, *and* she worked for the FBI. It said so right on her jacket.

Fan-freaking-tastic. The Feds had powers now.

"There's no time for a conversation," Chizara said firmly. "I can barely hold this place together."

For once, Ethan agreed with Crash. This prison was full of scary guys, guards and prisoners alike. He could see himself in the mirror that filled one wall of the room. His uniform was way too big, and his blond hair was rubber-duckie yellow under these lights. Without the voice, nobody would believe for a second that he belonged in this—

Bam! The mirror bowed inward, sending a funhouse ripple through Ethan's reflection. Everyone jumped.

"Shit," Flicker said. "Someone in there threw a chair against the glass. Can they break out, Crash?"

"All the glass in here is bulletproof," Chizara said. "And they're on the other side of an electronic door. I've got them bottled up."

She sounded certain, but when the glass shuddered again, Ethan felt his fear redouble in Kelsie's feedback loop, like a kick to his solar plexus.

The girl in the FBI jacket was still staring at Flicker. "You're the Sight-caster, right? Code name Flicker, according to Nate's files."

"Yeah, that's me. Pop those handcuffs, Crash."

The old guy in the suit nodded. "Crash—the Electro-kinetic—and Mob is your pet Predator. And you're Ethan Cooper, right? We've never seen one of you before."

"Aw, crap," Ethan muttered. He'd read his own name a hundred times in articles about the Cambria Five, but hearing it said aloud by a real-live FBI agent was too much. Plus, he was sick of everyone saying he wasn't a real Zero.

He wanted very much to insult this guy.

"'Electrokinetic'?" the voice said. "You suck at naming powers."

"Yeah, my bosses always laugh at that one," the guy said. "So let's use real names. I'm Special Agent Phan, FBI. Riley, Ethan, Kelsie, and Chizara—you're all under arrest."

"Hey, sorry we can't stick around for that," Flicker said. "We have a jailbreak to finish. Crash, the shackles!"

"I'm *trying*." There was sweat on Chizara's brow. "I can't get a grip on the mechanism!"

"Mierda." Nate looked down at his wrists. "I knew they were different."

"Made from an aircraft polymer instead of metal," Phan said. "A perfect insulator. Electrokinesis won't work."

"They knew you were coming," Nate said.

Phan nodded. "Eureka gave us plenty of warning. In another ten minutes, this prison will be surrounded."

"Sorry, but no," Chizara said. "I killed the comms."

"It's called a dead-man switch," Phan said calmly. "The moment our comms were cut, an alarm sounded in Sacramento. A hundred law enforcement officers are already on their way."

Ethan groaned. No way could the voice talk its way past that many cops.

"The only way this ends safely is if you all surrender," Phan finished.

"Nate," the lawyer said. "Listen to him."

"Where's the key?" Nate demanded, rattling the shackle on his wrist.

"A guard in the observation room has it," Phan said. "Too far away for you to charisma him. You aren't leaving here today, young man."

"Order him to bring it," Nate said.

Ethan shivered as the room filled with the bright familiar crackle of authority. Glorious Leader, back in charge.

But Phan only smiled. "I've met your kind before, Nate. And frankly, you aren't even average."

Ethan felt it hit them all. He would have felt it even without Kelsie's feedback loop. You could practically hear the pop of Glorious Leader's confidence bursting.

Nate visibly sank into his chair.

But Flicker stood straighter. "Scam. Please explain to this guy why he's going to get us that key."

Ethan didn't need to be told twice. *Okay, voice. You heard the lady! Threaten this guy with something!*

The voice rocketed up from Ethan's lungs.

"Listen, Phan. You know about Crash, right? How she can bring down electrical systems?"

"So what?" Phan asked.

"So your heart is a system too," the voice said. "Full of nerves carrying little sparks of electricity."

Beside him, Chizara gasped.

Ethan ignored her. Agent Phan was still frowning, unconvinced. *Double down, voice!*

"And not just yours. Verity's heart is also sparks and muscles, a little engine in her chest. One that Chizara can stop cold."

That got him. Phan looked ready to crap himself.

Ethan felt a grin warp his face as the voice delivered the

final blow. "So if you don't want her to die, you better order up that key. Now!"

Phan threw a panicked look at the girl—Verity—but she still looked calm.

"Apparently that's all true," she said. "But *would* you kill me, Chizara?"

"No," Chizara said at once, like she couldn't wait to say it. "Never."

Flicker raised a hand. "Don't toy with the man, Crash. I've seen you kill at least—"

Her voice choked off, her face spasming.

"Don't try to lie, Flick." Nate gestured at Verity. "That's her power: She makes you tell the truth."

They all stared at the girl, and Ethan felt it in Kelsie's feedback loop—the sudden realization that they were all screwed. The voice's threats were worthless when you couldn't lie about carrying them out.

The Zeroes were surrounded, outmaneuvered, and busted. Bellwether had been bait, like a goat staked out to lure a lion.

None of them were going anywhere.

For a second it felt like they were all about to give up and surrender. But then Kelsie slipped her headphones over both ears and shut her eyes. Nate's shackled hands opened, helping her pull the group's energy back to something halfway steady.

"Yes, it's true that Chizara would never hurt anyone. Neither would any of the rest of my crew." Nate stared straight into Verity's eyes, as if daring her to disagree with him. "But *I* would. Because I would rather burn the Zeroes down than let you take them from me."

"Then it's lucky you're chained to that table," Verity said.

Nate turned from her, the full force of his gaze falling on Chizara.

"You never hurt people on purpose. But we all know that accidents happen. Right, Crash?" The look of sadness on Nate's face grew more profound, and Ethan felt despair in his bones. "Like that time with Officer Bright."

She glared back at him. "What the hell are you doing, Nate?"

"You've read her file, Phan," Nate said. "You know all about what happened at the police station last summer. How she let all those criminals go. How deep inside, Chizara thinks she's a demon."

Her eyes were wide. "Nate, you said you'd never—"

"And now she's a wanted terrorist," Nate said to Phan. "And maybe wondering if her mother was right. If she'll always wind up losing control."

The lights flickered overhead.

"Oh God." Kelsie reached for the volume button on her phone.

But Ethan was pretty sure that louder music wasn't going to salvage this situation. Nate was playing chicken with an FBI agent. And instead of a car crash, they were headed straight for a prison riot.

Ethan opened his mouth—the voice could probably stop this roll Nate was on. But that would mean sitting here until reinforcements showed up.

Ethan didn't like throwing Chizara under the bus, but he also didn't like the thought of twenty years in prison. Nate's plan was the only one they had.

He felt the voice crawl back down his throat.

"Six hundred inmates," Nate said. "And the only thing holding them back is you, Crash. What if you can't manage it?"

Ethan felt the room grow colder. That Glorious Leader charm—normally it made you think you were awesome, that you could do anything. But this was like some switched-around version, making everyone in the room feel desperate and alone and worthless.

Prison, man. It changed you fast.

The lights flickered again, and Chizara whimpered.

Nate kept at her. "Last time we were in this situation, Officer Bright paid for it. How many will die this time? Hundreds?"

He turned back to Phan.

"And Verity will be among them. If our demon here opens all the locks, this room will be overrun in minutes."

Bam! The one-way mirror shuddered again with the efforts of the people behind it, making Ethan jump halfway out of his skin. Kelsie had her arms wrapped around herself, like she was wearing a straitjacket.

Then the lights went out. Total blackness.

"Sorry," Chizara gasped.

"Get the damn key!" Flicker cried. "He's not bluffing!"

"It's true." Verity's voice was hollow in the dark. "He's not."

Chizara let out an anguished bellow, and the lights sputtered on again. But the fluorescents were buzzing angrily, like the voltage was wrong, and alarms came from all directions. It sounded to Ethan like the whole prison was coming apart.

Phan hesitated another moment, his lips pressed tight together.

"Okay! Open the observation room door, Chizara." He turned to address the mirror. "But only Anderson comes out. Bring me that key, *now*!"

Chizara was trembling, covered in sweat. "I hate you, Nate."

Nate turned to Verity. "Come with us. You don't have to work for the government anymore."

"Dude," she said. "Are you kidding? I had enough of someone like you growing up. *Exactly* like you."

Nate stared at her. "Where are you from? New Orleans, where this big thing's happening?"

"Yes. And in about half an hour, after they gun you down, I'm going home for Mardi Gras to celebrate!"

Ethan swallowed. He imagined Verity in a wild, dancing crowd, firing pistols in the air.

"What's happening?" Nate kept going. "What's this bad thing?"

Verity was trembling with anger, trying to resist him. "Piper wants to break everything. That's all we know."

A prison guard burst through the door, holding up a key like it was the Olympic torch. Flicker grabbed it from him and freed Nate.

"I just have to ask her—" he started, but Flicker dragged him toward the door.

"Come *on*, Glorious Leader. We're out of here!"

About ten seconds later they were all following Flicker down the corridor, Kelsie bouncing on the balls of her feet, Nate rubbing his wrists, and Chizara shuddering at every shimmer of the lights.

But Ethan heard Verity call out, "If you survive this, where will you go?"

Before anyone else could speak up, he let the voice handle it, willing it not to reveal anything important.

"Who knows where we'll wind up?" he heard himself say.

It wasn't until Chizara had slammed the next electronic door behind them and they'd started running down the corridor that Ethan realized something unsettling:

The voice hadn't lied at all. The whole federal government would be after them now.

Where the hell *did* they think they were they running to?

CHAPTER 6
FLICKER

FLICKER SAW HERSELF IN A DOZEN GUNSIGHTS, ALL aimed at her heart.

There were eyes up in the perimeter towers, and cops crouched behind their vehicles, guns drawn. Some were confidently out in the open, taking deadly aim at the five figures who stood lonely, exposed, and unarmed. The prison plans called this empty stretch of concrete the Restricted Area, a barrier worse than any wall—a killing ground.

One word of command and the Zeroes were all dead.

"On the ground, *now*!" a voice called, barely audible over the wail of sirens. "Do *not* take another step!"

Flicker's mind raced. They could have survived the guards in the towers—Crash had already fiddled with the optics of their sniper rifles. But thanks to Phan's dead-man switch, dozens more cops had shown up.

The plan had failed. She'd led them straight into a trap.

Time to put aside the shit Nate had just pulled with Chizara.

"Any ideas, Bellwether?"

"I'm not Bellwether." He took her hand. "Call me Nothing."

The words didn't make sense, but they wrenched at her somehow. A sudden hole yawned in her chest.

Then Chizara took her other hand, and it hit.

Emptiness flowed into her from Nate, swept through them all. Her fear bleached out into irrelevance. The expanse of concrete was a sudden void around them, the alarm sirens hollow echoes.

And those eyes, the ones locked on the Zeroes with deadly intent, drifted away. Nothing to see here.

Nothing . . .

"What is this?" Her own voice sounded distant in her ears. "*Where* is this?"

"This is my real power," Nate answered. "I was always an Anonymous, inside out."

"What do you mean, anonym—" Suddenly it hurt too much to speak. A stray memory tore at her heart. A red leather jacket.

"I found this power in guilt," Nate said. "In my shame."

"In your shame about being an *asshole*?" Chizara asked.

"I'm truly sorry for hurting you," he said, and turned to Flicker. "Are they still looking at us?"

She swept her vision through the eyes around them. "No. But what *is* this?"

"This was always me, inside out. Maybe we should get moving?" Nate sounded like someone else. Someone uncertain, who'd never given an order in his life.

"Come on, everyone," Flicker said firmly.

The five of them started to walk, clinging to each other in the emptiness. She jumped into Ethan's vision on the towers overhead, full of marksmen searching the concrete for a target.

Chizara's eyes were dutifully trained on the ground, skimming a crack in the concrete with weeds pushing through. The sight chimed with another wisp of memory—a small green plant growing in broken stone. Something encircling her wrist, a phantom bracelet.

A memory of braille pulsed beneath her fingertips. . . .

T.

And there was that pain again, a shape punched out of Flicker's heart. She gasped with it.

Was Nate doing this? Was this anguish some side effect of being invisible?

"I can barely feel us," Kelsie murmured. "It's like we're in a dream."

"Just keep walking," Nate answered.

Alarms still sounded back at the prison, guards and police

scrambled and shouted orders in the distance, but no one paid any heed to the five of them. When they reached the tall fence that marked the edge of the prison yard, Chizara's hand jerked a little in Flicker's, and the gate's motors rumbled to life.

"Wait," Flicker ordered, and threw her vision behind them. The guards' attention had swung to the moving gate, and for a moment a few of them locked their gaze on the five distant figures and raised their guns. But a moment later those eyes had slipped away again, unable to keep focus.

A no-man's-land of empty field stretched in front of them.

"Hold *tight*," Nate said in a shaky voice.

His weakness roiled inside Flicker. She'd done a good job as leader, she knew. The fact that they were all alive proved that. But part of her had also hoped that Nate—*Glorious Leader*—would lift some of that burden off her when they got him back.

This boy beside her, who barely knew his own name, sounded like he would never take the reins again. And the way he'd gone after Chizara, purposely hitting her weak spot, threatening to get them all killed to save himself . . .

As if prison had changed him in a few weeks. Or maybe killing Swarm in cold blood had darkened his mind.

That left it to her to keep the team together. "Mob, how are the guards reacting?"

"Out here, confusion" came Kelsie's tentative answer. "But back inside they're full of purpose."

"Of course." Flicker sent her vision inside the prison walls, found video monitors that showed the five of them plainly. "The cameras aren't affected by whatever Bellwether's doing. Crash?"

"You got it." Chizara, at least, sounded certain of herself. One by one, the monitors filled with static.

"I can see the van," Ethan said.

Flicker jumped into his eyes. The getaway van was parked on the road that passed the prison—a big Honda, the metal of its hood ornament shining in the sun.

A big silver *H*.

The second letter on that phantom bracelet. *T-H . . .*

"No," Flicker said softly. A memory was welling up, something that threatened to knock her off balance. Something too big to push down. This anguish in her heart was sharper than her fear of being shot.

Chizara squeezed her hand and whispered, "What's wrong?"

"This new power of Nate's? I've seen it before."

Not just seen it, *needed* it. It was something she'd desperately missed all this time, but without knowing why.

But she had to keep control. She was the leader now.

"It's okay," she managed.

"It's *so* not okay." Ethan's voice sounded afraid. "A busload of freaking guards is coming right at us!"

Of course—someone had spotted the unauthorized vehicle sitting out here. With nothing else in sight, the van was the only thing they had to focus on.

When it started to roll away, the guards would start shooting.

"Crash the bus's engine!" she ordered.

"I can do better than that," Chizara said. A moment later: "Ha! I've got it going in circles."

"Whoa," Mob said. "Now they're *really* pissed."

"Move! Before they figure out how to stop it!" Flicker pulled them into a run.

"We're ready to go!" Crash cried, and ahead of them the van rumbled to life. Flicker heard the chunk and whir of automatic doors rolling open.

"Don't let go of me till you have to!" Nate warned.

Flicker cast her vision back. "It's okay. Everyone's watching the runaway bus now."

As they piled into the van, her fingers slipped from Nate's, and at last the world was sharp and real again.

Flicker sucked in huge breaths of relief. The anguish had snapped away.

It had been just been Nate's strange new power. There was no real memory behind this formless sadness.

They'd won! Nate was free, and *she* had led the rescue.

"Thanks for the assist, Bellwether," she said as the van began to roll. "Did you learn that trick in prison?"

"No. I learned it from Anon." He frowned at her; then his eyes darted around the van. "Where *is* Thibault? Didn't he come?"

Everyone looked at Nate in confusion.

"Who the hell is Teebo?" Ethan asked.

Flicker pulled her vision back into her own head. Her hand went to her wrist, where the guilty memory of a bracelet still lay against her skin. She felt braille letters there . . .

T-H-I-B-A-U-L-T.

Not a nonsense word: a name. And along with it came an image—a face with dark eyes and full lips, the pale curve of an ear peeking out from long dark hair. The boy called Nothing, whom she had created from stories with her own sister, and who had turned out to be real, to be beautiful, and yet—

She'd lost him. Left him behind like a kid leaves a toy on a bus seat.

"No." Flicker dropped her hand from her wrist, but the memories kept coming. His parents had abandoned him in the hospital, and now she'd done the same thing. "How did we all . . ."

"What's wrong?" Chizara asked from behind the wheel, her voice still bright with triumph. "Is someone following us? I'll crash the hell out of them!"

Flicker gave a low moan, like the sirens fading in the distance. She remembered everything now.

"I forgot him, Nate. We all just *forgot him.*"

The pain was just beginning.

CHAPTER 7

THE PICKUP PULLED OFF THE HIGHWAY AND stopped. The driver got out and slammed the door.

The boy lying curled in the truck bed woke up, saw redwoods the size of rocket ships rising around him, disappearing into morning mist.

He sat up and watched the driver walk into the woods to squat and pee. A path led off among the misty trees, signposted Damnation Creek Trail.

And now the boy knew where he was—where he'd been heading all along, following nothing but instinct. Knew enough to clamber up onto the rim of the pickup and drop his ratty backpack on the ground.

The driver had put some supermarket bags in the back, their contents showing through the plastic. The boy's stomach sent hunger pangs up to his higher self—they were connected like two tin cans with a string between them, sometimes taut and sharp, sometimes slack and useless. He pulled bananas and a box of muesli bars out of the bag and dropped to the ground beside the pickup.

His right boot made a clopping sound as he landed. The outer sole was starting to peel away. He didn't care much.

Making for the trailhead, he passed directly across the driver's path. His hand moved in some half-remembered gesture, but it wasn't necessary. She saw nothing.

Even this far from a crowd, no one saw him.

He was nothing.

Behind him at the pickup door, the woman paused to let out a belch, thinking she was alone. *Knowing* she was alone. Then she got in and turned the key in the ignition. The boy paused, enjoying his relief as the noise of that exhausted old engine faded.

It was good to walk away from the road. It was good to float among these enormous trees. They were so straight, so solid, so still. They smelled fresh and alive. Ferns and rhododendrons and giant huckleberry bushes crowded their feet.

He'd been here before, in summer, back when he'd had a name. Back then, the morning mist had slowly burned off in the sun. Now it was winter, and this lovely noise-dampening blanket would lie across the forest all day. It was cold but not freezing, nothing his distant body couldn't handle.

Far off he could feel the mist on his face, and it felt good.

He saw himself stumble, a tree root across the trail ripping away more of his boot sole. His stride adjusted, his right foot lifting a little higher.

The trail climbed away from the highway, crested, then took him downhill. The ferny, clouded quiet closed in, punctuated by water drips and a few birdcalls.

He heard his own footfalls on the trail, squelching on the damp leaves, cracking twigs, his broken sole clopping. The loudest creature in this world. All around him animals were frozen in their tracks, birds on their branches, alert to the noises of his body moving past.

Part of him wanted to sing out loud, to make the biggest noise he could, to prove to himself that he existed. But he also wanted to stand still, breathe silently, melt away into the quietness all around. Maybe forever.

He'd drifted back and forth between these two desires since the day he'd pushed the world away. Since he'd seen up close what a crowd could do, what he himself had done with a handgun.

Seeing that had made everything impossible.

Mostly he floated and drifted, admitting nothing, seeking nothing, content to belong nowhere.

But then the thought would niggle: He hadn't always drifted, had he? He *ought to be*, ought to exist. Someone, somewhere, had once remembered him.

And then he'd wake up somewhere new.

Like that impersonal hotel room, high above the town. There'd been a fridge full of packaged food, so he'd stayed there a while, staring out at the view, waiting for clearer memories to come.

Until the invasions of staff, exclaiming, whirling in and out. A big bowl of fresh fruit had appeared, and his body had almost cried out at the sight of it. He remembered fruit in his hands, the taste of it.

But then hotel guests had charged in. An executive shouting on her phone, her husband rushing to make them drinks.

He'd slid out the door unseen as their cart full of expensive luggage trundled in.

Another time he'd awoken on a scaly old leather armchair in an attic. He'd had the impression of sleeping there, *with* someone: skin-to-skin contact, long embraces. Were they his memories, or stories someone had told him? Things he'd once wanted, and didn't care about anymore?

A girl had come up the folding ladder while he sat there. She was his age, a little gothy-looking. She'd stayed a long time in the armchair staring at the wall. Not the girl he'd kissed that time, but close enough to be her twin.

She'd sunk her head in her hands. Apologized, not to him, but to someone whose name faded as it left her lips.

Then there was that other house, the room memory claimed was his, except that it was full of lace and chintz. He'd wandered around the unheated, vacation-empty house, down the stairs, and stood disoriented in the hall. Everything was tidy, every picture aligned neatly on the walls. But he could feel a storm in his gut, things torn, permanently disarranged. . . .

Then an old theater building in the Heights, barred with fluttering police tape. His body standing, shuddering on the trash-strewn sidewalk. Another room that was his, turned upside down. Steel doors and windows, barricaded stairs, a sick memory of people fleeing, hurting, disappearing from his life. And when he stepped out of the building—sweating in spite of the cold—the emptiness hit him from every direction. The empty used-car lot across the empty street. He shouldn't stand here, under this window. He shouldn't *be* here—

It's okay, he told himself. *I'm not there anymore.* He made himself take deep breaths of the piney air.

He'd drifted up the coast on buses, in RVs, in pickups and cars. He might have even driven a little way in an SUV he found idling outside a convenience store—he remembered concentrating hard to stay on the cliff road. It was easier to sneak into someone else's car and let them take him north.

Now the trail was winding along through slimmer, more thinly scattered redwoods, their bark pale gray, like ghosts.

And he still warred with himself. Was he here in this familiar place to reconnect with the world? Or to fade away forever?

He paused to get rid of a small pinecone that had wedged itself into his broken boot sole.

Someone else had been with him that summer, the last time he was here. They'd walked down this path together, and their voices had gone back and forth in conversation. Like normal people.

Who had that guy been? All he recalled was an impression of a person trying hard, putting in effort to see him, to know him, like no one ever had before.

A friend. Where was that friend now?

In a bad place, the boy's gut told him. Was he supposed to wake up from this misty dream and help him? What had happened?

You don't want to go there, his gut said.

He pulled back from thinking and just walked, carrying the food instead of eating it, following the switchbacks of the path through the fog-wrapped wood.

Scraps of jokes from that summer, puzzling and unfunny, floated through the boy's head. Carefully he skirted the places where the path all but slid away down the slope.

Up ahead was the sea. A foghorn sounded, and he smelled salt in the air. He could hear the creek running below, and searched the fog beyond it for the far bank.

His whole mind was full of this fog. Sometimes he had the energy for groping in it, catching hold of stuff. Sometimes he just wanted to let it blur everything from his mind forever.

At last he found a rough stairway that led down to a cove. The tide was out. He climbed down, crossed the gravel beach to the wet gray rocks.

A tide pool gleamed there, reflecting the fog. Two pink-legged crabs darted under a ledge at the boy's approach—animals could always see him. He crouched, leaned over the still water.

There was that face he'd glimpsed in shop windows. Thinner than he remembered, and the beard had grown in. He held his long hair back to get a real look at the uncertain face above the beard, the eyes that hardly knew what they were looking for.

Poor sucker. Maybe he should just walk into that ocean, let the waves take him at last.

The boy raised his gaze to the ripples rushing white on the beach gravel, to the rocks cragging up from the sea into the fog, remnants of a coastline chewed away by tides and storms.

This beauty would remain whether he was here to see it or not.

In the meantime, the sea sound would rinse away this troubled feeling. He would play the game that long-ago guy had shown him, whacking stones into the sea with a washed-up stick.

Driftwood baseball.

The boy smiled, pleased to have remembered.

As he stood, the sole of his boot caught on a rock and ripped again. Two thirds of it was flapping loose now. It was practically useless.

He bent down and untied the bootlace, pulled the boot off.

Pulled off the wet sock, too. The cold, solid rock underfoot felt good, real, right.

So he took off the other boot. He tucked the socks deep into the boots' toes and hurled them one after the other as far out into the water as he could. They splashed and then bobbed on the surface, like they couldn't decide which way to swim.

He turned and picked his way back across the rocks, scanning the beach for a good driftwood bat.

CHAPTER 8
BELLWETHER

"WE HAVE A FRIEND WHOSE POWER IS BEING FOR-
gotten," Nate said. "His name is Thibault."

The other Zeroes stared at him, their faces full of baffle-
ment and pain. They'd all forgotten Anonymous, and the frantic drive to the safe house had only confused them more.

The escape route had been full of police cars and roadblocks, a vast search for a gang of terrorists fleeing a supermax breakout. Flicker had taken command, guiding Chizara
to play havoc with the pursuit. They'd changed vehicles
twice and left a hundred stalled cars blocking traffic in their
wake.

But here at the safe house, Flicker had switched off. She sat
in the big armchair by the fireplace now, her attention hidden
away inside herself.

"It's not your fault you all forgot him," Nate said. "That's just how his power works."

This felt familiar, standing in front of his team, willing them to pay attention, but it was also different. Harder. They didn't accept his leadership as easily as they once had.

They kept looking at Flicker, but she was wrapped up in her pain.

"But we remember him now," Chizara said. "And we used to know him. How did we forget him all that time?"

Nate shook his head. He had a theory, but not one he could share. The truth would hit them too hard, especially Flicker.

The wind blew outside, and a cold draft coiled into the room. Ethan bragged that the safe house was one of several he'd talked caretakers into handing over the keys for. Remote cabins were easy to scam in the middle of winter, it seemed.

Maybe a little *too* remote for Kelsie. She looked lost in this crowdless place. Judging by the long private road to the cabin, the five Zeroes were the only people for miles around.

But after weeks in isolation, even this small group felt glorious to Nate. His power was easing back into his bones.

"He lived down the hall in the Dish," Kelsie said softly. "With a sign on his door to remind us how to pronounce his name."

Nate could feel her sadness pulsing in the group, her power linking their emotions. Chizara was still angry about what he had done back at the prison, and Flicker's heartache keened through them all like the cold wind outside.

She and Thibault had been in love, and she'd forgotten him.

"We were *buddies*," said Ethan from the far end of the couch. "He lived in that awesome hotel room, and we played this video game. I had to remember he was sitting there next to me!" His thumbs twitched at the memory.

"We all found ways to keep him in our minds," Nate said. "But somehow he was forced out of yours."

Chizara said darkly, "On the day you shot Swarm, right?"

Nate hesitated only a moment before nodding.

Too far away to see the shooting, the others all believed what the news said—that Nate Saldana was a murderer.

They couldn't learn that Thibault had pulled the trigger. Not while they were still reeling.

Nate needed to heal the group first. He needed them functional.

Something big was happening in New Orleans, something involving Zero powers, and he wanted to be there in full force.

Flicker spoke up. "What if this means Thibault's dead? He always worried that if he ever died, he'd just . . . disappear."

"That's not why you forgot him," Nate said. "Everything went to hell that day. You lost the Dish, you lost your families, and you've spent every moment since on the run. It's amazing you remember your own names, let alone Thibault's!"

He paused, letting that soak in, and for a moment he almost believed it himself. They all looked like they'd been camping for months. Bedraggled and exhausted, wearing cheap clothes scammed by Ethan from roadside stores.

"Wait," Flicker said, the fingers of one hand encircling her other wrist. "The day before we left Cambria, Thibault's mom was going crazy, because she never knew if he really existed or not. So he went through his family's house, trashing all the pictures they had of him, every reminder he could find. He erased himself from their memories once and for all."

"Harsh," Ethan said. "But why did *we* forget?"

Flicker's voice dropped. "He was so sad, so lost. Maybe in all the emotions after Swarm got killed, his power got too strong."

"Yikes." Ethan let out a low whistle. "Bad things happen when we level up."

He glanced at Kelsie, then stared guiltily at the floor.

"Don't worry, Ethan," she said. "I was just in a prison full of killers, and I didn't turn into a Swarm."

"Duh," he said. "You're over that whole thing."

"No" came a soft answer. "I'm not."

Chizara took Kelsie's hand, her eyes still alight with the power of crashing a hundred cars. "And I managed not to release any of those killers, even with Nate trying to make me. But if Anon leveled up that day, maybe he wasn't so lucky."

"Maybe," Nate said. They were closer than he liked to guessing that Anon had done this to himself.

Not because of his family, though. Despite all Thibault's self-control, his Zen distance from the world, somewhere down in his heart he was capable of shooting someone. Realizing that had been too much for him.

Guilt had sent Thibault spinning down into his own power. Nate was more certain of it every moment.

Chizara frowned. "How come he didn't erase *your* memories, Nate?"

"Maybe I had the deepest connection. I took notes on him for years, made sure to reread them every . . ." Nate trailed off.

All the attention in the room had gone to Flicker, whose fists were clenched.

Chizara shook her head. "Longest connection, Nate. Not the deepest."

"But it was probably simpler than that," he added hurriedly. "The cops dragged me away after the shooting. Maybe I was out of range."

Ethan nodded. "We were all back at the Dish by then, figuring out how to save you."

"You did the right thing, letting them take me away," Nate said with a smile. "It all worked out."

"No. It *didn't*," Kelsie said, her anguish spiking through the room. "We forgot Thibault and lost the Dish and . . . Craig got killed."

The room went silent. The sparkling lines of their attention shot off in all directions.

Nate tried to draw them together again, but his own will faltered. He had allowed Craig to stay with them for the showdown with Swarm. What kind of Glorious Leader let an outsider join a losing fight?

He cast around for something to say, but in the end he let the silence linger. Maybe the others needed it.

Nate had spent weeks in his cell thinking about what had happened that day—the battle with Swarm's police minions, the killing, Craig's death—but the other Zeroes had been on the run the whole time. Today's rescue should have helped, but the victory had been shattered by finding out that they'd left another Zero behind.

They needed a mission to focus them.

"Thibault's out there somewhere," Nate said. "We can find him and bring him back."

Their eyes lifted from the floor, and Nate smiled. It was good to feel his power coursing, even through this small assemblage. He would lead them again, guide them back to wholeness—and then to New Orleans.

Ethan spoke up. "How? He could be anywhere by now, and he's freaking *invisible*."

"He'll be somewhere important to him," Nate said.

"Like the Dish? Or his parents' house?" Chizara asked. "If we go searching in Cambria, we'll get arrested. Everyone in town knows our faces!"

A wave of homesickness went through them, and Nate resisted the urge to raise his hands and squash the feeling. They needed to process everything they'd lost.

"Actually, he's not there," Ethan said. "Cambria's full of surveillance cameras these days, and also weird-hunters. If those cameras were picking up some kind of ghost boy, I'd know about it."

"Still reading your friend Sonia's blog?" Chizara asked.

Ethan shrugged. "It keeps me up with news from home."

"Good work, Ethan," Nate said. It was strange to think how much their town had changed in the month he'd been in prison.

"But if he's not in Cambria, where is he?" Flicker asked. "What other places were important to him? I can't *remember*."

"Me either," Nate sighed. "Maybe if we had my notes. But the FBI found them."

"Yeah, I saw that," Flicker said coolly.

Anger rippled through Kelsie's connection—none of them had ever liked Nate keeping files about them. And now all that painstakingly gathered data was in the hands of Agent Phan.

"Wait a second." Flicker sat up straight for the first time. "I borrowed your Anon file last summer. That's how I found Thibault's hotel. It's still in my attic!"

"Then the Feds have it," Ethan said. "I mean, they found all Nate's stuff."

Flicker shook her head. "I was just a bartender at the Dish, not a murderer. And who searches the blind girl's house for a paper trail?"

They all looked at Nate hopefully. He nodded.

"So how do we get it?"

"My sister can bring it to us," Flicker said.

Ethan stared at her. "Lily? She wasn't a fan of the Zeroes even *before* we were wanted terrorists."

"Maybe not," Flicker said. "But she'd do anything for me."

Ethan started to argue again, but Nate silenced him with a glance. Flicker had already lost one certainty in her life—her connection to Thibault. She needed to trust her own twin.

"Can you get a message to her?" he asked.

"I guess. There's a fanfic board she posts on." A wan smile played on Flicker's face. "I could use one of my old names, from the stories we used to make up. She'll know it's me."

Nate nodded slowly. It was a long shot—trusting Lily, hoping the notes hadn't been found by the Feds. And it was possible that Thibault had just walked away into the desert, forgetting that he was a real person who needed food and water and shelter. . . .

But the Zeroes needed certainty, not doubts.

He had to bring them together.

"Okay, then," he said. "We ask Lily to bring us the notes. And we meet her somewhere far away from Cambria. Somewhere with big crowds, where we hold all the cards."

CHAPTER 9
BELLWETHER

A FEW HOURS LATER, WHEN EVERYONE ELSE HAD gone to bed, Nate went out onto the porch to stare up into the pinpricked darkness. It had only been a few weeks since he'd seen the night sky, but the stars were astonishing.

All those other suns, rendered in glimmers of ancient light. Too easy to take for granted when you weren't alone in a cell every night.

If the Zeroes hadn't pulled together to rescue him, he might never have seen the stars again. But they'd remained strong enough to break into a supermax prison. Flicker had kept them together.

He had a solid base to build on, and something important to pursue once the whole crew was back together—whatever was happening in New Orleans.

Nate remembered Verity's words. *Piper wants to break every-thing.*

What the hell did that mean?

"Nate?" whispered a voice from the shadows.

He turned. It was Chizara, walking softly on the porch's rickety boards.

"Everything okay inside?" he asked.

She nodded. "They're all asleep. Even Flicker."

"How is she?"

"Better. She got in touch with her sister already. We're meeting her in Las Vegas, like you suggested."

"Perfect. This gives Flicker hope." Nate turned back to the sky. "And Las Vegas means no shortage of crowds if things go wrong."

"Nope," Chizara said. "No shortage of pain, either."

"It'll be good practice."

She stared at him. "For what?"

He only shrugged. It was too early to talk about New Orleans to the others. They stood in silence for a moment, Chizara's attention shimmering among the stars.

Nate realized that it was up to him to start.

"What I did back at the prison," he said. "I never wanted to say all that, but it was the only way to convince Phan to let us go."

"Pretty smart trick, I guess. Worthy of Ethan's voice." She flinched, a small motion in the darkness. "Only one problem with it."

Nate nodded. "That I broke your trust. I'm sorry."

"Not that." She let out a sigh. "The Zero in the FBI jacket, Verity, her power makes you tell the truth, right?"

"Yes. I suspect she uses the social pressure of the crowd to keep you from lying. Some groups need to know the—"

"Yeah, whatever. But if she makes you tell the truth, that means you weren't bluffing, Nate. You really would have messed me up enough to let all those prisoners go? Killed hundreds of people—guards, inmates, cleaning staff? All of us Zeroes?"

Nate frowned. "Well, I knew it wouldn't come to that. Because I knew Phan would fold."

"But only because you *would have done it*. Verity's truth power is a guarantee of that!"

Nate nodded slowly. "My threat had to be real to work."

Chizara looked away, her attention dropping from the sky, splintering aimlessly into the darkness. They were silent for a while before she spoke again.

"Maybe this is why Thibault is gone."

He turned to her. "I don't understand."

"Because he doesn't want to come back. Not to us."

"He's just lost."

She shook her head. "You don't know how hard it is out here, Nate. Every car that passes by, every noise outside the window—there's always the chance that it's the Feds, and that we're about to go to jail forever."

"Can I point out that I've already *been* in jail?"

"Yeah, we noticed. But sometimes I actually want to get

caught, just so I can stop running. You'll see what I mean, soon enough."

Nate followed her gaze into the dark. The wind was rustling the leaves, like waves on a distant shore. "What does this have to do with Thibault? Or with what I did back at the prison?"

"Because he's running from *us*, Nate. Not from his family, but from the rolling disaster of the Zeroes!" As Chizara turned to him again, her attention narrowed down into a laser. "We break things. We get people killed. We spill each other's deepest secrets for some . . . *tactical advantage*! And after busting up a federal prison, we'll always be on the run. Why would Anon want to be part of that, when he can just disappear?"

Nate stared at her, and for a moment his confidence trembled. The prison seemed to wrap around him again—all that emptiness, that shame.

Why couldn't Chizara see that they had to find Thibault again? The Zeroes needed a mission, a way to practice for the crowds of New Orleans.

And more important than that . . .

"Flicker won't forgive herself until we find him," he said.

"And what if we find him and he doesn't *want* to be with us? How will she feel then?"

Nate didn't answer. His Zeroes were going to be whole again.

"And do we even want a guy who abandoned us?" she asked softly.

"That's not what happened." Nate sighed. "He *saved* us."

"What are you talking about?"

Nate hesitated only a moment. He needed Chizara on his side, and of them all, she could best handle the truth.

"He's the one who killed Swarm, not me. Shot him in the back, twice."

Chizara was stunned into silence.

Memories came surging in to fill the space. Nate had left the Dish to kill Swarm himself. He'd flipped his power inside out, thinking he was invisible. Quinton Wallace had seen straight through him, had laughed at him.

But then Thibault, who'd been Anonymous his whole life, had passed unseen through the entire swarm to do the deed.

"The Zen master shot someone? Whoa." Chizara shook her head. "No wonder he's gone. No way could he live with himself after that."

"Maybe. But we'll give him something better than Zen. Flicker loves him, and he saved countless lives by killing Swarm. What he did wasn't wrong."

"What he did was *murder someone*, Nate."

He held her gaze. "You all thought I pulled the trigger, and you still came to rescue me."

"Yeah, and look how you repaid me." At last the spotlight of Chizara's attention eased, and she turned away. "The thing is, Nate, I expect that kind of logic from you—taking one life to save many. But from Thibault it means something different. Something darker."

Nate blinked. In his prison cell, he'd gone through his own decision to shoot Quinton Wallace a thousand times, and every time he'd decided he was right. Why would it be different for someone else?

Of course, he knew Flicker wouldn't feel that way about Thibault killing someone.

"You can't tell them," he said. "Not yet."

"Are you kidding? You think I'm going to keep this . . ." Chizara's voice dropped off, and she shook her head. "I guess it doesn't matter. We'll never find him anyway. And if we do, he'll just disappear again."

"You're right," Nate said. Somehow Chizara had muddied everything in his mind. But without this mission the Zeroes could only keep running, doubting themselves, and falling apart. "It might take a while for Thibault to understand that he needs us, and that we need him. We should have a plan to keep from losing him again."

Chizara looked suspicious. "What kind of plan?"

He nodded and smiled his best, most persuasive smile. "You can help."

"With *what*, Nate?"

"Still working out the details." He gave her another winning smile. "Let's get that file back first."

"Ugh," Chizara said. "Something tells me I'm really going to hate Las Vegas."

CHAPTER 10
CRASH

"THIS PLACE IS THE WORST," CHIZARA SAID. "CAN'T I crash *anything*?"

"Not yet," Nate's voice answered in her earphones.

She suppressed a sudden urge to swear.

Las Vegas was much bigger than Cambria, and way more wired—like an electrified termite mound. Tech stings crawled all over her. The temptation to run downstairs, steal a car, and speed out of town and into the empty desert was overwhelming.

With one hand Chizara clung to the railing of the second-floor balcony overlooking the hotel lobby. The other gripped her phone in its leopard-skin cover.

Yep, even her phone was in disguise.

Her shiny, swooshy dress, scammed by Ethan from a market stall, pulsed like a migraine aura at the edge of her vision.

The red-and-gold turban was tacky, but it felt like the only thing stopping her head from exploding.

She was trying to pass as a dolled-up, carefree tourist, but probably looked more like she was nursing a Las Vegas–grade hangover.

All thanks to Glorious Leader, only back a few days and already running missions again. He was focused more on maximizing the Zeroes' powers than preserving Chizara's sanity.

The Strip was one long bustling, bristling flare of electricity. The lighting and the Muzak and the slot machines and the endless televisions, the stage-show tech, the castles-in-the-air of interlocked hotel circuits.

Threaded through all this brain-rattling tech was the machinery of surveillance. Widgets built into the slot machines making sure people didn't win too much. Thousands of cameras capturing every move. Rooms full of security people staring at monitors, keeping an eye on the staff, making sure none of the takings slipped into their pockets.

So much stuff to crash if things got tricky. So much power just *waiting* to be snatched up.

She was supposed to be keeping an eye out for Flicker's sister and federal agents. But she could hardly remember what Lily looked like, and spotting hidden microphones in this mess was impossible. The FBI could be all over the place, and Chizara would never know.

This was a disaster waiting to happen.

Even if Lily would never betray Flicker, what if the Feds had been watching her this last month? What if a sudden trip to Vegas looked suspicious, and they'd followed her?

All this risk, just for Nate's precious notes. To find a guy who'd abandoned them.

And why couldn't Lily just *mail* Nate's files? Because Flicker missed her twin sister, of course.

Like Chizara didn't miss her little brothers?

She lifted the earbud mike to her lips again, her teeth humming with signal. "I can't help you guys if my brain melts. Let me clear some space, so I can see better."

"If anyone's watching, a crash will tip them off," Flicker cut in. She was waiting for her sister in the diner downstairs, at the center of all of this. "Phan knew all about your power."

"But I need some juice," Chizara argued. "I've got nothing left from Eureka."

That was her excuse, anyway. The truth was, on top of the need for pain management, she *craved* fixing power these days. Without it she was prey to every little anxiety.

"What do you think, Flick?" Nate asked.

"Just make it small" came the answer.

Chizara smiled. "Maybe some slot machines. Far-off ones, don't worry."

She slid her attention along the busy street, snaked in through one of the bigger hotel lobbies, sought out the distinctive pattern of the slots in their sizzling rows.

They tumbled and whirred, each mini firework display indicating one more sucker, one more visitor emptying their pockets. Thinking *they'd* be the one to beat the whole rigged system.

A big ugly rip-off disguised as fun and glamour.

She sectioned off one of the busier avenues of machines and let it fail, a little shiver running up her spine. The lights tumbled over one last time and sank out of sight. A minor battalion of termite soldiers unclamped their mandibles from Chizara's flesh.

"That's better," she murmured.

See, Mom? she thought with a grin. *I'm saving people from themselves. Making the world a better place.*

Hmmm, came the answer.

Nate spoke up again. "Anybody see the target?"

"Is that what we're calling my sister?" Flicker asked, and Nate didn't answer.

Chizara shook her head. Those two had some issues to work out. The Zeroes had always had too many cooks in the kitchen, and now they had two head chefs.

She wondered how Nate planned to keep Thibault from leaving again, if they ever found him. Some kind of electronic tracker, probably, if he needed her help.

Chipped like a dog. From what she remembered of the guy, Thibault would *love* that.

"Um, is anything happening yet?" Scam said, filling the silence on the conference call. "My service isn't great out here."

"Nothing so far," Nate said.

Now that her head was clear, Chizara could make out Scam and the Zeroes' sedan down in the hotel turnaround, a football field away at the other end of the massive lobby. A taxi was dropping off some pastel-clad Midwesterners. A family immediately claimed the cab, a mom ushering two small boys into the back.

A picture slammed into Chizara—her little brothers Ikem and Obinna, staring at her, baffled. Through the ocean roar of Las Vegas electronics, she clearly heard the pain in Ikem's voice.

Why'd you run off, Chizara?

Around her the electronic pulse of the city skidded, a slip that the casino's wary monitors might register. She snatched back control.

Hold it together.

"Nothing down here," Kelsie said, sounding super cheerful. She'd loved Las Vegas from the moment they'd driven in.

Chizara blew out a breath across her teeth. Maybe she and Kelsie had some issues to work out too.

"Anything, Crash?" Nate asked.

"No Lily in the lobby," she said. "And no vans full of tech outside."

"Anyone wearing a wire?"

"Wires are small, Nate. But I'll try."

She forced her mind away from the tumult of the Strip, focusing on the people below. She tried to tune her ability to see the tiniest sparks.

Useless.

"It's like needles in a burning haystack, Nate." She tried to zoom in close. "I see . . . a pacemaker? That's a cochlear implant, and endless phones. Nobody wearing a wire."

She pulled back, letting the roar of the city's electronic infrastructure drown out the small things. She didn't want to be that close to the other faint whirring—the one *inside* people.

Your heart is a system too, Scam's voice had said to Verity. *Sparks and muscles, like a little engine in your chest.*

Since then, Chizara hadn't been able to ignore the ticks and whirs, those gradually more visible impulses that powered human bodies. Millivolt flashes prompted every heartbeat, powered arms to drop tokens into the slots, rippled across brains as new cards turned up at the blackjack tables.

She knew if she crashed this ruckus around her, she would have the power to zoom in on anyone.

Into their heart, their brain . . .

In the roar of this gambling-mad town, she could kill someone, anyone—that woman by the slots, that slob at the roulette wheel.

Really, a beer, at ten in the morning? Would anyone care if she grasped the sinus node at the top of his heart, blinking on and off, small and subtle? Just reached in and extinguished the rhythmic flashing like any machine made of metal and sparks?

Just like that.

There was a sick thrill in admitting she had so much power.

That she really was a demon. She could feel her judgment skewing under the weight of the possibilities.

Don't get distracted. You'll crash the whole town.

"How's the traffic on our escape route, Crash?" said Nate, as if he'd heard her attention slipping.

"Pretty good," she chirped back, fighting through the bejeweled nodes of traffic lights and signal boxes. A bus was holding up traffic on the Strip, waiting to turn in to the hotel with the crashed slots lounge. But if the Zeroes needed to make a fast getaway, there were other routes out. Chizara had memorized all the maps.

"You got enough juice to deal with the traffic lights?"

"Ha," Chizara said. "So easy."

She could *always* get more juice. Her body shook from holding up Las Vegas, from resisting the temptation to let it fall, to gorge on the power of the whole crooked place.

But just then down below, a slimmer, gothier, crankier-looking version of Flicker appeared. The girl was headed straight for the diner.

She didn't look up, but Chizara pulled back anyway, behind the clipped box hedge along the balcony rail.

In five minutes they'd be out of this awful place, speeding off into the desert's magnificent emptiness.

"Target spotted, entering the diner. Battle stations, folks."

CHAPTER 11
FLICKER

LILY SAT DOWN HEAVILY ACROSS THE DINER BOOTH, the plastic of the seat squeaking.

"You look like shit."

"I love you too," Flicker said, not hopping into her sister's eyes. She didn't particularly want to see herself. Her hair was ratty from a month of camping, and her skin was oily, thanks to a diet of roadside convenience store food à la Scam.

She didn't want to see Lily's look of disgust, either. So she stayed inside her own head, letting the other Zeroes keep watch.

Trust the plan. Get the folder and go.

"Dad's taking pills again," Lily said.

Flicker pulled her earbuds out and dropped them in her lap—the others didn't need to hear this.

"What kind?"

Flicker heard the faintest movement over the hyperactive rattle of the casino floor—a shrug, probably.

"He only takes them at night. So sleeping pills, I guess."

It was Flicker's turn to shrug. "That's not new. Is Mom seeing her therapist again?"

"What do you think?" Lily said. "She blames herself for letting you quit Dr. Bridges."

Flicker almost laughed. "Like *he* could've talked me out of being a Zero?"

"Yeah, no. That was my job."

"Don't even," Flicker said. "Listen, I'm sorry everything blew up. But it wasn't your fault, Lily. It wasn't even *our* fault."

"Because it was all some random accident, right?" Another plastic squeak as Lily leaned forward to take one of the french fries Flicker had ordered. She'd been too nervous to eat, and they smelled cold now. "Police stations and malls blow up on their own. Cops get torn to pieces every day. Shit happens, I guess."

"That wasn't us." Flicker hesitated. "Well, except the police station. But there are a lot of people out there with powers. They're all going crazy."

"Yeah, I watch the news," Lily said, chomping the cold fries savagely. She knew Flicker hated when people chewed while they talked. "We've got a front-row seat in Cambria. Everything is different since you left."

A sadness had come into Lily's voice, and Flicker cast her

power out to take a look. Someone in the next booth was staring at both of them over a milkshake, probably wondering if they were twins.

Lily was wearing a new jacket, black leather. Her eye makeup had gone seriously goth, like she'd decided to play evil twin.

An ironic touch, given that her sister was the wanted terrorist in the family.

"Different how?" Flicker asked softly.

"Cambria's full of reporters. And these randos called 'weird-hunters,' who are obsessed with you guys. Sometimes they come by our house in little groups, taking pictures, because you're weird famous. Mom *loves* it when that happens. There's even this company that wants to reopen the Dish. People are pulling it apart for *souvenirs*, for fuck's sake. We're like that town in New Mexico with the crashed aliens. But it's my sister in all the blurry photos."

"Damn," Flicker said.

"Yeah, hot damn." Lily hefted something. "I should probably sell this. To pay all those lawyers Mom has lined up for you."

Flicker shot her vision around the diner and found a set of eyes brushing across her sister. Lily was holding the familiar folder—the worn brown cover, the ragged edges of Nate's handwritten pages sticking out. Even the butterfly-clipped sheaf of photos she'd used to track Thibault's hotel down.

"This is what you wanted, right?"

"Yeah. Thanks for bringing it." Flicker reached across the table.

Her fingers closed on empty air.

"Seriously, Lily? Playing keep-away with the blind girl?"

"Tell me why this was so important."

"It's to help us find someone," Flicker explained. "There's this guy we all used to . . . Actually, it's complicated."

Lily snorted. "Um, I didn't forget Mr. Invisible Hotness. After all those stories you made me tell? He *lived in our house*, Riley."

Flicker's stomach clenched, hard.

Of course. Lily would have been miles from Thibault's meltdown, or his leveling up, whatever had wiped him from their minds. Much farther away than Nate. All this time, her sister had remembered her boyfriend, while Flicker herself had lost him completely.

Superpowers sucked sometimes.

"Just give it to me." Flicker hated the pleading in her own voice, but in those pages had to be a clue, a way to find him. The boy called Nothing, who was lost out there somewhere, torn from his family, his friends, her love.

Torn from himself.

"You need to *find* him?" Lily said. "What the hell? Did he bail on you?"

Flicker shook her head. "He did something to himself, made himself disappear."

"Small favors."

"Give me the folder, Lily. He's out there somewhere, hurting!"

"Gee, I wonder what that feels like for you," Lily said. "Missing someone. Not knowing if they're okay."

Flicker tried to swallow, but her mouth was too dry.

"Come home," Lily said.

"I want to. You know that."

"Then just leave with me now! It's not like *you* shot anyone."

"No, but my best friend did. And the moment I show up in Cambria, the government will grab me, Lily, and none of you will ever see me again." Flicker lowered her voice. "It won't be like on *Law and Order*, with due process and reasonable doubt. There's this FBI agent who knows about people with powers. He's already signed up one of us!"

"Yeah, I know," Lily said.

Flicker sat bolt upright. "Where'd you hear that? From some weird-hunter? Or the news?"

"You have to listen to me. Mom and Dad need you back." There were sudden tears in Lily's voice. "They're not going to make it unless you come home. We *love* you, Riley. I love you. That's why I did this."

"I know, and thank you. But you have to give me that . . ." Flicker paused. The roar of the slot machines seemed to grow, pulsing with the beat of her heart in her ears. She cast around again for a view of her sister. "Why you did what? Drove all this way?"

Lily spoke again, slow and clear. "I have to ask you something, Flicker. Are the other Zeroes here?"

"Why?"

"I have to ask if the rest of them are here."

"Shit," Flicker said. She found the eyes again, the ones across the diner that were on her sister again, watching the brown folder like it was the most important thing in the world.

Then they darted guiltily away, down toward a stack of pancakes that didn't have a single bite taken out of them.

"We cut you a deal, Riley. With this Special Agent Phan, who understands about people like you. Just put your palms flat on the table and it's done."

Flicker picked the earbuds up from her lap and stuck them in.

"Lily fucked us," she said. "Blow it up."

Then she threw herself across the booth to tear the folder from her sister's hands.

CHAPTER 12
MOB

THE LIGHTS WENT OUT. SURPRISE RIPPLED THROUGH the crowd, hitting Kelsie in her gut, like the boom of a giant bass speaker.

Flicker had hit the panic button, and Chizara was working the plan. The crappy mall music went silent, along with hundreds of slots and poker machines. The crowd wasn't panicked yet, but anxious voices rose in the darkness—friends calling for each other, parents looking for kids.

Within seconds, light came from countless bobbing phones, a chaos of scared faces around Kelsie. She pushed through them toward the diner.

Chizara's voice in her earbud. "Feds."

Kelsie saw them too. A corner of the diner had lit up.

Flicker and Lily, caught in the beams of a dozen powerful flashlights. Upheld badges sparkled metal in the air.

"Damn it, Lily," Kelsie breathed. "Narcing on your own sister?"

Flicker was going to be shattered. But there wasn't time to worry about that. The crowd's fear built as the lights stayed off, pushing into her mind. Kelsie fell sideways against the diner door, her feet unsteady.

The supermax had scared her. She carried it with her now. Another violent, angry stain on her soul, like the place Swarm still occupied in her chest.

And here she was, running toward the Feds—who would take her to the same kind of prison. She'd rather die.

"Guys!" Flicker shouted. "Do something!" "Pitch dark, Crash." Nate's voice was smooth. "No phones working but ours."

The flashlights flared brightly, then winked out, along with the jiggling light of phones—Chizara leveling the playing field for Flicker.

Kelsie took a breath and headed into the diner.

"It's getting gnarly out here," came Nate's voice. "Can you pull back the panic, Mob?"

Kelsie almost laughed. She *was* the panic. Las Vegas had been a relief from empty countryside, at first. But gradually she'd seen the truth of it, the pulse of greed that underlay it all.

Everywhere she went, Swarm followed.

"Federal marshals!" came a shout. "Nobody move!"

That tipped the crowd in the diner over into terror. Badges, flashlights, and their phones had gone dark.

Was this a bombing? Something worse?

But wedged inside their panic, Kelsie felt a new emotion—the grim determination of the marshals. Then a green luminance filled the darkness, worms of light like glow sticks at a rave, and she could see again. The marshals had linked arms and were advancing on Flicker, not leaving her any space to sneak past.

"Glow sticks?" Chizara whispered in her earbud. "I can't crash a chemical reaction!"

Of course. Phan knew all about Electro-whatevers, didn't he?

Kelsie felt it, the familiar spark of satisfaction from predators who'd cornered their prey. Acid rose in her throat.

It was up to her—Mob, Kelsie, Swarm, whoever she was right now—to fix this, while riding a wave of panic.

But maybe panic was the key.

"I can't get past them," Flicker cried.

"Sorry, everyone," Mob breathed, and seized the crowd's fear.

She looped it, fed it straight at the marshals in a screech of feedback. All at once their sickly green faces went wide-eyed, astonished. The crowd's horror pushed aside their certainty, made a home for itself in their veins.

Then Kelsie realized—the marshals' calm purpose had been the linchpin keeping the diner from falling into chaos, and she'd just yanked it out.

Fear burned through the crowd, spilling out onto the casino floor. In a single pure instant, the customers and marshals were part of one group, one beast.

A creature powered by raw, potent dread.

People stumbled and collided in the dark, with no place to go, shouting and screaming. They flowed through the diner's exits. Kelsie was shoved back out, bounced hard against a wall, and fell onto the floor.

"Reel it in, Mob," Nate said through her earbud. "Can you?"

Kelsie clenched her teeth. Running feet rumbled all around her. Trying to ride this beast was crazy. Dangerous.

But it was *awesome*.

Emotion thundered through her like a stampede. Lives were in danger, but she couldn't pull back. Couldn't rein it in if she tried.

She was the wild terror, the madness of the crowd.

She was the maelstrom.

The fear was there in her ear, Nate shouting, "Damn it, Mob! Bring it down!"

But she didn't want to. The crowd was *hers* now, her own swarm seeking its destiny at last. She was leveling up.

Then her girlfriend's whisper in her ear: "This isn't you, Kels."

Kelsie curled up tighter, took hold of herself.

"Help me, Zara."

For an endless moment there was no reply, and then she heard Chizara's voice again—

"How about this?"

Lights sprang on, blinking and whirling, and the air filled with buzzes and beeps and electronic whoops of joy. And Kelsie felt the ecstasy of money being won.

She shut her eyes against the glare, and heard Zara laughing a supervillain laugh as she cried out, "And *you* get a car, and *you* get a car, and *you* get a car . . ."

"Seriously?" Nate was shouting. "You're spilling all the slots? This is just a different kind of riot!"

"Yeah, but it's a *happy* riot!" Chizara cackled. "You want to talk them down? I just routed the speaker system to your phone. Go for it, Bellwether!"

"You did wha—" Nate began, and his words *boomed* through the casino.

The throng had cleared around Kelsie, everyone piling up near the rows of slot machines that shrieked free money.

The panic was turning to joy—but greed, too. Another facet of Swarm frothing inside her . . . Then she felt someone take her arm, and looked up.

Flicker, a folder in her hand.

"Come on. We don't have much time."

Kelsie stood on shaky legs, looked at the diner. "The marshals?"

"Swept away by your little greed swarm," Flicker said, dragging her into motion.

They fought against the surging crowd, toward the exit

where Ethan waited with the car. Kelsie remembered to keep her eyes on the floor, to help Flicker.

"Is your sister okay?" she asked.

"Safe. Got knocked out, right before the riot started." Flicker shook out her right hand, anger in her voice. "Sucker punched in the dark."

"Ouch," Kelsie said.

"Yeah. Hurts extra when it's your twin."

Kelsie wondered whether she meant her own fist or her sister's jaw.

"Sorry about that little glitch!" Nate's voice bellowed through the sound system. "But it's Everyone Wins Day here at World Casino! Please proceed calmly to the nearest machine to collect your money!"

As Kelsie glanced back, spotlights swung and found Nate. He stood on a craps table, holding his phone to his face, spilling his charisma across the crowd. And Kelsie felt something new in the mix of astonishment and greed.

His smile, warm and civilized and contagious.

"Yes, all that money is real, and it's all yours! But be nice to each other!"

Kelsie added a little something extra to the feedback loop. A bright anticipation, like they were about to find salvation in that money, all their problems solved. All they had to do was play nice.

All they had to do was not hurt each other.

Nate jumped from the table and was swallowed by the

throng. Kelsie couldn't see the marshals anywhere. They'd been in plain clothes, and there were too many people flowing toward the slot machines.

Then Ethan's voice was in her ears, sounding strained. "Um, guys? What's happening in there?"

"A shitshow," Flicker panted. "Is the car ready?"

"Sure. I'll start it up."

And then Chizara was coming at them, laughing as she ran. God, she ran so beautifully, even in that ridiculous costume.

"This casino is *so* going out of business." She took Kelsie's other arm. "My mother would be proud."

Kelsie smiled. Zara's mom disapproved of a lot of things, but she thought gambling was the worst.

Except maybe terrorism, inciting riots, and grand theft casino.

"Guys!" Nate's voice was in their earbuds again. "I'm right behind you, but the Feds are right behind me!"

Kelsie looked over her shoulder. There was Nate, with four burly men in street clothes in pursuit, along with a couple of casino security guards swept up in the excitement.

Her own legs were shaky, her body weak from fighting off Swarm inside her. Chizara took more of her weight under one strong arm.

Kelsie looked ahead. Fifty feet between her and the doors. She'd never make it.

But she'd die trying.

CHAPTER 13
SCAM

"THIS IS BAD," ETHAN MUTTERED.

He'd been standing beside the stolen sedan, watching people flee from the casino for the last three minutes. And now people were fleeing back *in*, shouting about free money.

That was usually a sign that a plan hadn't worked.

Seriously, the Zeroes had to stop trying to rescue people. That Anon guy was better off without them.

Reception was crap out here, but Ethan had heard Flicker shout something profane about Lily, which couldn't be good.

Then Nate's voice was in his earbud, loud and breathless. "Get the car ready!"

Yeah. Really not good. Ethan ran around the sedan, opening the doors.

Flicker and Chizara burst out of the hotel, dragging Kelsie

between them. Her face was pale, and she stumbled like her feet were on sideways.

"Into the back!" Chizara cried, and they hustled her into the car. Flicker took the passenger seat up front.

People were staring, and a guy in a hotel uniform was walking up.

Ethan turned on the voice.

"Food allergy! We're taking her to the hospital. Clear the turnaround!"

As the guy jumped into action, Glorious Leader came running out and dove for the driver's seat.

The casino doors whisked shut again, and a second later they rocked and swayed—six big guys hurtling against the glass and bouncing off it, stunned.

"That's just cold, Crash," Ethan said as he slid in next to Kelsie.

Nate gunned the engine, and Ethan was pressed back against his seat as the sedan burned rubber across the turnaround.

"Say," Ethan said, scrabbling to buckle up. "Did I hear the words 'Lily fucked us'?"

"Shut up, Scam," Flicker said, her voice hard. She shoved a thick folder into the glove compartment. So at least the mission hadn't been a complete fiasco.

But why did *he* have to shut up? Flicker had sworn up and down that her sister would never betray them. She'd declared

Lily the sole exception to the no-contact-with-Cambria rule, and they'd wound up screwed.

Damn. He'd always thought Lily kind of liked him.

"Head north," Chizara said from the other side of Kelsie. "I'll work the lights."

"Straight through the middle of Vegas?" Flicker asked.

"More cars to put in front of them," Chizara said.

She sounded like she had it under control, in a cackling, mad-scientist kind of way, so Ethan eased back into his seat. Nothing the voice could do in this situation.

Also, he kind of wanted to peek at his new burner phone.

Waiting in the turnaround had been boring, at least before the riot had perked things up. He'd really fought the temptation to send a message to Cambria. But it had been a long month of running and hiding, no contact with anyone who wasn't a superpowered freak.

So maybe he was a little homesick. And possibly he'd texted a certain someone to ask about ghost boys being caught on surveillance cameras back home.

Um, no, came the answer. *Is this who I think it is?*

It had taken him five minutes to come up with *Maybe.*

Holy crap, Sonia had replied.

Too bad the voice couldn't control his fingers. Then he could've texted something brilliant and funny right away. But he'd still been thinking what to say when all hell had broken loose.

Nate swung the sedan onto the Strip. Kelsie was flung sideways, jammed tight against Ethan. He realized she didn't have her seat belt on, and started to fumble for it.

"I'm sorry," she was murmuring. "I didn't mean to make them—"

"Not your fault," Flicker said from the front. "It's my DNA that screwed us."

Her voice was breaking. Ethan couldn't imagine being betrayed by his older sister, Jess. He figured having an identical twin do the honors would be even worse.

Nate was weaving back and forth across all six lanes of traffic. Ethan finally managed to get Kelsie's seat belt to click just as they darted through an intersection to a chorus of car horns.

Ethan's pocket buzzed.

Chizara stared at him. "Did someone just text you?"

"I set up a news alert," he heard himself say smoothly. "For crowd activity."

Hopefully they were all too distracted to spot the voice in action. He slipped the phone into his palm as Nate sped around an SUV.

Sonia's message was longer this time. *You guys anywhere near the Super Bowl? Some a-grade crowd weirdness happening.*

Ethan groaned. Seriously, were some Zeroes messing with the Super Bowl? Might as well declare war on apple pie.

The world outside the car windows turned liquid, they were moving so fast. Ethan didn't want to look at the blur of concrete, so he stared at his screen.

Another text from Sonia: *The ticket scanners all crashed, so they had to eyeball every ticket. But people got into the game with blank pieces of paper!*

Blank Super Bowl tickets? That sounded like Coin's power. But Coin was dead, killed by Swarm.

Swarm was dead too. And Ethan still missed the reassuring presence of the Craig every damn day. But maybe there was another Coin somewhere out there, just like there had been another Anon.

Maybe there was another Scam somewhere too. Someone who would understand that the stuff the voice said wasn't really Ethan's fault.

More Sonia: *My weird-hunter group is obsessed! And they hate sports!*

As Ethan tried to come up with something smart, the sedan went practically airborne through the next intersection.

Cool, he managed.

He looked up. "Um, those lights up ahead, are they red?"

"Backseat driver, much?" Flicker asked.

Nate sped up. Which Ethan hadn't realized was possible.

The traffic flowed across the intersection like a wall of metal.

Chizara leaned forward, her gaze set on the cars in front of them. "Don't slow down. I got it timed just right."

Ethan flung his arms over his face and braced for impact.

Horns went dopplering past, and Ethan twisted in his seat

to look back. At the intersection behind them, the cars had all stopped dead, leaving an exact sedan-width gap between front and rear bumpers.

"Red lights don't matter," Chizara said with a chuckle. "I went straight for the engines."

"Close it up!" Nate ordered.

Chizara swirled a hand in the air, and a few of the cars jerked forward to block the gap.

"Nobody can catch us!" Ethan crowed.

"It's not over yet," Kelsie said softly. "Those marshals felt pretty determined."

Ethan untwisted to face forward. All along the Strip ahead of them, the traffic lights switched to green. Chizara had built a path right through town.

They sped along the wide, sun-drenched Strip, between the rows of palm trees. Tourists were everywhere, walking wide-eyed, taking pictures. It hardly felt like a car chase at all now.

Vegas sprawled around them like an upended toy box. The buildings were random shapes and sizes. None of them matched, except for their shifting light shows. Which, Ethan realized, were starting to go dark.

"Is that you?" he asked Chizara.

"Yeah," she muttered. "Charging up, just in case."

"In case what?" Ethan said as a vast swath of the city's signage sputtered out.

"In case they catch us," Crash said with an ominous smile, "and I need to show them who's boss."

Five minutes later the city trailed off abruptly, like a mirage. The buildings and palm trees were gone. A tall sign flashed past. DRIVE CAREFULLY.

Good luck with that.

Ahead of them was only desert and a long, straight highway.

Ethan looked at his phone again.

You guys busted Saldana out of prison, didn't you? That was badass!

He smiled. Sent her a thumbs-up.

So where are you now?

Top secret, he typed. Though not really, given that Crash had just darkened half of Las Vegas. So he added, *Just watch the news. I BET you'll never guess.*

The reply came about five seconds later.

BET? So you guys are in Las Vegas?

Crap. Too easy. Ethan had always sucked at making up clues.

Not anymore. We've got another rescue mission to get to.

Whoa came her reply, and the word made him shiver. *Vegas is all over the news, dude.*

"What are you looking at?" Chizara asked, peering over. "Your phone keeps needling me."

"We made the news already," Ethan squeaked, managing to stuff the voice down into his chest.

"Thanks to Lily," Flicker said. "We should ditch this car as soon as possible. And the phones. Crash?"

"Wait a second!" Ethan started typing. "There's this story about the Super Bowl that—"

"Really?" Flicker said. "Since when did you care about sports, Scam?"

"But it got Zeroed!" Ethan stalled.

Got to ditch this phone soon but hit you later, he sent.

"What kind of power?" Nate asked.

"Blank paper turned into tickets. Sounds like Coin."

Nate breathed out of clenched teeth, like the getting-Davey-killed scars were still fresh.

Hope to hear from you soon, Sonia replied. *You already made me famous twice. Maybe the third time's the charm!*

Ethan blinked, rereading the words. What kind of charm was she talking about, exactly?

Before he could ask, another Sonia text appeared. *Btw, I'm going out of town soon. Weird-hunter conference.*

"You can read about the Super Bowl later," Nate said. "The Feds are probably scanning for us."

"Just give me one more—" Ethan started, but Chizara snapped her fingers and the screen went blank.

"Crap." He dropped the dead phone to the floor.

He didn't even know where Sonia was going to be. But there were more burners in the trunk, and Chizara had to sleep sometime.

"We've got more immediate problems, Flicker said. "Eyes in the air."

There was a thwacking sound above them, like short booms of thunder.

"Great," Chizara said, twisting toward the back window. "Choppers are the worst."

CHAPTER 14
BELLWETHER

"WHAT DO YOU MEAN?" NATE ASKED. HIS PALMS were slick on the steering wheel.

"Helicopters aren't as simple as cars!" Crash said.

"Can you force it down?"

"Not without risking everyone inside." Chizara paused, and the traffic lights half a mile ahead turned green. "The tail rotor has to balance the torque, or the chopper goes into a spin. It's not like I can do that math in my head! Maybe if I'd had a helicopter to practice with . . ."

Nate swallowed. Things had changed since he'd gone to prison. Two months ago Chizara had been controlling lights at a nightclub. And now?

Give me a helicopter to play with. No big deal.

And the Feds were way too smart these days. Showing

up with no tech, just glow sticks that Chizara couldn't crash. Forewarned and forearmed.

The Zeroes had worked every advantage, meeting in the densest crowd he'd ever seen, and Phan had almost grabbed them.

But prison had also taught him patience. There was no need to panic.

"Okay," he said. "What can they actually *do* to us from up there?"

"They can shoot us," Flicker said. "I've got eyes looking through sniper scopes—aiming for the tires."

"Got it," Chizara said.

Flicker smiled at Nate. "We practiced for snipers during the prison break."

He didn't answer, not daring to interrupt Chizara's work.

"Okay," she said a moment later. "Their scopes are useless now. They'll miss by ten feet."

"Can you make it twenty?" Ethan asked.

"Good work, team," Nate said. He swerved around a slow-moving pickup truck, wide-eyed kids in the back watching the sedan shoot past. "So they can't shoot us. Well, until they get close enough to open up with handguns."

"They won't," Flicker said. "They want us alive."

"Are you *sure* about that?" Ethan asked.

"Afraid so." Flicker's voice dropped. "Lily said she'd made a deal. She was trying to recruit me."

Nate tore his eyes from the road to stare at Flicker. Of course. They had Verity working for them. Why not a Sight-caster?

"Um, *just* you?" Ethan asked from the backseat.

Everyone looked at him.

"I mean, being a junior G-man might not be so bad," he added.

"Can it, Scam," Flicker said. "No one's joining the FBI. But at least if they want us alive, they won't go all Bonnie and Clyde on this car."

"Which means that chopper can only track us," Nate said. "But they'll put up roadblocks."

His thoughts drifted back to what Flicker had said. The whole time he was in prison, nobody had ever offered him a deal. Because they'd thought he was a murderer, and maybe also . . . what had Phan said?

You aren't even average.

Phan had known other Bellwethers. Better ones.

What kind of better, exactly? What part of Nate's own power hadn't he explored yet?

"Spikes on the road would be bad," Chizara said. "I can move cars out of our way, but not some dumb piece of metal."

"Can you tweak the chopper a little, like a fuel leak?" Flicker asked. "So they'd have to turn back?"

An exhalation from Crash. "That might start an engine fire. I told you, helicopters are finicky. We did enough damage back in Las Vegas."

Nate's hands tensed on the wheel. This was a great time for Chizara to get safety conscious.

All they needed was half an hour out of view, and he could pull off into the desert and disappear. He'd mapped out a dozen nearby places to hide—ghost towns, abandoned mines—and a couple of used-car lots for a quick vehicle switch. And Chizara could stop anyone who followed them off-road, unless they came on horses.

"Crap!" Ethan cried. "Another chopper!"

"Yep," Flicker confirmed. "And it's got snipers too. Crash?"

"On it."

The helicopters grew louder. One made a close pass overhead, swirling dust across the sedan's front windshield for a moment. The skitter of sand and pebbles on glass set Nate's teeth on edge.

Were they trying to force him off the road?

Screw that. He would drive until they shot his tires out.

Junior fucking G-men.

Not even average.

Then a small voice came from the back.

"I can handle them." Kelsie, sounding grim.

"What do you mean?" Flicker asked.

No answer came.

Nate adjusted his rearview. Kelsie was huddled back there between Ethan and Chizara, pale and shivering.

He'd felt it back in the casino—what she'd almost become.

"No," he said. "You're not using that side of your power. Ever."

"Easy for you to say!" Kelsie cried. "The rest of you can cut a deal. But I was there when a cop got torn to pieces. They'll put me in isolation!"

Chizara spoke up. "It's okay, Kelsie. Nobody's going to make a—"

"I almost didn't make it out of that casino. Do you know what I'd turn into in prison? *What I'd turn the prison into?*"

A helicopter buzzed overhead again, drowning her out, but the nightmare answer came unbidden to Nate's head.

A Swarm would turn any prison into a slaughterhouse. Guards, prisoners, janitors—nobody would survive.

Maybe he could make Chizara understand: A locked-up Mob would be a hundred times worse than a couple of helicopter crashes.

But he'd already played the moral-calculus card with Chizara once this week. She wouldn't listen to him now.

He wasn't the leader anymore.

He felt the weight of that insignificance settle on him. Like in the empty corridors of the supermax, when there weren't enough prisoners for him to feel the Curve at all. Like Phan calling him less than average in front of the other Zeroes. Like Flicker being coleader now.

It was almost enough to make him contemplate surrender. Let the others take their shot at making a deal. Maybe even

Kelsie could swing something. Hadn't Swarm hunted other Zeroes, as if by smell? Surely Phan would find a use for her.

Nate shook himself. What the hell was he thinking? These were his friends. His allies. They'd saved him from life in prison.

He had made the Zeroes what they were—cemented them together, taught them to pool their talents. Fate had put Verity and Phan in that interrogation room with him, pointing him toward New Orleans.

He wasn't going to give up now.

Then one of the helicopters swept past again, so close that the skids almost touched the ground, and he smiled.

Maybe he *was* going to give up.

"I know what to do," he said. "Hold tight."

CHAPTER 15
CRASH

THE SEDAN PULLED OFF THE ROAD, KICKING UP A clatter of gravel.

Chizara leaned forward in her seat. "So *this* is your plan, Nate? We bust you out of jail and you want to walk straight back in?"

"And take us with you?" Scam squeaked from beside her.

Nate threw a grin back at them. "Trust me, guys."

One of the helicopters was directly overhead. The dust of its rotor wash flew up around the car, like a twister was lifting them. The noise was unbelievable, and Chizara's head filled with a light-speckled cloud of airborne electronics.

Her Crash brain kept searching for a way to bring the helicopters down safely.

Or you could just drop them, it nagged.

But the balance of the spinning blades was so precise, she couldn't stop the engines without the choppers spiraling into the ground, killing everyone inside.

No, that wasn't her. Not yet, anyway.

The sedan crunched to a stop. Leaving the motor running, Nate unlatched his door. Dust and thunder poured in through the crack.

Chizara felt a kick of Glorious-Leader power from him as he flung the door wide.

"Everyone out! Act like you're giving up!"

"We *are* giving up!" Ethan cried.

But they all leaped to obey. Chizara grabbed Kelsie's hand and stumbled out, screwing up her eyes against the whirling sand. Tiny pebbles stung her bare arms and legs.

The giant mechanical insects whap-whapped downward. The nearer one fumbled delicately for a foothold, then settled its monstrous weight on the dirt.

"Do not move!" came a shout through a megaphone. A man in a flak jacket stood in the open side bay door, the sniper beside him aiming through his scope.

Chizara nudged the scope's optics another few degrees, just in case.

"Keep everybody calm, Mob!" Nate yelled.

But Kelsie looked too wobbly to control a crowd. The rotor wash was practically blowing her off her feet.

Chizara leaned closer. "It'll be okay. He's got a plan."

Apparently.

The five of them arranged themselves in a line, hands up. Kelsie shut her eyes against the wind and sand, started bopping to the beat of the blades.

"Crash!" Nate's shout was like a cricket's chirp against the engine roar. "Don't mess with the choppers till the second one lands. Do what you can with the guns!"

She nodded. Of course—once the helicopters were on the ground, she could wreck their engines without killing anyone. But by then they'd be surrounded by armed marshals.

Had Nate really thought this through?

Four men had already spilled from the doors of the grounded helicopter. Sidearms drawn, they scuttled along in a crouch beneath the spinning disk, taking up positions. They peered nervously at the empty sedan and the line of kids beside it.

Chizara scanned the pistols—Glocks, made mostly of plastic polymers instead of metal, no electronics. All she had to play with were the tiny metal springs in the firing pins. Even full of power from the crashed Strip, she'd find it tricky to disarm the pistols.

She started on the first one, doubts attacking her:

There isn't time.

You've never even tried this before.

A 90 percent success rate won't be good enough!

But Kelsie's loop hit her then, calming her, helping her focus on the metal spring wrapped around the firing pin of the

Glock. Focus deep, focus hard, until she could see the lattice-work that made up the alloy, that gave the metal its elasticity. She brought her power to bear, working with the faint charge in the tiny component to overexcite the molecules, to make heat, to dislodge them from their places in the lattice. Slowly, surely, she welded the spiral onto the pin.

Distracting her were the tiny pounding lights in the cops' chests, strung out in a line, begging to be crashed. Maybe she could make their hearts flutter a little? Drop them to their knees in a swoon . . .

Chizara gritted her teeth. This wasn't the time to experiment. A stopped heart would kill someone just as surely as a helicopter crash.

At least the pistols were all the same model. She went onto the next and attacked the firing pin, quicker and more confident now.

The second helicopter was landing, farther away. The rotors' wind pummeled Chizara's ears, fluttered her clothes. Soon there would be more boots on the ground, more pistols aimed at them—too many to disable.

"It's almost down," Nate said. "I hope you've fixed those handguns."

Chizara crushed the third Glock's firing pin with a burst of energy.

"All but one. And that sniper's close enough to fire from the hip."

"He won't be a problem. Give me two engine fires, *now*."

Chizara had to smile. So easy.

She took hold of the digital engine controls in both heli-copters. Flattened the rotors so that the choppers couldn't take off again, opened the fuel lines wide, revved their engines up as fast as she could. The torque began to make the skids shift across the ground.

Inside, the pilots started yelling, grappling with their useless controls.

Chizara grunted, jamming all the safeties and forcing an oil leak through the closer chopper's engine casing, where it splat-tered on scorching metal. Alarms sounded and smoke began to pour off the helicopter's roof.

The agents looked up, began shouting. One waved her arms, and the others started scurrying away from the spinning blades.

"Panic them, Mob!" Nate shouted over the din. "Everyone link up!"

He grabbed Chizara, and Chizara took Kelsie's hand.

A dullness came over the world as Nate sucked them into anonymity. All Chizara's anxiety, her battle readiness, her deter-mination not just to survive but to *win*, whipped out of her.

Smoke whirled from the burning helicopter. Two of the marshals retreated into the dust cloud. Others went to help the pilot and the sniper, who were out of their seats, spraying fire extinguishers up at the ceiling of the chopper bubble.

"No eyes on us!" Flicker shouted. "Back in the car!"

She pulled Chizara and Nate along, with Scam and Kelsie at the ends of the chain.

A second engine fire seemed like overkill, so Chizara simply zapped the controls of the just-landed helicopter. It began to slew across the dirt as its tail rotor lost its battle with the main disk's torque.

Then she let all the choppers' electronics fail, like huge Christmas trees toppling in on themselves, splintering, their strings of winking lights sputtering out.

They scrambled back into the car, clumsy and awkward, like this was some kind of wild dare at a traffic light, changing handholds so no one would be visible even for a second.

"They're totally freaking," Kelsie said, scooting along the backseat. "I'm keeping them that way!"

Once they were all inside, Nate let go. The tumult of reality rushed back in at them, dust and noise and acrid smoke.

Chizara focused her power, starting the car.

"How are those guns, Crash?" Flicker shouted.

"I jiggered three of the pistols' firing pins—I think."

"I guess we'll find out," Nate cried. "Heads *down*!"

He floored the accelerator, and the sedan took off, fishtailing on the sand before steadying. Dust filled the windows.

"The marshals are getting their panic under control!" Kelsie shouted, throwing an arm around Chizara and dragging her down.

"They can't even see us," Flicker scoffed.

But a moment later the front windshield cleared, the sedan bursting out of the cloud of rotor wash and smoke.

"Here we go," Flicker said. "Someone's looking at us through a scope. Aiming for the right rear tire!"

Chizara tried to remember which way she'd nudged the sniper's optics—left or right?

The answer came when a sharp smack went through the car. Something dunking against the bottom of the chassis, dead center.

"Crap!" Ethan shouted next to Chizara, lifting his feet up off the floorboard. "I *felt* that!"

But she was laughing now, full of juice and adrenaline. "They can't hit anything. At least not on purpose!"

"By accident is still a bullet!" Ethan cried.

"Whatever you did with the handguns worked," Flicker said. "One of those guys is stripping his pistol."

"But I didn't get all of—"

A glassy *pop* cut her words off. Tiny ice cubes cascaded over Chizara's back and into her curls.

"Whoa!" Nate said. The car veered for a moment, then found the highway's center and accelerated again.

Still laughing, Chizara rose up to peep out the back window. Blue-green cubes of glass danced away across the trunk lid, carried by the car's vibration and the wind. The helicopters and the hapless marshals had shrunk to toy size behind, wreathed in swirls of smoke and dust.

But one man in a flak jacket stood there, still taking aim. She glimpsed his heart—

"Get *down*." Kelsie dragged on Chizara's shoulder, pulling her back under cover.

The sound of the shot reached them, but nothing hit the sedan. They were too far away, moving too fast for pistols and rifles with broken sights.

They all sat up, Ethan, Chizara, and Kelsie brushing glass off themselves.

"Man, they're *pissed*," Kelsie said. "They hate a bunch of kids beating them!"

"And now we're barreling down the highway with no back window," Flicker said. "We need to ditch this car ASAP."

"Let's just take a moment to breathe," Nate said.

Flicker stared at him. "Since when are you Zen Boy?"

Nate only shrugged. "I don't have to be. You'll get the real one back soon."

Flicker yanked open the glove compartment, pulled out the folder, and pressed it to her chest.

I hope this guy's worth it, Chizara thought. Her body was burning through its nervous energy as the battle fervor faded. Every cell was back in its usual place, primed at maximum watchful anxiety. The elation gradually faded, and she felt hunted again, homesick.

That had only been two helicopters. How many did the federal government have? Thousands more?

The Feds were too smart, too numerous and well equipped. It was only a matter of time before they ran the Zeroes down.

But she was glad of this churning in her stomach. In that anonymous world with Nate, she'd felt not quite human. Like a helicopter herself, hovering above reality, disconnected, not responsible for anything she did.

Like a demon might feel.

The hot desert air spilled through the car, buffeting her clothes and hair. Up ahead, the highway was empty. As was the wide blue sky, and the road behind.

A laugh bubbled up in her, but not the evil-villain laugh that came with crashing stuff. Something light, relieved, astonished.

"So basically we won that one by surrendering?" she said. "That is *so* not you, Nate."

Nate ran a hand over his prison buzz cut.

"People change."

CHAPTER 16

COLD EVENING WAS COMING DOWN. THE DAY'S
sounds were all gone—the sea hissing on the gravel beach, cars
roaring past along the highway, the fog-bound oaks and maples
dripping.

Now silence, all around the boy, beckoned him deeper into
the forest. He'd made it, to the last place that connected him
with the world.

Beyond this there was only peace, freedom from the pain
he'd been fleeing. Freedom from everyone and everything. A
final chance at nothing.

A last disappearing.

He forced himself to make a fire first. Fire would warm that
distant, complaining creature, his body. His bare feet, sore where
they weren't numb with cold, *really* liked the idea of a fire.

The fire had been the focus the last time he'd been here, with that guy who'd known his name for a while. It had been easier to talk at burning wood and crackling sparks than to face each other.

He could remember the guy's manner, thoughtful and curious.

Had he smiled a lot? Or just given off the *feeling* of smiling?

The campground was closed for the winter, so there were no other people. He was alone with the deep memories that drifted up to keep him from melting into the Nothing.

The fire he made was small and nearly smokeless. But it brought life to the dimming, dripping forest. For now it kept him anchored to his body, to the pain of his thawing feet.

But when it was gone, he would go too.

His friend had sat right here next to him, beside this same concrete fire pit. He'd brought all sorts of equipment—keyboards, cameras, a notebook. Recording everything. Siphoning their conversation into his devices, like some collector who'd found a prize specimen. Saying that as soon as he got home, he'd print it all and wipe the devices. A promise of trust and secrecy.

The boy had been grateful for all the talking. Back then he'd craved being seen, recognized. He'd curled up in his sleeping bag that night with a quiet mind, happy.

He fed a fresh stick into the fire. Did he even want that happiness now?

It didn't matter what he wanted. What he'd done stood in the way.

Something cold and wrong.

A burning coal popped in the fire, and a roar filled his buried memories. His right hand ached. The fire wasn't a fire anymore—it was a fallen boy, his back and his head blown open, two awful fiery craters.

There was no coming back from that.

His body panicked for a moment, all thumping heart and taut muscles. He stared down the vision, until it was a fire again—small, hungry for more wood, harmless.

His pulse slowed, and a different rhythm throbbed behind it. A car engine, off in the woods toward the gate. Would these trespassers force him away from the warmth?

He waited by the fire, his body soaking up heat while it could.

The engine sound drew closer along the looping trail, cruising past one empty campsite after another. The time had come. The forest waited, ready to take him in, to absorb him completely.

He stood up, kicked dirt over the fire.

The vehicle was nearly here.

Music was pouring from it, rolling out among the ferns and stumps and trees. Music he knew.

And a girl was calling out the window. He knew her, too, and she knew him.

He turned away, pushed into the fog and the cold, into the forest that would dissolve him completely.

She called again, her voice shaky. *Please be here!*

But he wouldn't. He wouldn't be anywhere. He wanted to be nothing.

The van pulled into the campsite, its doors opening. He ducked and crept farther into the trees, letting go, pushing away from this reality.

It sank and flowed away behind him, the world he'd once known and belonged in. Ahead yawned the darker nothing— peace and emptiness lived there, and, at the very farthest edge, no coming back.

Nothing! called the girl into the dripping quiet.

That made him stop. He remembered someone naming him that.

The van's engine went silent.

Are you sure this is the place? A scratchy voice, male.

One hundred percent positive. That voice, bone-weary, was the guy from that summer. Right here. He'd remembered this place too, damn it.

The boy eased away through a patch of ferns, climbed a small slope. He was edging behind two oaks growing close together when the girl called again.

She called his name, his real name. Her voice carved a hole through the fog, through the dusk. It banished the distance he'd been working so hard to keep . . .

Are you here? she cried. *Don't hide from me.*

She was closer than the others, right at the edge of the

clearing, about to plunge in after him. *You've got to be here, Thibault—where else would you go?*

She was in pain. She was in tears.

It was very simple all of a sudden.

He couldn't let her cry.

He opened his mouth, and a voice came out of it, hardly a voice at all, hoarse with disuse. . . .

"Flicker?"

Instantly he wanted to snatch the word back. That single sound was reeling everything in—all his pain, his guilt, what he'd done.

But already she was hurtling toward him, feet thudding, breaking twigs, tearing past foliage. "Yes, it's me! Where are you?"

He stood among the oaks, motionless, giving her no more clues. It was better if he went, for everyone. She would hunt for him, and not find him, and go away thinking she'd imagined his voice—

But she drew closer. Her face a pale circle in the near dark, turning this way and that. Her attention glittering in the darkness, not a spotlight from her eyes, but diffuse and coiling, like sparks rising up from the fire.

She struggled on for another three steps.

"Thibault," she whispered, as if she knew how close he was. "Say something. Say my name again. That's all you have to do."

As if she knew the way into him, the key.

As if she understood how hard this was for him, how impossible.

Flicker, he mouthed soundlessly. His being wasn't floating free anymore, but rocketing back toward this tiny, singular body of his. This body that yearned for that girl in the ferns.

"I can feel you," she said softly.

And she came toward him through the curling cloud of her senses, stumbling up the slope.

He stood silent, shrinking from that world where he'd done that thing, broken every rule he knew. He didn't move. He gave her nothing, not a rustle, not a catch of his breath.

He lifted a hand, but couldn't bring himself to slice away her attention.

Her focus reached for him, the nerve endings in her skin, her hearing, her sense of smell. She came around the oaks and spread her cloud around him. She put out her hand and his chest was there, the heart pounding inside it, betraying him.

She lifted her face as if she could see his. Her other hand came up and touched the ragged beard, the bare skin of the cheek above.

Then both her arms were around him, and they were pressed tight together.

He was someone again.

They helped him back to the campsite.

They sat him down at the picnic table, built up the fire tall and hot. Flicker washed and bandaged his feet and put socks and Ethan's spare sneakers on him, while the others went to make camp in the neighboring sites, each divided from the next by thirty feet of redwood stumps and undergrowth.

Ethan sat with him while Kelsie helped Flicker pitch her tent and Chizara and Nate got dinner ready. They all watched him nervously, as if worried he would slip back into the night.

Steaks. Potatoes wrapped in tin foil. Thibault's hungry self was a lot clearer to him now. Everything was turned up way too loud—the fire smoke and cold air, the smells of food, everyone's attention shafting to and fro. If they would only stop moving and talking, give him a rest. If only they'd go away, and leave him to the forest, to the birds and the trees and the fog.

He looked down at pages in the brown folder, which they said would help him find himself again. He looked so neatly dressed and shaved in the photos. Like a schoolkid.

The folder was fat with pictures, transcripts, notes—all those campfire confessions with Nate were here, and they were the least of it.

Thibault was slowly paging through, not knowing what to feel. Every artsy photo he'd taken, every line he read triggered rafts of other memories, inching him closer to the real world. The hungry part of himself was just fine with that, but the rest was holding back.

He should never have said Flicker's name. Just another minute and she would've given up, they would have driven away.

He'd be alone now, dissolving into the forest, transforming into leaf and bark and bird wing.

Kelsie thumped a six-pack of beer on the table. Her hair was dyed dark now. Like she'd changed from a good fairy into some creature of shadow.

"So, you know we're wanted terrorists, right?" she said.

Everyone's attention swung to her, then back to Thibault.

"It's not the most relaxing gang to be in." She passed out the beers. "Nate's a murderer, and the rest of us are suspects in crimes they don't even have names for."

"Especially Crash," Ethan said. His hair was bleached blond. It looked ridiculous. "She's fucked up an *awesome* list of things since we saw you last."

"No human was harmed in the course of our escapes," Chizara pointed out.

"Not *seriously* harmed." Ethan laughed, popping a beer. "But Las Vegas got pretty dicey. Who knows how many federal marshals lost their jobs?"

"No loss of life," Chizara said earnestly to Thibault. "Not since Quinton Wallace and Craig."

All their attention lines firmed and brightened. Not even Ethan dared to crack a joke.

"Right." Thibault felt faint, like he was fading out. "We killed people, didn't we? In between dance parties."

"*Swarm* killed Craig," Ethan said hotly. "So Nate had to kill Swarm, to stop him from wiping us out."

Thibault looked up, and his silence spread through the group. He turned his stone head on his stone neck and stared at Nate.

Nate, his hair shorn close, pretended to be busy checking the steaks. But finally he looked up.

"You let them believe that?" Thibault asked.

"I . . ." Nate gave an awkward shrug. "It was simpler that way."

Flicker's fingers were suddenly tight on Thibault's shoulders. "Let them believe what?"

"That I killed Quinton Wallace," Nate said. "But now that we're here, and everyone's together at last, I should explain."

Nobody said anything. The fire popped once, like a distant gunshot.

Nate cleared his throat. "Thibault shot Swarm, to save my life. To save all our lives."

And Flicker's warmth was gone from behind Thibault. The others stared at him openmouthed—and then they were all gone, along with the rest of the world, wiped out by a cataract of memory.

CHAPTER 17
MOB

"I COULDN'T IMAGINE ANYTHING WORSE THAN prison," Kelsie said. "But being in there for something you didn't even do? Poor Nate."

Chizara shrugged. "It's not like he had a choice. You can't tell a judge, 'It wasn't me, your honor. My friend did it, in front of a bunch of cops, but everyone forgot.'"

Kelsie stared at her. "I wasn't saying he should snitch. Geez."

"Of course you weren't," Chizara said with a laugh, and nudged her aside. They were alone in their tent, trying to zip two sleeping bags together into one. Kelsie had been camping for most of three weeks now, and she still couldn't get the sleeping-bag thing to work.

It was warm and cozy here in the tent, but around them

the forest was rain-drenched and empty. As lonely as one of Scam's borrowed cabins. A few hikers had passed by a while ago, but that little taste of the Curve only made the isolation worse.

Kelsie reached out for the other Zeroes but found no threads of connection. Everyone was in their own headspace tonight.

She'd spent all day trying to keep them focused and upbeat as they searched for Thibault. It had been exhausting, partly because they knew she was doing it. And when Flicker had gone off with Thibault to put up their tent, she'd asked Kelsie to ease up.

Let everyone feel what they need to feel.

Flicker had said it nicely, but Kelsie felt ashamed for trying to control the group. Maybe she was still a baby Swarm.

They should all be happy now—for once a plan had worked from start to finish. But there was nothing binding the group. The six of them kept becoming five, like Thibault couldn't stayed linked with the others.

"He still wants to disappear," Kelsie said quietly.

Chizara looked up from the sleeping bags. "Sure. He can't live with what he did."

"It was self-defense. And he was protecting the rest of us, too!"

"I know. But you shouldn't be comfortable with killing. There's nothing wrong with feeling guilt."

"Nothing wrong with it?" Kelsie said. "Zara, it *erased* him!"

This new Thibault was gaunt and quiet. He had a faraway look, like he was listening to music only he could hear.

Kelsie knew what killing could do to you. She could still feel every moment of that night in the church, when she'd been part of the swarm. There was a mark on her soul from what Quinton had made her do.

"It's in me, too," she said. "Guilt about killing Delgado."

Chizara gave her an almost angry look. "But Swarm had control of you!"

"At first, yeah. But then it was both of us—and I *liked* it, Zara. Quinton was connecting with something that was already inside me. Do you want me to disappear too?"

Chizara shook her head. "When you ran away, you took me. Guilt made you need me *more*, not less. You ran away to protect the other Zeroes, not to erase yourself."

Kelsie sighed. Maybe that was why she couldn't understand any of this. She just wanted everyone to understand and support each other. But the Zeroes kept flailing and fighting.

She wished they could just start all over. No grudges, no shame.

The sleeping bags were finally aligned, and Chizara zipped them together in one elegant sweep of her long arm. They climbed in and lay staring up, shoulders touching. The plastic of the tent rippled above them with the wind and the movement of the moon-cast shadows.

"He scares me now," Chizara said.

Kelsie turned to face her. "Thibault? Why?"

"He spent his whole life trying to be Zen. To be at one with everything." Chizara shook her head. "But when it came time to choose, he turned his back on that."

"He was protecting his friends."

"At the cost of his faith. I don't know much about Buddhism, but I'm pretty sure shooting people isn't in the program, no matter how good the reason."

"You can't judge him," Kelsie said. "He *saved* you."

"I'm not judging him. It just scares me that he could be a killer, when he was trying so hard to be something completely different. What does that mean about him?" Chizara's voice dropped to a whisper. "What if we all keep forgetting him because . . . there isn't really anything inside him?"

Kelsie flinched. There might be a lot of anger and hurt inside Thibault, but he wasn't nothing.

"You don't really think that," she said. "Why did you say that?"

"Because I might be the same," Chizara whispered, her arms wrapped around herself. "Remember when Ethan threatened Agent Phan? When he said my power could stop hearts?"

"He didn't say that—his voice did. You can't listen to it."

"But Verity was sitting right there," Chizara said. "What if her power makes even the *voice* tell the truth?"

"Oh." Kelsie turned back to the ceiling of the tent, stunned. Ethan's lying was bad enough. But an all-knowing voice telling inescapable truths was somehow scarier. "But you can't crash *people*, Zara. They aren't machines!"

"In a way they are. Since the voice said that, I've started to see more. Hearts, lungs, brains. They're all one giant electrochemical system, not all that different from a network. I could switch someone off like *that.*"

She snapped her fingers, and Kelsie jumped. Being in the tent out in the wilderness suddenly felt scary, right out of a slasher movie. And the look on Chizara's face wasn't helping.

"But you won't," Kelsie said. "You're all about doing no harm, remember?"

Chizara stared down at her hands. "I've worried about hurting people my whole life. Even when I'm asleep in the car, we could pass a hospital or an airport and I could have a nightmare and wreck it all! I feel like I'm carrying A-grade plutonium everywhere I go."

Kelsie turned and hugged her. "But that's never happened. Because you're strong."

"Strength works both ways. Like when those marshals were coming at us in the casino. I would never have let them take you, Kelsie. Push me hard enough, and I'm a killer too. Maybe we *all* are."

Kelsie didn't answer. She'd already answered that question with Swarm. In the right circumstances, she was exactly what Chizara feared.

Suddenly she felt the emptiness around her. She reached out to her friends, but the Curve was tenuous. Ethan was somewhere out of range, and she could feel Thibault slipping in and out of the loop of sadness and uncertainty. Exactly how it'd felt when her dad had died, his consciousness coming and going.

Like losing someone, over and over.

She had to say something to make it better.

"I trust you, Zara."

"You shouldn't." A sigh in the darkness. "I need to tell you something."

Kelsie pulled away and waited. This couldn't get any worse.

"Nate already told me he didn't kill Swarm," Chizara said.

Kelsie looked at her. "When?"

"A week ago, at the cabin." Her words came out in a rush now. "Flicker was already freaked about forgetting Thibault, so Nate couldn't just tell her that her boyfriend was a killer. He asked me not to say anything."

"To Flicker, sure. But why didn't you tell me?"

"I could barely remember the guy. And I never thought we'd actually find him! And you're so lonely out here, I didn't want to talk about murder."

Kelsie shook her head. Another thread of connection was breaking.

It felt as if the winter could swallow her.

Chizara was staring up at the ceiling of the tent, where the shadows of windblown trees danced. "Nate only told *me* because he wanted me to make a tracker. So if Thibault disappears again, we can find him."

"A tracker? Like a chip in a pet? That is such a Glorious Leader idea." Especially the old, before-prison Glorious Leader. "You said no, right?"

Chizara only shrugged.

"Zara! What was the point of finding Thibault if we have to *force* him to stay with us?"

"The point is, now that we've found him, we're responsible for him. You saw how skinny he was. If we hadn't gotten here in time, he would've starved to death. Do you think Flicker could take it if we lost him again? Forever this time?"

"I guess you're right." Kelsie shook her head. "But you have to trust me. Don't get drawn into Nate's lies. I'm not some child who has to be protected."

She turned over and curled up with her back to Chizara.

"I know," Chizara said. "I'm sorry."

"It's okay," Kelsie said, deciding to be strong. "I'm not mad."

"You forgive everything, don't you?"

Kelsie shrugged. "I had a lot of practice with my dad."

"Yeah, maybe." Chizara put her arms around Kelsie. "But most people with a father like yours would've turned out the opposite."

"Trust issues aren't my thing," Kelsie said. The weird thing was, she'd forgiven Zara just to sound strong, but uttering the words had made them true. A burden lifted from her, and the threads between the two of them pulled tight again.

The cold wind ruffled the tent. But Kelsie felt safe, even if it was just the pair of them.

When Chizara spoke next, Kelsie felt the breath on the back of her neck. "I used to love camping, you know. Nothing to crash. No hospitals, no cargo ships."

Kelsie smiled. "No haywire dance parties. No deadly mall crowds."

"No twin sisters to betray us," Chizara added softly.

Even with the group's energy scattered, Kelsie could feel her grief, her homesickness for her brothers.

"Forget all that," she said. "Let's just be us for a while."

Chizara smiled sadly. "You think you can handle that? All alone out here, just you and me?"

"Sure." Kelsie felt herself smiling. "For a while."

Chizara drew her fingers along Kelsie's shoulder and down across her back. Kelsie breathed in the smell of her girlfriend's skin, and sent her delight spiraling out across the emptiness around them.

But the few sparkling connections with the group fed it back to them.

"Not exactly alone." Chizara chuckled. "There's no privacy with you, is there?"

Kelsie shrugged. "That's just who I am, Zara."

She was too relaxed and glad to stop the emotions from getting loose.

Chizara kissed her deeply. "I love who you are."

CHAPTER 18
FLICKER

"WHOA," FLICKER SAID. "DID YOU FEEL THAT?"

Thibault shifted on the plastic floor of the tent. He was huddled by the propane lamp, watching the flame dart and dance. He'd stared into the campfire all evening, too, like it was some awesome new video game.

"Maybe," he said. Thibault's voice was so different now. Dry and gravelly, like he'd forgotten to drink water all that time away.

"Maybe?" Flicker had to smile. "If you can't feel the nightly Mob-and-Crash feedback loop, you should check your pulse."

"Nightly?" There was a pause, and then a smile in his voice. "Oh. Right."

"That's why we use propane lamps," Flicker said. "They're smelly, but at least Chizara can't crash them. We even wrap the burner phones in foil at night so she doesn't brick them when they . . . by accident."

"Wow," he said, and then silence. Nothing but the wind stirring leaves, and the far-off rumble of ocean.

Am I talking too much? Flicker wondered. She kept explaining the Zeroes' survival procedures to Thibault, like he was some new Zeroes recruit, anxious to learn everything. But he felt a thousand miles away.

She wished she could see through his eyes, to know if he was looking at her. But she'd fallen in love with the only person she'd ever met whose vision she couldn't hijack.

Superpowers interacting. Like mixing the wrong kinds of medication.

At least she could smell him, here in the confines of the tent. The laundry soap of his fresh clothes, the tang of shaving cream, but also the pine-needle scent that hadn't washed away. A cleaned-up mountain man.

And Thibault's own smells—his skin, his hair. Every breath of it brought back those fugitive memories of other nights, and redoubled the guilt of having forgotten him.

He was so thin now, all angles. What would he feel like to lie next to?

This silence was getting long—but she couldn't think of what to say.

He spoke first. "Kelsie must be used to broadcasting her emotions, but how does Chizara cope with no privacy?"

Flicker smiled again. It was the longest sentence Thibault had said since they'd found him.

"I wouldn't exactly call it coping," she said. "You can't mention it in the morning. Like, no teasing or jokes or *anything*. Sometimes Ethan doesn't even show up for breakfast, just in case he smiles wrong."

Thibault didn't answer.

She counted silently to ten. Still nothing.

"This one time he smiled wrong, Chizara set him on fire," she said.

Only the resounding silence of a joke being ignored. Maybe he wasn't listening at all.

Flicker shifted uncomfortably. What she needed to say wasn't going to come up in casual conversation, so she might as well just say it.

"I don't care that you killed Swarm. What I care about is that you ran away. You just left me."

The wind picked up then, thousands of leaves rattling against each other, fluttering like cards thrown in the air.

Or maybe the roaring was in her head.

Why wouldn't he just *answer*?

"It feels like you died," she went on. "But I didn't get to mourn you. Even when people kill themselves, the ones left behind get to be angry about it. But I didn't get to be *anything*."

She couldn't hear his breathing. What if he'd already crept away into the night, and they never found him again?

Flicker resisted the urge to reach out and confirm that he was there. A warm drop was rolling down her cheek, but it felt like someone else's tear.

"You were just gone out from the world. Gone from my—"

"It happened when I saw Craig's body," Thibault broke in. "That's when I lost myself."

Flicker waited. That was all she could do now.

"After I shot Quinton, I helped Ethan get away from his mom and the cops. Quinton's blood was on me, and somehow the sight of it leveled me up. I took hold of Ethan and made us both anonymous."

Flicker nodded. "Nate can do that now."

"He was just figuring out how to make himself Anonymous back then. We have the same power, inside out. We're just different people, I guess."

Flicker felt a chill. She'd already figured most of this out. But the idea that her oldest friend and her boyfriend were different *versions* of each other was too squicky to think about.

"What happened then?"

"Ethan and I got back to the Dish, and that's when I saw Craig."

He paused for a long time. Through the wind, Flicker could almost make out the crashes of individual waves on the faraway beach.

"It wasn't really him, though. Just his body. You know how Nate and I see attention? All those sparkling lines of awareness between people? The ones I chop away and he manipulates? Craig's were *gone*. Whatever human connection gives us our powers, he was cut out from it. Dead."

"I saw his death too, kind of," Flicker said. "He was looking over the edge of the truck when he got hit. I was in his eyes, using him like a periscope. His vision broke into little shards of light. Scattered away."

"Oh." Thibault reached out and took her hand. Even his fingers were thinner.

"Kelsie felt him leave the loop," Flicker said.

"We always knew our powers were about crowds," he breathed. "But maybe they're about something bigger."

"Like what?"

"Life, maybe?" His hand tightened around hers. "Whatever binds everyone together? When I realized that I'd sliced Quinton Wallace out of that web, it was too much. If I could cut someone else out, then I didn't deserve to stay connected myself."

"What about what *I* deserved, Thibault?"

He went silent. Flicker wasn't sure where that sudden pulse of anger had come from. But it was growing inside her.

"It's super awesome, how everyone is connected," she said. "Yay for us. Yay for our freaky superpowers and the web of humanity. But zoom in a little. There's also a thing when there's just two people. Like what's between us."

"We were *all* in shock that day," she insisted. "Craig was

dead, Nate under arrest. But nobody else ran away. And didn't *I* matter—didn't *we* matter—enough for to you to stay with me?"

He was silent.

Crap. That had all come out wrong. Selfish and crazy-sounding and way too soon. What if yelling at Thibault only made him disappear again? What if she could never be honest with him again, without worrying that he'd run away?

But she couldn't take it back now.

So she went all in. "Why wasn't I enough to keep you here in reality?"

For once she didn't have to wait long for an answer.

"Because everything is harder with you," he said

Flicker blinked. "Harder?"

His slow sigh joined with the sounds of wind and leaves. "Living with this power, I learned not to be attached to anyone. It was easier that way, and safer, because everyone would always forget me. But then you learned to see me. That made me think I could connect. That my family could learn too."

Flicker looked away, remembering him storming through the halls of his parents' house, tearing pictures off the walls. "And that didn't quite work out."

"No. It didn't."

"My bad," she said. "I pushed it too fast."

And then, when everything had gone sideways, she'd forgotten him too. Abandoned him just as cruelly as his parents had.

"You tried to help," he said.

Flicker shook her head, taking hold of his shoulders. His bones were too near the surface, sharp. "All I care about is *if you're going to leave me again.*"

She heard him try to answer, to reassure her—the first breath of a word coming from his mouth. But it lay there, strangled into silence.

The wind died outside.

"I don't know," he finally said.

"Okay." Maybe this was also too soon, but it was all she had. "Nate has an idea that might help."

"Of course he does."

"Chizara made a tracker. It doesn't send out a signal all the time, just when her power activates it. Like a chip in a passport, she says. She can home in on it. She'll use it to help find you if . . . you get lost again."

Flicker felt his response with her hands. His body turning inward on itself, pulling away from the idea. It was everything he hated—an invasion of privacy, an erasure of will. It was someone tagging him, tracking him, owning him.

But what he said out loud was "Will that make it easier for you?"

Flicker pretended that she hadn't felt the shudder in his body, in his voice. In her own heart.

"It will," she said.

"Okay, then. A tracker sounds perfect."

CHAPTER 19

BELLWETHER

NATE WAITED TILL AFTER BREAKFAST, WHEN CAF-
feine and blood sugar were glittering in everyone's attention.
The sun speckled down through pine needles, chasing away the
night chill.

"There's doughnuts in the van," he said. "Also, I think we
should go to New Orleans next."

Kelsie looked up, her attention shimmering like a string of
glass beads. He knew he didn't have to convince her. Her dad,
on his deathbed, had said her mother might still be in New
Orleans.

Plus, the ultimate party girl, in the ultimate party town?

Too easy.

Chizara was the first one to argue, of course.

"What the hell, Nate? Did you *miss* what happened in

Vegas?" She lowered her voice. "We almost lost control. The first time we're in a big city in weeks, and we had a riot going inside five minutes!"

"We were betrayed, attacked," he said. "But there's no one setting a trap for us in New Orleans."

"Every city is a trap." Chizara looked around for support. "All those people. All those eyes. All those wanted posters! Do you really want to be looking over your shoulder all the time?"

Nate glanced down at the palm of his hand, where he'd written a message for Flicker.

Help me?

But if she was looking through his eyes, she didn't respond.

"What kind?" Ethan asked.

Nate stared at him, uncomprehending.

"Of doughnuts," Ethan added.

"Stale."

"Cool. My favorite." Ethan slouched off toward the van, coffee mug in hand.

"I think going to a city makes sense," Kelsie said. "We lost it in Vegas because we're out of practice. I mean, how are we supposed to learn to control our powers if we're in the wilderness all the time?"

"Good point," Nate said.

"But New Orleans isn't your average city." Flicker spoke up. "And isn't it almost Mardi Gras? That's like learning to swim at the Olympics! Thibault just came back to the real world. Do we want to throw him straight into the deep end?"

So much for Flicker helping him.

"This isn't about training, is it, Nate?" she said. "What's the *real* reason you want to go there?"

"Because of Mardi Gras. The world's biggest party will be a Zeroes magnet. We'll find other people like us."

"People like us mostly suck," Chizara said. "And didn't Verity say she was from there?"

Nate spread his hands in surrender. "She did. Agent Phan is too, I'll bet."

"Seriously?" Ethan was back, standing at the edge of the campfire circle, chewing a chocolate-glazed doughnut. "You want to risk bumping into the guy who almost trapped us—twice—*and* his superpowered sidekick? What the hell for?"

"Listen." Nate let the word hang for a moment, then gently pulled the strands of their attention tauter. "Something's happening out in the rest of the world. Something big. People with powers are everywhere, and they're doing important things."

"They're doing *stupid* things," Flicker said. "Messing with the Super Bowl? That's a great way to get us all shot on sight!"

"That's why we can't just sit here." Nate swept his gaze across the group, trying to connect them. "Before you interrupted my interrogation, Phan was telling me about someone called Piper. She's also in New Orleans, planning something. He thought I might know about it. Think about that for a second."

Everyone stared at him, listening now.

"I was stuck in jail a thousand miles away, in isolation most of the time, not allowed to talk to any other prisoners. And he asked me about Piper's plan." Nate looked around at their uncomprehending faces. Why were they being so thick? "Whatever it is, Zeroes from all over must be joining up with her!"

"So *you* have to be there too," Chizara said. "Figures."

"This isn't about me," Nate said. "This is about who we are. Do we want to hide for the rest of our lives, not using our powers? Or do we want to be part of whatever's going on out there? Part of what this all *means*?"

"He's right," came a voice from the edge of the circle.

Everyone looked up.

It was Thibault. He'd gotten lost in the bickering. But now he stood there, clear as day behind Flicker, connected to her.

"These powers have to mean something," he continued. "You think they just popped up for no reason, all over the world at once? And even if they're dangerous sometimes, they can also work for good. I mean, look what we did back at the Dish, bringing people together. What if there's some bigger version of that happening? Don't you want to be a part of it?"

"Not if it's a bigger version of what Glitch and Coin used to do," Flicker said.

"Or Swarm," Chizara added.

"Then we should be there to stop it," Thibault said. "If

there's a battle happening, we should pick a side. I'm tired of drifting, of running away."

Nate blinked, not quite believing what he was seeing. Thibault was holding their attention, for a moment at the radiant center of the group.

Then those sparkling lines started to slip from him, and he became Anonymous again.

"Okay," Flicker said. "Let's vote. But if it's three to three, then we figure out somewhere else. Someplace a majority of us want to go."

She turned to Nate and smiled sweetly.

"Is everyone okay with that?"

Murmurs of agreement went around the circle. Nate tried to think of a reason to disagree, to keep the argument going. But they all listened to Flicker now.

Voting? Things really had gone haywire in his absence.

"I say no." Flicker turned to Thibault. "Sorry. But it's too dangerous."

"*Way* too dangerous," Chizara chimed in. "No for me, too."

"Zara!" Kelsie stared at her girlfriend. "What about my mother?"

Chizara shook her head. "We don't know if she's still there. But a million Mardi Gras revelers will be. You can't handle that yet."

"I can't wait to," Kelsie said. "I vote yes."

"So do I," Thibault said.

Nate shook his head. Both couples were in disagreement. However this worked out, things were going to get awkward once night fell.

And worse, Flicker had engineered this so that Ethan had the deciding vote.

Mr. Bravery himself, standing there chewing a stale doughnut.

Nate turned, hoping that the sugar had reached Ethan's bloodstream. He marshaled every ounce of charm he had, all the shards of his power dulled by weeks in an isolated cell, every argument he could think of, every appeal to Ethan's ego and cowardice and short-term thinking.

"I vote yes," Nate began. "Because this is without question the most important—"

"Me too," Ethan interrupted.

"Wait," Nate said. "What?"

"What?" Flicker spat.

Ethan stared at the ground. "Uh, I heard there was this conference in New Orleans. Kind of wanted to check it out."

Nate frowned. "A conference?"

"Yeah," Ethan said. "Like, a weird-hunter thing. I mean, about Zeroes. Could be . . . informative."

Chizara gave him a death glare. "Where the hell did you hear about that?"

Ethan was wearing a look, one that hadn't changed much in the weeks Nate had been away—the look he wore while deciding whether to use the voice on his friends or not.

"The internet," Ethan finally said in his real voice.

Chizara swore. "You've been using the burners to go online again."

"Not since you yelled at me!"

She glared at him another moment, then groaned. "Well, I guess the motion passes. Hell, it might be worth going to NOLA, just to get Scam in a room with Verity again."

"That's cold," Ethan said.

Nate frowned—*would* the voice be affected by Verity? Or were Scam's lies the stronger power?

Lies versus truth. A sudden thought shook Nate.

"Ethan," he said. "Have you ever tried to use the voice to make someone *else* talk?"

Ethan stared at him. "What do you mean?"

"Concentrate, right now. Use your power to make *me* tell the truth. Draw it out of me!"

"How the hell would I do that?"

"Just *try*!" Nate yelled, hoping the shock might nudge something in Ethan's brain. If his Bellwether power and Anon's were opposite sides of the same coin, why not Verity's and Scam's?

"You mean . . . ," Ethan murmured. He got a determined look on his face, his attention narrowing like a spotlight on Nate. The rest of the Zeroes were riveted, the Curve fully present.

"I love stale doughnuts," Nate said. "And sharing a tent

with Ethan. And it's great when Flicker reminds me to signal my turns."

All of it came out without the slightest hesitation.

Ethan slumped. "That was pointless, dude. My power's not the reverse of Verity's. Swarm didn't even think I was a real Zero. I keep telling you guys—that's why he didn't eat me!"

"Well, this is why we're going to New Orleans," Nate said with a shrug. "For answers. Maybe we'll find another one of you there."

And the question of another Scam was only the tip of the iceberg. There could be hundreds of Zeroes among the vast crowds of Mardi Gras. More Crashes, Flickers, Anons, Glitches, Coins . . . Mobs halfway to Swarms. And better Bellwethers, it seemed.

New powers, probably, with infinite new ways for all of them to intersect.

So much to see. So much to learn.

Worth any risk.

CHAPTER 20
SCAM

"WE NEED GAS," ETHAN SAID.

No one answered. Probably napping. Ethan had been driving for three hours already, and New Orleans was still twelve hours away. Apart from visiting his dad one time in Chicago, Ethan had never been this far from Cambria.

He glanced at Nate, who lay with his head against the side window of the van. Lucky asshole. Ethan could never sleep in cars.

"Gas," he said louder.

"There's a station half a mile ahead," Flicker replied from the backseat. "Only a couple of people inside."

Ethan grunted his thanks.

A friendly yellow filling-station sign loomed into view a minute later, and Ethan coasted off the highway and up to a gas pump.

"I'll do it," Thibault said. "You pay."

Ethan jumped. "Oh. Thanks, Tee."

Thibault smiled. It looked weird on him, like he had to remind himself how.

Ethan still felt guilty about forgetting the guy. But that guilt didn't help him remember Thibault in the here and now, especially when they were all crammed into a car together. The Curve really liked tight spaces.

"I need to stretch," Flicker said, pulling a floppy hat on. Apparently she didn't want Thibault getting more than a few feet from her. Didn't she trust Chizara's tracker thing?

The Zeroes just got more paranoid every day.

"Get some snacks, too, Scam," Nate said, hunkering lower in his seat. His face was the one on the wanted posters, so he never had to do anything.

"Duh," Ethan said under his breath. Like he served any other purpose in life. Snacks and gas and fresh clothes.

He grabbed his cap and pulled it down low over his sunglasses. Then he unfolded himself gratefully from the van.

This road trip was giving him cabin fever. One thing about growing up as Ethan Cooper, he'd always spent a lot of time on his own. But now it seemed like the entire rest of his life was going to be like this. Holed up in some cramped space with the same four—no, five—people.

What a freaking mess.

He was sick of being on the run. He had permanent neck

cramps from always looking over his shoulder. Plus no video games or internet.

Chizara was keeping the burner phones wrapped up tight these days, and Ethan hadn't even gotten a chance to tell Sonia that he was headed for her weird-hunter conference.

But maybe that was the smoother move. Just send her a text when he got to New Orleans, like it was no big deal.

Hey, in town. Wanna hang?

Yep, an international man of mystery.

Or interstate, anyway.

"Get salsa!" Kelsie yelled across the forecourt. "I'm starving."

Ethan flinched. Didn't Kelsie understand the concept of lying low?

He wondered what Sonia was doing right now. Probably going to weird-hunting parties, meeting cool people, and bragging about knowing the Cambria Five.

Ha! Nobody even knew there were six of them. Maybe he could casually drop that into conversation.

Yeah, no. If that info wound up on the weird-hunter message boards, it would just make it easier for the law to spot them.

Inside the convenience store, he headed for the snack aisle to load up on salsa and chips. At the checkout a guy stood sucking a giant soda.

Ethan could just make out the guy's name tag through his sunglasses. Dwayne. Name tags really took the fun out of things when you had the voice to fill you in.

Ethan dumped the snacks on the counter, and the voice came charging up his larynx, glad to have company at last.

"Hey, Dwayne," the voice said. "Brittney says hi."

Ethan felt better already. Having only Zeroes for company meant these pit stops were the sole chance he had to exercise his power.

Dwayne looked at him. "Do I know you, man?"

"We met once, at Randal's," the voice said. "She's been talking about you."

Dwayne looked pathetically hopeful. "Really? I thought she was ghosting on me. She hasn't answered my texts in, like, five weeks."

Ethan nodded wisely while the voice kept going. "Because of that fifty you owe her. She's kind of pissed."

"Yeah, but how'm I supposed to pay her back? She won't even talk to me!"

"That's a tough one." Ethan felt the voice shift gears in his mouth, twisting into a menacing growl. "That's why she asked us to come round and collect."

Dwayne stared at him. "Us?"

"Me and my friends." Ethan jerked his head toward the van, which seemed appropriate. Dwayne looked, and his eyes widened.

The van was pretty scary, Ethan supposed, with its shitty paint job and dark windows. Nate hunkered down in the passenger seat, wearing a cap. A girl outside in dark glasses, and a guy pumping gas who you couldn't quite get your eyes to stick to.

"I don't want any trouble here," Dwayne said.

"So you're good for the fifty?"

"Uh, I don't have it on me." The poor guy gulped. "But I can give it to her if she'd just—"

"How about this?" the voice interrupted. "Front me for the gas, and this stuff, and the slate's clean."

"Seriously?" Dwayne looked at the register. It read $57.14. "Um, that's more than I owe her."

"Finder's fee." Ethan didn't feel great about this, especially since this guy was still going to owe Brittney fifty bucks. But the voice didn't really do victimless crimes.

Ethan felt himself wanting the guy not to hate him.

The voice apparently felt that desire, because it said, "Look. You know that other girl you like? Clara?"

"Uh, how did you know about that?"

"Brittney told me. Girls notice this stuff." Ethan smiled.

"Aw, damn it." Dwayne was really having a bad day now.

Come on, voice. Throw the guy a bone!

"She's cool with it," the voice said. "And now that you're finally paying up, she says to relay that Clara really likes you. And she'll be at Jason's party Saturday."

"Huh," Dwayne said. "Really?"

"Only one way to find out," the voice said, sounding sympathetic. "Show up there."

Dwayne bagged the salsa and soda, looking hopeful. "Yeah. Maybe I will."

Ethan pulled his cap lower. Chizara had probably already crashed the closed-circuit camera above the till, but Dwayne had been staring at him way too much. That was the problem with the voice's confidence games. They required a personal connection that penetrated dark glasses.

"So are we straight here?" Ethan said. "No need for me to call my friends inside?"

"Yeah, man. I got this." Dwayne pushed buttons on the register. "Tell Brittney I'm sorry it took so long. And I didn't mean to ruin her dress like that. I hope she found a new one."

Ethan kept himself from wanting to know what the hell that meant. He did *not* need the voice inquiring.

"Thanks, buddy." As Ethan reached for the bag, he accidentally bumped Dwayne's supersized soda. The giant cup spilled bright orange catastrophe all over the newspapers in the rack.

"Crap!" Ethan muttered.

"Aw, hey, man, I ain't paying for those!" Dwayne shouted, headed around to survey the damage.

Ethan was about to unleash the voice, but then he stopped.

On the front page of the local rag were five high school yearbook photos. Nataniel Saldana, Riley Phillips, Chizara Okeke, Kelsie Laszlo. And of course Ethan Thomas Cooper, his not-dyed-blond crew cut sharp the way it used to be, grinning at the camera like a total goof.

"Holy freaking crap on a stick," Ethan said under his breath.

He dropped the bag and took hold of the papers. Dwayne grabbed the other end of the pile like they were playing tug-of-war.

"Let go, man! You're spreading it everywhere," Dwayne said.

But then Dwayne went quiet. Too quiet.

He was staring down at the pictures.

"Damn." He looked up at Ethan. "Brittney sent *you guys* to collect?"

Whatever will delay him the longest, voice.

"Brittney knows some powerful people, Dwayne. And she's going to keep an eye on you. Just keep this little story to yourself."

Dwayne just stared at him.

Ethan grabbed the snack bag and ran for the door.

The other Zeroes were already in the van. He could feel the rush of panic from Kelsie's feedback loop as he leaped for the driver's seat.

"I saw the papers," Flicker said. "Did he recognize you?"

"Yep," Ethan admitted. "Everybody in? Crap, where's—"

"I'm here," Thibault said from somewhere in back.

Ethan dumped the bag of snacks on Nate and started the van.

"Head east," Flicker said. "Fewer eyes."

"Which way's east?" Ethan asked.

"Left," Nate supplied, putting the bag in the footwell. "Take the access road, not the highway."

Ethan gunned the engine, breathing hard. His knuckles on the steering wheel were white. Panic tinged the air like tear gas.

"Trying to drive, Kelsie!" he pleaded. "Dial it back a notch?"

"Sorry," Kelsie mumbled from the back of the van.

The knot in Ethan's stomach began to ease. Not completely, though. There was only so much Kelsie could do.

"He's staring at his phone," Flicker said. "But he hasn't done it yet."

Ethan headed for the forest. He hated forests. Bad things happened in forests. Drug dealers, for one. Serial killers, probably. Also, romantic feedback loops that he did *not* need to know about.

But a few minutes later they were among the dark trees, the highway lost behind them. The road they were on gave way to dirt. Leaves whipped at the windshield, and low branches scraped the roof. The forest was so thick it turned the daylight green.

"He's out of range," Flicker said. "But last I could see, he hadn't made the call."

"The voice was being pretty scary," Ethan said. Though if Dwayne ever did call the Feds, Brittney was due for a disturbing visit from the FBI. Hopefully, Verity would clear her name.

"There's no signal out here," Chizara said in awe and wonder.

"That's because nobody's stupid enough to live here," Ethan said. "Are we lost?"

"No." Nate was looking at the paper maps that Anon had stolen at an old gas station. "Keep going."

Ethan drove on over the bouncing road. Would Dwayne back at the convenience store really go to that party this weekend and hook up with Clara? He kind of hoped so. Maybe the lies the voice had told would create a ripple in that little town, changing lives in a positive way for once.

He'd been wondering more than usual lately about all the stuff the voice said. Where it came from. How it chose one thing to say rather than another. Why it sometimes lied wildly and sometimes homed right in on alarming truths.

Was it *trying* to mess things up? Or was that Ethan's fault somehow?

Did his voice have an inside-out version? Like Chizara fixing things, or Nate going Anonymous? What the hell would it even be?

He also wondered what would happen when he met other people like him, with a voice inside them too.

What would two voices say *to each other*?

In those precious moments when he snuck off with a burner to text her, Sonia always asked him questions like that. He hated not knowing the answers. He needed to know more about his power, and the only way that would happen was if he met someone else who shared it.

And the best place to do that would be the current center of Zeroes action in the country.

New Orleans.

The fact that Sonia Sonic herself was headed there too didn't hurt either.

So Ethan Cooper kept driving along the scary country road, even as night descended and the others all fell back asleep.

CHAPTER 21
ANONYMOUS

"THAT PLACE ON THE RIGHT LOOKS EMPTY," Flicker said. "Pull over."

Thibault stared up at the shuttered house as Ethan brought the van to a halt. Everyone sat quiet, tired from the long drive, nerves jangled from cruising New Orleans, hunting for a hide-out, trying not to flinch when police cars drove past.

At least they'd finally stopped. Thibault's body wanted to move, to stretch. To be free of this van.

"Yeah, no eyes in there," Flicker said.

"Nobody's sleeping?" Ethan asked. "No insides of eyelids?"

"I wouldn't see that in deep sleep. Anon should check it out to make sure."

Thibault was already looking along the street for the

sparkling attention lines of nosy neighbors. No one was watching the house.

Through the honeysuckle on the front fence he saw a side gate.

"Feels like they're on vacation," Chizara added. "No wifi groping around. Not much power coming off the grid. Pretty sweet security system."

She snapped her fingers.

"It *was*, anyway."

"Can you turn the boiler on, Zara?" Kelsie pleaded quietly. "I'm dying for a hot shower."

Chizara smiled. "Me too. Done."

"Take a phone, Anon," Nate said. He was sitting in the center backseat, his usual trucker cap pulled low over his eyes. Redneck Glorious Leader.

Chizara solemnly passed Thibault a burner from the foil bag.

"I'll text you if it's clear." He gave Flicker's hand a squeeze, and she clasped him back, keeping him in the van for another moment. A gentle reminder to return.

He stepped out into the damp cool of New Orleans winter.

There wasn't a padlock on the side gate. The sound of a faintly babbling TV came from the house next door, but no attention glittered from the windows. Televisions were useful that way, magnets for wayward eyes.

In the sunny back courtyard, all the signs were good. The

pet bowl was dry, as was the soil around the drooping potted plants. The owners had been away for a while, with no one coming to water while they were gone.

But did that mean they were coming back soon?

A brick sat by the steps, looking significant, and sure enough a key was under it. Thibault blew the dirt from it, shaking his head. This must be a safe neighborhood. Or were the neighbors supposed to be watching the house?

A few spiderwebs clung between the screen door and the jamb. Thibault parted them and unlocked the door inside.

The kitchen was clean, the counters bare. Nothing in the fridge but mustard.

He was definitely alone here.

After the bright sunshine outside, the shuttered interior was a shadowy dream world. A dark hallway skirted a staircase, the walls lined with framed photos. They glimmered with needles of light from the door glass at the end.

A hallway lined with photos . . . A memory rushed at him of snatching down picture frames, throwing them into a trash bag. A roar built in his head, threatening to pull him into that storm of self-obliteration again.

He took a slow breath.

This was *not* his parents' house. He had to stay in this moment, in this body. His friends needed to find a safe spot to rest, and he could help them. Flicker needed him to come back to her.

His footsteps creaked the floorboards under the hallway rug—he had weight. He wasn't a ghost, a lost spirit. He was part of the Zeroes.

He felt the leather strap on his wrist. Chizara's wafer of circuitry hung from it. He imagined her power reaching in, feeling for him through the walls. Lighting up the tracker on his wrist.

Claiming him. Or maybe watching out for him.

Off to his left the dining room opened, full of dark, polished furniture. More photos hung on the walls. A skier throwing up a great arc of powdered snow. Family arranged by a big fireplace, ski tans the shape of goggles around their eyes. Hopefully, that was where they were now, another week's vacation in front of them.

The sight of a happy family sent a pang of envy through him, of yearning and subdued rage. And of fear. What if he'd missed something, that day when he swept through his parents' house with Flicker, grabbing photos and gifts and birthday cards? If he'd just left one thing, and Mom found it, she'd latch on and drive herself crazy again.

He turned to the next room, forcibly leaving the thought behind.

Shelves full of books, padded chairs and ottomans, carved side tables. Envy hit him again, of people who felt at home in the world. Who could *make* a home, claim a space, fill it with their own stuff, trust it to stay how they'd left it.

But envy was useless. He checked for exits, escape routes in case the Feds came knocking. The hall was narrow, the walls cluttered with Mardi Gras masks and photos. Tight enough to bottleneck a stampede of FBI agents barreling through the door.

A folded copy of the *Times-Picayune* lay in the kindling box, two weeks old. The occupants had left well ahead of the first parades of Mardi Gras.

They were rich enough to just shut up their house and go. No renting it out to visitors. Just switch on the security system and leave.

He should text the others. They were waiting out there, nervous, in need of showers and beds. But being alone in this lived-in, cared-for space felt so good after that long drive.

They'd camped in out-of-the-way places, shared cheap motel rooms. Always in each other's faces. Flicker right there, her senses all over him, worrying he was about to slip away again. The tracker always on his wrist, a reminder that no one trusted him.

Thibault had spent years making his home in different places, bedding down in unseen corners. But the rest of them weren't so used to roughing it, and Ethan complained nonstop.

He was sick of breathing the terror that hung around them now, trapped in the feedback loop of Kelsie's power, like a herd of prey animals attuned to each other's fight-or-flight signals.

Even something as simple as lunch took so much planning.

Where to park the car. Whether Scam should swindle or Anon steal. Who wanted what kind of sandwich.

Yesterday, lifting all those subs from the deli, it had all suddenly seemed so stupid and petty and *wrong*. Hadn't he had enough of ripping people off at the Hotel Magnifique?

His memory coughed up the friendly face of Charlie Penka, the hotel manager whose career he'd ruined. And that was back in the good days, before any of this. Before . . .

His hand twitched.

Thibault stood staring at it, smelling gunpowder.

It was dangerous for him to be away from the others, to be this far away from Flicker. Here at the top of the stairs, surrounded by doorways, he felt the Nowhere tug at him again. He didn't need a forest to dissolve into. He could just pull off the bracelet, step away, fade, go.

He could do it now—leave the constant ringing in his ears, the keening of his guilt. Lose the ache from the gun's kickback. Rid himself of the vision of Quinton Wallace lying there with his head blown apart. Of Craig, who'd been so strong, so loyal, dead on the truck bed—

He pulled at the tracker on his wrist. He could throw it out the window, grind it under his heel. He had any number of ways to escape. He was constantly noticing them, resisting them.

The Zeroes couldn't go on forever like this. The others were too visible. They'd done too many illegal things. Eventually they'd be rounded up by the cops or the Feds, and he'd have to watch.

He'd have to watch them take Flicker. . . .

Thibault shook himself, pulled himself back into the present. *You're checking the hideout. Making them all safer.*

He went into each bedroom. Furniture and life clutter. Bathrobes hung from the backs of doors, odd things were strewn on a couple of the beds, leftovers from packing. This was what real lives looked like, nothing like what he and his friends had.

He texted Nate:

Come on in. Looks like we can stay all winter.

Or forever. He pocketed his phone, unable to shake the thought that this family was gone for good. Like they'd known that something evil was coming to New Orleans, and had fled for their lives, never to return.

CHAPTER 22
FLICKER

"WE'RE GOOD," NATE SAID AS HE READ THE TEXT, sounding relieved.

Flicker felt her own relief. Not just for a shower and a real bed, but that Thibault was still with them, not faded away into the city. He'd taken an oddly long time to check the house. It had taken an effort of will not to have someone text him with a *You okay in there?*

"Let's go," she said. "If anyone challenges us, let Ethan handle it."

Kelsie opened the car door. "Okay, but I call first shower."

"Noted," Ethan said. "Just like the first five times you called it."

Flicker gave him a nudge. "Move. Thibault's alone in there."

"He's upstairs," Chizara reassured her. "His tracker's reading fine."

Ethan opened his door and stepped out onto the curb, and soon the five of them had unloaded the car. The bright sun was welcome on Flicker's skin. Her dark glasses wouldn't look out of place, in case the neighbors had read about the hapless blind girl who'd fallen in with the evil Cambria terrorists.

Flicker moved into Nate's eyes, searching for threats.

He was scanning the plant-hung porch of the house across the street. It had three chairs, and a couple of glasses glittered on a metal table.

"We should keep the front windows of the house shuttered," she said. "The neighbors opposite like to hang out on their porch."

The balcony next to that one was leaf-strewn, and a small lockbox for spare keys was attached to the iron fence. Somebody who rented their house? Short-term stayers wouldn't be very nosy. On the other side, a watering system was spraying the flower beds. Another good sign—owners who'd rather stay inside than come out and water their lawn.

Next door to the chosen house was the problem. The side windows were open, the sounds of talk radio trickling out.

"You see that?" Nate asked her softly.

"Yeah," she said.

They crossed the front lawn in a pack, carrying backpacks

and plastic grocery bags—nothing suspicious here!—and arrived at the front door just as Thibault opened it. Kelsie's exhaustion, spiked with nervousness, finally broke into relief as they piled through.

"Close the door," Nate said. "Keep the shutters closed."

"Wait a sec," Flicker countered. "Crash, go dump the car. About—"

"About a mile away, unlocked, keys in view," Chizara recited. "And check the neighborhood for security cameras."

"Shouldn't I dump the car?" Thibault asked. "If it gets reported, we don't want anyone to remember who left it."

Suddenly everyone was waiting for Flicker to answer. They knew she didn't want Thibault wandering off alone.

"Both of you go," she said. "Anon can practice keeping someone else hidden."

She checked his expression through Chizara's vision, but he wasn't giving anything away. Did he buy her reasoning?

"Yeah," Ethan said, heading into the kitchen. "You're going to have to work hard to beat Bellwether at that shit."

"Okay," Thibault said. "Take my hand, Crash?"

"Away we go," she answered, and a moment later the room felt a little emptier.

Flicker listened for them leaving through the front door, but got distracted by Ethan moaning about the lack of food. Kelsie's light footsteps flitted upstairs, and the rumble of running water soon filled the old house's pipes.

"I could've gone with Chizara," Nate said. "I can always flip my power inside out."

"If he runs off, she can read the tracker."

"Good point." A zipping sound came, and the thump of wadded dirty clothes hitting the floor.

Glorious Leader getting ready to do laundry. Maybe the prison industrial complex was actually good for something.

Flicker cast her vision out into the neighborhood, checking to see if their arrival had drawn any interest toward the house. There were people watching TV, staring at computer screens. (Porn. Yay.) Someone playing a sax, far enough away that her ears couldn't catch the sound.

"What do we do next?" Nate asked.

"Why ask me? Coming to New Orleans was your idea."

"That was strategy. This is tactics."

"Whatever," Flicker groaned. "Okay. Thibault and I should head out to the local FBI field office. Check if our friend Agent Phan is in town."

"And Verity," Nate said. "We should send Ethan to that weird-hunter meeting. In case they know something about Piper."

"Right. And let's send Crash and Mob out together," Flicker said. "Kelsie's seriously crowd-starved, but I don't want her starting a ten-block conga line. Chizara's grumpy yin might calm her raging yang."

Or was it the other way around? Thibault had explained yin

and yang to her a dozen times, but Flicker could never remember which was which.

She hoped he was okay out there, with the Curve of a real city threatening to pull him away.

"Okay," Nate said. "But what exactly are those two looking for?"

If he was testing her leadership skills, it was annoying as hell. But maybe prison had changed him in some profound way, and he was willing to cede control.

"Mob can search the crowds for weird stuff," she answered. "Anything that smacks of other Zeroes. And Chizara can look for surveillance vans and other signs of FBI."

There was a moment of silence, and Flicker went into Nate's eyes. He was sorting the laundry, separating darks from lights.

Wow. He should have gone to prison *years* ago.

"Does that make sense?" she asked, then hated herself for sounding needy.

Nate looked up at her—her hair was a disaster, and what color even *was* this T-shirt?—and his vision shifted with a shrug.

"Seems like you've got it all under control."

Flicker frowned. Was he being sulky? Or just admitting that she was the leader now?

She wasn't even sure she *wanted* to be in charge. She had Thibault to think about. And she missed Nate simply being her friend. Not a rival.

A sudden absence of sound tugged at her ears—the TV from next door had gone silent. She sent her vision searching, and found eyes staring at the kitchen window.

Ethan stood there, drinking a glass of water.

"Shit." She turned and called softly toward the kitchen. "Ethan! Someone's watching you. Go out and make with the voice!"

She crept into the kitchen in a crouch, jumping into Ethan's eyes. He stepped out onto the back porch, leaving the door open.

"Hello there?" he called in his calm, assured Scam voice. "Mrs. Lavoir?"

"Yes, that's me." An older woman emerged onto the veranda.

"Well, hi there!" Ethan said, taking a step forward. "Mr. Barrow said I should introduce myself."

"I see," the woman said. "And you are?"

"Karl Lucas," the voice said warmly. "I'm a friend of the Barrows' son, Max. They're having a great time in the Tetons!"

"Are they?" Mrs. Lavoir looked unimpressed. "He didn't mention you were coming."

Nate, crouched behind her, took Flicker's shoulder.

"Last-minute trip," Scam chattered on. "There's a few of us here, but we won't be around much. It's our first Mardi Gras!"

Flicker could practically see his cheerfulness bouncing off the woman.

"Well, I don't know. It isn't like Ed Barrow, letting a crowd of young people stay over. He's very particular about his house."

Ethan gave a friendly laugh. "I know what you mean. He made us promise to set the alarm every time we leave. Said his system was the best money can buy."

Mrs. Lavoir folded her arms, but gave a curt nod like she'd heard that line before. In his bedraggled camping clothes, Ethan probably didn't give the impression of a master thief who could disarm a high-end security system.

"Well, see that you behave yourself. This is a quiet neighborhood, and we like to keep it that way."

"Of course, Mrs. Lavoir. We'll do all our partying on Bourbon Street!" Ethan backed up on the veranda, nearly into the door.

"And how long are you folks planning to stay?"

"Till Fat Tuesday."

Four days, Flicker thought. The voice would have chosen a date that made sense to Mrs. Lavoir, which meant the Barrows wouldn't be coming back before then. Unless she didn't know the exact date.

You could never trust the voice.

Mrs. Lavoir gave Ethan one last suspicious look, then turned and went back inside without a good-bye, which seemed like a bad sign to Flicker.

"Think she bought it?" Nate asked softly as Ethan came back in.

"Course she did," Ethan said. "The voice wouldn't say anything if it wasn't going to convince her."

"Well, there's impossible and there's fifty-fifty," Flicker said, throwing her vision next door into Mrs. Lavoir's eyes.

"What's up?" Kelsie was in the kitchen doorway, smelling of wet hair, soap, and shampoo.

"Nosy neighbor," Ethan said.

"Damn," Kelsie said, sending a spike of disappointment through the room. "I really like this place."

"Relax. The voice handled it," Ethan said. "Not that we have a choice. We've got no car, Crash and Anon are gone, and our stuff is spread all over the house."

"Hang on," Flicker said. Mrs. Lavoir was pacing down the hallway, eyeing a landline phone on a small table. "She's thinking about calling the Barrows. Or the cops."

"If only we had someone who could crash phones," Ethan said. "But no, we sent her off to *park the car*."

"Be quiet, Ethan," Flicker said. But he was right. She'd separated the group before the situation was secure, like a general dividing her force in enemy territory. Maybe she'd been too busy worrying about Thibault.

Nerves spread through the room.

But then Nate spoke, sending out a shimmer of calm. "Kelsie, get the Anon file. If we have to run, everyone grab one bag."

"She's *right* by the phone," Flicker whispered. Her vision

blurred for a moment as Mrs. Lavoir took off one set of glasses and put on another. "Rummaging in the drawer . . . damn."

Kelsie and Ethan thumped off into the other room. Flicker heard the whisper of vinyl as dirty clothes were shoved back into duffel bags. A zipper closed too fast, caught on something. A muttered curse.

Nate stayed beside her, his hand still on her shoulder.

"If she's looking for a phone number, she's not calling 911," he said, radiating calm. "We'll have plenty of time to get away."

"She's found it." A sticky note from deep in the drawer, the yellow edges faded with age: ED BARROW—JACKSON HOLE. And a number. "Looks like she hasn't called them in a while."

"Should we head out?" Nate asked. "Your call."

Flicker hesitated. Having to run so soon would send the group reeling. It would put them all out on the street, with Crash and Anon alone and invisible.

She couldn't leave them out there if there was any alternative. "We wait."

The woman lifted the sticky note, pressed it to a corkboard on the wall above the phone. Its aging adhesive peeled away, so she stuck it with a red pushpin.

Flicker smiled. "Hot damn."

"What?" Ethan's duffel bumped into the door frame as he came back into the room.

Mrs. Lavoir was walking down the hall, away from the phone.

"She believed you," Flicker said.

"Told you!" Ethan said. His bag hit the floor with a thump. "The voice doesn't waste energy. It gets shit *done*."

"Big talk, Ethan," said Kelsie with a giggle. "But I saw your face when you were packing that bag."

"She's got their number ready," Flicker warned. "We have to be *perfect* neighbors."

"Um, okay," Ethan said. "That really doesn't sound like us."

Flicker couldn't argue. How long would it be before some Zeroes-borne disaster descended on the neighborhood? Or before Mrs. Lavoir called the Barrows for a friendly chat about their motley house sitters?

Typical. Scam's lies might work in the moment, but the voice never thought more than five minutes ahead. Flicker was going to have to monitor the situation closely.

The thought exhausted her. Was she ever going to relax again?

"Maybe we should relocate once Crash and Anon get back," Nate said.

He wanted her to decide? Or was this another test?

Whatever.

"No," she said firmly. "This place is perfect."

Kelsie cleared her throat. "Except for the impending doom part."

Flicker ignored her. "Here's how this works. We learn our escape routes, but also behave like perfect neighbors. And the moment Anon gets back, he goes over to switch that sticky note for a forgery—with Ethan's burner number. So if Mrs. Lavoir decides to call the Barrows, we'll get a heads-up."

Nate chuckled softly. "He can pretend to be some family member she's never met. Sing the praises of their fine, upstanding house sitters."

Kelsie laughed. "Hilarious. I hope she *does* call now!"

"Not even slightly funny," Ethan said. "The voice hates phones. Whatever mind-reading trick it pulls doesn't work long distance."

Flicker turned to him.

"Really, Ethan? After sixteen years of riding on the voice's coattails, it's about time you learned how to bullshit on your own."

CHAPTER 23
SCAM

ETHAN PACED BACK AND FORTH ON THE PEDES-trian bridge into Crescent Park, too nervous to stop moving.

His shoulders were hunched. His Saints cap was pulled so low over his sunglasses he could barely see. Keeping a low profile was in his veins now, but it was giving him serious neck cramps.

"You made it!" someone shouted. Sonia's voice.

Ethan spun, hissed, *"Keep it down."*

Sonia ignored his frantic gestures to play it cool, marched right up, and hugged him. She squeezed the air from his lungs, and when he could breathe again, he caught the chlorine whiff of hotel pool—she smelled like vacation.

"You recognized me?" he said, when he got his breath back. "Even with the bleached hair?"

"Duh!" Sonia said. "You could use some serious help with that, by the way."

She reached for his cap. When Ethan pushed her hand away before she could whip it off, she laughed. It was weird. He hadn't seen someone this relaxed in weeks.

His neck unclenched a little.

Seeing Sonia in the flesh made him miss home even more. It felt almost normal, talking to someone from Cambria.

Well, not *normal*. Her lip gloss was so shiny it hurt his eyes. Her hair was bright purple. She was strictly *not* a low-profile kind of girl.

It was ridiculously dangerous meeting up with her, but he needed to talk to someone who wasn't a Zero. The cabin fever was sucking his will to live, especially after that two-day drive to NOLA.

"Can we walk?" he asked. "I have to watch out for cops. All the time. It's like an instinct now."

"Cool." Sonia swung her head around, taking in the park, the train tracks under the bridge, the broad, still river. "Can I watch too?"

"Sure," Ethan said. "But try not to *look* like you're watching."

They crossed the bridge into the park, and he chose a direction at random. There weren't many people, and none of them looked like an undercover Fed.

"Are the others here?" Sonia asked.

"We split up," Ethan lied. "In Saint Louis."

No point in Sonia knowing the truth. She might blab it to her weird-hunter friends.

"Smart move!" Sonia said. "You guys are too recognizable in a group. They're looking for the Cambria Five, not the Cambria One."

Ethan grunted. "How's your conference?"

"WeirdCon is the best. You should come and see!"

"No way." She'd wanted to meet at the con hotel, but a whole *crowd* of weird-hunters? He'd be recognized inside a minute.

Like one weird-hunter in his life wasn't enough.

Was Sonia in his life? In the last month they'd only texted a handful of times, whenever he could get a burner and some privacy. But somehow those moments had seemed more real than his endless hours with the other Zeroes.

And here she was, in the flesh. Talking to a non-Zero he wasn't trying to scam felt wonderful. The FBI-Most-Wanted tension was slowly leaking out of his body.

"Get this," Sonia continued, grinning. "The local ghost hunters hate us for invading their turf. And the vampire hunters are even—"

"*Vampire* hunters?"

"Duh. This is New Orleans," Sonia replied. "Centuries of monetizing the uncanny! But why are *you* here?"

"The others sent me to check something out." Ethan

rummaged his brain for the name. "Do you know someone called Piper?"

Sonia froze. "Know her? She's, like, a legend here. The local boss of weird."

Ethan came to a halt beside her. "Does anyone know what she's up to?"

"Something big. Everyone says she hates us normals." Sonia's voice dropped. "Is that what you guys call us? *Normals?* So rude."

"Well, I don't think of you as normal," Ethan said.

"Awww." She smiled and took his hand. "Anyway, no one knows specifics, but it sounds like Piper wants to blow up normal world. Which seems like a bad thing."

Ethan nodded. It did. "Can you try to find out more?"

Sonia beamed. "On it. I'll get everyone asking around. Knowing you personally makes me a total celeb."

He stopped dead in his tracks. "You told them about me?"

"Everyone's seen my video, and they know I used to hang out at the Dish." Sonia shrugged. "Besides, it's not like I can spill *that* much. You're a mystery wrapped in an enigma!"

Ethan stared at her, his shoulders winding up tight again. Flicker had been betrayed by her own blood, and here he was trusting someone he barely knew.

He looked around. No federal marshals jumping out of the bushes yet.

"You didn't mention I was *here*, did you?"

Sonia looked serious. "Would I ever put you in danger, Ethan?"

"No?" Ethan felt himself relax. "I guess not."

Sonia smiled at him. "Exactly. I'm not giving up my exclusive rights to the Cambria Five."

"Six," Ethan murmured, out of habit.

"Huh?"

"Nothing." Ethan started moving again.

Maybe meeting Sonia hadn't been completely stupid. Nate had told them to scout New Orleans for federal activity, after all. What better way to do that than talk to the world's nosiest blogger?

"What can you tell me about the FBI?" he asked.

"They questioned me a few times back home. I didn't tell them a thing!"

"What did they ask about?"

She shrugged. "This was before the big prison break. They mostly wanted to know about your parties at the Dish. Like, were you giving out drugs."

"Great," he said. Mom would love seeing DRUG DEALER next to TERRORIST on his wanted poster. "How's Cambria?"

"Paranoia City," Sonia said with a disgusted noise. "That awkward moment when someone brain-melts your whole police force."

"That wasn't us! It was that guy who . . . got shot." He pushed the uncomfortable picture of Quinton Wallace in a pool of blood out of his mind.

"Yeah, us weird-hunters know all about him." Sonia shuddered, then her voice lightened. "I saw your sister on TV, by the way."

"Jess? On TV?"

"With your parents, doing an appeal for your safe return," Sonia said. "They think you have Stockholm syndrome."

"What syndrome?" Ethan asked. "Wait, *both* my parents? Were they, like, together?"

"Yeah. He had his arm around her."

Ethan turned away, feeling *really* homesick now. He hadn't seen his folks in the same room for five years.

"How'd Jess look?" he asked.

"Halfway scared for you, halfway seriously pissed."

"Yeah, she learned that expression in the army."

He'd never meant to upset his family like this. But one thing had led to another—which it always did in Ethan's life—and now there was no way to contact them without putting the Zeroes in danger.

Of course, he wasn't supposed to contact Sonia, either. And here he was, blabbing away.

"Just to be clear," he said. "You haven't told *anyone* in Cambria you're still in touch with me, right?"

"As *if*. And I snuck away from WeirdCon without . . ."

She paused, her scowl fading.

"What?" Ethan asked.

Sonia shrugged. "I *may* have mentioned that I was meeting a friend from home. It just slipped out."

Ethan froze in his tracks. "What do you mean, 'slipped out'?"

"I was leaving the con hotel, and this girl I'd been hanging out with asked where I was going. And it just came out of my mouth, you know? Like some kind of brain fart." Sonia laughed at his expression. "But it's not like I said who you were."

"I have a feeling you didn't have to." Ethan spun on one heel, looking in all directions. "Listen, I gotta—"

But there she was, halfway down the path, hands in pockets, casual as can be. An all-too-familiar figure.

"Verity," Ethan hissed.

"Huh?" Sonia said. "You know Verity too?"

"She's a federal agent," Ethan said through gritted teeth, dragging Sonia behind a hedge.

"No way. She's a local weird-hunter. I've been reading her blog for months."

"Shhh! We have to—"

"Ethan Cooper," called Verity from the other side of the hedge. "I can see you. Come on out."

CHAPTER 24
SCAM

ETHAN FROZE.

For a moment he considered making a run for it. But then his head filled with images of cops bringing him down in a flurry of shotgun blasts.

So he put his hands in the air and slowly walked out from around the hedge.

"Relax," Verity said. "I gave my bodyguards the slip."

"Bull." Ethan kept his hands in the air. "You just want me to get shot."

"Put your hands down," Verity said, glancing around. "They'll be looking for me. Plus, you look stupid."

Sonia took a step forward. "Did you follow me here, Verity?"

"Gee, cool hair *and* smart," Verity said. "Yeah, I figured if the Cambria Five were in town, you'd know where."

Sonia looked pissed. "You *used* me? That's totally against the weird-hunter code!"

"Oh, please."

Ethan finally lowered his hands. Verity was also scanning the park. Was she looking for her backup?

Or maybe she was telling the truth.

"Okay, one question," he said. "Why aren't there a bunch of marshals busting me right now?"

Verity raised her phone. "There will be if you try to run. But I'd prefer to have a private conversation."

"Holy crap." Sonia stared at them both. "She really *is* a Fed?"

"Afraid so." Ethan turned to Verity. A conversation was fine with him. It meant he could use the voice. "What do you want to know?"

"Is the rest of your crew here?" Verity asked.

When Ethan hesitated, the force he'd felt in the interrogation room hit, pushing against his throat. No, he was going to beat it. Verity didn't have a crowd, after all.

But then he felt it—a need to answer, to tell the truth. And it was building.

He turned at the sound of laughter. On the other side of the hedge, four kids were rolling up the path on bikes. They took their time, winding along in meandering loops, the Curve building as they came.

Ethan hated those kids. He hated their slow, easy banter

and their wobbling progress. The closer they came, the worse his throat got. Like tonsillitis and mono rolled into one.

But then Sonia blurted out, "They split up in Saint Louis!" She looked confused. But she'd told the truth as she knew it.

Ethan felt the pressure ease from his throat. Sonia answering the question had helped a little, and the kids were finally rolling past.

"What the hell was that?" Sonia asked.

"She makes you tell the truth," Ethan said. "That's her power."

"You mean, she's one of *you*?" Sonia's eyes went wide. "*And a Fed?*"

"Yes!" Ethan said. Telling the truth felt *amazing*.

But Verity was still going. "What are they doing in St. Louis?"

Oops. Time for power versus power.

Come on, voice, razzle-dazzle her.

"Nothing," it said flatly. Which was technically true, Ethan supposed, because if you weren't in a place, you weren't doing anything there. But he wanted the voice to straight-up lie, to beat this girl at her own game.

"Have you heard from Piper since you got here?" she asked.

Damn. There was that pressure again, like a burning hand around his throat. Luckily, this one was easy.

"I don't know who . . . ," Ethan began, but it was too hard. "Only that she's a big deal in this town."

"And she hates normals!" Sonia chimed in.

A big group of kids was coming into the park now. Kids in matching T-shirts, with a few adults guiding them. Great. Some kind of extracurricular excursion.

Verity's power was catching a tsunami-level Curve.

"Listen carefully," she said. "Have you heard anything about a secret meeting tomorrow? With a guy called Beau?"

A crushing weight came down on Ethan, and he didn't even try to use the voice. "Never heard of any meeting, or him."

"Me either!" Sonia practically shouted.

Verity gave her a bored look. "Yeah, you weird-hunters don't know shit. Total waste of my weekend."

Sonia glared at her. "Hang on. Your truth power is why I told you all about Timmy Hofferson in fifth grade, isn't it?"

Verity chuckled. "Yeah, that *was* funny. So maybe not a total waste."

Ethan took a step back. If looks could kill, Sonia's expression was pretty much a flamethrower right now.

"You should leave, Sonia," Verity raised her phone. "I'm calling in the freak collectors. You don't want to get busted for aiding and abetting."

She started to tap at her screen, and Ethan opened his mouth.

Voice, distract her! Freak her out.

"You don't trust Phan, do you?" it said. "That's why you wanted this conversation to be private."

Verity stared at him. "Pretty insightful for a guy with a C-minus average."

Damn it. *That* was in his FBI file?

But at least her fingers had stopped moving.

Melt this girl's brain, voice.

"You don't trust anyone," it said, totally sure of itself. "Pretty ironic, for a girl who's never been lied to."

"You don't know me," she said coldly.

"The scary thing is," the voice answered, "I *do*."

Verity sent a confused look at the kids, who were still right there and boosting her power. But the voice was telling the truth, after all.

It knew everyone.

As long as it kept her from calling in those bodyguards.

Go, voice!

"When you were at school, no one ever lied about knowing how poor you were. Your secondhand clothes. Your shitty house. You heard about your father's affairs when you were way too young to understand. You knew *everyone's* awful secrets—until your whole family all hated you for it. The truth is humiliation and pain, isn't it?"

"That's my power causing pain," Verity said softly. "Not me."

Ethan swallowed. He hated it when the voice got all dark like this. But he also hated the idea of life in prison, so he let it keep pounding away.

"People may not lie to you, but they still break promises.

Phan says you'll lead a team of superpowered agents one day. But you know it's never going to happen. His bosses hate us. They'll never trust you." Ethan managed to grab a breath. "And he's putting you in danger for this meeting, isn't he? You know you're expendable. Because to the government, you'll always be a superpowered freak!"

For a moment, Verity looked stricken. All her worst fears confirmed.

The voice had nailed it.

"What the hell is your power?" she asked.

The voice got all proud in Ethan's mouth, coming out bigger than he'd ever heard it before. "It's more than you can understand. More than anyone can grasp. You only have the truth. But I have knowledge, the annihilation of the unknown. Past, present, future. Thoughts, feelings, fears. *I know all of it.*"

"Damn, Ethan." Sonia was staring at him. "I would not have called that."

"Well, I've heard enough." Verity raised her phone again. "Someone needs to shut you down."

Ethan opened his mouth, wanting more than anything to keep distracting her, but nothing came out.

The voice was fresh out of diversions.

"Here's how this works," Verity said. "When I slip away from my guards, they scramble a team. Too many for you to get past. If you try to run, you'll only get hurt. These guys don't play nice with freaks. Understand?"

Ethan's mind spun. The voice couldn't just throw shade anymore. It had to say something that made Verity *want* to let him go.

And with that new desire, it came charging back up his throat.

"If you do this, I'll be working for the Feds inside a week!"

She gave him side-eye. "Yeah, that's kind of the point."

"Really, Verity? You want a government that knows everything you're thinking? Everything you're scared of? A government that knows about the pencil you shoplifted when you were seven, just to see if you could keep a secret? That knows how all you want is to keep Piper safe? That you still call her up some nights? That you still wish she and you—"

"Shut *up*!" Verity cried out, pushing him back with both hands, hard.

Ethan stumbled but kept his footing. The group of kids went silent, and suddenly all of them were watching. Like Ethan was in a play and didn't know his lines.

But the voice did.

"You don't trust Phan to keep you safe tomorrow," it said. "Why would you trust him with *omniscience*?"

Verity stared at him for what seemed like a solid minute. Finally she lowered her phone.

"Get the hell out of here," she said. "Both of you."

Ethan turned away and started walking, fast. Sonia was beside him, tapping notes into her phone.

He wanted to tell her to stop, but his head was pounding too hard with what he'd heard the voice say about itself.

Omniscience really *was* scary, when you thought about it. Especially since Ethan didn't know where all that knowledge came from, and was never really in control of what came out of his mouth.

But hadn't Nate promised that New Orleans would be full of answers?

More than ever, Ethan wanted to find another Scam.

CHAPTER 25
ANONYMOUS

"YOU'RE SPOOKING THEM, THIBAULT," FLICKER'S voice chirped in his earbud. "That place is crammed with cameras."

"My FBI jacket's not fooling them?"

"Maybe it's your haircut. Or the fact that you're sixteen? No alarms yet, but the guy at the security desk's on the phone. Be ready to move."

"Great," Thibault said under his breath. He was halfway across the third floor of the FBI's New Orleans field office, a rabbit warren of corridors kinking around offices and meeting rooms. It was a little after five, and the place was busy enough that chopping away attention was easy, but there was nothing his power could do against cameras.

He didn't want to leave. There was information here, and

he was the Zeroes' boots on the ground. It kept him real, being on a mission.

And he liked having Flicker in his ear, guiding him. It made him feel safe, connected.

"Is Phan coming back to his office?"

"He's headed for the security desk," Flicker said. "Maybe they always call him when weird shit happens."

Thibault froze, wondering if Phan knew about Stalkers. If so, this mission just got a lot trickier.

"You're *right* in front of a camera!" she said. "Move! Or at least turn your back to it. They might have your face on file from the Dish photos."

Thibault moved. A bell pinged as he passed the elevator doors. They hissed open behind him, and someone's attention zotted into the back of his head.

"Hold up, buddy," a nervous voice said, and a radio spat and squawked.

Thibault turned to see a portly man standing, hand on his gun. He severed the man's sightline with a swipe of his hand.

"Uh . . ." The security guy blinked and looked around.

His radio crackled again: "He was five yards in front of you, McEvoy. What's the problem?"

"He who?" The guard's gaze swept the corridor.

Thibault stood back and let the guy stride past and around the corner, his attention whipping around, his radio exclaiming on his hip.

"Still want to stay in there?" Flicker asked.

"Yes."

"Okay. Head to room three seventy-eight."

Thibault walked, the numbers climbing to his right. He passed an open door, and a woman in a blue suit glanced up from a monitor.

"Looking hot in that raid jacket, Anon," Flicker murmured.

Thibault grinned, chopped the agent's attention away, and kept going.

There was no wood paneling along this hallway, and the doors were closer together. Like these were temporary offices.

Behind him, Thibault heard McEvoy: "You see a kid come past here? Tall, dark hair, raid jacket?"

"A kid? Nope."

The hallway turned left and left again. Thibault hurried along it, still checking door numbers. "I'm at the three seventies . . . here it is."

The squawk of a radio was coming around the loop in the hall.

"You aren't on camera," Flicker said. "Go!"

Thibault pushed through into 378, closed the door behind him.

The office was a mess, a chaos of folders and binders. Thibault stood with his back against the door, taking it all in.

"Man, these guys print *everything* out."

Two tall file cabinets were jammed up against the back wall.

An ancient PC was pushed back to one corner of the desk, the keyboard on top of the monitor to make room for more papers and files.

The security radio squawked past outside the door.

"You're clear," Flicker said. "Let's get some photos, Anon."

"You got it, boss."

"That still sounds weird," she said. "I prefer 'Your Magnificence' or 'Your Worship.'"

"Whatever, boss," Thibault said, smiling. Flicker owning her place as the group's leader was the only pleasant surprise in his return to the world. She might be uncertain about being in charge, but that only made him want to support her more.

He started with a panorama of the grubby, Blu-Tack-marked walls, the beat-up desk, the veneer peeling off the cupboard doors.

Phan must be at the bottom of the pecking order of this place. The local agent in charge must not be taking his crowd theories *that* seriously.

Then he saw it on the wall. "Whoa, there's a map."

"Of what? New Orleans?"

"The whole US." It took up most of the wall opposite the desk. Thibault leaned back against the desk to fit all of it on the phone screen. "It's got pins all over it—red, white, and blue."

"God bless America," Flicker said. "That's *so* FBI."

He took the picture. His hands were shaking, so he took a few more.

"One problem," Thibault said. "There's no key to what the colors mean."

"Let's Rosetta Stone this," Flicker said. "Find Cambria."

"Right." Thibault leaned closer, lifted an unsteady finger to the California coast. "Yep, there's a bunch of pins here. All three colors, mostly white."

"Count them."

"Um, sixteen white. Two blue, just one red." He scanned the area. "Also a red and a white out in the Arizona desert."

"Arizona? As in the Desert Springs Mall?"

"Right. Whoa." Thibault felt sudden nerves in his stomach.

He ran his fingers back to Cambria. So many white pins. They couldn't all be Zeroes.

One red. Two blue.

He looked from Cambria to Desert Springs and back again. Then down at Houston. Another cluster of white.

Of course. Training sessions, pranks, crimes.

"White is crowd-psychosis events, Zeroes screwing around," he said, and took a step back. "The whole map is full of it."

"What about the other colors? Actual Zeroes?"

"No, there's just two blues in Cambria, not the famous five. None at the mall. And one red in each place."

A chill passed through Thibault at the sight of the single red pin at Desert Springs.

Davey.

The guy they'd called Coin. The guy they'd watched being torn to pieces. The fellow Zero who he, Thibault, had handcuffed to a sculpture right in the swarm's path.

Thibault swayed on his feet.

And the single red pin in Cambria. That had to be Quinton Wallace, collapsing in front of Thibault's gun.

Both red pins were his doing.

Darkness fringed his sight and began to close inward. The shape of a pistol grip filled his hand. That smell of shooting, fireworks gone sour, prickled his nostrils. Blood spread on the asphalt, its edges gleaming in the sun. . . .

"Anon?" Flicker's voice came from a hundred miles away. But it stopped him from fading out, pulled him back to his body. This was important. The Zeroes needed him to stay in this blood-soaked world.

"I'm here. Just checking something."

He followed a line of pins, a jagged string of red, upward from Cambria. Quinton Wallace's kills, leading all the way back to Portland.

A final red pin sat there in a cluster of white. Thibault reached out and touched his fingertip to it.

The other Anonymous. The one who Swarm had taken.

Someone like him. Dead now, but not forgotten by everyone. Marked with this pin, at least.

Thibault's gaze slid down the map, past other flocks of white. Reds and the occasional blue blurred among them.

"Red means dead Zeroes," he said. "They're all over the country. Dozens."

"Damn." Flicker's voice was soft in his ear. "What about the blues?"

He stared at the two blue pins in Cambria again, and it came to him.

"Officer Delgado. Officer Bright."

"Of course," Flicker said. "Blue for cops, dead or injured."

"Man," Thibault said. "No wonder they hate us."

"Speaking of law enforcement, Phan just left the camera room. You don't have much time. Get some close-ups of New Orleans. We need to know what we've gotten ourselves into."

Thibault pulled out his phone again. Finding NOLA wasn't hard. Dozens of pins spilled into the Gulf of Mexico. There wasn't room to fit them all. Mostly white, but also—

"Six . . . seven of us dead in New Orleans." As he took pictures, his voice sounded thin and far away in his own ears. "And four blues."

"Shit, *four cops*? Let's get you out of there, Anon. You don't sound good."

"I'm okay," he said. "I'm not fading on you."

She hesitated, like she'd somehow felt him trembling at the edge. "Okay, but you do *not* want to get arrested in this town."

"Yeah. Maybe not."

Thibault took in the eastern half of the States. It was

clumped with Zeroes activity, especially around the major cities. But nothing as dense as New Orleans.

It would have felt so amazing a year ago—finding out about all those other Zeroes. But his excitement was curdled from the start, because that white sea of possibilities was stained with red and blue.

"He's in the elevator. Get out of there."

"Not yet, Flick. We need to know more."

His hand went to his wrist, to Chizara's tracking device.

"Anon! What do you mean? You're not going to *talk* to him, are you?"

"Hell no. But I have to go quiet. You too. No sound leaking out of my earbuds."

"Damn it, Anon," she hissed, then a whisper: "He's right outside."

On cue the office door opened.

CHAPTER 26
ANONYMOUS

THIBAULT SPUN TO FACE THE MAN, LIFTING A HAND to slice the shaft of his attention before it could lock on.

Phan hesitated in the doorway. He scanned the room carefully.

Yep. He'd dealt with Stalkers before.

He was just like the others had described him. Older, graying, Asian. His suit a little too large, like he'd been losing weight lately.

Finally the suspicion faded from his face. He came in, sat down at the desk, and leaned backward. In the crowded space, Thibault had to suck in his gut.

He was pinned now. Maybe this hadn't been a brilliant idea.

Phan pulled a wallet and phone from his back pocket and

slapped them down on the corner of the desk. He pulled the keyboard off the computer and balanced it on the folders.

Then he stared for a moment, his attention glittering at the blank screen.

"Your reflection in the monitor!" came Flicker's whisper.

Thibault reached out and snipped the thread.

Phan shook his head, as if rousing himself from a daydream. When he tapped a key, a lock screen came up: the FBI seal, bright enough to outshine any reflection.

Thibault breathed out slowly.

Phan typed in his password in a blur, then scrolled and clicked until an e-mail filled the screen. He reached for the landline phone on the far side of the desk. Punched a few numbers, drummed his fingers.

"Koslowski? Phan here. Got a favor to ask. I got this team flying in from Houston for an operation tomorrow morning—"

There was a pause as Phan listened. Thibault raised his phone, trying to get the computer screen in focus.

"But I *still* need a vehicle that can take the whole detail, seven people. And it's gotta look legit. The target's gonna be wary. Grew up down here, and knows my consultant from way back."

Thibault took a few pictures and pocketed his phone. Now for the other thing.

He pulled the leather strap from his wrist, untied it. The curled wafer of tracker circuitry slipped easily off the end.

Chizara had said it could take a lot of punishment—water, impact, anything short of lighting it on fire.

He rolled it flatter between his fingers. Perfect.

Behind Phan's elbow, under his phone, lay his wallet, fat with a badge. A sliver of Phan's awareness coiled around the pile—some people were always aware of their phones. Thibault reached out and snipped the sliver of attention, then pulled the badge case free.

He slid Chizara's tracker into the pocket behind the gold shield.

It felt dangerous, like throwing away an anchor. And it was a huge, dangerous relief, to have that anchor's weight lift from him.

No more tracker. He was free. He could shed the Zeroes at any time. Could flee reality itself if he wanted, and Chizara couldn't follow.

They would all forget him again. Flicker's fear would be over.

But Phan's voice brought him back.

"You see my problem," he was saying. "Since my thing at Dungeness went wrong, it's always the same half-assed shit. They give me the people and no transport. Or the right vehicle and nobody with crowd-psychosis experience. That's why Las Vegas was such a shitshow. I know, I already owe you for backing me up on letting Saldana go, and I've *still* got nothing to offer you in return, but us crowd crazies gotta stick together. This is our chance to get one of these freaks all alone. Someone we can *break*."

Thibault wedged the badge wallet back under the phone.

"This guy scares me," Flicker whispered. "You need to get out of there."

No kidding.

But the door was shut, and he was still pinned in the corner.

"A Ford Transit? Perfect," Phan was saying. "Anything without fancy electronics. This town's crawling with Electrokinetics. No, we don't need it till morning. I owe you."

He put down the phone and stared at the screen. Then he looked all around the little office, clearly uneasy.

Thibault stayed motionless, trying not to breathe.

"He *feels* you in there," Flicker whispered. "Let me fix this."

The bud in his ear went dead. What was she up to?

Long minutes of silence stretched out. Thibault let go of the mission, of urgency and fear.

The room dimmed and grew partial around him. Maybe he was letting himself fade too much. He could disappear now, away from those little red and blue accusations on the wall map—

The desk phone rang, jolting Thibault back into the world.

"Phan here." The man listened for a moment, then sat up straight, his whole body rigid. "Are you serious? She mentioned Verity by *name*? Why didn't you put her through?"

Thibault squeezed his eyes shut. Damn it, Flicker.

"Right now? Where?" Phan stood up as he listened, logged off the computer, gathered his wallet and phone.

A moment later he was out the door.

Thibault stood there, alone, solidly in his body after that surge of adrenaline. His phone vibrated in his hand.

"What did you tell them?" he answered.

"The truth," Flicker said. "That I was a superpowered kid who'd met Verity. I heard the FBI was hiring, and I wanted to talk to him."

"That last part isn't true, is it?"

"Maybe one day," she said. "But not in half an hour at the corner of Bourbon and Saint Ann."

Thibault laughed, relief flowing over him. Flicker had extracted him from this brilliantly. He could walk out of this office, free of the FBI. He was free of the tracker, too. But he wanted nothing more than to walk out into the sunlight and into her arms.

Sometimes reality was worth sticking around for.

"You need to ditch that phone," he said. "We both should, since you called me."

"Not till I feel your hand in mine."

He couldn't help but smile. "Okay. I'm coming."

He winced at the thought of losing all his photos, and took another long look at the map, trying to memorize every region. Just in case the Zeroes found themselves in another city and needed to know the situation there.

But for now New Orleans was the front line of this war.

CHAPTER 27
MOB

KELSIE DANCED TO THE ANTHEM BLASTING FROM
a brass band on a street corner.

Trumpets and trombones blared over the tuba's spine-shaking riffs, and the crowd sang and clapped along in the evening
cool.

"Oh my God! Everybody knows the words!" Kelsie shouted
into the air.

She'd never been part of anything like Mardi Gras. The city
was full of noise and the smell of cooking crawfish. People ate
and drank and danced. Music made the cool air feel sultry and
alive.

She could almost forget she was on the FBI's Most
Wanted list.

This city didn't have the corporate glitz, the desperate

fun, of Las Vegas. This was a real party town, and it was in her blood. She danced at each new corner full of music and breathed in the wild, crazy energy of the crowds. She could feel tangled mobs like melodies, separate but intertwined.

After weeks of hiding in empty campsites with grungy shower stalls, New Orleans was scrubbing her soul clean. It felt like home. A place she'd missed without even knowing it existed.

Kelsie imagined herself here at three years old, soaking it all in, and suddenly her whole life made much more sense.

She needed to tell Chizara, and searched the crowd for her—for that pulse of deep concentration, like a pure, rich bass note.

There she was, back against a wall and lost in the city's tech, a distant frown on her face. Busy searching for surveillance vans, agents wearing earpieces, signs of other Crashes playing with technology.

Serious stuff.

Kelsie danced closer, a hand out, beckoning Chizara into the sound and life of the New Orleans night. She pushed the crowd's party atmosphere at her.

Chizara's concentration softened into a smile. "Stop that."

Kelsie grinned back. "Relaxing is good for concentration. I read it somewhere."

"Yeah, well, *dancing* is not good for concentration."

But Kelsie kept pushing until she could see Chizara's chin bopping to the pulse of the brass.

"It's been *weeks* since we danced!" Kelsie shouted above the music.

"We're supposed to be working," Chizara replied.

Kelsie took her hand, locked eyes with her, and started moving to the beat. Dancing was Kelsie's link to the good things in their past, before evil Swarms and vengeful Feds and supermax prisons.

Chizara put her hands lightly on Kelsie's waist, a gentle weight against her rise and fall. "We're supposed to be on the lookout, remember?"

"We can look *and* have a good time."

Chizara shook her head, still grinning.

"Come on, Zara," Kelsie pleaded. "How long's it been since we enjoyed ourselves?"

"We're running for our lives. Enjoyment isn't on the agenda."

Chizara said it like she was joking, but Kelsie felt the moment she shook off the feedback loop, like stepping off a dance floor.

Kelsie eased back, letting the crazy-happy vibe of the crowd slow down around her.

"Okay," she said. "Let's check the next street over."

They walked on, passing a bar with its windows open wide to the sidewalk, selling beer in plastic go-cups. Kelsie was thirsty, but she'd never get Chizara to drink, not while they were on duty.

"Do you remember any of this?" Chizara asked over the music.

Kelsie shook her head. "Only in my bones. Seems like I'd remember *something* specific, though. An address? A street name?"

But soon after her mom had broken Kelsie's wrist, Hurricane Katrina had laid waste to the town. Dad had fled that disaster as well as his marriage. To protect his daughter.

She could never blame him, though she'd lost this vibrant place in the bargain. She hated to think of him having to run. Like she was on the run now, except he'd had a tiny daughter in tow.

She missed him more than ever.

"So, your mom," Chizara began. "Where do we start?"

"I found some old paperwork in Dad's stuff. Just a name: Zoe Moseley. I used to search for her online all the time." Back when the internet had been a casual convenience, before burner phones and remote cabins.

"Didn't you tell me she was in a band?"

"Easy Vice. A jazz quartet," Kelsie said. "But the last time she played with them was five years ago."

Chizara shrugged. "Let's see if they're still around."

She pulled out her burner, turned it on. Stared at the spinning boot-up wheel on its screen, Kelsie felt the street's energy turn sharp and nervous along her spine.

Zoe Moseley was a stranger. The Zeroes couldn't trust

strangers anymore—even blood relations. Kelsie's mom couldn't break her wrist anymore, but she could destroy her with a phone call.

"Wait, Zara. Don't we have more important things to worry about?"

"Let me worry about the Feds." Chizara stared at her phone. "Easy Vice, right? They're playing at the High Blues club tonight. That's, like, six blocks from here."

Kelsie looked down—so close. Her anxiety spiraled out into the crowd. A stir traveled down the street, and when the brass band at the end of the block blew a few sour notes, the crowd's dance turned ragged and agitated.

Chizara's arm came around her. "Hold it together, Kels."

"Sorry," Kelsie mumbled into her shoulder. She squeezed Chizara hard, and with a shuddering breath drew back inside herself.

"You don't have to be scared of her anymore," Chizara said. "Maybe you never did. We don't even know your mom's side of the story."

Kelsie nodded. Dimly, she felt the call of the crowd, which had recovered its good cheer on its own. She reached out for that warm, reassuring party vibe. Her tribe. Her town.

And her mother was part of that connection. Part of her.

"Okay, Zara. As long as you're with me, I'm not afraid."

CHAPTER 28
MOB

WHEN THEY REACHED THE HIGH BLUES CLUB, THE bouncer on the door fell wordlessly victim to Kelsie's feel-good vibe and waved them inside.

Kelsie breathed slower in the safety of the club. The low lighting, the friendly crowd paying serious attention to the music. Nobody looking for the Cambria Five.

"Nice place," Kelsie said.

Chizara's wide eyes were scanning the lighting setup. "It's all analog!"

They sat at a small table and watched a jazz quartet finish their set of Dixieland and ragtime. When the musicians wrapped up half an hour later, Kelsie felt her anxiety leaking out into the crowd again.

"I need a drink," she said.

"No, you don't." Chizara pointed to the stage. "That's Easy Vice."

Three women in feather boas and fedoras were coming on stage, testing their instruments. One played a riff on the keyboard, while the others tuned the open strings of their fiddle and bass.

"They used to be a quartet," Kelsie said softly. Had Zoe joined another band? Left town? Died?

Kelsie searched the faces in the audience, just in case she was here for old times' sake. Would she even recognize her own mother?

The band launched into their first song. Music streamed through the room. Deep, soulful music with a crying edge that made Kelsie want to weep for her losses. But also to take account of every narrow escape, every stolen moment with Chizara.

The crowd mellowed, and Kelsie fell into their soft energy. She felt soothed and protected and safe. She was home. *This* was home.

Chizara looped an arm around her, and they sat with their heads touching, watching the stage.

Forty minutes later, the band laid down their instruments for a break. They nodded to the crowd's applause, and two of them disappeared into a back room. The bass player stepped offstage and went to the bar.

Kelsie got to her feet and cut across the room toward her. She felt Chizara following, close and protective.

Just as Kelsie was about to tap her shoulder, the bass player glanced her way. The woman blanched.

"Damn. I'm seeing ghosts!"

Her gaze was so intense, like it was finding something Kelsie hadn't known was inside her.

All she could say was, "Do I really look like her?"

The woman nodded, and they were both silent for a moment.

Finally she said, "I'm Edie. Good to see you . . . Kelsie, right? You've grown. I mean, of *course*."

Kelsie laughed in spite of the fact that she was trembling. She gestured shyly at the audience. "I was hoping my mom would be here."

Edie shook her head. "She quit the Easies years back."

"Yeah, I saw that," Kelsie said. "Is she in another band?"

"Quit the business," Edie said sadly. "Quit singing. She took it hard when your daddy stole you away—"

"That's not what happened!" Kelsie said hotly.

Her sudden ferocity spiraled out, catching Edie in its wake. Edie's hand tightened around her drink. A bus boy dropped a tray, and people leaped back from the broken glass like it was glittering snakes and spiders. There was a rattled silence as he scrambled to collect the pieces.

Chizara stepped forward, putting an arm around Kelsie, and Kelsie remembered to breathe.

"Sorry," she mumbled. She pulled back on the anger.

Edie stared. "That was you? Are you one of those—"

"We're just looking for Zoe, okay?" Chizara said gently.

"Okay," said Edie, but she didn't look convinced. "It's true, she was drinking hard back then. She saw things a particular way. But after she sobered up, she wanted to move on, you know?"

Kelsie nodded, but wondered exactly what that meant.

"She's part of something now," Edie said. "Call themselves the Clarity Circle. It's a . . . spiritual group."

"A cult?" Kelsie asked. Cults were the worst kind of group, and they loved to prey on former alcoholics, Fig always said.

Edie waved that suggestion away. "Not as far as I know. They preach truth and recognition, stuff like that. Zoe loved their meetings. Made her feel whole, she said. Like she'd found something she'd lost."

Kelsie nodded slowly. She knew that feeling. "Where can we find them?"

"They used to meet up in a community hall somewhere here in town, every Monday afternoon," Edie downed her drink. "Don't know if they still do. Not my scene."

The rest of Easy Vice was back on stage, tuning their instruments.

"Can I ask something?" Kelsie said. "You guys are so good together. How could she give this up?"

Edie's face softened. "Because of you, child. Everything she did after your dad left, it was because of you. She was punishing herself."

Kelsie wanted to ask Edie more about when she was a kid. What Zoe and her father had seen in each other. How long they'd been together. But her throat was too tight.

"If you go see Zoe, take care," Edie said. "Your mother loved you. But it'll be a big shock for her."

She turned for the stage, and Kelsie watched her go, tears welling in her eyes. A feedback loop began to build, carrying her sadness across the crowd.

Chizara took her hand. "Come on. Let's get out of here."

CHAPTER 29
CRASH

"IT'S OKAY, KELS," CHIZARA SAID. "WE CAN FIND her now."

"I know." Kelsie's voice was steady, but tears still trickled down her cheeks. "It's just . . . a lot. She gave up everything because of me."

"Moms do that," Chizara said.

The party swirled down every street, but she could see Kelsie's tears muffling the mood nearby, like a rain cloud tethered to them.

The feeling sank into Chizara's bones as they walked. She didn't want to think about moms. Or dads. Or little brothers. Or coming home to the smell of egusi soup.

It was tough being back in a crowded city. *Everyone* had their phone out, snapping and uploading pictures. Chizara didn't have much juice left to fend off the stings. She'd crashed the Las Vegas Strip more than a week ago.

At least New Orleans was pretty basic, electronically. More than ten years after Katrina, the infrastructure still had an improvised feel. Anything new and shiny stuck out a mile.

And she had great range here, with these crowds filling the nighttime streets. Their bee swarms of phones showed her the avenues and squares in bright outline, thinning out into the residential districts. The place was a glittering quilt, thickly sewn with biting sequins.

A flurry in the crowd ahead made her jump. Drums were pounding.

"What *is* that?" Kelsie said.

There was a lot of shouting. Plumes of crimson feathers stuck up from the throng, the top of a headdress. People were craning to see, grinning.

The drums came closer, and the shrill rattle of tambourines. The crowd tightened around them until Chizara couldn't take a step in any direction.

A second, turquoise headdress reared up. She tried to read the crowd's mood, but it was a confusion of crush panic and excitement.

At least it had washed away Kelsie's sadness.

Chizara could hardly tell what *she* was feeling. Were her emotions her own, or were someone else's being forced on her?

Were there Bellwethers up ahead? Mobs? Swarms? Glitches?

The crush was pushing her and Kelsie backward, up against an iron fence. The two sets of plumes came together, half crimson and half turquoise. Two armies of percussionists beat their rhythms out against each other, the noise bouncing off building fronts.

Kelsie hoisted herself up on the fence to look out over the crowd.

"They're facing off!"

"Who? Is it some kind of crowd battle?"

"I can't—there's so many—"

"Any powers?"

"Not sure," Kelsie laughed, motioning with her free hand, as if pushing Chizara's fear out of the way. "But it's *awesome*."

Chizara tried to let go of her anxiety, but she hated being trapped here, her body unable to move, her brain pin-stuck with phones and cameras. Everyone was taking pictures of the confrontation.

But much worse were the jiggling, pulsing sparks of heartbeats all around her. A thousand fragile lives like fireflies dithering over a dark field.

She reached for thoughts of the Nevada desert—flat, empty, signal-free—to keep herself calm.

Shouted chants went back and forth. The crowd whooped and hollered around the combatants. The drums and tambourines joined with the phone signals to grip Chizara's head.

"I think it's just Mardi Gras stuff!" Kelsie called down from her perch. "Don't you love those drums?"

Helplessly Chizara listened for something to love about the drums. Could she trust Kelsie's joy washing through her, looping through the crowd around them?

"Zara, you should see these guys' costumes—so many feathers! And the *beads*!"

Kelsie's face was the brightest Chizara had seen it since back at the Dish, cueing her next track, guiding the crowd with music. Of course this crowded carnival was her idea of heaven. And the tumult had washed away her uncertainty, her anguish and anger about her mother.

But did Kelsie have to be up so high, where the whole crowd could see her? They were still fugitives.

A big cheer erupted in front of them.

"It *was* a battle!" Kelsie cried, laughing again. "The red guy's letting the blue one through! That's what it was all about—territory!"

The crowd began to loosen, and she jumped down.

"So no Zero powers?" Chizara asked. "Just a normal day at Mardi Gras?"

"No such thing." Kelsie was still surveying the throng. "I love this town. It's all about crowds. Traditions that pull people together, give them a reason to dance and sing."

Chizara shrugged. "I guess."

"The parades, the music." Kelsie smiled. "Of *course* Zeroes would all come here."

"I'd rather be *elsewhere*." Chizara took Kelsie's hand and pulled her through the crowd's jigging phones and cameras, all those heartbeats and brain sparks. "We're looking for your mom, remember? Or the FBI, or more Zeroes. Anything that's not another parade—or whatever that was."

She dragged Kelsie into a quieter cross street, where the balconies were hung with planters. The familiar patterns of domestic tech eased Chizara's pain, the row houses forming a barrier against the eddying background of New Orleans's carnival crowds.

Kelsie was her bouncing self again. "I think we're going to learn a lot here."

Chizara groaned. "I wish education wasn't so *painful*."

Kelsie gave her a sympathetic smile. "You need to wind down. Come on."

She led Chizara farther from the crowd, in among darkened warehouses. They were mostly abandoned, the arteries of dead tech slumped and dangling inside them. Their walls were striped with faded muddy watermarks from bygone floods. Windows were broken or boarded up, and rusted padlocks hung on gates and doors. Half the streetlights here were broken.

"Look at all this," Kelsie said, doing a spin in the middle of the road. "Empty. Cheap. But so close to Bourbon Street.

Perfect for setting up another Petri Dish, right?"

"I'm not sure that's a good . . ." Chizara scanned the area ahead, frowning.

Something was wrong. A chunk missing from the horizon.

Yes, *there* it was—a blank spot, a hole in the crazy quilt of signals. At the end of the block was an old warehouse with no electronic pulses coming from it. Not so strange in this half-derelict neighborhood, except that the building was also blocking the city *behind* it. And sitting beside one of the loading-dock doors was a piece of bright circuitry that didn't belong.

"Hmmm," she said.

"What?"

"Looks like you aren't the first Zero with that idea. Turn off your phone."

Kelsie followed Chizara's gaze, staring with widened green eyes. "Why?"

"Because that warehouse is a Faraday cage."

"You mean like at the Dish? You think some *Crash* lives here?"

Chizara shrugged. "I can't sense inside. Let's get closer, in case you can feel a crowd in there."

Kelsie mercifully powered down her phone as they walked up the street, keeping to the shadows. A cold wind came off the river, and the darkness was suddenly freighted with dread.

"You know, it could be a government lab," Kelsie muttered. "For experimenting on Zeroes."

"Doesn't feel like it." The shiny tangle of electronics at the loading dock was an invitation, created by a kindred spirit.

"There *are* people inside," Kelsie said softly. "Fifteen? Twenty?"

The grimy brick building loomed, its windows starred by thrown rocks. And there, hidden inside an old junction box, the pretty, intricate *thing* called to Chizara.

"They're busy, all working hard," Kelsie whispered as they hunkered beneath the lip of the loading dock. "Focused and loving what they're doing. If this was the Dish, I'd say they were getting ready for a rave."

"Twenty Zeroes?" Chizara wondered what could be done with that much power. More than just mischief and mayhem.

Something larger. World-changing, maybe.

But they didn't *all* have to be Zeroes, did they? Even at the Dish they'd had Craig helping out.

Chizara scanned the surrounding warehouses for any spark of a phone, or the ghostly smudges of organic electricity: beating hearts, brains full of firing synapses. Nothing. "Anybody watching us?"

"Not that I can sense," Kelsie said. "But maybe we should get Flicker here."

"I'm not waiting around." Chizara pulled herself up onto the loading dock. Beside a thick roller door painted charcoal gray sat the junction box. The other doors were all welded shut.

There was no other way into the signal void, that refuge

from the city's constant needling attacks. Except through the junction box, sizzling with power, alluring in its intricacy.

Chizara gave a soft, astonished laugh.

"What's funny?" Kelsie hissed.

"This thing." She pointed at the box. "It's a puzzle."

Kelsie stared at it. "It looks broken. Like it'll electrocute you if you're not careful."

"It's hooked up to the roller door. It feels like a lock, or more than a lock. A test."

"Or maybe a *trap*?"

Chizara felt around inside the circuitry, deeper and deeper. "No, it's a challenge. A special treat for Crashes. This might take a minute."

Kelsie laced her fingers tight among Chizara's. "Are you sure? What if this is the Feds? Or just straight-up bad guys?"

But Chizara barely heard her—she'd already dived into Lockworld.

She felt right at home, and at the same time everything was brand-new. It was like negotiating the cramped, labyrinthine innards of an Egyptian pyramid, carrying a spirit lamp and fighting off rats and demigods along the way. She had to hold some parts aside, break other pieces and repair them behind her, crash *and* fix simultaneously, split her efforts along two routes, then a third . . .

She was vaguely aware of sweat trickling down the small of her back, of Kelsie's worried whispers, of every muscle in her body rigid with concentration, with anticipation, with the effort of ten-dimensional thinking.

Maybe not thinking at all, so much as *being* this lock.

She had passed the point of no return, the puzzle teaching her more, asking more of her, with every gleam and surrender of its circuits.

At the heart of the thing, she saw the traps they'd laid. She built a great antlered flowchart in her mind, showing everything that could go wrong. Every way the lock could try to trick her, fool her, sting her.

Finally she turned her head to stare at the big steel door, and sprang the final release.

The roller door jolted to life, rumbling upward. Kelsie made to leap away, but Chizara's grip held her firm.

"*I* did that." She was cold all over, exhausted. "Do they know we're here?"

"They must. They feel surprised." Kelsie moved her head like she was twitching an insect off herself. "Let's just get out of here and tell the others what—"

But Chizara was walking toward the door. "Whoever did this *wants* to meet another Crash. No one else could figure that lock out."

"That's what I'm scared of, Zara!" Kelsie squeaked.

Chizara raised her hand to Kelsie's mouth and stared into her eyes.

"What do you *feel*? What do their emotions tell you?"

Kelsie hesitated. "They're curious. And *really* impressed."

"They should be." Chizara stepped into the darkness, pulling Kelsie with her.

The door rolled closed behind them. The Faraday cage resealed, and a fantastic silence fell. Chizara had that floaty feeling she used to get whenever she entered the Dish, the weight of the city's blather lifting from her shoulders.

It was dark, and cool. Her footsteps echoed—the whole warehouse was one open space.

"People all around us," Kelsie breathed.

Chizara nodded, her mind probing the darkness.

Heartbeats. A few high up, as if they could levitate. And, everywhere, equipment like she'd never seen. A theme park of electronic tools and components, laid out neatly in places, or piled up, glittering like a dragon's treasure.

And in the middle of the vast space stood something tall and metal and very weird. Something that was asleep for the moment, but Chizara felt strange, huge capacitors waiting, hungry.

Bringing that thing to life would take a *lot* of power.

"Okay, we're here," Kelsie announced to the darkness. "Where the hell are you?"

For a moment there was no answer.

Then a wall of bright white seared Chizara's eyes, banks of spotlights hitting her from all directions.

CHAPTER 30
CRASH

"YOU BROKE MY LOCK," A BOY'S VOICE SAID.

A snicker ran through the crowd behind the dazzle.

Chizara squinted from behind her raised hand, trying to see something in the glare. She made out silhouettes, people on walkways along the walls, hanging from ladders around the huge device in the middle of the warehouse.

This was another test—a much easier one.

Chizara waved a hand, and the bank of spotlights faded a little.

There were at least twenty of them.

A New Orleans mix—more dark skin than white, a few Asian kids—but all teenagers. No adults like the Craig helping out here.

What powers did they all have? Was there a Bellwether in charge? A *council* of Bellwethers?

What about a Sight-caster? No one was wearing dark glasses. But maybe Flicker's blindness was just a weird coincidence.

The Cambria Five didn't know much about the world.

"Thanks for that lock," she said. "It was fun."

The girl standing closest to them eyed her coolly. She was light-skinned, her hair short and natural, like Chizara's. She wore work coveralls, tools heavy in the pockets.

"You worked it pretty fast," she said.

"*Real* fast!" A white girl in paint-stained dungarees was springing down a ladder and across the concrete. "No one's made it through the Madbolt that quick since Truc built it. Where you *been* all our lives?"

She stopped short of Chizara, hands on her hips, looking her up and down with grudging admiration.

"We *know* where she's been, Jaycee" came from a catwalk above. A pale Asian guy with a long ponytail called down. "Knocking over police stations back when you were pranking your high school graduation. My poor little Madbolt didn't stand a *chance*."

So that was Truc, who'd spoken first. Chizara tried to read his expression. Was all this praise sarcastic or admiring?

Whatever it was, at least she didn't have to introduce herself. Everyone knew about the Cambria Five—the least-secret gang of Zeroes in the land.

"Graduation was last year," Jaycee said. "More recently, I did kinda let everyone into the Super Bowl for free."

"Not on your own," said a young male voice from the shadows. "All you did was crash the ticket readers."

"Quit your squabbling," said the black girl in coveralls. "This girl took down a *supermax*. That took teamwork. Loyalty. Cojones. Maybe you two could learn from her."

A little "ooooh" went though the crowd.

She was their leader. But tools weighted her coverall pockets.

Was a *Crash* in charge of this crew?

They were certainly builders here. With the lights on, Chizara could see the strange device in the center of the warehouse. It was covered with metallic bunting in Mardi Gras colors—purple, green, and yellow—and the whole thing was built onto a truck, like a parade float.

Somehow that only made it more ominous.

The girl looked like she was waiting for a comeback.

"You know my name," Chizara said. "What's yours?"

"Essence." The girl bowed a little.

"Well, Essence, the Madbolt was interesting." Chizara gestured at the machine in the middle of the warehouse. "But nothing compared to that thing. What the hell are you making?"

For a moment, all eyes went to the device, and their faces filled with pride, satisfaction. Ownership.

A realization pulsed at the corners of Chizara's awareness.

But Kelsie said it first: "Oh my God, Zara. They're *all* Crashes."

Chizara's mouth dropped open, and laughter spread through the room.

"That is the worst name," Truc said from above. "We're *Makers*, dude."

"For sure," Essence said. "But you got to admit, the girl is a Crash. Break any cities today?"

When she turned to Kelsie, her smile faded.

"And Kelsie Laszlo. Becky with the predator tendencies. Shouldn't you be blond?"

Kelsie held her gaze. "Yeah, I was. But then a guy called Quinton Wallace screwed up my life."

The warehouse went silent, quick. Chizara felt the spike of Kelsie's anger looping through them, mixed with their own nerves.

The white girl in dungarees, Jaycee, took a wide-eyed step backward. "You're right, Essence, that *is* her."

"I never even *seen* one of them," Truc said from the edge of the catwalk. "And you brought her in *here*?"

The fear spiraled, Kelsie half smiling in the middle of it. She was bouncing on her toes like she was ready to fight, not dance, and Chizara felt an echo of the street vibe they'd been absorbing all day. The mood was turning into something dangerous.

"So you know about Wallace?" she asked.

"Everybody knows about Swarms," Essence said. "They aren't exactly subtle."

Kelsie held her gaze, still bouncing a little. "Then you must know that he wanted me to eat my friends. And that I didn't."

Essence nodded slowly. "Not yet, anyway."

"Your boss man shot him before he could turn you," Jaycee said. "What does that prove?"

"That shooting Swarms is the right idea!" Truc called down.

And now fear glimmered on Kelsie's face.

Chizara raised a hand. She was about to shut the lights down, and a whole lot more. Like the permanent fusing of every circuit in their precious parade float.

But Essence spoke up first.

"Don't get rowdy, everyone," she said. "That's what the predators want."

Kelsie shook her head. "I *don't* want that! We came here to learn. We heard that something big was happening in New Orleans."

It was Truc who gave it away—his head turned just a little to look at the device.

Chizara reached her mind inside it again, trying to figure out its purpose. It was full of circuitry she'd never seen before, and didn't follow the plan of any kind of machine she knew. Those giant capacitors—they weren't designed to hold an electrical charge at all, but some completely different kind of energy.

All she could tell was that all that potential was pointed

straight up, as if the device was some kind of challenge to heaven itself. . . .

"I have to kick that question to the boss lady," Essence said, pulling a phone from her coveralls. "Come with me, Chizara Okeke. Your baby Swarm is freaking out my crew."

She lifted a finger, and the roller door jolted back to life. She beckoned Chizara and Kelsie to follow her toward the opening in the Faraday cage.

And as the city's tempest of signal stormed back in, a wonderful thing happened. Chizara winced—

And everyone else winced too—everyone but Kelsie.

This was how it would feel to belong. To live among people like her. With the same power, the same way of seeing. The same every-minute-of-every-day pain.

They'd all had to pretend in front of their families. To dream up ways to make the constant flinches look normal. Chizara didn't know most of these people's names, and she didn't trust them much. And yet they *knew* her better than anyone else in the world.

In a daze she followed Essence and Kelsie out onto the loading dock.

The signalscape of New Orleans descended like mosquitoes in a whining cloud, sinking its stingers in all over her skin. Chizara felt her mind juggling and compensating, holding up the city's scrappy infrastructure. She felt the strength of the effort, the weight of the responsibility.

But for the first time ever, she wasn't doing this alone.

"Yeah," Essence was saying into the phone. "I figured you'd want to. Okay. I'll tell them."

The moment she was done talking, the pinprick of Essence's phone died. Chizara had begged her friends a hundred times to shut down when they finished a conversation, and yet they always had to be reminded.

Essence lowered the phone.

"Boss lady says welcome to NOLA. She hopes you enjoy Mardi Gras."

"Is that all?" Kelsie asked.

Essence shrugged. "She's going to make contact with your pal Nataniel. Soon."

She waved her hand, and Chizara felt the phone in Kelsie's pocket squawk as its circuitry melted into slag.

"Hey! What was that for?"

"So you don't tell your buddy what's coming." Essence smiled. "Piper likes to make her own introductions."

CHAPTER 31
BELLWETHER

THIS WAS WORSE THAN PRISON.

There was a huge city out there, roiling with happy people, and Nate was stuck in this tranquil neighborhood. Trapped by his mug shot decorating all those FBI Most Wanted posters, and by Mrs. Lavoir's attention shimmering from her kitchen window every few minutes.

Alone with the thirsty tendrils of his power.

He paced from room to room. Sending everyone off on separate missions had been a terrible idea.

Flicker had called from a borrowed phone to report that she had big news but couldn't say more. Her burner was compromised—she'd called the local FBI office and Thibault's burner as well. So both of them had ditched their phones.

Then Ethan had reported in. He was walking home the

long way from WeirdCon, dodging FBI agents, or something equally preposterous.

Kelsie and Chizara weren't answering at all. Either in trouble or just making out somewhere.

It was chaos out there without him.

Not surprising. After weeks cooped up together on the road, their powers starved of the Curve, Nate had tossed them into this boisterous cauldron, three nights before Fat Tuesday. Even here on this quiet street, gaggles of drunken tourists kept stumbling by, offering Nate a tantalizing glimpse of the party.

And now something bigger was coming his way.

Nate felt the parade before he heard it—the rattling drums, the saxophones soloing over a spare, persistent tuba riff. Between stabs of brass, ecstatic shouts and cries echoed down the dark streets.

He went down the dim, narrow hallway, lined with mocking Mardi Gras masks, and knelt close to the front windows. Still parched from his prison stay, Nate drank in the glorious coordination of the approaching crowd. Like the double Dutch champions he'd taken Gabby to see last summer, the whole procession was fused into one being.

When he heard them turn onto the Barrows' street, a shiver went down Nate's spine.

He peered out from the darkened front room. Yes, there was Mrs. Lavoir's sparkling line of attention. But aimed at the parade for once, instead of at the suspicious house sitters next door.

The musicians came first, with at least a hundred marchers following close behind. According to what research he'd managed on the way here, this was a "second line" parade, a traveling procession welcome to any who wanted to join.

Nate wanted to join—or take control. He wasn't sure anymore.

He remembered long ago back in Cambria, riding one night with Flicker on his handlebars, gathering a mass of cyclists from across the city. These jazz musicians had managed the same trick, pulling in followers with music as their superpower.

But maybe it wasn't just music.

He saw it now. The crowd was so sublimely unified, a clockwork machine. As if someone was guiding them, molding them.

But who, exactly?

An older man marched in front of the procession, his drum-major uniform sparkling yellow in the streetlights. He kept time with a large baton, and the wandering gyres of the dancing musicians' attention grew bright when he let out short bursts on the whistle clamped between his teeth.

But he was too old to be a Zero.

Next to him was a white girl, Nate's age, looking out of place. She wore black and gray, almost invisible in the darkness beside the brightly costumed marching band. She danced with small, lonely movements of her arms, a wallflower at the party.

Then something odd happened—the procession halted.

The band didn't stop playing. The followers didn't stop dancing. The seething energy of the crowd didn't go slack. But without any signal given, they all came to a bouncing, drum-beating stop . . .

Right in front of the borrowed house.

They were waiting for Nate to come out and join them.

He knew it then without question, felt the tendrils of power reaching across the front lawn. The *need* building inside him—to join, to become one of the crowd, to revel with the others.

To follow.

For the first time in his life, he was being bellwethered.

He could see it now, the subtle coils wrapped around the girl in black and gray. Her style wasn't at all like Nate's. She was wreathed in barely visible shimmers. It wasn't even attention, really, but something more stately and sublime.

Influence. Quiet authority. A queenly confidence that the revelers would follow her to the ends of the earth.

A certainty that Nate would come forth and join her parade.

Mrs. Lavoir's focus was locked angrily on the noisy invaders. If he walked out now, she would realize they'd stopped by for one of the Barrows' house sitters.

But every moment the band lingered, it only drew more attention.

In the end, the girl's power solved his dilemma—he couldn't keep away from her. The hunger from his weeks in prison was too great.

And she was too strong.

He grabbed one of the Mardi Gras masks hanging in the hallway. Stole into the kitchen and out, around the rear of the house. He jumped across backyard fences, putting distance between himself and Mrs. Lavoir.

But he couldn't resist the girl's call for long, and soon he slipped between two houses and out onto the middle of the street, half a block in front of the parade.

The Bellwether girl smiled, nodded a little.

The procession lurched into motion again, coming at him. As it grew closer, the lines of its force, boisterous and obedient, shot out like lightning bolts. And he wanted to be struck, wanted to be overtaken and drenched. This storm was finally filling the aching hole left by solitary confinement.

The music—thundering percussion, heart-kicking tuba, commanding sax—made its way into him as well, and on that dark street he found himself doing something he'd never done in those long nights at the Dish, surrounded by the fiercest energies that Crash and Mob could generate.

He danced.

The procession swept him up, carried him along. With every footstep, his hunger to stay with the girl, to join her in everything she did, grew.

Something unexpected and perfect happened then, both halves of his power uniting, completed. He felt the procession dancing behind him, hundreds of limbs strung to the twitches of his muscles. And also the safety, the anonymity, the glorious emptiness of being a conduit of Piper's will.

This submission, even sweeter than control.

When the girl spoke, it was clear who was the better Bellwether.

"I'm Piper," she said. "We're going to change the world."

CHAPTER 32
FLICKER

"NO IDEA WHERE NATE IS." FLICKER CHECKED THE house for eyes again—nothing. "When I talked to him, he was still here."

"Ditto," Ethan said, his voice muffled by a cushion. He was lying facedown on the couch.

Flicker sat in the big armchair, trying for some authority. The others were spread around the living room, hyped up from their day in the Mardi Gras crowds.

"We never talked to him." Chizara's voice was breathy. "The Zeroes we ran into melted our phones—they were Crashes. Plural!"

"Yeah, yeah. Multiple Crashes," Ethan said. "We heard you the first time."

"A Crash was in charge," Chizara said softly.

Flicker checked next door. Mrs. Lavoir was either asleep or not home. Probably Nate had just stepped out for a little crowd magic. He'd sounded pretty stir-crazy on the phone.

"Let's not wait for him," Flicker said. Chizara was itchy enough to black out the whole neighborhood. "Sit up, Scam. Crash, you report first."

"We found a building like the Dish," Chizara said.

Flicker felt a moment of homesickness at the name. "Like the Dish how?"

"Faraday shielded. So I figured somebody like me lived there. And when we tried to get in, the door was controlled by this weird device. It was halfway between a lock and a puzzle, like only a Crash could solve."

Flicker, in Ethan's vision, saw that Chizara's face had a shine of excitement, like when she crashed something big.

Flicker tried to sound calm. "But you solved it, of course."

"It was tricky, but yeah." Chizara's voice dropped, like she was telling a ghost story at a campfire. "And there were at least twenty of them inside."

Ethan's eyes went wide. "Twenty Zeroes?"

"Twenty *Crashes*," Chizara said.

Flicker swallowed. That *was* plural.

Kelsie wasn't chiming in. She sat in the corner of Chizara's vision, arms crossed as if to protect herself.

Something out there had upset her. Flicker could feel it in the feedback loop, sadness mixed with a slow trickle of fear.

"With twenty Crashes in town, how is this city even running?" Ethan said. "Shouldn't it be a smoking crater?"

Chizara glared at him. "Hey! I fix stuff too, you know. *We* fix stuff. They call themselves Makers, not Crashes."

"Maybe that's why they're all here," came a voice from the corner of the living room.

Flicker's breath caught. She must have lost Anon as the others had come home, building the Curve of his anonymity.

And he wasn't wearing the tracker anymore. . . .

"What do you mean, Thibault?" she asked, making sure to say his name.

"To make things work," he said. "The city was almost destroyed more than ten years ago. And it's still pretty messed up. Maybe all those Makers came here to help out."

Ethan's eyes were doing the slidey thing, drifting off to the masks on the hallway wall. But Flicker saw Thibault just long enough to see that he'd replaced the borrowed raid jacket with a black hoodie.

Ethan snorted. "Zeroes, helping out? Like they helped the Super Bowl?"

"Ethan's not wrong," Chizara said. "Those Crashes were building something, but it didn't look like useful infrastructure for the good people of New Orleans. It was disguised as a parade float, and designed to channel a lot of energy. What kind of energy, I couldn't tell."

"Now *that* sounds like Zeroes," Ethan said. "As in deeply scary."

Chizara looked up. "They mentioned Piper, that person that Nate was talking about. She's the boss here."

Flicker pulled in her vision. She needed to focus. "After what we found in Phan's office, I doubt she's up to any good."

"Probably not," Thibault said, the optimism in his voice flattened.

Flicker turned to the others. "There was a map—the whole United States, full of pins to mark events. Most were superpowered pranks, all over the place. But some of the pins were for Zeroes getting killed. Or unlucky cops."

"Oh," Kelsie said softly. Her anxiety hummed low in the room, jarring with Chizara's excitement.

"Two police casualties in Cambria," Flicker said. "And a pin for Quinton Wallace."

She went into Kelsie's eyes, which were on Chizara. The spacey glee on her face had faltered for the first time since she'd gotten home. You could always sober Chizara up with a reference to Officer Bright, beaten into a coma at the Cambria police station.

Flicker went on. "But Cambria had nothing on all the pins in New Orleans. Nate was right. This place is ground zero for Zeroes mayhem. And casualties, cops and us both."

"Eleven, to be exact," Thibault said.

"So why are *we* the famous ones?" Kelsie asked. "Everybody's obsessed with the Cambria Five!"

Flicker tried to sound reasonable. "After Delgado's funeral? All that footage of the police marching on the Dish? It's no wonder. And Nate's picture has been on TV nonstop since the jailbreak."

"Everyone knows about Quinton Wallace, too," Chizara said. "After the Desert Springs Mall, it must have been obvious exactly what he was."

"One of the Crashes called me a baby Swarm," Kelsie said softly. "They even used the same word for it. Like the Zeroes here knew Ren and Davey."

"Huh," Flicker said. So these Crashes had been afraid of Kelsie. That's why she was spooked. Flicker went into her eyes, which were staring down at the floorboards.

Flicker had to lift her despair. The Zeroes couldn't afford to spiral like this. Where the hell was Nate?

"You already faced that, Kelsie, and you won," she said.

"So far."

Ethan chimed in. "I'm not worried about you, Kelsie. It's all those other Swarms who could be out there. New Orleans is full of Zeroes, and don't predators show up wherever there's prey? Like lions hanging out at a watering hole!"

Flicker thought of all those red pins, and a shiver ran down her spine. Maybe this war wasn't just between Zeroes and the FBI. . . .

A sound tugged at Flicker's awareness—a scrabbling at the side door.

"Guys. Hush."

The sound came, louder, the door opening, and a sudden shot of panic rang through the feedback loop.

She cast her vision out and found a pair of eyes coming in through the kitchen door. A border hovered around what she saw—the intruder's vision edged with black.

"Shit," she said. "They're wearing a mask."

The others stood up, someone rattling a poker from the fireplace. The intruder crossed the kitchen to the hall door—swiftly, like they knew this place.

Then a figure rose up in their vision, silhouetted against the front-door glass—Thibault, his fist pulled back for a punch.

"You guys are back? Great!" came a familiar voice.

The mask was whipped off. Thibault let his arms go slack.

"Nate!" Flicker cried. "Way to scare the *shit* out of everyone!"

CHAPTER 33
SCAM

"*TWO* GLORIOUS LEADERS." THIS WAS RIGHT OUT of one of Ethan's nightmares. "Are you sure she's like you?"

Nate nodded. "She's not just like me, she's . . . better. She guided a *parade* up to our front door to say hello."

Glorious Leader, admitting that someone was more awesome than him? Ethan's spine chill was getting worse by the second.

"But how did she *find* this place?"

"She's got this town locked down." Nate turned to Kelsie and Chizara on the couch. "One of those Crashes you met can scoop the data out of phones. Not just calls—location tracking too."

"Whoa," Chizara said. "That's some serious code, right there."

Ethan stared out the window into the dark night. Were Piper's forces gathering out there right now, ready to strike?

"Should we be running?" he asked.

"She's got bigger things to worry about than us." Nate flashed a thousand-watt smile. "She was just welcoming the Cambria Five to town. We're famous!"

Kelsie groaned softly at this, and Ethan felt the pulse of her anguish in the wash of Nate's excitement. She must hate the idea that Zeroes everywhere were terrified of her—of what she might become.

"What bigger things?" Flicker asked.

Yeah, *that* was the question, Ethan thought. What sort of multi-Bellwether nightmare had Nate dragged them all into?

And not just Nate—Ethan had himself to blame too. He had actually voted for coming to New Orleans. Why had he done that, again?

Two words: Sonia Sonic.

"Piper won't tell me her plans—yet." Nate smiled again.

Ethan cringed. Hadn't Sonia said something about Piper *hating normals*? That didn't sound like the jumping-off point for a very happy plan. But he couldn't bring that up without mentioning his secret rendezvous.

"Next time you guys hang out, ask about the big machine they're building," Chizara said. "It's dressed up like a float, which means they're going to use it during Mardi Gras."

"Tell me everything," Nate said.

As Chizara described her time with the Crashes yet again, Nate sat on the edge of an ottoman, fingers steepled and elbows on bouncing knees. Ethan figured he was hyped up about meeting another version of himself, presumably one of his longtime dreams. His Bellwether power had everyone else wrapped up, but Ethan wrenched his gaze away, lingering on the darkness outside.

The thought of all those red pins in a map was just plain creepy. Zeroes were dying on a regular basis in this town, and Ethan himself had almost gotten snatched by the Feds today.

His voice might have saved him by scaring off Verity, but it had scared him, too.

What had it been talking about, with all that *omniscience* crap? Was Ethan just a random meat puppet for some all-knowing brain somewhere? That was a fricking terrifying idea.

Nate leaned forward as Chizara wound down. "If Mardi Gras is when this all goes down, we only have a few days to get up to speed."

"Less," Flicker said. "We found out something at the FBI office."

"A map of death!" Ethan cried.

"Something worse" came from the corner.

Right. Thibault was here.

"There's some kind of FBI operation happening tomorrow," Tee said. "Phan's bringing in a team to grab someone. He wants to start a collection of Zero agents."

Ethan nodded. The voice had said something about that to Verity, too.

"Does he know *we're* here?" Kelsie asked. Her fear blared across the room, and Ethan flinched.

"Will you quit panicking, Kelsie?" he grumbled. "You're stressing me out."

"Phan doesn't know anything about us," Flicker said calmly. "The target is someone from New Orleans."

Her certainty doused Kelsie's panic, but Ethan still had a knot in his stomach the size of a fist. Someone at the FBI *did* know that Ethan, at least, was in New Orleans. Even after that voice whipping, Verity might have reported him to her boss.

He should probably fess up right now. . . .

"Whatever they're up to, we'll know about it," Thibault said. "I stuck my tracker into Phan's badge case."

"Good thinking." Nate turned to Chizara. "How close do you have to be to pick up that signal?"

"A quarter mile?" She crossed her arms. "Which is way too close. Do you really want to follow an FBI agent around all day?"

"Not all day," Flicker said. "The operation's planned for tomorrow morning."

Nate frowned, and Ethan felt the familiar discomfort of a boss fight building.

But in the end Nate only nodded. "You're right, Flick. We can't let a fellow Zero get picked up by the Feds. It could be Piper they plan on grabbing. If we save her, we'll earn her trust!"

"So you've already chosen a side?" Chizara asked. "You don't even know what she's up to!"

"Exactly," Ethan said. "Piper could be evil and hate regular people or something. Why not let her and the Feds duke it out while we drink daiquiris in Mexico?"

"No," Nate said, standing. "We do what's right. Which means keeping anyone with powers out of prison until we know what's going on."

It was an inspirational little moment, and Nate knew it. He wasn't jittering anymore. He drew himself up to full leadership height and looked down at everyone else.

In fact, it was the most commanding he'd looked since getting out of prison. Whoever this Piper was, she'd given Nate some kind of Glorious Leader recharge.

Ethan waited for Flicker to step in as the voice of reason, to say they were all going to Mexico. But she was sitting there in the big armchair, nodding along.

"Things are coming to a head," she said. "The FBI knows about Zeroes, and weird-hunters are having conferences. We can't just hide anymore."

"We can't?" said Ethan. He'd never really thought very far into the future. But he always figured he'd have one. Now he was stuck between a federal retrieval force and multiple Glorious Leaders.

Life sucked.

And if the Zeroes were all going to march into the jaws of the FBI together, it was time to confess.

"So guys," Ethan said. "Verity's in town too. I saw her."

Nate turned on him. "Where?"

Everyone else looked at him too. He squirmed in his seat.

"She was at WeirdCon. Using her power, trawling the weird-hunters for intel."

"So what?" Flicker said. "None of those dimwits know anything about us."

Ethan cleared his throat. "Well . . . except that Verity kind of saw me."

"What?" Nate cried.

"It's okay! The voice threw her off the scent. She thinks we split up, and that you're all in Saint Louis!"

Nate eyed him sidelong. "So your voice can lie to Verity?"

"Uh, not quite." Ethan squirmed again, but there was no point hiding anything. "I lied to Sonia Sonic, and then she kind of repeated it to Verity, thinking it was the truth. Booyah, right?"

He looked up at them all, waiting to be praised for this brilliant end run around Verity's powers. But all he got were grim expressions.

"Sonia Sonic?" Flicker said. "*She's* here too?"

Ethan nodded.

"And you just happened to run into her?" Nate asked.

"I kind of . . . told her I was coming?" Ethan said. "But the whole thing was worth it! I found out that Piper hates normals. That seems important, right?"

They were all still staring at him, but Flicker and Nate were looking at each other, more thoughtful than angry. For a moment Ethan thought he'd weathered this shit storm.

Then his phone buzzed in his pocket.

"What the hell?" Chizara asked.

Eep. It had to be Sonia. Nobody else outside this room had this number.

He yanked the phone from his pocket, trying to read the message before Flicker hijacked his eyeballs.

Saw Verity with weird-hunters, had to warn them!

She asked for your phone number. Couldn't help but spit it out!

Ethan leaped up. "Phone's compromised!"

He threw it to the floor like it was on fire.

Chizara snapped her fingers and the phone let out a death bleep before it hit the rug.

Nate pulled out his phone and dropped it to the floor. That was the plan. If one phone got compromised, every phone it had contacted had to be destroyed.

"Good thing we stocked up on burners," Chizara said wearily.

"Care to explain, Ethan?" Nate asked, his voice neutral. "Maybe tell us *why* you've been talking to Sonia?"

Ethan sighed and sank back into the couch. He didn't want

to go into all this, but Nate and Flicker weren't going to let him off the hook.

Say something to shut them up for a minute, he pleaded with the voice. *Anything to give me time to think!*

"I have this huge crush on her," the voice said.

Ethan let out a squeak and curled up in a ball of shame, but, true to form, the voice's words had worked. Everyone was silent. Most of them looked stunned, except for Kelsie, who was smiling for the first time all night.

"Called it," she sang softly.

CHAPTER 34
CRASH

"I COULD GO FOR A SECOND BREAKFAST ABOUT now." Ethan peered at the next table's array of French toast and waffles slathered in whipped cream.

Chizara elbowed him in the ribs. "Keep your eyes on the door, Scam."

"And your mind off Sonia," Kelsie added with a snicker.

Ethan stared at the table, sulking.

Chizara took her attention off the distant tracker for a moment, looking around the diner. Just the sort of greasy spoon law enforcement liked to patronize, only a minute's drive from FBI headquarters.

And all six Zeroes were here, ready to get busted.

"I'm watching," Ethan said. "But we've been sitting here for *two hours*. Are you sure this is even the right *day*, Tee?"

"Tomorrow morning, Phan kept saying."

Chizara realized that she'd forgotten Thibault again, even though he was right there, squeezed between Nate and Flicker. Hadn't she been better at remembering him before?

"I just need something to cut this coffee," Ethan was gibbering. "If I have too much caffeine I get all—"

"Lovelorn?" Kelsie pulled the coffeepot toward herself for a refill.

"Everyone, be quiet," Flicker said. "Some of us are working here. Tell me when you need a break, Crash. I can just barely get my eyes in there."

Chizara nodded absently, again pushing her mind past all the ruckus of the diner. The place was crowded with families eating breakfast. Kids transfixed by cartoons on noisy tablets, without the saving grace of being her brothers. She was so wired, and homesick, she wanted to slap the noisy little devices out of their hands.

And everyone had their damn phone out, bleating signal into Chizara's brain. It was killing her to stay hooked into the irritating scratch of the tracker a quarter mile away.

Phan hadn't moved much this morning. Just a few short trips away from his office, a bundle of computer noise and wireless buzz.

"What if he doesn't go with his team?" she asked, keeping an eye on the tiny twinkling signal. "He could direct the whole thing from his desk, you know."

"Phan would never let Verity go into the field alone," Nate said. "At Dungeness he let all of us go, just to save her."

"He was sweating every detail of this op. He's not going to leave it to outsiders." That was Thibault again. Staying aware of the guy was tricky in this crowded place, especially without the extra spark of the tracker.

No one had asked Chizara to make a new one, and she wasn't about to volunteer. Flicker and he looked pretty cozy over there, not like a couple who had to keep tabs on each other. Maybe sneaking into an FBI headquarters together was a good bonding exercise.

"I'm ordering more food," Ethan said. He straightened and waved his arm to catch the waitress's eye.

"What if Phan's target is a really evil Zero?" Kelsie said. "Someone who *should* get arrested? Like Piper?"

"Piper's not evil," Nate said.

"What part of 'hates normals' did you miss?" Ethan said.

Nate shook his head. "That's just a weird-hunter rumor, Scam. Or do you believe everything Sonia says now?"

"Okay, fine." Kelsie shifted in her seat. "But what if the Feds are after another Swarm?"

Silence fell over the table. Before anyone answered, the waitress came over and Ethan started in.

"Two slices of white toast, extra butter? And a big order of bacon. Like, a last meal–size order. Anyone else?"

The others all shook their heads, and the waitress moved on.

"If it's a Swarm, the Feds will need our help," Nate finally said. "We'll have to play it by ear."

"FBI zombies," Ethan muttered. "Bonus fun."

Chizara resisted the urge to slap him. People had died the day of Delgado's funeral. He'd been zombified *himself*, for heaven's sake. How could he make light of it?

Then the distant, twinkling star shifted.

"Hang on." Elbows on the table, Chizara closed her eyes. "He's moving."

Beside her, Kelsie pulled her daypack into her lap.

"But my toast," Ethan whimpered. "My bacon."

"Forget it," Chizara said—the tracker was gliding downward. "He's in the elevator!"

Nate plonked a saltshaker down on a pile of already counted bills.

"Let's go!" Flicker pushed up from the table. The others followed.

"But I *see* my bacon! It's under the heat lamps. . . ."

Chizara dragged Ethan along behind the others. "Come *on*. If we lose this guy because of you, you're dead."

"I could die anyway. Starvation."

Together they sprinted for their latest car, the gray SUV taken from the Barrows' garage. Chizara waved a hand, and its motor rumbled to life.

CHAPTER 35
CRASH

"THERE IT IS," CHIZARA SAID, POINTING. THE tracker shimmered ahead on the highway, a ghost hitching a ride among the weaving cars. "That white van up ahead. Phan's riding shotgun."

"Five in the back," Flicker said. She was next to Chizara in the front seat, beside Nate at the wheel.

"Seven agents." Thibault's voice came from the back. "That's what the e-mail said."

Nate accelerated, pushing a little closer to the van. "Is Verity with them?"

"No, it's all guys." Flicker frowned. "Street clothes, no suits. One dressed like he's homeless. A couple of them have bouquets in their hands."

"Flowers?" Ethan said. "That's pretty random."

Chizara felt for electronics in the van but sensed only the usual sensors and wires. No serious gear.

The van headed south, past a tech-free expanse of golf course. Suburban houses followed, each behind a rectangle of lawn, the interiors spangled with wifi appliances gently chewing on streams of incoming data.

"They're going into town?" Kelsie sounded hopeful.

"Doubt it," Chizara said. "Phan's too smart to grab a Zero in a Mardi Gras crowd."

They flew along with the traffic, above the sparkling spread of New Orleans's electronic life. Up ahead rose the Superdome, which Chizara could never see without thinking of the hurricane. She imagined the roof peeling off, disaster all around. Her mom had made her watch every minute of Katrina coverage— a teachable moment about how the world couldn't always be counted on to help.

But then the white van swung off an exit, and Nate followed it back down into the quilt of stabbing electronics. They looped around and under the highway, took a left, cruised along among warehouses and medical centers, and slowed to a halt beside three blocks of old brick walls.

Whatever was behind the walls was blessedly tech-free. Chizara breathed a little easier.

Nate parked well back from the Ford. "What can you see, Flick?"

"They've left the homeless-looking guy at a gate," she said.

"The others are going inside the . . . it's a cemetery. Whoa, a really old-school one. All crypts and creepy statues."

"Hence the flowers," Chizara said. Also the tech silence inside the walls. The graveyard was a long rectangle of stillness in the blare of the city.

"That's just cold," Ethan said. "Kidnapping someone in a graveyard? What if they're visiting their granny or whatever?"

"No crowds, no Curve," Kelsie said softly.

"Phan's agents are spreading out." Flicker leaned her head back, addressing the ceiling of the SUV. "Everyone's got a view of the middle of the graveyard, where two paths cross. That's where this arrest is going down."

Chizara closed her eyes, reaching out her power. "They've switched off their phones, like in Vegas. But I can see Phan's tracker."

And when she concentrated harder, she saw the faint flash of hearts, the signals washing faintly through nervous systems. The sight sent a faint shiver through her.

The agents' formation appeared, ghostlike among the crypts. Six of them hovered at the corners of the cemetery, the seventh still out front. Phan's tracker was closest to the center.

But where was Verity?

"Scam, guard the gate," Nate said. "If anyone young enough to be a Zero comes near, use the voice to warn them off. Maybe we can stop this before it starts."

"What about Agent Hobo?" Ethan said. "He's gotta know my face!"

"Anon's staying too. Keep yourselves invisible." Nate turned to Flicker. "Find the rest of us a side entrance. We'll set up where we can see everything. These guys don't have any tech, so we might as well keep our phones on."

As the car speckled with stabs of signal, Chizara opened the door and stepped out into the blinding New Orleans sun.

CHAPTER 36
ANONYMOUS

"QUIT TWITCHING, SCAM. I'VE GOT TO FOCUS."

Ethan looked down at Thibault's grip on his arm and twitched again.

"Sorry, dude," he said. "Too much coffee. And it's kind of weird in here."

"Yeah. Welcome to my world."

It wasn't just weird here in the Nowhere; it was dangerous. With his power amped up enough to keep Ethan and himself invisible, Thibault hovered at the border between reality and gone.

After yesterday's successes with Flicker, he'd felt so tuned in to reality. But every day he had to start the fight again.

"You guys okay?" Nate's voice came in his earbuds.

"We're great," Thibault said, and reached up to mute his phone mike. He gestured for Ethan to do the same.

The problem with Bellwether's plan was there was no crowd at the cemetery's front gate. Keeping two people invisible needed at least some Curve. So Thibault had pulled Ethan across the street, closer to the crowded waiting room of a walk-in medical center.

It wasn't much to work with, but when the sparkling attention of the FBI agent at the gate swept the street, it passed right through him and Ethan.

"Is it like this for you all the time?" Ethan asked.

"Only when I make someone else anonymous."

"Good, because this would suck," Ethan said.

Thibault didn't explain that it had been this way for weeks after he'd erased himself. But it hadn't sucked, because he hadn't cared.

Caring was what hurt.

"But hey, I remember more now!" A muzzy delight lit Ethan's face. "Like hanging out at the Dish, you and me and Kelsie. Playing tunes on that sound system, *super* loud. I can't believe I forgot all that."

Thibault shrugged. "Don't beat yourself up. I made you guys forget me."

"I know, but still." Ethan frowned up at him. "Friends should remember each other."

Thibault got a firmer grip on Ethan's arm, trying to navigate his way between guilt and the call of the void.

"Neither of us had a choice. I had to disappear."

"Because you shot Swarm?" Ethan murmured, like he was having trouble remembering that, too.

"Quinton Wallace." The name was a mouthful of ashes. Thibault's hand buzzed with the gun's recoil. The world slipped away a little, and he held on harder to Ethan's arm.

Ethan was staring up into the sky, which always seemed stuck in twilight here in the depths of Nowhere. Like even the sun could forget who Thibault was.

He searched for something to focus on, to drag himself back to the real world. An FBI agent dressed as a homeless man and a crumbling graveyard wall weren't doing it.

"So, Ethan. How're you going to work this, exactly?"

Ethan stared at him, his expression fuzzy. "What do you mean?"

"Well, what if people come to smoke weed here? While we're warning off some random kid, we could miss the real target."

Ethan smiled. "Not to worry, Tee. The voice is great at stuff like this. I'm going to wish *real hard* that whoever shows up doesn't go in that cemetery. And what the voice says will give us a clue."

Thibault shook his head. "I don't follow."

"If it was some kid playing hooky, the voice'll say, 'Don't go in there. It's crawling with teachers!' But if it's Phan's target, it'll say, 'It's crawling with Feds' or 'They know about your powers!' See what I mean?"

"Right." Thibault had to admit, being on the run had focused Ethan. "So you're pushing the voice to leak information."

"Yeah, does that all the time." Ethan got a funny look on his face. "Just yesterday, it said something kinda scary. About me being omniscient."

Thibault stared at him. "How is that scary?"

"I was using the voice to freak out Verity, so she didn't sic her bodyguards on me. And it said that if I ever worked for the Feds, the government would know everything about everyone. Like, game over for the First Amendment."

"I think you mean the Fourth Amendment." Thibault frowned. "But yeah, that's probably good-bye to *all* of them."

What could his own powers do, if he worked for the FBI? Or, hell, why not the CIA? He'd erased himself from his friends' minds. Could he make people forget *any* inconvenient truth?

The sky was dimming, and Thibault shook himself.

"Can we get off the topic of governments with superpowers? No Swarm talk either. All that stuff makes me want to let go of the real world—and if I fade out, I don't know what happens to you."

"Whoa. What?" Ethan took a step away.

Thibault held firm on his arm. "Just remind me of something happy and fun."

As he said it, happiness and fun had never seemed like more pointless, abstract concepts.

"Well, I guess . . ." Ethan looked blank-faced, as if the Nowhere was calling him too. Then he brightened. "Remember that time you let me stay in your hotel suite, when the Craig was looking to beat me down? All that room service! And we played *Red Scepter* for, like, six hours straight!"

Thibault tried to nod along, like this was a happy memory, but the name Craig stabbed him in the gut.

He remembered the man's lifeless face staring down from the truck bed, the bullet wound red and gaping in his throat. The exact moment when Thibault had torn himself out of reality.

Ethan scowled up at the darkening sky. "Flicker! She makes you happy, right?"

The name seized Thibault, and he felt reality within his grasp again.

"Yeah. She does."

More important, she had stuck by him, even when he'd abandoned her. She was more amazing than she knew.

"Equally exciting and fun is . . ." Ethan cast around, then pointed. "That bus! The target could be on it!"

"About time." Thibault took a firmer hold of Ethan and walked him across the street. The waiting-room crowd faded behind them, but the approaching city bus was half-full, more than enough to keep the Curve going.

It squealed to a slow, gliding stop. Thibault peered through the darkened windows and made out a shadow moving forward between the seats.

"Teenage girl," he said. "Could be the target."

He glanced at the FBI agent, maybe twenty feet away. The guy was pretending to be homeless and detached, but his attention was focused on the bus. When Thibault reached out to slice it away, it drifted back. The bus was too big and loud to hide.

"Get ready to say something calming when we grab her," he told Ethan. "Explain that we're friends, or whatever."

"The voice is always ready, Tee."

The bus door sighed open. A girl stepped down—jeans, puffy jacket, black hair in a ponytail. Casual and confident.

Thibault took a step forward, his free hand outstretched.

"That's Verity!" Ethan hissed, digging in his heels. "From the prison! She's a Fed!"

The girl was only a few feet away, and at the sound of Ethan's voice, her eyes lifted from the pavement and stared at him. Recognition glimmered across the space between them.

"What the hell are . . ."

Thibault sliced through the line of her attention.

The girl's expression softened, and her gaze shifted to the agent dressed in rags. A glimmer passed between them.

The bus door closed, and it eased away from the curb—taking its crowd with it.

Thibault hustled Ethan back across the street, back to the Curve coming from the medical center. "Damn. That was close."

"Yep," Ethan said. "And there's the target!"

Thibault followed Ethan's stare. A guy was coming down the

street on foot. He was the right age, wearing ratty jeans and a shapeless pullover. He had an indistinct face and needed a haircut.

As Thibault watched, a glitter of connection sprang out and joined him to Verity, who still waited by the gate.

Thibault unmuted his phone mike. "I'm not sure this is going to work, Bellwether."

"What's up?" Nate's voice answered.

"The target's on his way in, but Verity got here first. She's already spotted him, and I don't have a crowd to work with!"

Silence.

Damn it, where was the old decisive Nate when you needed him?

"She knows about Stalkers, right?" Thibault hissed. "Do we risk tipping her off? Or just let him walk in?"

Still no answer. The guy's slumped posture straightened for a moment as he met Verity. They hugged like old friends.

"Bellwether? Flicker? Any guidance at all would be appreciated."

Ethan was thumbing his phone screen.

"Dude, it's dead," he murmured. "As in *crashed*."

Thibault stared at his own blank phone screen, then at Ethan. He pulled them both against the medical center wall, deeper into the Nowhere, as a wordless thought passed between them.

Twenty Crashes, Chizara had said.

CHAPTER 37
MOB

"OUR PHONES JUST WENT DOWN," KELSIE HEARD Chizara whisper. "All of them."

"The Feds have jammers?" Nate hissed.

Kelsie looked back at Chizara, who was staring at her blank screen.

"The chip's fried. No machine could do that."

Nate's eyes lit up. "Maybe this guy's a Crash. The town's full of them."

"What the hell?" Flicker said. "Scam and Anon are just letting him walk in!"

Kelsie felt jitters wash through the group. The four of them were at the edge of the graveyard, crouched on top of a crypt the size of a container truck. Coffins were interred three high beneath them. A row of gravestones thrust up like broken teeth along the outer wall.

The thought of all those bodies only made Kelsie more aware of the emptiness around her. The keening of her friends' anxiety was almost a relief in the silence of the dead.

"Melted," Chizara said again, and dropped her phone. "No way to fix them."

Nate shook his head. "Doesn't matter. That would just blow our cover."

"Our cover?" Flicker whispered. "We're not staying hidden, are we? We're here to save this guy!"

"We're here to figure out what's going on."

Kelsie looked from Flicker to Nate and back, feeling the group cleave. Since he'd rejoined the Zeroes, no one knew who was in charge anymore.

Sometimes he was the old Nate, but then he would fade away into the background again.

"Bellwether," Kelsie said. "I thought you wanted to pick a side."

"Not until we know who crashed our phones. Besides, maybe this guy can take care of himself. Let's see what he's got up his sleeve."

Kelsie had to look away from his eager expression. Like this was some kind of science experiment and not a fellow Zero about to lose his freedom.

"Okay," Flicker said. "We'll figure out who needs saving once we know what the hell is going on."

That settled it. Kelsie gritted her teeth against her own emotions and reached her power across the graveyard.

The Feds were spread out, their connection tenuous. But they were joined by shared goals—ambush, dominate, capture.

Kelsie raised herself a little and made out two figures on the cemetery's central path. The guy was pretty unremarkable, and she didn't recognize him from the Crashes' warehouse the other night.

A moment later they were lost from view behind the crumbling family vaults. Kelsie sank back to the sun-warmed stone.

"They're smiling and talking," Flicker said. "A little awkward. Like old friends who haven't seen each other for a while."

"Friends?" Chizara whispered. "She's leading him into a trap."

"The Feds are moving in now," Flicker said. "Slow. Staying hidden."

Kelsie wondered what the new guy's power was. Was he another Crash, or something more dangerous? With an operation this size, it seemed like the Feds wanted him bad.

Maybe they were happy to get any Zero in custody.

She scooted up to the edge of the crypt, peering past a statue of a winged angel. The closest FBI agent was a stone's throw from her, making his way among the crumbling mausoleums.

As the agents converged, their group bond became more solid.

"This is weird," Flicker said. "He looks . . . different."

Nate looked at her. "Who? The target?"

"Yeah, he was super average-looking a second ago. But he's changing."

Kelsie and Chizara exchanged a glance.

"I mean, he looks exactly the same," Flicker continued. "But he's kind of . . . *getting hotter*."

Everyone looked at Nate.

After a long moment he let out a whistle. "Maybe that's his power."

"Hotness?" Chizara snorted.

Kelsie felt it now. The FBI agents were close enough to form a crowd around Verity and the boy, nine of them altogether. But their professional focus had been dented.

"It's hitting the agents," she murmured. "They're surprised. Kind of awestruck."

"He's so damn *gorgeous*," Flicker said. "I can't even figure it out. His face is the same. He's still got that *awful* haircut. . . ."

Nate dropped into his nature-documentary voice. "Beauty is a social construct, after all. Coin made money from crowds—maybe this guy creates attraction."

"I repeat my question," Chizara said. "His power is *hotness*?"

"It's not going to save him," Kelsie said. The agents were confused, but they were professionals, still intent on their target.

"If he's not a Crash, who wrecked our phones?" Nate asked. "Flicker, any extra eyes looking on?"

"Nope. Mob?"

"No big groups anywhere." Except for the converging Feds at its center, the cemetery felt empty—

Then suddenly it wasn't. Like a door in reality opened, and a crowd pushed through.

"Oh my God," Kelsie said.

Flicker gasped. "Shit. A ton of eyeballs just came out of nowhere!"

"Heartbeats," Chizara murmured. "A whole mass of them."

"What are you all talking about?" Nate asked, standing for a better view.

Kelsie pressed her fingertips to her temples. The new group was as determined as the FBI agents, but wilder, looser. Full of frantic energy, like a bunch of kids let out of school onto a playground.

She rose unsteadily, shielding her eyes from the sun.

At the center of the cemetery, Verity and the boy stood arguing, ignoring the agents closing in from all directions. And from an open mausoleum out of their view, a gaggle of people poured into the sunlight. Kelsie felt the group swelling as they emerged.

"They've been here the whole time!" she cried.

"That crypt, it's like a Faraday cage," Chizara murmured beside her. "But for Zero powers. The walls blocked us from sensing them!"

"A double cross," Flicker said, then flinched. "One of Phan's agents just went down. No idea why, but his vision just *fritzed*."

"Come on," Nate said, sliding his feet over the edge of the crypt. He turned around and skidded down the side to arm's length, then dropped.

Chizara followed. "Are we saving him now? Or Verity?"

"Still figuring that out!"

Kelsie slid down, her sneakers skidding on the protruding lips of tombs as she clambered down. *Sorry, dead people.*

As her feet hit the dirt, she felt a moment's dizziness. A familiar slant in the slippery new energy that filled the cemetery. She racked her brain, trying to place it as she ran.

The four of them skidded onto the main path.

The new Zero boy beside Verity was slumped and disheveled, his face kind of lumpy. And yet he was radiant, filling Kelsie's heart with happiness just to look at him.

The Feds were staggering, confused. Their faces went slack, and they fell, dropping from the feedback loop one by one. There was Phan, running toward Verity, his pistol drawn. But whatever had knocked out the others hit him, too, and he dropped like a rag doll to the ground.

Then Verity dropped too.

Chizara came to a halt, placed a heavy hand on Kelsie's shoulder. She swayed like she was about to pass out.

"Whoa," she said. "I've felt this before."

Kelsie nodded. From the moment she'd locked onto the

other group's energy, it had all been familiar. That terrible sense of the world slipping and shifting, of meaning leaking away.

For a moment she hardly knew Chizara's face.

The new crowd stared at the Zeroes across the fallen agents, wary and ready to fight. Kelsie dimly recognized a few of the Crashes that she and Chizara had met the day before.

But at the head of the group was a face she knew all too well.

"Oh my God," she said. "It's Glitch."

CHAPTER 38

BELLWETHER

SPARKLING LINES OF ATTENTION CRISSCROSSED among the old stones.

Two dozen Zeroes stood there on the path, blinking in the sunlight, as if they'd teleported in. The boy the Feds had tried to kidnap was glowing now, his beauty amplified by the sudden crowd.

Though maybe it wasn't really *beauty*. It was something more primal, some group need to worship an idol, a king. Every angle of his face was a hook sunk deep in Nate's visual cortex. A demand to keep looking, to drink in that face. To gaze along with every other eye in the cemetery . . .

But Nate didn't have time to analyze this new power. With every ounce of his will, he tore his eyes away and stared at Glitch.

Also known as Ren, the girl who'd attacked the Petri Dish just before Christmas. She stood at the head of the new group, her eyes lit with pleasure from knocking out Verity and the federal agents.

Her power's focus had improved since Christmas. Nate felt dazed, but nothing like the awful disorientation of her full-on assault.

But he needed to assert himself before she struck again.

"You owe me a car," he said.

Ren stared at him, stony-faced. "You owe me a husband."

Right, yes. There was that.

"But *you're* still alive," he said. "And we took care of Swarm."

"Too little, too late. Still, this crowd's big enough to lobotomize you. *That* might make up for it."

It look Nate a moment to answer. Every night in prison, he'd seen Davey handcuffed to the fountain in the middle of the Desert Springs Mall, the deadly mass of Quinton Wallace's minions descending on him.

He had processed all that. But he'd never had Ren right in front of him.

"I'm sorry," he said.

"Sorry doesn't cut it!" Glitch cried, and the world tipped sideways. The lines of attention wavered as confusion rippled through the crowd. The words on the gravestones turned into an alien script.

Nate raised his hands high, trying to gather the disordered glimmers. Maybe if he could focus the group on himself, he could dampen Ren's power long enough for one of the others to do something.

But instantly those shimmering strands pulled away, slipping through his fingers. The disorientation hit him full force again.

"Stop this nonsense," someone ordered.

In the head-spinning confusion, Nate wouldn't have recognized his own parents, but he recognized that voice. And Glitch obeyed, the world falling raggedly back into place.

But she yelled out in protest, "He killed my Davey!"

"Swarm did that, and he's dead now. Are you okay, Nataniel?"

It took Nate a moment to form words.

"I'm fine. Everyone, this is Piper."

She stood next to the beautiful boy, basking in reflected glory.

"Someone's been snooping," Piper said. "Are you *stalking* me?"

Nate shook his head. "We knew the FBI was planning to grab someone. Just trying to help a fellow Zero."

"The Cambria Five to the rescue!" Piper looked around at Chizara, Kelsie, and Flicker. "Four of them, anyway."

Her smile fell on him like pure, undiluted honor. And he felt it again, the need to please Piper, to join her.

He knew it was just her power, the same ability that he put to work every time he met a stranger, every time the Zeroes argued with him. But the gift was so much more magnificent in her.

Late last night, unable to sleep after meeting her, he'd realized why—Piper had grown up here, in New Orleans. A city that swelled with huge crowds once a year. These massive parties, these glorious parades, these weeklong celebrations were her birthright.

She could teach him all of it.

"Looks like you had it under control," he said.

A ripple of laughter went through Piper's gang. Like the word "control" was an understatement.

Chizara stepped forward. "Are these *normals* going to be okay?"

Nate looked down—damn. Seven federal agents out cold on the ground, an open gate forty feet away, and he'd been too distracted by Piper to worry about any backup they might have.

"Relax," Piper said. "Special Agent Phan has been tracking my crew for years, which makes him the only normal who really understands us. We're going to need him soon."

"So this was all about getting Verity," came a voice from behind Piper—*the* voice. Ethan stood there, looking nervous and ready to run. But when he spoke, it was with perfect ease. "You've got plans for her, huh?"

Piper looked at him, then back at Nate. "Ah, the mysterious fifth Cambrian. What's his power again?"

"Asking good questions," Nate said.

Piper smiled again. "Verity is an old friend. I'd never hurt her."

"Then why knock her out?" Ethan said. "And what does she have to do with that weird machine you're building?"

For a moment Piper's closure slipped. The voice was hitting a nerve.

Then she reached out and tapped Ren on the shoulder. Ren raised a hand, glitch light gleaming in her eye, and Ethan went wobbly on his feet. He sat heavily on the dirt, head in hands.

"Knock it off!" Kelsie cried, and ran to him.

Piper turned back to Nate.

"I like you, Nataniel—your crew is charmingly chaotic. But my sources say Agent Phan is in trouble for letting you out of prison. A suspicious person might think you two made a deal."

"We did," Nate said. "Phan let us go, and I didn't blow up his supermax."

Piper narrowed her eyes, and Nate felt the full swell of her power. Even with Verity out cold, she wanted to pull the truth from him.

"Why did you show up here, Nataniel?"

He basked in her gaze, felt his power shift inside him.

He let himself submit.

"To save a fellow Zero," he said. "We don't work for the FBI."

She held his eyes for a moment, then glanced down at Verity and sighed.

"Too bad we had to knock you out, babe. Could've used you about now." Piper looked up again. "My plans are too important to share with strangers. But come see me on Ash Wednesday, Cambria Five. That's when the real work starts."

"How do we find you?" Nate asked, almost pleading.

Another ripple of laughter.

"That won't be hard," Piper said. She raised a finger, and two of her gang swept in and lifted Verity up. The group headed toward the cemetery gate.

"Do we follow them?" Kelsie asked.

"And give Glitch another excuse to fry our brains?" Ethan coughed. "No thanks."

Nate wanted to follow, to stay close to Piper, to ask how he could help. But he shook himself.

"That'll only make Piper angry. But we have to get out of here."

"Not till I get a look at that hiding place," Chizara said, turning away. "Its walls blocked our powers!"

"We leave *now*," Nate commanded. "Remember Phan's dead-man switch at the prison? His backup could be on the way."

That got them. Everyone headed toward the gate.

"We can come back later, Zara," Kelsie said.

"Not too much later," Chizara said. "You heard what she said—this'll all be over by Ash Wednesday."

"Which is when?" Ethan asked groggily.

275

"The day after Mardi Gras," Kelsie said. "Like we thought, Piper's plan goes down on Fat Tuesday."

"The day after tomorrow." Nate swore. "And we don't even know how to find her."

"Not a problem."

They all looked up. It was Thibault, joining the group as they passed through the graveyard gate. Spellbound by Piper, Nate had forgotten all about him.

"What do you mean, Anon?"

"Ethan was just stalling, giving me time to get the tracker out of Phan's badge case." He gave a shrug. "I put it in Verity's back pocket."

"You're a genius!" Flicker cried, and ran to hug him.

"Perfect," Nate said.

They had a way to track down Piper. He and his Zeroes could be a part of this.

He still didn't know what she was up to, and maybe the weird-hunter rumors were true and they'd have to stop her. But Nate knew for certain that he *didn't* want to be on the sidelines.

And that his heart still rang with what Piper had said just minutes ago . . .

I like you, Nataniel.

Mierda. He liked her right back.

CHAPTER 39
FLICKER

"WHAT IF THIS THING DOESN'T WORK? WOULD WE even know?"

Flicker waved the phone in the air. The carnival-choked streets roared around them, full of music and the smell of cheap beer.

But from the phone, no beep, no buzz. Nothing.

The burner was heavy. Chizara had rebuilt it last night practically from scratch, along with two others. It was crammed with new parts, including a few glued to the outside. With its ungainly new antenna, it felt like a cell phone from the Stone Age.

"We tried it on a test tracker while you were asleep," Thibault said. "It works. For a couple of blocks, anyway."

"Nothing like searching an entire city on foot," Flicker muttered.

Chizara had said not to take any cars. They'd zoom past the tracker too fast to pick it up.

Why on earth had Nate sent her and Thibault to search the downtown area? The thick of Mardi Gras seemed like the wrong place to test Anon's tenuous connection to reality.

A passerby jostled Flicker, and she pulled Thibault closer.

"Maybe you should've worn the test tracker," she said. "You know, just in case."

He shook his head. "Not while we're looking for Verity. We can't have two trackers out there."

"Right. But after we find her . . ."

Thibault didn't answer, and in the silence Flicker felt her face flush.

Or maybe it was just the leather mask she'd borrowed from the Barrows' wall. Here on the day before Mardi Gras, pretty much everyone on the streets of New Orleans was incognito. Which was handy if you were on a most-wanted list, or hiding a blushing face.

"Sorry," she said. "I know you're past that. Right?"

She felt him shrug. "I thought it was getting easier. And I want to be here for you, for all of you. But sometimes the world seems like too much."

"You don't have to tell me that." The throng here was thick enough that Flicker had to keep one arm locked with his, her senses wrapped around him. She stayed in her own head, not daring to split her attention. "I just don't want to lose you again."

He pulled her closer. "I'll be fine, as long as I don't have to shoot anyone."

Flicker smothered a startled noise. Was that a *joke*?

The phone pinged three times, and she tensed.

"False alarm," Thibault said. "Just a bunch of texts from Nate. 'Everyone in position? Keep to your search areas! We don't have time to overlap!'"

"Send him a thumbs-up," Flicker said. "He hates emojis."

"Ha," he said. "I'm surprised this thing still works as a phone."

"No escape from Nate and his plan," Flicker said, though she wasn't sure Glorious Leader ever had *plans* anymore. He switched between commanding certainty and this weird passiveness left over from prison. And his face when he was gazing at Piper . . . like she was the answer to everything.

His plan, such as it was, went like this:

One: Find Verity and grab her.

Two: Truth-zap one of Piper's minions to find out what she was up to.

Three: ???

"This whole trip to New Orleans was about one thing," Flicker said. "Nate wanting to be in the middle of all superpowered things."

"So you agree with Scam?" Thibault asked, guiding her one step up onto a boardwalk. The crowd's hubbub changed as the wall to her right became more sound reflective—stone or brick instead of wood. "We should be in Mexico, waiting this whole thing out?"

Flicker snorted. "There has to be a middle ground between charging in cluelessly and running away."

"Well, *I* want to be out here looking," Thibault said, guiding her past the smell of bubbling fish stew. "If I'm going to stay connected to this world, I should be ready to protect it, right?"

Flicker pulled him to a stop, scanning the passersby for a glimpse of his face.

There it was—his old expression, without that distant look he'd had since returning from the void. He gazed intently down at her.

And for a moment the mass of people around them didn't matter. She was *connected* to him.

"Okay," she said. "As long as we're together."

She leaned forward into a kiss.

With her lips against his, Flicker felt herself drawn into another world. Not some shapeless void, but a private space that shut out the churning crowds. Their own reality, in no danger from Piper's mad plans.

"Me too," he said when they pulled apart, then, "Huh."

"Huh, what?" she asked.

"There's a girl over there. She's acting kind of strange. But no one's paying any attention."

Flicker laughed. "Dude. It's Mardi Gras. You're saying there's only *one* weirdo in the French Quarter?"

But his whole body had gone tense. And he spoke softly, as if he were telling her a secret.

"The play of people's attention. The way they're looking at her. Or *not* looking—their attention just slides past her. Just slips off, like . . ."

"Holy shit, Thibault, is she another—"

Then her hands were empty. There was no one beside her, no one to talk to. Some vital meaning had been yanked out of reality, leaving her grasping at air.

Who had she been talking to?

Her fingertips fumbled on her lips, at a spark of heat, of taste.

Who the hell had she been *kissing*?

CHAPTER 40
CRASH

"DAMN," CHIZARA SAID. "IT'S CRAWLING WITH FEDS."

"Told you this was pointless."

Chizara looked at Kelsie. The whole way here she'd been nervous, full of arguments for staying away. "Are you *afraid* of dead people, Kelsie?"

"Not really. But the city's so alive right now." Kelsie was staring at the cemetery entrance across the street, where yellow police tape fluttered in the breeze. "And nobody in there wants to party."

Chizara frowned. She felt a dozen heartbeats among the graves, and a painful spangling of tech. Not as crowded as Bourbon Street, but hardly an empty wasteland. The FBI was as interested in the cemetery as she was.

She had to find out how Piper had hidden her gang. What had shielded them from the Zeroes' crowd powers?

A man came around the far corner of the stone outer wall, his dark suit screaming *FBI*, and Chizara took a step back into the shadows. She and Kelsie were wearing Mardi Gras masks, but the purple feathers framing her face only made her feel more conspicuous.

"Maybe Piper wasn't using technology at all," Kelsie said softly. "What if she has Anons in her gang? Or maybe she can flip her power inside out, like Nate."

Chizara shook her head. "Her gang came out of one of those crypts. If they were using Anonymous powers, they could've stood in the open. If they have some kind of Faraday cage for Zero powers, I need to see it."

"If you say so," Kelsie said, adjusting the green foil mask over the top half of her face.

Chizara was sweating under her own mask. She was exhausted being in this mad city, which grew madder every day as Mardi Gras approached. She was tired of juggling its ratty infrastructure 24/7. Even Kelsie's pleasure in the pumped-up party vibe was starting to wear on her. She longed for the Zeroes' safe houses in the tech-free wilderness.

Her lack of sleep wasn't helping. It had taken all night to rebuild three burner phones so they could detect the tracker chip. Now the Zeroes were spread across the city, hunting for Verity.

At least, that was what Chizara and Kelsie were *supposed* to be doing.

But this was more important.

"We could go around the back."

"Forget it," Kelsie said. "The vibe in there is hard-core. As in *shoot Zeroes on sight.*"

Chizara sighed. "I guess that's what happens when someone kidnaps the FBI's pet Zero."

"Why do you need to see this shielding so bad?"

"Because *nothing* has ever blocked you from feeling a crowd before, right?"

Kelsie shuddered a little. "No. It was weird. Like they were spilling out of a portal from . . . another world."

"Flicker said the same thing—all their eyes just appeared. So maybe our powers are some kind of signal, like a radio wave. Something that technology can influence!"

Chizara thought again about the weird device in the Makers' warehouse. If it had some kind of crowd power, it would soon have more than a million people to work on . . . or to fuel it.

Kelsie was nodding slowly. "Makes sense, I guess. A lot of what we do is like a remote control. The way me and Nate influence crowds, or Glitch jams up brains. So there must be *some* kind of signal going through the—" She stopped, and her voice dropped to a whisper. "Hey, is that Phan?"

Chizara's heart beat faster—Kelsie's fear in the air, trying to find a crowd to loop with.

Agent Phan was on the central cemetery path, striding

toward the exit. He turned onto the sidewalk, heading toward a couple of white vans parked there.

A moment later, a stab of pain went through Chizara's head. Some flavor of signal she hadn't encountered before. Maybe Phan was testing the shielding inside the crypt, trying to pierce it with his own transmission.

Whatever it was, it hurt.

She spoke through her teeth. "We're not getting inside there any time soon. We should go back to that warehouse. Figure out what Essence and her people were building. Come on."

She turned away from the cemetery, walking back toward downtown. Kelsie followed.

"Nate said not to go back there." She pushed her mask up so that Chizara could see her frowning. "They won't hide Verity in a place we know about."

"Screw Nate. And screw Verity. I need to see that machine again."

"Pretty sure Piper doesn't want us poking around."

"Screw Piper, too."

"Zara!" Kelsie was laughing now, scandalized.

But this was serious. "Essence's machine was decorated like a parade float. And Mardi Gras is *tomorrow*!"

"But Piper told us to stay away. If we get up in her business, we could get our brains glitched!"

Chizara turned and started walking. "She tries to stop us, I'll stop her heart."

Kelsie caught up and pulled her to a halt. "You wouldn't."

Chizara met her girlfriend's eyes. Wouldn't she?

She just didn't know. It would depend on the threat, and how full of rage and fear she was—and curiosity. Her deepest demon self wanted so much to know what it felt like to seize someone's heart. To flex that ultimate power.

That self looked back at Kelsie now.

"Zara? Tell me you wouldn't—"

"Of course I wouldn't." Chizara let her gaze soften, felt her better self win over. Of course she wouldn't stop anyone's heart. *Do no harm.*

Kelsie kept eyeing her.

"Just come with me, okay?" Chizara asked.

Kelsie pulled down her mask.

"Okay, Zara. At least if I'm there, I can keep you on the straight and narrow."

CHAPTER 41
ANONYMOUS

DAZED, THIBAULT STEPPED CLOSER TO THE GIRL. IT meant stepping out of the world, tempting the boundary between here and gone.

But this was it. At last he'd found someone like him. A living person, not the fuzzy memory of one of Swarm's victims.

Back in Thibault's body, the sensations of shock and wonder raged: the thundering heart, the held breath, goose bumps scrambling over his skin. But inside this bubble with her, it was all Zen calm. The crowd noise was muted, their darting attention strands passing straight through the girl.

Like him, she had retreated from the real world, slipped into the Nowhere behind everything.

She didn't look very Zen. She looked homeless and dirty, when she could stroll into any hotel she wanted for a room, a shower. Starving, when she could grab food from any market or restaurant.

But Thibault remembered the redwoods, living in this world-behind-the-world, not sure what the point of eating was. He'd been like this. She was just like him. He'd lost his own body, his friends, even—

He spun round. No one but strangers. No Flicker.

He'd forgotten her again, for an instant. And she in turn had lost the memory of him, the thought of him, and walked away.

Of course, there were two Anons here—twice the power of forgetting.

That felt dangerous.

But he couldn't retreat. She was *another Anonymous*, right here in front of him.

"Hey there," he said.

"Not this again." She wasn't looking at him. She kept pacing, tossing back her dark hair.

"You've seen me before?"

She waved him off with one dirty hand. "Don't have time for ghosts today. Too much going on."

A sightline flicked out from the crowd, brushed her, slid right off again. It was so strange to see that happen to someone else. Recognition rushed through him—along with a pang of pity.

She was gone so far into the Nowhere, she thought Thibault

was from her own imagination. How long since she'd talked to anyone besides herself?

"I'm not in your head—I'm real."

"Real?" She turned to the crowd and flung her arms wide so that he had to jump back out of the way. "What's real is carnival! Beautiful weather, tourist money flowing in, every sparkle and feather in place. The stage is *set*. We're ready for a *show*!"

No one looked. No one listened.

He tried again. "You're not making me up. My name's Thibault Durant."

She still didn't face him, but her expression shifted. Suspicion.

"That sounds exactly like a name I'd come up with. Fancy and French."

Thibault sighed. "That's my parents for you."

He dared to put his hand on the shoulder of her sweaty shirt. She went very still.

"I'm Anonymous, like you," he said. "Some people call us Stalkers."

Her hand came up and touched his, exploratory, disbelieving. She kept gazing out into the crowd.

"You've got to understand," she said. "My brain's always splitting off and chatting with me. I'm probably not well."

"I'm sorry," Thibault said. "Maybe I can help."

Her hand dropped away, and so did his.

She looked down at her shoulder, pushed out her lips

thoughtfully. "When people start talking to me, means I need to drink water."

"Let me get you some."

He took her arm again and led her through the jostling crowds, toward a store with vaporizers and Mardi Gras beads in the window. A cooler sat outside, full of sodas and waters swimming in ice.

He grabbed a bottle and thrust it, cold and dripping, into her hand.

"There," he said. "Could an imaginary friend do that?"

She took a long swig, then another. Her gaze skated past into the crowds, though her attention was very firmly attached to him.

"Some days, yeah."

"You know there are other people like you, right?" he asked. "People with powers?"

She snorted. "Oh, I know *all* about that. This town is full of them."

Thibault swallowed, remembering the cluster of pins in the map. And Chizara had found *twenty* other Crashes? The thought of twenty Anons was too much.

He pushed it away. "What's your name?"

She flashed a false grin. "I don't need a name."

Her faraway look gave him the creeps, and his own gaze darted between her and the crowd flowing along behind her. He was afraid one or the other would fade from sight.

This girl was like he'd been a week ago. Held here by the

faintest scraps of her individuality, poised in this fragile balance, one step away from merging with the universe.

But his friends had saved him. Hanging on to reality was all about staying connected to other human beings.

"So you know people with powers. You have friends, right?"

She looked at him, straight on at last, that eyebrow raised again.

"I *had* friends, yeah."

"What did they call you?"

"They called me . . . Rien."

Thibault stared at her—*Rien* was French for "nothing." The same name Flicker and Lily had called him in their stories.

It hit him again—she was someone just like him.

"If you're real, you have to be careful." Rien took hold of his shirtfront. "You think you're solid, with your fancy name and your nice manners. But we nobodies have trouble with big crowds like this. Last Mardi Gras, we lost a couple of guys just like you. Nice-dressed boys, who shaved every day and laced their shoes up tight."

"I know all about it," he said. "I almost faded out once."

Rien's eyes widened, and something like respect shaded her expression.

"And you made it back? Good for you. I wouldn't stick around for Fat Tuesday, though. You can only hold out for so long, if you're not used to it. I was born here, so I'm good. But you . . ."

"I hear you." Thibault was already having to lean away from the force of the Nowhere that surrounded Rien. He tried to focus on solid, real things—the ground under his feet, the smell of spilled beer.

He wondered where Flicker was now. Lost in the crowd? Still trying to find Verity with the tracker?

Looking for her boyfriend?

"And this Fat Tuesday's going to be special," Rien said.

Thibault stared at her. "What do you mean?"

She stared off into the distance, like she was trying to remember something. For a moment he thought he'd lost her again, but then her eyes came back to him, fixed and certain.

"Piper. The girl who gave me my name."

He nodded, holding her gaze. "She's the boss around here, right?"

She recoiled. "You work for her?"

"No." He reached out, took her shoulder again. "But she kidnapped someone, and I'm trying to find them. Do you know where Piper is? What she's planning?"

Rien shrugged his hand off, took a long drink of water.

"She used to care about knowing me. Remembering me. Taking notes to keep me in her head."

Thibault had to smile. "I've got a friend like that."

"Piper's an *ex*-friend. But for a while she had me recruiting. All over the damn country, picking up people like us. Extending her reach."

Now her voice had lost all its vagueness and had turned hard and bitter.

"Not anymore?" he asked.

"Not once I found out what she was up to." She shuddered, and the shudder went through the world itself. . . .

The backdrop of crowds and music shimmered, froze. The last threads of noise and boisterousness stopped leaking through the veil, leaving them both in a vast silence. The crowd faces turned gray, mouthing and flickering like old silent movies.

Thibault felt himself slipping away, thinning out, like when he thought of Quinton Wallace, like when he smelled acrid gunpowder.

"Stay with me." He took her arm, squeezed hard. "Stay here in the real!"

She looked right into his eyes, unblinking. "I realized what I'd helped set in motion. But it was too late to stop it."

"To stop what?"

Rien's eyes closed and her brow furrowed, like thinking about it was too much. Behind her the crowd's movements slowed and faded, and Thibault felt himself waver again.

"She's going to raise the Mardi Gras flag," Rien said. "Purple, green, and gold."

Thibault shook his head. "What does that mean?"

"Purple for justice, green for faith, gold for power."

Now he could see the crowd moving, not just beyond Rien but *through* her face and her body.

And through his own grasping hand.

He let go as if she'd stung him. "Try to stay with—"

"Justice for the bankers who did us wrong. Faith in the truth. And power for *us*."

Far away, Thibault's body shuddered, his spine turning to ice.

"Power for people with powers." Rien's voice was racked with guilt. "But ashes for everyone else. And I *helped* her put it together. Millions of people, and it's all my fault."

"What's going to happen?" he demanded. But she was fading. . . .

Everything was fading, paling, bleaching, the crowd turning to blobs on the backdrop. Thibault felt himself tipping forward into the blur of Nowhere, joining her, disconnecting too. For a moment he felt the lure of namelessness, the luxury of stretching out thin, letting holes open up in him. . . .

"Flicker."

His body had said it. His mind reached out to grasp the thought as the girl's sleeve dissolved between his fingertips.

And when he reached for the girl again, there was no arm for him to grab, no body at all. Her name was gone, that wisp of meaning, in the roar of the massive carnival crowd, in the fast, bright attention thronging among them.

The girl had gone to nothing.

Leaving him at the edge, his own name in tatters, about to topple over.

CHAPTER 42

SCAM

"ETHAN? IS THAT *YOU* IN THERE?"

Even in the roiling crowd of costumed Mardi Gras fans, Sonia stood out. She wore silver microshorts and a tight velvet vest, and her purple hair fell to her bare shoulders. The sun shone through a spray of white feathers that stuck straight up from her beaked mask.

She was astonishingly hot.

Ethan sighed. He'd never thought of Sonia as out of his league before, but ever since his stupid voice opened its big mouth about his crush, that was *all* he could think about. Sonia was the kind of girl he'd always be playing catch-up with.

"*That's* your costume?" She bent forward, laughing. "Teenage Mutant—"

"Hey, it was cheap, okay!" Ethan said.

Free, actually, with a little help from the voice. He'd found it in a bargain bin on Lafayette—the only costume he'd seen that would cover him from head to toe. Now that Ethan had the Feds *and* Piper's crew watching for him, there was no such thing as too much disguise.

Sonia was still laughing. "I can barely hear you!"

Ethan lifted the mask a little to free his mouth. "What are you supposed to be? A giant bird?"

He flinched at the way it sounded. His first attempt at a compliment, and it had come out snarky. He should have used the voice.

But Sonia grinned. "Exactly what I was going for. A raptor hunting for weirdness!"

Ethan smiled as he pulled his mask down. Somehow he and Sonia were on the same wavelength. Maybe he could use his own words with her.

"We have to keep moving," Ethan said. "I'm supposed to be hunting too."

"For who?" Sonia held up both hands. "Wait! Don't tell me anything! I don't want to blab if Verity shows up. That's why I wore a mask—so she couldn't follow me again."

"Not a problem," Ethan said. "She's the person we're looking for."

Sonia stopped, stared. "Shouldn't we be *avoiding* her?"

"You'd think, right? But finding her leads to Piper, who's,

like, the Zeroes boss of this town. And who has some kind of big, city-destroying plan." Ethan shook his head. "If it were up to me, I'd be halfway to Mexico."

Sonia smiled. "Then I'm happy it's not up to you. It's kind of fun having you around."

Ethan was glad for the costume then. He could feel his face burning.

He didn't dare say anything, in case it came out in a squeak. It had been humiliating enough, telling the other Zeroes about his crush on Sonia. He didn't want to make the same slip in front of *her*.

Maybe that was why his fellow Scams were so hard to find. They'd all embarrassed themselves so much that they'd taken Buddhist vows of silence and were now hiding in caves till the end of the world.

Which was scheduled for tomorrow.

He pulled out the bulky rebuilt phone Chizara had given him. "This is supposed to find Verity. She got kidnapped, right in front of me. Glitch was there!"

"That cow who busted up the Dish?" Sonia said. "Man, she messed up my wrist that night. Still hurts when I type."

"She sucks," Ethan agreed.

Sonia pointed at the phone. "How does that thing find someone?"

"There's a tracker on Verity. This little baby makes a noise if we get within range." He showed her the phone's screen—a street map. "My search area is here, east along the water. It's out of the crowds, at least."

Ethan realized he was telling Sonia everything. Was that because he trusted her now? Or because he had a crush on her?

Maybe it was the same thing.

She was nodding, taking it all in. But then her eyes narrowed.

"You didn't build this thing, did you?"

"Hell no. How could I even . . ." He froze for a second. "Oh, right."

Sonia was giving him the hairy eyeball of suspicion. "So your Zeroes pals are in town? Not in Saint Louis anymore?"

He'd forgotten that lie. There was no point in sticking to it. Verity couldn't pump Sonia for information if she was Piper's prisoner.

"About that—the others were always here," Ethan said. "I made up that stuff about Saint Louis."

Sonia nodded, like she'd already figured that out, and punched him on the arm. Nowhere near as hard as Jess would have. His army-trained sister could leave a bruise with her pinkie finger.

"That's for lying," Sonia said.

"Ow," Ethan obliged.

"No, I get it. You had to be careful what you told me, because of Verity. It's just . . ." She turned away, letting out a huff of frustration. "It's one thing, helping you out—the

Feds just want you for questioning. But your buddy Nate is an escaped fugitive. That's serious aiding and abetting. Like Verity said, I could go to prison!"

Ethan hadn't thought about it that way. He was used to the idea that any slipups meant the slammer for him and all his friends. But Sonia, too?

"I guess that changes things," he mumbled.

"I cannot do prison, Ethan."

"It's not high on my bucket list either!" He shuffled his mutant-toed feet. "So I get it if you just want to . . . stay away from me."

"Ha!" She punched his arm again, this time harder. "As *if*. Just promise that if they put me in jail, you'll bust me out like you did Nate. Then I'd *really* be famous."

"Well, I can't exactly promise," Ethan replied. "But I'll try."

And he realized that it was true. He would march back into a supermax if it meant freeing Sonia Sonic.

Geez. He had it bad.

"Come on," he said. "If we can find Verity and rescue her, the Feds might give you a medal instead."

They walked on Rampart, along the edge of Ethan's search area. It was crowded this close to the Quarter, even in the early afternoon. Styles of music clashed from every direction, and people elbowed past each other, drinking from plastic cups, eating street food wrapped in wax paper.

No pings from the rebuilt phone, though.

After a few minutes Sonia said, "So I've been thinking about what Verity said. About your power."

"Me too. It's so not fair."

Sonia stared at him. "What isn't?"

"Everything!" He had a voice inside him that was omniscient, but it never talked to *him*. How about telling him whether he was going to die in prison or not? Or if Sonia was really into him, or just liked him because he kept making her famous? "I've got this awesome power, but it's really hard to control. I just wish I could find another person like me. We could compare notes!"

Sonia nodded. "Yeah. I've been asking around about that."

Ethan came up short. "About what?"

"About your power. Whether anybody at WeirdCon has heard of someone with omniscience."

Ethan grabbed her elbow and steered her gently off the main street, until they were huddled against a brick wall.

"You told them about *my power*?"

"Relax," Sonia said. "I didn't tell them you were in town. Just that I had a theory about what you are. Everybody's seen my video of you talking to the bank robber. It's, like, Weird-Hunter 101."

"Stupid video," he muttered.

"Yeah. My bad." Sonia hoisted off her mask and frowned. "But I didn't *know* you then. You were just some guy who tried to talk to me about Patty Low."

"But at least that video gives me an excuse to ask about you. Do you want to hear what I found out or not?"

Ethan hesitated.

What he really wanted was to find out if Sonia liked him. Because if he died during Piper's psycho parade, he wanted someone to remember him not as a superpowered terrorist, but as a messed-up, freaked-out human being. A guy who'd always thought he'd live long enough to flunk his SATs.

But he didn't know how to ask that, so he went with "Okay. What did they say?"

"People have figured out a lot of powers," Sonia said. "We all know about people who mess up technology. People who control crowds. Who give you brain freezes. But as far as we can tell, there's no one else like you."

Ethan blinked. Seriously? Not one nutball weird-hunter had ever read a half-baked news story that screamed *Ethan Cooper is not alone*?

He had a lump in his throat the size of a bowling ball, and for once it had nothing to do with the voice.

"Crap."

"You're unique," Sonia said. "Why is that so bad?"

"Because Chizara met all these other Crashes, and she got really excited. And there's another Nate who runs this town, God help us, and he's practically in love with her! Even when Kelsie turned out to be like Swarm, she figured out how to stay nice. It made her stronger!" Ethan looked away. "Meeting other versions of themselves, it helped them figure out who they are. But what if I'll always be alone?"

Sonia said carefully, "Being special is cool too."

"Yeah, awesome. Except once people know how my power works, they don't trust me anymore. Even my friends call me *Scam*. But hey, we're all going to prison anyway, right?"

"You know, you're a real pessimist, Ethan," Sonia said. "I bet the other Scams are just hard to find, because you can all lie your way out of anything. But I've got a plan to track one down!"

"What kind of plan?"

"Think about it," Sonia said. "We're in New Orleans, a town full of magic and voodoo and vampires. If you wanted to scam people here, what would you be?"

"A flood-insurance salesmen?" Ethan asked.

"Nope." Sonia laughed, and pointed at the shop across the street.

It had a neon sign that blinked the words PAST, PRESENT, and FUTURE in bright red, and a giant diagram of a palm with its lines labeled LIFE, FATE, and HEART.

Ethan looked back at Sonia, whose eyes were bright.

"You'd be a fortune-teller," she said. "The oldest scam in the book."

CHAPTER 43
FLICKER

FLICKER MOVED THROUGH THE JOSTLING CROWDS, hopping among the eyes around her.

So *much* to see. Shiny sequined costumes, bare flesh, and masks. Trumpets and banjos and hand drums. And the *beads*: thousands of them strung around necks, hung in the trees, flying through the air, scattered treacherously on the ground . . .

And none of it was what she was looking for—though Flicker still couldn't remember what that was.

Who that was, right? She'd been talking to someone, right before her brain had slipped away.

She looked down at the ungainly, glued-together phone, which was warm against her palm. Burning battery, busily scanning the airwaves for Verity's tracker.

But Verity wasn't who she'd lost. It was someone more important. Someone she'd sworn never to forget.

Her vision darted among the eyeballs around her, searching for a clue, a glimpse, anything that would jog her memory. The awful dizziness of trying to see through too many drunken, dancing eyes threatened, but then something happened. . . .

The collective gaze of the crowd began to gather on a single face.

Flicker stopped in her tracks. He was so beautiful. His dark hair rippled to his shoulders. His face was alight with purpose and intelligence. Those eyes—what would she see if she stared deeply into them?

Was it *him* she was looking for? No, that was crazy. She never could have forgotten a boy as lovely as that.

Flicker shook her head. What the hell?

It was just the guy from yesterday, with the hotness power. Except the crowd here was about a hundred times bigger than in the cemetery. The Curve was pushing his beauty to nuclear levels.

He marched at the head of a small parade, a brass band outnumbered by drummers and dancers. He wore a cape with an upturned collar. A werewolf mask was pushed up onto his head to reveal his irresistible face.

The crowd was going crazy for him. Every eye in the street was turning his way, drawn by his glamour, his sheer flawless-ness. And the more people stared at him, the more splendid he became. Girls were screaming, guys, too, like he was a pop idol at the center of mass hysteria.

It *hurt* to look at him, to have those exquisite features scalded into her brain from a hundred viewpoints. Flicker felt herself swaying on her feet, her brain starting to fry. But just as she was about to draw back inside her head, the boy reached up and pulled the mask over his face.

She steadied, but then a new agony came—his absence cutting at her heart.

A moan passed through the crowd. All of them felt the same anguish at losing his beauty. The throng was surging forward, trying to see the boy's face again. He turned and ran through the musicians, dodging flashing drumsticks, ducking outstretched arms.

Flicker followed.

She leaped from eye to eye, keeping him in sight, blundering through the crowd. He was fast, and soon the next jam-packed street swallowed him. His pursuers pushed ahead, slower and slower, defeated by the many bodies. Until finally they came to a ragged, confused halt.

But Flicker kept moving. Yesterday in the graveyard, he'd been the FBI's target, and he was Verity's old friend. He must know something about Piper's plans.

Someone in these thousands of eyes had to catch a glimpse of that werewolf mask.

CHAPTER 44
CRASH

BACK INTO THE CITY, INTO THE MAELSTROM OF phones and wifi. Blaring TV camera trucks here to capture the revelry, all of it flying past the cab's windows in a roaring blur, pounding in Chizara's head.

"It's getting scary out there," Kelsie said as traffic slowed on the expressway. She was peering down at the city. "More crowded than yesterday."

"You don't have to tell me." Chizara winced at the mass of phones boiling below them.

"And tonight, when they've all been drinking all day . . . what if we run into a bunch of assholes looking for a fight? I'm worried about my feedback loop."

Chizara stopped rubbing at her temples and took Kelsie's

hand. "You aren't Swarm, okay? With you around, they'll all have a great time."

Kelsie looked reassured. But Chizara was glad when the cab was finally past the French Quarter and out into the relative emptiness of warehouses and factories.

Mardi Gras was the real problem—it made Zero powers too strong, too hard to control.

And Piper had grown up here. Her personality had been forged in this ego-amplifying cauldron of humanity. She was Nate on steroids.

No wonder she thought she could take on the world.

A few minutes later they were across the street from the Makers' warehouse, the cab pulling away.

"This is weird," Chizara said. The Madbolt sat dead in its box like an empty chrysalis, all its magic flown. "They haven't reset that lock."

Kelsie pulled off her mask, frowning. "I can't feel any crowd inside."

"So no Glitches to worry about, at least."

The closer they drew to the warehouse, the emptier it looked. The roller door was wide open, but no signals reached from inside—not so much as a phone bleeping.

"They've moved out," Chizara sighed.

Kelsie peeked nervously into the yawning doorway. "It *feels* empty. But what if they have a crowd-hiding room in here? This could be a trap."

"They had us trapped yesterday," Chizara said. "And they let us go."

She stepped into the cool darkness, but the warehouse's Faraday cage was broken by the open roller door. She was tempted to close it and cut out the city's blare. But the door was their only escape route.

As Chizara's eyes adjusted, though, it soon became clear that the place really was abandoned. In the middle of the warehouse floor, where the machine had sat, bright with meticulous and inscrutable circuitry, there was only darkness.

Disappointment swept through her. "It's gone."

"Why would they move it?" Kelsie looked around.

"Maybe they thought we'd call the Feds," Chizara murmured.

Her mind was already pushing through the shadows, looking for evidence. She felt the tools strewn across the table, the dragon's hoard of other equipment left behind. There was a Dumpster full of discarded parts and packaging. From these things and her memory of the machine, she tried to piece together its history, its function.

And then she saw it in the corner, a giant box marked with the logo of a satellite-dish company. The box looked to be eight feet across, the sort of dish you'd use for internet access out in the country, off the grid.

"Oh my God. That's what was mounted on the float." Chizara's voice echoed in the vacated space. "Some kind of transmitter."

"Transmitting what?" Kelsie said, her green mask glinting in the light from the roller door. "Bellwether Radio?"

"No." A shiver ran down Chizara's spine. "Powers."

"Are you serious?"

"Zero powers are just a signal," Chizara said. "Something you can block. So maybe Essence and her crew figured out how to *project* them too. What if Piper can throw her influence out onto a million people? Worse, what if *Glitch* can?"

"Whoa."

Chizara pulled her phone out of her pocket and switched it on. "Nate needs to know about this."

At the warehouse. Empty. The machine is gone.

I think it transmits powers.

"You know what he'll say," Kelsie said. "Something like, 'Get back to looking for Verity! We only have a day!'"

Chizara shook her head. "He's not wrong, if this is what she's planning. Our search area's half a mile from here. Come on."

"Sure." Kelsie's voice was light as a ghost. "There's just one thing."

"What?" Chizara asked.

Kelsie pulled her phone out. "It's nearby. I don't know if I actually *want* to go, but . . ."

"Go *where*?"

"No, forget it." She shoved the phone back into her pocket. "We're supposed to be saving Verity. We should just . . ."

Kelsie jittered there in the middle of the floor, a solitary puppet on a dimly lit stage.

"Tell me."

"That group my mom joined? They're meeting five blocks away, on Bartholomew. Right about now."

"Whoa," Chizara said.

"Yeah." Kelsie shrugged.

Chizara crossed the unswept floor. Of all the Zeroes, she could detect the tracker the farthest, using her power instead of some jerry-rigged device. She should be out there right now, searching for Piper.

But this was Kelsie's mother—the only family she had left. This might be their last chance to connect, before Piper visited another disaster on the whole city.

"Are you up to it?" Chizara asked. "Meeting your mom now, in the middle of all this?"

Kelsie's eyes were huge, the pupils big and black in the dimness.

"I don't know," she said in the softest voice.

Chizara smiled. "Let's go find out, huh?"

And she took her girlfriend's hand and led her out into the sunlight.

CHAPTER 45
FLICKER

FLICKER FOUND THE BEAUTIFUL BOY IN A CAFÉ with a tiled floor and arched ceiling. It was long and narrow, lit by a row of chandeliers down the center.

He sat in a corner, staring down at his coffee like he was trying to figure out how to drink through the mask.

But then he pulled it off.

Flicker waited for a sudden explosion of beauty—nothing. He was back to the straggly hair and indifferent chin he'd had before turning beautiful in the cemetery. Apparently this guy could control his power in a crowd.

She walked over and sat across from him.

"Do I know you?" he began, but when Flicker lifted her mask, the frown in his voice changed to a smile. "Oh. You're one of those celebs who showed up yesterday. Cambria Five?"

"That's us," she said, making a quick scan of the room's eyes. Everyone was talking, reading their phones, too intent to listen in. But she pulled the mask back down and kept her voice low. "We thought Phan was going to grab you."

"Like Piper would let that happen. She *runs* this town."

"No kidding," Flicker said. "That's why we're looking for—"

"Wait!" the boy interrupted. "You're Riley Phillips!"

Flicker hesitated. But there was no point hiding it.

"Yeah. But maybe not so loud."

"Ha!" His chair squeaked as he leaned forward, his voice dropping to a whisper. "I'm Beau. Always nice to meet a fellow Sight-caster!"

The words didn't make sense. Flicker shook her head.

"I think you're confused."

"Oh yeah?" Beau turned. "That guy to your right? He's reading about Troy's Super Bowl party."

Flicker frowned, but sent her vision into a nearby set of eyes flicking across a phone screen.

> . . . *bar-code scanners crashed, and backup verification methods mysteriously failed as well, despite sophisticated anti-fraud methods including holograms and watermarks. Later, many of the fraudulent tickets turned out to be nothing more than blank pieces of* . . .

"Shit," Flicker said. "You can see that?"

Beau let out a laugh. "What, you never met another one of us before? I thought you guys knew *everybody*. The Cambria Five are supposed to be the bomb."

"We are, but not in the sense you mean," she said, then shook her head. "Wait. If you're like me, why were you so damn *pretty* a minute ago?"

"I didn't know about the beauty thing either," he said. "Not till Piper's Stalker brought me here. Then I started learning stuff. The thing is, every power has two sides."

"Of course," Flicker said.

Chizara could crash and fix. Mob could make a crowd happy or turn them deadly. Nate could flip his charisma around to become Anonymous. But Flicker had never come up with even a *theory* about how her own power would reverse.

Yet here the answer was, sitting in front of her.

"So I could be . . ." She imagined herself at the center of a screaming, worshipful crowd, and the idea almost made her giggle.

"Totally hot?" Beau supplied. "You bet. Just stop throwing your vision into other people. Instead, draw their vision toward *you*."

"It can't be that simple."

"You've already got the muscles." He was leaning forward again, his voice intense, his weight scooting the table an inch toward her. "Just turn them around."

Flicker focused for a moment, feeling the eyes around her. She could leap into this gaze, or that one—but to drag them all toward herself?

It seemed kind of pathetic, *forcing* people to stare at her.

At a concert once, she'd seen a natural version of Beau's power. The group's singer had been pretty average-looking, but the mere fact of *everyone* staring at him made him seem irresistible. As if the lemminglike focus of the crowd had formed its own superpower.

But Flicker had never imagined herself as a rock star, any more than she thought of herself as a great beauty. The whole thing made her feel giddily undeserving, like when she'd found out about the fuckton of money she was down for in Gramma's will.

"You aren't even trying," Beau complained.

"I'm a wanted terrorist," she said with a shrug. "Unnecessary attention is not my friend."

"Trust me. No one will recognize you when you're beautiful."

"Ouch."

"Just get over yourself and *try* it. Imagine flipping your power inside out, like when you're cleaning a contact lens."

"A contact lens? Is there something wrong with your eyes?"

She jumped into Beau's vision and saw herself with perfect clarity—the crappy roadside-store T-shirt, her hair disheveled from a day of frantic searching, the ill-fitting mask.

"Just a little shortsighted," he said. "Why?"

"I just thought . . . ," Flicker began, but she didn't know *what* it was she'd thought. It had always been a lingering question.

Then Beau got it. "Oh, right. You're the blind one. You thought that was part of sight-casting?"

"Um, I guess so?"

"Nope." The frame of his vision moved as he shook his head. "I've met two other Sight-casters. Neither of them even wore glasses."

"Huh," she said softly.

So being blind was part of who she was, not some side effect of her power. That was how she'd always thought about it—or at least the way she'd *wanted* to think about it. But she'd never been completely certain. And Nate had always insisted that her blindness had to *mean* something.

"Are you okay?" he asked.

Flicker nodded. "It's just, sometimes my blindness feels the same as being one of us. A different kind of awareness. A different way of being in the world."

"I guess," Beau said, his eyes on her mask. "I always thought it was cool that you guys can hear better."

"We can't," Flicker said. "We just listen better."

"Okay. But that's *sort* of like a power."

"That's not what I meant. It's more about how the world isn't designed for blind people. And we freak some people out, just by being who we are."

He shifted back in his chair. "You don't freak me out. And having a power isn't going to feel out of place for much longer either. Piper's going to *do* something about that shit."

The words brought Flicker back.

"What do you mean, 'do something'?"

"She's going to break everything down," Beau said, awe in his voice. "We're gonna start from scratch and build it all up again. I even get to be on the float tomorrow. To keep everyone focused on us, you know? That's when it all goes down."

"When *what* goes down?"

He hesitated, and when he spoke, disappointment colored his words. "Piper doesn't tell me everything. My job is just to look pretty."

"Pretty," Flicker murmured. It was just too weird to think that, if she wanted, she could be earth-shatteringly, crowd-addlingly *gorgeous*.

Of course, she knew what Zen Boy would say about that.

She sat up straight—*Thibault.*

He was the one who'd disappeared. Faded into the massive crowd, and she'd just forgotten him!

Flicker stood up. "Oh shit."

"Trust me, it'll be okay." There was a smile in Beau's soft voice. "We're all going to be okay, us people with powers. The world's going to get remade . . . for *us*."

"I have to go." Flicker turned, making her way toward the door.

Unbelievable. How could she have sat here philosophizing about beauty and blindness while the boy she loved was *missing*?

She ignored Beau calling after her. She had to get back to where she'd lost Thibault, before he slipped too far into the Nowhere and was gone forever.

CHAPTER 46
MOB

"DO YOU KNOW WHAT YOU'RE GOING TO SAY?" Chizara whispered beneath the murmur of the gathering. "If your mom's even here?"

Kelsie tensed. "Don't call her that, okay?"

Zoe Moseley had broken three-year-old Kelsie's wrist, scared her dad so much he'd run halfway across the country. She didn't deserve the title of mother.

"She never looked for me, you know?" Kelsie said. "Even now, when my name's in the news."

"You don't know that," Chizara said gently. "We've been on the run. If the Feds couldn't find us, how could she?"

"I guess." Kelsie adjusted her mask. It felt weird to be wearing it here, but other people were dressed up. Mardi Gras seemed inescapable, even out in this quiet part of town.

"Dad told her never to contact us, but still . . ."

It hurt, having to be the one to show up searching, begging for recognition from her own mother.

Kelsie had been waiting for this moment since they'd arrived in New Orleans. But now that she was here, she wanted nothing more than to be out looking for Verity again. She had a mission. She had the other Zeroes.

She didn't *need* a mother.

The Clarity Circle meeting was being held in an old converted church, which seemed to be someone's house—someone who liked to cook. The kitchen wall was covered with fancy pans, each fitting snugly in its own outlined spot, but the rest of the ground level was wide open. There wasn't much furniture, but streaks of discolored wood showed where pews had once lined the floor. Most people sat on cushions.

There were about thirty of them gathered, all ages, lots of different types. A solid crowd with a friendly, expectant vibe. Too good-natured for Kelsie's anxiety to build a feedback loop. But somehow their warmth didn't settle back into her either.

Kelsie used to love the feel of a group like this. But since Swarm had hijacked that AA meeting, Kelsie knew how quickly an earnest gathering could turn bad. What she could turn them into if she really tried.

She hoped the meeting started soon. It was already ten minutes late.

"Any whiff of Verity's tracker?" she asked.

Chizara shook her head. "Nothing. Nate's gonna be pissed."

Kelsie sighed. Between their side trips to the graveyard and the Crashes' warehouse—and now this—she and Zara were way behind schedule. "We should go. Zoe Moseley doesn't care if I'm alive or dead."

Chizara laid an arm across Kelsie's shoulders. "We don't know her side of the story yet."

Kelsie started to speak, but was silenced by a sudden ripple of energy in the room. As a murmur passed through the crowd, all eyes went to an old woman in the doorway.

The woman gestured for quiet, and the noise stopped at once.

A young guy in a purple shirt got up from the floor. He led the woman to a leather armchair at the front of the room.

"I'm Madame Laurentine," she said, her voice lightly accented with a Cajun lilt. "I know it's Mardi Gras, but we are here for clarity—to show ourselves. So please reveal your faces."

People started taking off their masks, looking around at each other, smiling and blinking, like it was the end of a masquerade party.

Kelsie's stomach clenched. Every instinct she'd developed over the last month screamed against revealing her face among strangers. But being the only people in masks would only attract more attention.

She dipped into the group's positive energy and held it level, hoping to short-circuit any alarm of recognition. Then she reached for her mask.

"Are you sure?" Chizara whispered.

Kelsie wasn't sure about anything. But this might be her last chance to find Zoe Moseley and ask what had really happened fourteen years ago.

The world might change tomorrow, after all.

She pulled off her mask. Chizara did the same.

No one was looking at them. The crowd continued to smile up at Madame Laurentine, caught up in a heady gratitude for her presence.

She gazed intently back at her audience, like she was getting to know each and every person. There was a new energy in the room.

Recognition. Acceptance. It was calm and steadying.

Kelsie felt herself smile.

"That's funny," Chizara breathed.

"You feel it too?"

Chizara's gaze met hers. "Are you thinking what I am?"

Kelsie shook her head—Madame Laurentine was way too old to have a power. They had to stop seeing Zeroes everywhere. They had to remember that there were people in the world who were simply *good*.

"Thank you all for being here," the woman said. "For taking time out of your Mardi Gras festivities. And for coming all the way out to the boondocks. You know how clarity doesn't do well in rowdy environments."

A murmur of laughter went through the room. That

feeling of an old joke they all shared, reminding everyone that they belonged here.

Madame Laurentine let the sound subside, then said, "And special thanks for sharing your home with us, Zoe."

Kelsie froze.

Madame Laurentine was nodding to someone in the front row. Someone she couldn't quite see.

Her mother.

Kelsie tried to breathe, to keep herself steady. But the floor had dropped out from under her. She caught a glimpse of long ash-blond hair tied up in a bun. A glimmer of eyeglasses as the woman nodded back at Madame Laurentine.

Her mother wore glasses. She had blond hair, like Kelsie used to.

Kelsie looked at the kitchen again. All those pots so cozy in their spots, hung by someone who cared about everything she owned. Was this really the home of someone who would hurt her own daughter?

And then a man in front of her leaned to one side, and she saw something else. . . .

Sitting next to Zoe were two small boys. Also fair-haired. They sat quietly, content and happy, full of the certainty that they were valued and loved.

And *everything* became clear.

She'd been replaced. That was why there'd been no

search, no tearful letter out of the blue. No appeal on TV, her mother standing next to FBI agents, asking for Kelsie to give herself up.

Nothing in fourteen years.

Her mother had moved on.

Kelsie knew that she should be upset, angry, humiliated. But another wave of understanding struck—it didn't matter, because Kelsie was still whole.

She knew who she was. Who her friends were. Who she loved and why. Her life had its own melody.

When Fig had taught her about music, his first lesson was repetition and alteration. The same number of beats in each measure, but different notes occupying them.

Life was change.

When her father had died, she'd bonded to the Zeroes. Her mother had simply done the same thing—the Kelsie-sized hole in her life was filled twice over.

No one was irreplaceable. Kelsie was like a note shimmering in the air—perfect but transitory.

Everything was so clear, so easy to understand. The only thing she didn't understand was why everyone in the whole room felt the same way. . . .

They were all having their own moments of clarity.

The boy who had led Madame Laurentine to her chair was standing now, gazing at the crowd. He was as dark-skinned as

Chizara, with a square face and a wisp of beard on his lower jaw. Exactly the right age for a Zero.

Damn. This *was* a power.

And in her moment of sublime recognition, Kelsie knew exactly which power it was. . . .

She'd seen it just yesterday in the cemetery. But flipped around. The opposite of recognition, the reverse of knowledge and self-understanding.

"Zara," she whispered. "He's a Glitch. But inside out."

She turned. Chizara stared back at her, tears in her eyes.

"It hurts all the time," Chizara said. "Every day, I'm in pain."

Kelsie swallowed. "I know this city's hard for you, Zara."

"No—my family. I miss them so much."

Another wave of understanding, far more terrible, passed through Kelsie. She had always been a wanderer, alone in a crowd. Ready to head off to the next party with anyone who was game.

And the Zeroes, even on the run, were the most solid thing she'd ever had. A family of people like her. But in leaving Cambria, Chizara had lost something deeper—her real family. Her beautiful brothers. Her perfect mom and dad.

Kelsie saw it now, with awful clarity: She needed Zara more than Zara needed her.

"I'm lost without them," Chizara said. "And all I want is for the Feds to put an end to this so I can see my family again. Before I kill someone."

Kelsie shook her head. "Zara. You'd never."

Chizara's eyes closed. "I could, just by *thinking* them dead. Hearts are just machines ready to crash."

Kelsie caught a clear, steady glimpse of what Chizara's words meant, and a gasp rose up from deep in her chest. This new power was just another thing that Chizara had to fight every day.

Kelsie's anguish finally pierced the feedback loop of goodwill that lay across the group. A murmur of surprise and anguish shot through the room.

The guy in the purple shirt was staring straight at her.

"Oliver?" Madame Laurentine stood, laying a hand on the guy's shoulder. "What is this? Another power?"

He nodded.

A jolt of real fear went through Kelsie then—and it too spilled across the room. If Oliver knew how to reverse his power, he could switch it around and glitch them on the spot.

"Not just any power," the boy said gently. "One of the famous Cambria Five."

Chizara was scrambling up now, trying to pull Kelsie to her feet. But Kelsie could only watch, frozen, as Zoe Moseley turned and stared, drawing her little boys close. Her eyes widened, and she mouthed something that could've been Kelsie's name. Again with perfect clarity, Kelsie saw every emotion on Zoe's face—guilt and sadness, longing and confusion, and a dread underlying it all.

325

Her daughter was a wanted terrorist, after all.

Chizara's strong arms lifted Kelsie to her feet, and the spell was broken. The two of them darted through a crowd of people who cowered as they passed, their fear almost sending Kelsie sprawling to the ground.

"Don't be afraid, everyone," Oliver called out. "You can't always believe the news."

But his friendly tone didn't break the feedback loop, and didn't stop Kelsie from running, from needing to escape the turmoil of emotions in her mother's eyes.

No one chased them out the door.

CHAPTER 47
BELLWETHER

PING, PING, PING . . .

Nate turned off the rebuilt phone.

He looked up at the decaying factory building—more likely it had been a power station, with that nest of transformers off to one side. Two giant smokestacks rose up against the blue sky, their crumbling brick spires braced by metal splints. Half the panes in the big industrial windows had been shattered by flung stones. Graffiti the size of billboards covered the lower stories, and the metal doors looked rusted shut.

Like an empty ruin. But according to Chizara's improvised tracker, Verity was in there somewhere. Which meant that Piper and her crew were too.

It was a pretty awesome lair, Nate had to admit. Decrepit and magnificent. Powerful-looking, but no one driving past would give it a second glance. New Orleans had plenty of abandoned buildings here along the river, away from the French Quarter and the surging crowds.

He had to get closer and scope out a plan of attack for tonight. There was no time to come back later with Anon or Flicker. Tomorrow was Fat Tuesday, when the streets would be choked by the largest, climactic Mardi Gras parades. When Piper's plans would unfold.

It was time to become Anonymous.

Nate breathed in slowly, letting his mind fill with the antiseptic reek of his prison cell, and his power withered. All his tendrils of dominance, hungry for obedience, wilted on the breeze. He let the building awe him, allowed its majesty to make him feel small. Staring across this vacant lot at the edifice that Piper had seized for herself, Nate realized how tiny his schemes had always been.

An amateur nightclub, a sleepy hometown, five other Zeroes—nothing compared to Piper's lair, her boisterous city, her army of powers. Whatever her plans turned out to be, he knew they were not small.

As his own insignificance settled over him, Nate's power turned gently inside out, until he was nothing. Beneath notice.

He turned off his phone and walked across the vacant lot under a veil of inconsequence.

Nearer the factory, he felt a crowd inside. Enough people to make his smothered ego thirsty. . . .

But prison had taught him how to lie low. How to stay small enough to disappear. If Dungeness hadn't been full of cameras and automatic doors, he could've walked out unnoticed after that first awful week.

It was scary, how good he was at anonymity now.

He breathed the thought away, focusing on the factory's windows at ground level. They were secured by metal grates, but he spotted one that looked rusted and worn. Nothing a crowbar couldn't peel back. He reached for his phone to take a picture—stopped himself in time.

Chizara had texted that the Makers' warehouse was empty now. They were probably here, preparing for the final part of Piper's plan. They would spot a switched-on phone in a second.

Brushing the brickwork with his fingertips, Nate counted the steps from the corner to the rusted grate, until he was certain he could find it in the dark.

A truck rumbled past, pulled in at one of the warehouses across the street. They seemed to be still in business, their loading docks freshly painted, with boxes stacked outside. Whatever Piper was up to in her lair, it wasn't so obvious that her neighbors had called the cops.

Of course, Nate could call the FBI himself. Explain to Agent Phan that a gang of terrorists was assembled on the edge of town. Let the Feds handle this.

But what if Piper's plan was something wonderful?

Something that would help Zeroes everywhere against a world that feared them?

Wrapped up in this insignificance, Nate wanted to join something, *anything*, even if it meant serving under another Bellwether. The way Piper had guided that parade two nights ago had been so elegant. This seething, musical city had taught her how to play a crowd like an instrument. He could learn so much from her.

But he had to make his own decision, and rescuing Verity was the key. With her truth power, all the Zeroes had to do was grab one of Piper's confidants at the same time and they'd learn what she was planning.

As Nate walked away back across the field, his body shuddered, and his power flipped again, like a cat's bent ear flicking back to its normal shape. He smiled as the last threads of anonymity fell away.

He was ready to fight for recognition. For his rightful part in deciding whether Piper's plan would go forward or not.

Nataniel Saldana was a Bellwether, not some pawn.

But he was still cautious, walking for half a mile before he powered up the phone and sent a text to the others.

Found her. Get ready. We're breaking in tonight.

CHAPTER 48
SCAM

ETHAN'S PHONE BUZZED.

He pulled it out of his pocket. It was from Nate.

"Crap," he said to Sonia. "They found Verity. I gotta go."

"No, you don't," Sonia said. "We're finishing this!"

Ethan just stared at her. They'd tried three fortune-tellers already and found out nothing. New Orleans had a lot more psychics than that, of course, but Sonia had narrowed the search down to the ones who looked Zeroes-aged on their website pictures.

She was pretty damn smart.

But it had been a bust so far. Every so-called psychic had had a different answer to Sonia's brilliant question, but no one had given the *right* answer. As far as Ethan could tell, psychics weren't real and other Scams didn't exist.

"Maybe we can pick up again tomorrow?" he said. "If I'm still alive."

"Hush." Sonia looked down at her phone. "The last one on my list is just up the street."

"Whatever," Ethan agreed.

Sonia led him beneath iron second-floor balconies with potted plants hanging from them, to the entry of a shadowy alley. Even in daylight it looked kind of creepy.

At the far end was a single red door. Ethan was pretty sure he'd seen the exact same door in a horror movie.

Ethan hesitated. "You sure about this one?"

"Totally. She gets great reviews. I figured that's a good sign, right? And they all mention how young she is." Sonia pushed her mask to the top of her head. "Sucks that Zeroes have to be born in two thousand. I was two years early."

"Superpowers are overrated," Ethan assured her. "What kind of town has teenage psychics, anyhow?"

"Same kind that has twenty-three voodoo stores," Sonia replied.

When they reached the end of the alley, Sonia tapped out a complex rhythm on the door.

"It's a code from her website," she said. "She's really into secrecy. Another good sign that she's hiding something, yeah?"

Ethan blinked. Maybe this one really was a Zero.

Someone like him . . .

Sonia pressed her ear to the door. Ethan stood back, half

hoping the door would never open. This alley was scary, and part of him was starting to get nervous about all this.

What if this girl was another Scam, and *her* life sucked too?

What if the voice's life-suck power was inescapable?

The door swung open. Sonia stepped back, colliding with Ethan.

A girl their age stood in the doorway. She wore a long paisley skirt and a headband of twinkling gold coins. A veil covered her face up to her dark eyes.

"Aha! Young lovers," the girl said confidently. "You want to know your future."

"Uh, not exactly," Ethan said. His future scared the crap out of him. So did romance. On the other hand, he *did* like Sonia. A lot. "We're looking for, um, psychic advice."

"Congratulations, you found a psychic," the girl replied. "I'm Madame Deidre. Let me guess. Sonia Sonic?"

Sonia gasped. "Holy crap! That was amazing."

"Nah. I read your blog. I'm DeeDee in your forum." She turned to Ethan. "And you must be . . . Raphael?"

"Ha! Wrong." Ethan turned to Sonia. "Come on, let's go."

"Um, Ethan." Sonia looked him up and down. "I think she's right."

"Oh. The costume."

"Retro," Deidre said, and gestured them inside. A small, round table waited in the center of the room. It was a cramped space, lit by a couple of table lamps. Big-eyed puppets hung from the ceiling, with straw poking out of their sleeves. There was a bench along one side with a collection of bones and feathers and stuff Ethan didn't have names for. And it smelled like wet fur. Ethan tried not to breathe.

"What year were you born?" Ethan asked.

"Two thousand," Deidre said. "Which is why you chose me, isn't it?"

Good answer. But he didn't buy that she knew everything. She was a weird-hunter, after all. They all knew about the 2000 rule. Maybe she was just trying to get people to *think* she had a power.

There was nothing like having a lying voice living inside you to make you a skeptic.

"Shouldn't you have a crystal ball or something?" he asked.

"Props are for fakers," Deidre said. "Shall we get started?"

Ethan took a breath. Then he pulled out all the money in his pocket, piled it on the table, and told Madame Deidre exactly what he'd told the others.

"This is all my cash—three hundred bucks and change. It's all yours if you say the exact words I'm dying to hear."

Yep, Sonia's plan was that simple. Easy money for one tiny little answer. Surely *any* Scam worth her salt would be thinking to her voice right now, *Three hundred bucks? Tell the guy in the turtle costume what he wants to hear!*

And, of course, the answer Ethan craved was, *Hey, I'm a Scam too!*

Nobody else would say those words in millions years of guessing. It was sheer elegance in its simplicity. Sonia was a freaking genius.

Deidre smiled. "You're on. But it may take a second."

When she closed her eyes, Ethan and Sonia exchanged glances.

Deidre had to be fake. The voice didn't take time. And what kind of psychic said, "You're on"?

They waited. Ethan tried not to gaze at the seriously disturbing puppets hanging from the ceiling. One looked just like his old gym teacher at Cambria Junior High.

"Shit," Deidre said at last. "It's not coming to me."

"Ha." Ethan reached for the money, disappointed and also relieved.

"But I do have something to tell you," Deidre added. "You will get everything you want. And yet you'll lose the very thing that makes you special."

"That's pretty generic," Ethan said. "And what does it even mean?"

"Everything," Deidre said. "Or nothing. The choice is yours."

Ethan groaned. They'd bombed out again.

"Yeah, no. That's *not* what I wanted hear." He shoveled the money back into his pocket, except for one twenty-dollar bill. Even fakers needed to eat.

But when he offered it, Deidre held up her hands.

"Keep it, Turtle Boy," she said. "Any friend of Sonia Sonic's is a friend of mine. Besides, I've got a feeling you'll need it soon enough."

Ha. Off target again. He was a Scam—apparently the one and only Scam. He could get money anytime.

And maybe this fortune-teller racket was where he could go for the big bucks. If this girl could make a living spouting nonsense like that, imagine what the voice could rake in.

Deidre reaffixed her veil and stood. She ushered them to the door. As Sonia moved to step past, Deidre hugged her.

"Your blog will do great things," Deidre said.

"Really?" Sonia asked.

Deidre shrugged. "Maybe. Blogs aren't really what they used to be. And Twitter's all trolls now."

"I know, right?" Sonia said.

Ethan waved Deidre off as she tried to hug him, too.

A moment later he and Sonia were back in the alley, which no longer seemed creepy at all.

Sonia said, "That was—"

"Totally crap," Ethan supplied. "It's like she wasn't even trying."

"She was awesome!" Sonia argued. "But no, I guess she wasn't another Scam."

Ethan shook his head. "Not with a capital letter, no."

"Like I said yesterday, is being unique so bad?"

Ethan shrugged. "Being alone blows."

"You're not alone, Ethan." Sonia looked at him. Really looked at him, in a way that made him nervous. "You've got me."

Ethan tried to laugh it off, but Sonia stared him down.

"Um," he said after a nervous moment of silence. "Got to get back. Time for whatever sucktastic plan Glorious Leader has come up with."

Sonia blinked. "You mean Nate, right?"

"You've met the guy—you tell me."

Sonia laughed and Ethan joined in. For a moment he felt like there was someone on his side. Someone he could joke around with, someone to distract him from how serious his situation was, while still hoping in her heart that he'd make it out okay.

He wished he could say just the right thing to make Sonia stay with him forever. But he didn't want to use the voice. And the voice was the only surefire way Ethan knew to say anything.

So, yet again, Ethan Thomas Cooper's life was set in suck mode.

"Hey, um," he finally said. "In case I don't get another chance, I wanted to say thanks. For helping me. It was a really smart plan."

"But it didn't work," Sonia sighed. "And it took me all night to come up with it."

Ethan grinned. "You thought about me all night?"

"Well, I thought about omniscient superpowers in general," Sonia said. "But as we now know, that's pretty much just you."

She punched him again.

"Anyway, we're friends, right?" she said. "We're supposed to help each other out."

Ethan felt a little part of himself die. He had enough friends already, and mostly they didn't particularly like him.

"Sure," he said, trying to think of something *friendly* to say. "Listen, if you ever run into my sister back in Cambria, or my mom, can you tell them that . . . I love them."

Sonia got very still. "That sounds pretty final, Ethan. Are you guys hitting the road again?"

"No. But it could all go sideways tomorrow." Ethan shrugged. "You can never be sure what's—"

But then he stopped talking, because Sonia was kissing him, and not at all like a friend.

CHAPTER 49
ANONYMOUS

AFTER THE GIRL LEFT, HE STAYED FOR A LONG time at the edge of things, fighting against the pull of the Nowhere.

The girl had been right—this vast crowd was dangerous. A whirlpool that could suck him in. Here at Mardi Gras, people were after their own little slice of anonymity. The right to drink and dance and misbehave, and have it all forgotten the day after tomorrow. To leave the world behind without a care.

The force of all that willful oblivion threatened to pull him away. But a spark of certainty held the boy firm—a promise he'd made. He was meant to stay in the world. He had a purpose here.

If he could only remember it.

He couldn't remember his own name, was the problem.

The only name he knew was the one that had kept him from following the Anonymous girl into the Nowhere.

"Flicker," he kept saying.

Until finally the answer came.

"Thibault?"

And he was tumbling backward away from the cliff edge, falling back against another body, becoming himself again.

She wrapped him up in her arms, in her familiar scent.

"Where did you *go*?" Her mask was half pushed up, and tears streaked her face.

"Flicker," Thibault said again, dazed. He looked around at the street corner. "I was here the whole time."

She pulled back and struck his chest once with an open hand. He'd never felt more in his body. "You were *gone*, Thibault! You're lucky I found you!"

"You found me," he repeated softly.

"I've been looking for hours! Stumbling around, feeling for you, *smelling* for you, everyone thinking I was drunk off my ass. It was worse than in those woods—I'd thought you'd left me again."

"There was a girl," Thibault said.

She drew a racking breath, thought a moment, like she half remembered. "Tell me what happened."

He put his arms around her, steadying himself as much as Flicker. "She was Anonymous, like me. I had to follow her—"

"Bullshit," Flicker interrupted. "What you have to do is

keep yourself *here*. It didn't cross your mind that another Anon might be dangerous?"

Thibault shook his head. It hadn't occurred to him at all.

"I'm back. I'm here. It's okay." He kissed the top of her head. He didn't even know how frightened he should be. What had just happened?

He looked over his shoulder, trying to fix the memory in his mind.

Rien—that was her name. But there was no sign of her, just the swilling Mardi Gras crowds in their gaudy costumes and their masks, some eerie, some beautiful, some grotesque. A nightmare world of pretend.

He closed his eyes. "She was just about to tell me something. Piper's plan. The purple and the gold. What everything meant."

Flicker pulled closer. "She works for Piper?"

Memories were falling back, but in fragments. "She used to. But whatever Piper's planning has her freaked. Bad enough that she . . ."

"That she might help us stop it?" Flicker provided.

Thibault shook his head, remembering the shudder in Rien's voice, like when he himself talked about Quinton Wallace. "It freaked her out enough that she went away. She's gone."

"Gone? Like what happened to you?"

"I don't know. I can't see her anywhere." He took Flicker

by the shoulders. "If Piper's plan is that scary, we should get back to finding Verity!"

"We found her. Nate texted—we're going in tonight. And there's something else I should tell you. . . ."

Her voice trailed away, and Thibault steered them into a little park, a tiny pocket of less chaos than the street.

"I saw the guy from the cemetery," she said. She was holding his elbow tight, like they were walking along the roof edge of a tall building. "The one the Feds wanted. I talked to him, and it turns out he's a reversed *me*."

"He's a Flicker too?" Thibault came to a halt. "The kid who turned beautiful?"

"Yeah." She made a face up at him. "Can you believe I level up into . . . a raging beauty?"

"Yes," he said.

A laugh burst out of her, and she turned away, shaking her head.

But this was Flicker, after all. He could still see her addressing the Zeroes before that last battle at the Dish. Magnificent and in command.

"Ridiculous, right?" she muttered. "Let's sit down. I need to get my head straight before we go back and deal with Nate."

As they sat on the bench, Thibault realized something.

"We both just met someone with our own power. First time ever, exact same day."

"Huh. What are the odds?"

He looked around at the swirling crowd. How many more of them were Zeroes? "It's not random. It's Mardi Gras. Nate was right about coming here."

"I guess. But only because we need to knock this evil Bellwether on her ass."

Thibault nodded. "You should have seen Rien when she tried to tell me about Piper's plan. She had so much guilt about helping, it was enough to suck her away into the Nowhere."

"More proof that Piper has to be stopped," Flicker said.

"Will Nate believe that?"

"I don't know. Half the time he sounds like he's in love with Piper. And being in prison didn't help his opinion of nonpowered humanity." Flicker sat up straighter on the park bench. "But we have to stop her, with or without him."

Seeing her fierce expression, Thibault grinned. "You know, I wouldn't mind seeing you level up."

She half pulled away. "I thought surface appearances weren't your thing, Zen Boy."

"They aren't," he said. "But it's not like you'll turn into some corporate pop star. More like an avenging angel—flaming sword, turning people into pillars of salt."

She laughed, leaning back in to him. "I can't even tell if that's a compliment!"

"Trust me, it is." He stood. "Come on. Let's go see what Nate's planning for tonight."

CHAPTER 50
CRASH

"NO PHONES IN THERE," CHIZARA SAID. HER SENSES coiled around the ruined power station. "No wifi, either."

"Maybe the FBI has a pet Crash," Nate said. "Someone who'd spot an abandoned building blaring with tech. So Piper keeps it dark."

Chizara shrugged. "Or maybe she's just a good boss. Doesn't want her Makers dealing with all the noise."

Nate lowered the binoculars and looked at her.

She shrugged. "You're an okay boss too, Nate."

She turned from him and sent her power at Piper's headquarters again. No pesky phones, but so much glorious old tech in there—all of it scaled for giants! Deactivated turbines and coal chutes, the great yards of transformers on the far side. Even lifeless, the ancient shapes of it hulked in her mind. She would love to explore those ghost-systems, reverse engineering how they had all fit together in the olden days.

"We could have the wrong place," Ethan said. He'd been twitchy all evening, like he had somewhere better to be.

"No, this is it," Chizara said. "There's a trickle of juice running through the wires. They've got lights, and maybe intercoms."

"And a ton of people," Kelsie said.

"A hundred, at least," Chizara breathed. Even from this range she could see a galaxy of hearts inside.

"Want me to go ahead?" Thibault spoke up, appearing out of the shadows. "I could scout around."

"She knows about Stalkers," Flicker said. "We stick together. And keep your phones off!"

The Zeroes slipped through a ragged fence into the weedy concrete lot beside the power plant. It was full of moonlit scooters and bikes, junked cars, and a few newer vehicles. Perfect cover for sneaking.

"Think these all belong to Piper's crew?" Ethan whispered.

"I could crash them, just in case," Chizara said. "Just like I'm going to wreck that machine of hers."

"Don't wreck anything till we find out what her plan is," Nate said firmly.

"Like we haven't heard enough!" Chizara hissed.

The empty satellite-dish box had been plenty for her. Piper planned on projecting powers, either fueled by or pointed at the massive Mardi Gras crowds. That couldn't be good. Flicker's pretty boy had talked about starting from scratch—great for making cakes, not so much for industrial society. And Anon's quotes from his mystery friend had sounded apocalyptic.

What more evidence did Nate need?

"Once we have Verity, we can find the truth," Nate said. "Until then, do no harm."

Chizara rolled her eyes. Using her own words against her was a cheap shot. Well, she could always crash the damn machine *without* Glorious Leader's permission.

"Okay, I'm getting some eyes," Flicker said when they were halfway across the lot. "Everyone's hard at work. They're organizing everything on paper. Clipboards, checklists, very old-school."

Chizara had to smile. *No noisy devices.*

Maybe if she'd been born here in New Orleans, she'd be in there right now, working in electronic peace and quiet. . . .

No. She didn't believe in tearing everything down just to get your way. What Piper wanted was anarchy and chaos.

"We need to see if Verity's okay," Nate said. "Give Flick a location, Crash."

Chizara came to a halt, pressed her power harder.

"It's weird. I can't feel the tracker anywhere. Maybe one of the Makers noticed it? But there's also couple of blank spots in the building—on the second floor near the front. They could be power-shielded. Flicker?"

"I see what you mean. Can't get inside them, so they must be shielded. But I found Piper." Flicker came to a halt, concentrating. "In the front of the building. Ground floor. She just looked up at your parade float. Like a big truck covered with Mardi Gras bunting?"

"That's the one," Chizara said, her eyes closed. She felt it in there too.

The machine was powered down, but she could sense it hulking behind all that brick and mortar, waiting to be activated. The traceries of juiceless wiring, the aluminum curves, and the steel feed horn of the transmitter dish.

A little closer and she could pull its guts to pieces.

"It's got a big sign on it," Flicker said. "'Krewe de New World Order.' Piper's not into subtlety, is she?"

"That's how we get in." Nate was pointing at a ground-floor window covered with a metal grate. "Think we can pry it off?"

"No problem," Thibault said.

Chizara shook her head. "Don't touch it."

All the windows had sizzling lines of current around them. Some kind of sensor . . .

A motion alarm? High voltage? Unknown Crash magic?

The nearby door had a fancy lock—standard biometrics, so that non-Crash members of Piper's crew could use their fingerprints to get in. But the windows were simply designed to keep people out.

"It's going to take some work," she said.

"Is there time for a pee break?" Ethan asked.

"Scam," Flicker said.

"I know, I know. Should've gone back where we parked the pickup."

Their conversation blurred to nonsense in the background as Chizara pushed her mind into the window alarms, mapped out their tricks and traps.

So much sheer near-nonsensical creativity had gone into this! All those redundant-looking functions, maybe backups? At the center of it all was a black box her power couldn't penetrate—it was shielded. Something crucial had to be lurking inside, something unexpected and beautiful.

Then she felt Kelsie startle, a jitter that pulsed through the group, dragging her mind back to the real world.

"Guys," Kelsie said. "It's not just this building."

"What do you mean?" Nate asked.

Kelsie was staring across the street. "Those other warehouses, they're full of people too."

Nate shrugged. "Could just be civilians working."

"Regular people wouldn't be this intense. Nobody at a warehouse is ever this *committed* to what they're doing."

"Oh shit." Flicker leaned back against Thibault, as if her legs had gone rubbery. "It's all the way down the block, as far as I can see."

"*What* is?" Nate whispered.

348

"Food, mostly. Canned stuff on pallets, boxes stacked to the ceiling. Medical supplies—bandages and disinfectant. Crutches, even surgical instruments. And survival gear. Tents and sleeping bags. Knives and hatchets and . . . guns."

Ethan went wide-eyed. "What the hell?"

Chizara swallowed. She could feel the low-tech activity from here—forklifts and conveyor belts. Heavy stuff moving around.

"Boxes of ammo—shelves, *rooms* of it!" Flicker flung an arm out. "That long warehouse near the water? It's full of nothing but bottled water. This whole area is Prepper Central."

"Except they're not prepping for a hurricane," Thibault said in a hollow voice. "They're bringing down the disaster themselves. That's what scared Rien away."

"Holy crap," Ethan said. "I *told* you we should've gone to Mexico! We should've built our own bunker and gone underground!"

Chizara stared at Nate. "So you still think we should hold fire on that transmitter?"

He met her gaze, his eyes invisible in shadow. For a few seconds he was silent, his uncertainty curdling the air around them.

When he finally spoke, she hardly recognized the snarl in his voice.

"Let's get in there and burn this sucker down."

CHAPTER 51
CRASH

TEN MINUTES LATER, CHIZARA WAS A SWEATY, shaking mess, but she'd mapped every wire and circuit of the window alarm.

She was as ready as she'd ever be.

"Okay," she said. "I'm about to go in. Get ready to run."

"Run?" Ethan shook his head. "I thought we were sneaking."

"It's an *alarm*, Scam," she hissed. "If I blow this, they'll know we're here."

He opened his mouth, but she waved a hand.

"Don't say a *thing*. One wisecrack at the wrong moment and I'll slip up."

Chizara turned back to the window and grasped the locks in her mind, staring sightlessly at the moonlit concrete. She checked through the circuits again, made sure she hadn't missed anything, lingered on the black box.

Speak to me, she thought at it.

But it gave up nothing.

Still—there was only one wire that led into the box. If she cut it off from the rest of the system, it had no way to complain.

She focused her power on that one slender wire, probed the metal gently. Plain old ordinary copper.

With a twitch of power, she snipped through the wire.

The black box let out a little squawk of signal.

"Oh crap," Chizara said.

"Crap what?" Ethan asked.

She waved him silent. From the box's labyrinthine depths, it had signaled its failure—wirelessly. She'd been a fool, thinking that just because they didn't want phones buzzing around, Essence and her Crashes wouldn't use a single hidden antenna.

But it had only been that tiny squawk. Maybe that lone, vulnerable wire hadn't been a trap. . . .

And then into her brain rushed madness.

It was like the buzz of crashing a city, to the power of ten. It hit Chizara and decompressed into her head, her chest, her loins. Pure hot bliss lit up her body, springing her from her crouch, arching her back.

She felt like she was hanging a foot off the ground, out flat and rigid, power jagging out all around her. Jolt after jolt went through her. The air rang with cries. She couldn't tell which were hers, which weren't.

And she couldn't stop it. They'd stored this power up somehow, maybe in all those ancient transformers on the building's far side, and the whole *building* was broadcasting it now, soaking her with bucket after bucket of buzz.

It was like holding a live wire, the power contracting her muscles in a grip that would surely snap her bones. This trap had been designed just for Crashes, and she'd sprung it, and now she was helpless in its grip.

Dimly she felt the others try to save her, to pull her out of the seizure. Their shaking and pinching was featherlight compared to the force racketing through her. The trap had crashed her body, just like she'd imagined crashing all those wisps of hearts and nervous systems.

Alarms were ringing, people shouting, distant behind the frothing of her blood, the thudding of her bones, the ecstatic screaming of her muscles.

She didn't want to be saved. This was *everything*.

But then she was coming out of it, her lungs raggedly pumping, her muscles booting back up. Her friends were dragging her away. Fleeing her mistake.

Chizara laughed like a madwoman, floppy as a length of cloth. Her legs wouldn't work, skidding like a rag doll's across the concrete, bouncing over the sprouting weeds. Her brain pushed commands at them. They didn't listen.

Floodlights blasted down, bleaching everything stark white, the road and the parking lot, the broken windows and crazy old brickwork of the plant—and Thibault and Nate carrying her. The HQ door had burst open and people were bundling out.

"Look!" she tried to shout, but it came out squashed and foolish. "Got their own army of Craigs!"

"Oh my God, that's *Glitch*!" Kelsie said, snatching a look behind. Her panic flitted across Chizara's ecstasy, not ruffling it in the least.

"Drop her, Anon," Nate said. "I'll stay."

Her right arm was dropped. It didn't hurt to be dropped. Nothing hurt when you were made of champagne bubbles. She flopped there, admiring the angles of the warehouse corner, the plant's two big smokestacks towering among the stars.

"Just leave me," Chizara said, trying to sound sensible.

"Nate!" Kelsie's voice. "We can't—"

"Move!" Nate screamed with every ounce of command he had, and Kelsie fled onward.

Chizara didn't mind—champagne couldn't hold a grudge.

Nate crouched above her, a spotlight flowering over his head, lighting his prison haircut.

"You're a *good* boss!" Chizara said delightedly. Against her back the concrete vibrated with the approaching thunder of Piper's crew and the fading footsteps of her own team, retreating . . .

Retreating toward the pickup.

"So noble," she burbled to Nate.

The noise, the floodlights, the warm rush of the seizure's

afterglow, they were all going to engulf her like a wave. She was going to be dazzled to death. And she was so, so ready to accept the dazzlement.

With her last scrap of sense she reached around the corner, sprang the door locks on the pickup, kicked the engine into life.

"Easy-*peasy*!" she murmured.

And then new figures were looming over her and Nate, and she was dissolving in their hands, into shreds of streaming light.

CHAPTER 52
MOB

"FIRE HYDRANT!" FLICKER SHOUTED FROM THE backseat.

"I see it! They're *my* eyes!" Ethan screamed, and spun the pickup truck right.

Kelsie clutched the passenger-door handle—the truck jolted beneath her, leaping over the curb and hurtling straight at a chain-link fence. The fence hit with a bone-jarring *thwack*, wrapped around the truck, then slid away under the front wheels with an unholy scraping sound.

The truck rattled across the empty lot, swerving around patches of broken concrete and scrubby plants. Behind them, the glare of floodlights glowed in the sky. Was Piper's crew starting up all those motorcycles and cars to give chase?

Chizara was back there—injured and confused—and Nate had given himself up to stay with her!

Kelsie faced forward again: A silhouette loomed.

"Look out!" she shouted.

Ethan jerked the steering wheel left—too late. With a crunch, a rusty old shopping cart spun into the air, landed on its side, and skidded off into the darkness. It had taken out the truck's right headlight, dimming the light in front of them.

"Why is there so much *crap* everywhere?" Ethan cried.

Kelsie reached over and took his arm, trying to think calming thoughts. But Chizara flashed before her eyes—the way her whole body had stiffened and shuddered, like someone being electrocuted.

Piper's lair was a fortress, and it held an army. Going up against her had been madness.

Kelsie began to shudder with delayed panic, but the Curve didn't take hold. Not enough people in the car—thank God. The last thing Ethan needed was a feedback loop while driving.

If you could call this driving.

At the other side of the empty lot, a thin line of stunted trees came at them. Ethan gunned the engine and aimed between two of them.

"Can you slow—" Flicker started.

Branches whipped at Kelsie's window. The side mirror snapped and dangled, thudding against the door. And then they were through.

"—down?"

The truck jolted off the curb and skidded onto asphalt, tires squealing. But finally Ethan had control, straightening out and heading away from the river. More fences sagged in front of a warehouse with smashed windows and graffiti-marked walls.

"Fast is good!" he cried in triumph.

"Zara and Nate," Kelsie murmured. "We just left them there. She could be *dying*."

"That trap was designed for Crashes," Flicker said. "Do you really think they'd make it lethal? Kill one of their own?"

Kelsie shook her head. But she didn't know why any Zero would create something so awful. And the *joy* their mob had felt as they'd poured out of the power station . . .

The remaining headlight caught a pile of trash in the middle of the road. Ethan swerved, and Kelsie slid sideways into the door. A jolt of pain went through her collarbone.

The truck was squealing now, a low whine coming from the front left wheel.

"Shit, Ethan," Flicker muttered. "Where'd you learn to drive?"

"My dad. He sucks at it too."

Kelsie sank back in her seat. Fast cars were fun with a happy crowd. Less so with panicked Zeroes trying to outrun a gang of psychos, leaving their friends behind.

"So Piper won't hurt them?" she asked.

"Never," Flicker said. "She needs Zeroes to rebuild the world."

Ethan snorted. "I notice we didn't stick around to test that theory."

"Because we don't *want* to help her!" Flicker cried.

"But she's a Bellwether," he argued. "You know how cold-blooded Nate can be."

Flicker shook her head. "Nate tries to convince people to join him. He wouldn't hurt another Zero."

"Tell that to Quinton Wallace!" Ethan cried. "Nate may not have pulled the trigger, but he *tried*!"

They flew through an intersection, rusted warehouses on either side. Parked semis and a Dumpster. No signs of life this late, this far from the center of town.

It felt bleak and empty to Kelsie. At least Piper's headquarters had been full of life and intensity. She hoped they knew how to help Chizara recover from their trap.

"Keep your eyes on the road," Flicker said. "Not the rearview."

"Keep your eyes out of my head!" he replied. "There's a motorcycle back there. I think it's following us."

"Mob, take a look," Flicker ordered. "You focus on driving, Scam."

Kelsie turned, and for a moment only saw dark and empty asphalt. Then a lone motorcycle cornered into view. The rider wore no helmet. She was a light-skinned black girl.

"I know that face. . . ."

"Why only one?" Flicker asked. "They had a shitload of vehicles!"

At that moment the engine sputtered and stalled. The truck kept rolling, dashboard lights flickering.

"Piece of crap!" Ethan shouted, frantically trying to restart it.

The car radio came to life, blaring static. Kelsie stabbed at the controls. The buttons were useless, but the radio began to skip between stations. Music, talk, some kind of preacher.

"It's her!" Kelsie shouted over the noise. "She's a Crash! The head Crash. Essence!"

Ethan swore. "So that means we're—"

The engine gurgled to life.

"Huh." Ethan put his hands back on the steering wheel. The truck was picking up speed, turning, rattling onto the sidewalk.

A moment later they had turned a hundred eighty degrees.

"Scam?" Flicker asked.

"It's not me!" He grabbed the wheel harder. "Power steering, man!"

The motorcycle ahead turned around as well, Essence giving them a smile before speeding off.

"She's taking us back to Piper," Kelsie said.

Flicker leaned forward. "Hit the brakes!"

A squeal filled the truck as brake pads clamped down, fighting the engine, and Kelsie was thrown forward against her seat belt. But then the car spasmed ahead again.

"Power brakes, too!" Ethan shouted. "Any other genius ideas?"

Kelsie reached across and yanked hard on the parking brake. The engine strained, but the truck still roared forward, convulsing.

"We're moving too fast to jump." Flicker rattled her door handle. "And this piece of crap has power locks!"

Ahead of them, Essence turned right, throwing them a smile. She was enjoying the fight.

As the truck followed the motorcycle around the corner, a burst of fresh panic went through Kelsie. She was trapped, sealed up in metal and glass in the middle of nowhere with engine and brakes at war, the truck jolting and shuddering. Captive out here in the empty darkness.

She tore open the glove compartment and scrabbled for anything to break the window—the cold metal of a flashlight filled her hand.

Perfect.

Kelsie reared back and brought the butt of the flashlight against the glass beside her. Nothing but a loud smack.

Anger filled her veins like fire, and Kelsie swung again. This time the glass buckled, spiderwebbed.

The next blow shattered it into a thousand tiny diamonds. A sudden cold wind blew though the cab.

Ethan looked over at her, impressed. "Okay. Now all we have to do is stop this thing."

"Crash the truck," Flicker said.

Ethan turned to face her. "Are you nuts?"

"It's the only way to stop it," Kelsie said. "Essence has to drive us *and* her motorcycle, so we mess with her. Next time we're about to turn, I pop the brake and you hit the gas. If we jump the curb hard enough, we'll break an axle!"

"We are softer than axles!" Ethan cried.

"Do it, Scam," Flicker commanded

He didn't answer.

Before them, the motorcycle was turning right again. Splayed out straight ahead was a small park surrounded by a wrought-iron fence.

"This is our shot!" Flicker cried. "Three, two, one . . ."

Kelsie released the parking brake as Ethan planted both feet on the gas pedal, his hands over his face. The acceleration pushed Kelsie back into her seat.

The wheel spun on its own, but too late to turn the rocketing truck. At the curb, Kelsie felt the passenger side lifting into the air beneath her, the left tires skidding across the sidewalk with a birdlike shriek. Then the truck crunched sideways into the fence.

Kelsie's teeth snapped shut, and she was thrown toward Ethan—her left elbow hit him hard. The seat belt snapped against her torso, knocking the wind out of her.

The truck fell back onto all four wheels. Kelsie's head bounced against the headrest.

No airbags.

For a moment there was nothing but quiet and the ticking sound of the engine settling.

Kelsie sat, gasping. Her vision spun. She felt sick to her stomach.

"Everyone okay?" she croaked, when she had the nausea under control.

Ethan groaned. "No."

"Everyone out!" Flicker reported.

Kelsie undid her seat belt and squeezed through her own window, stumbled on solid ground. Flicker knocked out more glass from the shattered back window, then emerged onto the truck bed.

Both of them turned back to where Ethan still sat in the driver's seat.

"Scam," she said. "Move!"

There was an answering groan from Ethan.

Kelsie walked around to the driver's side, wincing as her bruised muscles flexed. There was a narrow space between the truck and the wrought-iron fence.

She gasped when she saw what the fence had done to Ethan's door. Like a giant bird of prey had raked it with iron talons.

She reached for the handle. The door angled open with a pained metal shriek.

"Are you okay?" she asked.

Ethan turned to stare at her. His eyes were glassy.

"We have to *go*," Flicker urged.

Kelsie reached to help him out. Her whole body felt made of jelly. Ethan eased himself down from the seat with a grunt.

"Damn," came a voice. "You guys trying to *kill* yourselves?"

Essence sat there on her motorcycle, staring at them from the middle of the street.

A dark thought crossed Kelsie's mind—did Essence know what Zara had realized, the trick of crashing hearts and brains?

"Stay away from us!" Kelsie cried. "You know what I am!"

"Harmless is what you are," Essence said with a laugh. "No crowd here."

Ethan looked up, his eyes glassy. "There will be soon. Crowds love accidents. Blood excites them."

A shudder went through Kelsie. She knew it was the voice, but it was the creepiest thing she'd ever heard.

Ethan pointed at the convenience store down the block. A few people had emerged to check out the sound of the crash.

"Fine, I'm gone." Essence grasped the bike's handles, revved the engine. "But stay away from us!"

With a last nervous look at Ethan, she sped away into the night.

"Nice work, Scam," Flicker said. "Now look for a car to . . . what's wrong with your vision?"

No answer.

Kelsie turned. He was just standing there. His arms hung loosely and his face was slack in the moonlight. "Ethan?"

He didn't answer. Just started walking away from the wreck like a zombie.

Kelsie ran to him, pulled him to a halt. She touched his

temple and felt something warm and sticky. Her hand came back dark with blood.

"Call an ambulance," she said.

"That means cops." Flicker came toward them. "That's a stolen truck. They'll hand us to the Feds!"

"He needs a hospital!"

"We need to *disappear*. Anon, can you . . ." Flicker's voice faded.

Kelsie looked around. Of course—Thibault! She didn't remember him getting out of the car. Had he ever been *in* the car?

"Thibault, are you here?" she cried.

Flicker waited a moment for an answer, looking stricken.

"He must've stayed behind," she finally said. "Or Piper got him. Or maybe he . . ."

She shook her head.

"Find a car to hot-wire, Kelsie. Let's get Ethan home."

CHAPTER 53

BELLWETHER

"RELAX," PIPER SAID. "YOUR FRIEND WILL BE FINE."

Nate looked up at her, trying not to show how dizzy he was. Glitch had hit him with a jolt of her brain-addling power out on the vacant lot. His whole body felt wrong, like someone had replaced his organs with off-brand duplicates. Even his clothes seemed borrowed, ill-fitting and unfamiliar.

"She'd better be," Nate managed. He tried to stand straighter as he looked around.

He was in Piper's headquarters at last.

The broad concrete floor was bright and buzzing. Harsh work lights illuminated a parade float in the middle, decorated with purple, green, and gold bunting. Workers swarmed in all directions, and the dark corners were full of barrels and boxes.

But everyone spared a splinter of their focus for Piper, who soaked up their adulation effortlessly.

"Chizara is safe. We don't hurt special people." Piper swung herself down from the float, navigating the glittering trusses like an acrobat. "Except Swarms, of course."

Nate stared up at her. "And kidnapping doesn't count as hurting?"

"You were trespassing. Did you want me to call the cops?" She smiled, her glorious attention narrowing on him. "You're still a wanted man, Nataniel."

He tried to sound defiant. "Verity wasn't trespassing when you took her."

Piper shrugged. "She was working with the FBI, trying to grab one of my people. Trying to make him spill the beans. Can't have them breaking down my door this close to show-time. Also, I needed her for my little project."

She gestured at the parade float behind her.

Half a dozen other Zeroes—Crashes, presumably—were working on the float. It was built onto a truck chassis, and the hood was open, revealing an engine alongside things Nate couldn't recognize. The Crashes were wrapping the interior in a shiny hexagonal metal mesh.

The biggest part of the structure was a huge bowl, eight feet across, brightly painted, and full of strings of Mardi Gras beads. Three raised seats sat behind that—green, purple, and gold. Across the front hung a crooked sign with big sparkly letters:

KREWE DE NEW WORLD ORDER.

"What is this thing?" Nate asked.

"It's called Nexus," Piper said. "It's like me and you."

"I don't follow."

"We channel a crowd's power. Take all that unfocused energy and make something useful out of it." She reached up to run a hand along the giant bowl of beads, and Nate saw that beneath its garish paint job, it was just a satellite dish. "Nexus is just a high-tech version of the same trick."

"You mean it's a machine with *superpowers*?"

Piper rolled her eyes. "Nataniel, haven't you realized? *All* our powers come from machines. From the simple truth that humanity is connected now—by our phones, our feeds, our endless pinging each other with texts and tweets and posts. We are *Homo nexus*."

"Seriously?" He let out a laugh. "This is about the internet?"

She sighed. "That word makes you sound so old, Nate. I'm not talking about the wires, but about the encircling flood of data that binds humanity. People used to think that one day it would all become conscious and start talking to us. But instead it gave us superpowers. A *much* more interesting outcome, don't you think?"

Nate didn't answer. His brain, which still thrummed from being glitched, was now infected with Piper's madness as well. It all sounded ridiculous, except that this was exactly how Chizara described the world she saw—a vast chorus of connections, a noisy sea of information sloshing between humans and their devices.

Crash's power had always seemed different from the rest—more about machines than people—but maybe it was at the center of them all, the key to understanding the others. And that was why Piper had gathered twenty Crashes in her city.

"That glitch that was supposed to happen in the year two thousand? Y2K?" Piper said. "We were it."

"Huh. Okay." Nate started at the parade float. "So this machine is a . . . Charismatic?"

"Yes, a—what did your friends call you? *Bellwether?* You know that's a kind of sheep, right?"

Nate sighed. "It's the head sheep, okay? But yeah, it never really worked as a name."

"Another symptom of your small thinking, Nataniel." Piper shook her head. "This machine is a change in scale. You and I are a couple of matches, and it's a flamethrower, hooked up to the biggest source of fuel there is—Mardi Gras."

He managed to hold steady against the wattage of her gaze. "What are you actually planning to *do*?"

She turned toward the three raised seats on the float. "Nexus will project three powers. Three things the world desperately needs."

"That's why you grabbed Verity? You want to force *truth* on New Orleans?"

"Not just my city. The whole world." Her smile was radiant.

"Think of it. No politicians lying about how they'll help us rebuild. No crooked businessmen stealing our houses. No lies."

"Maybe. But total honesty might lead to some awkward situations."

Piper shrugged. "More than awkward, I hope. But the effect won't last forever. Maybe a few months, maybe a year. But even a *day* with no bullshit would change the world forever."

Nate finally had to turn away from Piper. Her certainty was infectious. "Yeah, it might. But I've got a feeling you're not storing up food and guns for an outbreak of honesty, are you?"

"No." Her smiled faded. "You were there when Davey Masterson died, weren't you?"

"Every night in my dreams," Nate said.

"Then you know how my friend Troy's power works. But he's managed to reverse himself. Something a show-off like Davey never would've considered."

Nate shook his head. "You mean, he can turn things into . . . *not* money?"

"Clumsily put. But yes, money is the most fragile weapon our bosses wield. Once we stop believing in all those dead presidents, they're just paper."

"Jesus, Piper." Nate took a step backward. "Troy's going to *break money?*"

She nodded. "After the hurricane fucked up my town, it was the bankers that twisted the knife. I'm going to return the favor."

Nate closed his eyes. Suddenly the stockpiled food and medicine and guns all made sense. If people stopped believing in money, even for a week, he couldn't imagine what would happen.

Would people still feed each other out of the goodness of their hearts? Would doctors trade medical care for chickens?

"Think, Nataniel," she said. "No debts. No stock market to manipulate. No one tossed out of their home because they miss a payment."

"I think you're missing a step," he said. "The part where everyone starves."

Piper gave him a smile. "Not everyone."

Nate swallowed. "Should I even ask what the third power is?"

"You should. Because that's where things get *really* interesting."

CHAPTER 54
FLICKER

"GET ICE ON IT!" CAME KELSIE'S VOICE FROM THE Barrows' kitchen.

She and Ethan were in there, her vision darting around for a hand towel to put the ice in. Ethan's eyes stared at the mist inside the open freezer with that sickly waver they'd had since the accident.

Accident. Flicker pulled back inside her own head.

Not an accident. Crashing had been her brilliant idea.

But the brutal fact was, Flicker had bigger things to worry about than Ethan's concussion—Piper's city-crashing parade could be starting in a few hours.

She could still see those stacks of boxes in her mind's eye. Thousands of them filling the warehouses near Piper's headquarters. Food and medicine. Guns and ammunition.

Piper was expecting everything to shut down, leaving her in charge.

Flicker sent her vision into the next house—Mrs. Lavoir was awake and watching. She must have heard the three of them getting back in the middle of the night, in yet another new car, one of them drunkenly staggering. Her eyes were focused on the kitchen window, watching Ethan's silhouette as he applied an ice-filled towel to his head.

Then the eyes went to the phone in the hall, where the Barrows' vacation number was still on that sticky note. Ethan's number, really, but that only meant she'd get a disconnected burner and call the cops.

Unless Thibault had snuck over and updated it since they'd last switched out the . . .

"Thibault," Flicker said, remembering again. "He's still back there."

"You think they got him?" Kelsie asked. She was leading Ethan into the living room, the ice rattling in the towel. The two sat heavily on the couch.

"They couldn't have seen him," Flicker said. "Piper's army would give him all the Curve he'd need."

"Unless he got glitched," Ethan said.

"Or . . . ," Kelsie began. "You know."

Flicker stared at her. What if he'd faded out, drifted into nothingness? Because an imminent disaster was too much for him to face?

"He'll be fine," Flicker said. "He's probably rescuing Zara and Nate right now."

"We should go back," Kelsie said.

"Knock yourselves out," Ethan said, his words slurring a little. "But don't expect any help from me. I am pre–knocked out."

"We'll take you to a hospital on the way," Kelsie offered.

Flicker jumped inside Ethan's eyes—they blurred the room double.

Definitely concussed. What was she supposed to do?

"We can drop you at Emergency," Flicker said, "and leave before anyone sees us."

"Too pretty for jail," he mumbled.

Right—jail. Ethan had no ID, so someone would call the cops. He'd be arrested, taken to the local FBI headquarters, and presented with the choice between prison or working for Phan.

Flicker knew which Ethan would choose. And Scam would be even worse in an interrogation room than Verity.

Of course, this might all be irrelevant in a few hours.

"We can't just sit here," Flicker said.

"But Piper's got Glitch on her side," Kelsie said. "And all those Crashes. She has an army!"

"You know who else has an army?" Ethan said. "Like, a *real* one? The US government. Why don't we call the FBI?"

Flicker shook her head. "And tell them to attack an abandoned power station in the middle of the night?"

"We could tell them who we are," Ethan said. "Phan would listen to us. We nuked a supermax!"

"You think some flunky would call him at home at five a.m.?" Flicker asked. "And it would still be, 'Hi. It's your least favorite terrorists, and we'd like to tell you where some *worse* terrorists are.' That sounds like a productive conversation."

Ethan shrugged, making the ice click. "I could do it. The voice could, I mean."

"Ethan," Kelsie said, leaning forward to put a hand against his forehead. "Did you forget your power doesn't work on the—"

"I know! So take me to the hospital and let me do my thing."

Flicker stared. Was Ethan volunteering to go to jail? To sacrifice himself? His head injury had to be worse than it looked. "Are you serious?"

He shrugged. "To save a whole city, sure."

"But it wouldn't be just you," Flicker said. "If the FBI shows up at Piper's headquarters, Nate goes back to prison. We'd be making that choice for him, too."

"Like he wouldn't sacrifice one of us?" Ethan cried. "When I was tied up in the Whatever Hotel about to explode, Nate was, like, 'See you later, pal!'"

"Zara's in there too," Kelsie said softly. "How many years would she get for busting him out of a supermax?"

Flicker's head swam for a moment. Were they really talking about sacrificing three of their friends?

But then she saw the endless rows of boxes again—food, medicine, guns. A million people glitched. A whole city crashed. Maybe the whole country.

The whole world?

"Maybe it's worth it," she said.

"No," Kelsie said. "I know a better way. Talk some sense into Piper. Make her see that lots of people might die."

Flicker almost laughed. "She doesn't care about who gets in the way. She only cares about the plan!"

"That's Bellwethers for you," Ethan murmured.

Flicker shook her head. Nate would never sacrifice a whole city.

"I'm not saying *we* can convince her," Kelsie said. "But I know someone who can."

"What are you talking about?" Flicker asked.

Kelsie hesitated, then spoke carefully, softly. "Today, when we were supposed to be looking for Verity, we took a little detour to find my mom."

"Your mom?" Ethan said. "Did you find her?"

Kelsie nodded. "We did . . . and also this guy. He has a power, one that makes you *see*."

CHAPTER 55
ANONYMOUS

THIBAULT DOUBLED BACK TO THE POWER PLANT.

Flicker had been right—these guys were preparing for a straight-up apocalypse.

Slipping inside the warehouses had been easy. The long rows of loading-bay doors were open to the chill night air. Trucks were still arriving, bringing labeled boxes: survival gear, fuel, generators, emergency rations. And long, unmarked cases that had to be guns.

Piper and her crew could last for months with everything they had stored here. Maybe years.

And they weren't looking to share. The warehouses were receiving goods tonight, but they were ready to be locked down at any time—alarm systems, dogs, and lots of people.

Piper had her own army, like some kind of mad dictator. Watchful attention lines sizzled down from roof corners, loading docks, entryways. Armed men and women of all ages. Piper hadn't just been recruiting teenage Zeroes. She had mercenaries.

Piper could mint her own money, of course. She had at least one Coin, who'd honed their skills by faking the Super Bowl tickets.

How to stop all this? It was too huge, too unthinkable.

But busting out Nate and Chizara was a good place to start.

The main doors of the power plant were big enough to drive a truck through, but they were closed. All the windows had the same wiring that had zapped Chizara, so Thibault wasn't going anywhere near them.

Circling to the waterfront side of the plant, he found a smaller door with people flowing in and out. The two security guards gave him a puzzled look as he followed someone in, but he snipped away their interest.

The Curve was in full effect inside, the air hazed with attention lines. People on high alert, keeping an eye on everything. The smell of instant coffee filled the dusty hallways.

No guns or food in here. Thibault came to a whole room full of parade costumes on racks—boned and bouffant, sequined and beaded. Spiked and feathered headdresses hung on the walls. Everything was in gold, green, and purple, just like the float Chizara had described.

Just like Rien had said. What did the colors mean? Purple for justice? Green for faith . . . whatever.

These were uniforms, for an army posing as Mardi Gras revelers.

A guy was going through the racks, reeling off numbers to a girl with a clipboard. The two looked as deadly serious as army quartermasters the night before a battle.

But when the sound of a revving engine echoed down the halls, both of them went silent, their eyes alight.

The sound sputtered a moment later, but Thibault was already looking for the source. Everyone's awareness bent toward it, threads of excitement spilling over from their immediate tasks. The closer he got, the brighter the lines of attention burned.

Until there it was, framed through a large doorway—the parade float, glinting with colored foil bunting.

But above the doorway a camera pointed right at him. Thibault ducked his head, stepping back into the shadows.

Piper knew all about Stalkers, of course. She'd even had one in her army.

Maybe she was worried Rien would come creeping back to try to stop this plan. Whoever was watching that camera feed would sound an alarm if anyone unfamiliar approached the float.

Besides, Thibault was here to rescue Chizara and Nate—and maybe Verity, if he was lucky. He had to focus.

What had Crash said before trying the lock? Something about a power-shielded room on the second floor, near the front of the plant. Perfect for holding prisoners.

He went looking for the stairs.

A lone guard was posted outside the door.

The guy was a little too old to be a Zero. He looked bored, immune to the restless energy buzzing in the rest of the power plant. He kept reflexively dipping a hand into his pocket, then pulling it out empty. Of course—Piper didn't allow phones or tablets here.

Thibault couldn't see any cameras, either. A couple of prisoners weren't as important as the parade float.

He stepped lightly along the hall. Up here on the second floor there wasn't as much Curve, and each footstep summoned a subconscious shred of the guard's attention. Thibault trimmed them all away, staying out of his direct line of vision.

The door had a keyboard on the lock. It also had a little lens at eye level—for iris scanning?

Great. So Thibault needed a code *and* an eyeball? Those Crashes knew how to complicate a rescue mission.

The guard was solid, muscle-bound. A rattlesnake tattoo crawled up out of his collar. Thibault was pretty sure that the first punch landed was going to be the end of the fight. Force was out of the question.

But maybe he could spook the guy.

Thibault leaned casually against the wall and whispered as softly as he could, "What's your name?"

A shaft of troubled attention shot at him—Thibault snipped it. The guard turned away to look up the hallway. He was just the right amount of unsettled, confused.

"Your name," Thibault repeated.

The guy froze, then spoke uncertainly. "Noah?"

"Noah, I think you have a problem in there. You should check the prisoners to see if—"

"I know what you are," Noah said softly, without turning. "We trained for people like you."

Thibault felt his plan crumbling. But maybe if he kept talking . . .

"What did they tell—"

The guy's elbow swung back, catching Thibault in the ribs. The blow sent him stumbling back, sliding along the wall.

The guard turned, bringing the full glare of his attention to bear. Thibault tried to slice it away, but Noah's eyes were alight with focus.

His fist shot out at shoulder height. Thibault half dodged it, but the shallow contact sent him staggering again, until the wall at the end of the hallway thumped into his back.

He sucked in air. "Wait, I can—"

Noah was still closing in, ready to strike again. His focus was the sharpest thing Thibault had ever seen—except for at a gym once, a woman pummeling a bag, her eyes like lasers.

And this time, Thibault was the punching bag.

CHAPTER 56
MOB

"NO EYES INSIDE," FLICKER SAID. "ARE YOU SURE this is the place?"

Kelsie nodded. The building looked gloomier in the darkness, more like an old church than a home. But the handwritten sign welcoming everyone to the Clarity Circle was still on the door.

She knocked again, louder this time. No answer.

"If anyone's here, they're fast asleep," Flicker said. "Do you really think this guy can change Piper's mind?"

"Definitely! He's as powerful as Glitch, but inside out. He makes you recognize yourself. Piper has to see that what she's doing is wrong!"

Flicker snorted. "You think that would've worked with Swarm?"

Kelsie winced at the name. She turned away and struck the door again—more of a blow than a knock.

She knew exactly how Swarm thought, in a way Flicker never would. But this was a different situation. One that needed to be resolved peacefully to keep Chizara safe. This had to work.

"Okay," Flicker said. "Somebody's eyes just opened."

Kelsie stepped back, feeling a trickle of fear. Weird. The world was maybe ending tomorrow, but she was more afraid of seeing that stricken look on her mother's face again. Guilt and sadness and loss.

Why care? She didn't owe that woman anything.

This afternoon, it had all felt resolved. Kelsie had been okay with the fact that her mother had moved on. But that had been a Zero power at work. Was Oliver's power any more long-lasting than a feel-good night of dancing, or being charmed by Nate, or Swarm's madness?

And if so, how could it get through to Piper?

"Get ready," Flicker whispered.

The door opened. Zoe Moseley stood there, frowning and sleepy, holding back her blond hair with one hand. When she saw Kelsie, a fragile smile touched her lips.

"You came back," she said gently. "I hoped you would."

A rush of pain ripped through Kelsie. The three of them weren't enough for a feedback loop, but from the expression on Zoe's face, she was hurting too.

Zoe's gaze swung toward Flicker. She frowned, confused.

"This is my friend," Kelsie said. "We need your help."

Zoe swung the door wide at once.

Flicker went through, but Kelsie hesitated on the threshold, hope and fear mixing in her stomach.

This was the woman who'd hurt her when she was little. The woman her dad had run from. Who'd replaced her with two other children.

It was too much to process now, in the middle of the night. Kelsie felt like turning around and heading back out into the darkness.

But they needed to get Chizara and Nate back safe—not by fighting or calling in the police. This was the only option left.

She followed Flicker inside.

The room looked larger without people spread across the floor. In the dim light from the hall, chairs and cushions were still strewn around the walls. But it was empty of all the under-standing, all the *recognition*, that Oliver's power had called into being. Kelsie missed it.

Zoe switched on a lamp and took a seat on a low armchair. She gestured for them to sit. Flicker navigated to a couch, look-ing right at home.

Kelsie stayed where she was, standing near the door.

"We need to find Oliver," she said.

Zoe frowned at her. "Oliver? Oh, I thought you came here to . . ."

"Talk to you?" Kelsie turned away. Suddenly it was hard to speak.

"It always happens after your first jolt of clarity," Zoe said. "You feel like everything's resolved, but then there's backsliding. All those habits of thought creep back in."

Kelsie stared at her. The words sounded smooth, as if Zoe had said them before to people knocking on her door past midnight.

"Especially with an old hurt," Zoe said. "Like what's between you and me. But what you need isn't more of Oliver's gift. You and I should talk."

Kelsie felt her lips trembling.

She did want to talk to her mother, but not when Chizara's life was in danger. Maybe later, if they survived Piper's plan.

"I'm not here for that," Kelsie said. "Something's happening, something big, and we need Oliver's help. Please."

Zoe nodded sadly. "You lost hold of clarity, and you need it again right away. But I've agreed to protect his privacy. We all have, especially from—"

"Your own daughter?" Kelsie asked sharply.

"That's not it." Zoe leaned forward. "I've read about you in the news. You're one of them, aren't you?"

"Yes, I have a power," Kelsie said. "If you'd known that, would you have stayed in touch?"

The words were out before she could stop them. But it felt good to flash with anger, to cause pain. Payback for the woman who'd never even sent her a letter.

"I promised Jerry not to look for you," Zoe said firmly. "So I didn't. I wouldn't have known he'd passed except the papers said you were an orphan."

"An orphan," Kelsie said. "I guess you didn't bother to correct anyone about that."

"I couldn't bring attention to Clarity," Zoe said. "We can't afford to have the FBI here. I had to protect Oliver."

"Like you protected me?"

Zoe looked away. "I failed you—you and Jerry both. But that's no reason to break Oliver's trust. You and your friends are dangerous."

Kelsie's anger was blunted by the words, and Flicker spoke up.

"We're trying to *stop* people from getting killed, Zoe. Oliver can help us. Will you get him over here or not?"

"I can't risk it, after all the good he's done for us. Not even for my little girl."

"Don't call me that!" Kelsie's face burned.

"Hush," Flicker whispered. "Someone else just woke up. Who's here with you?"

"Only my boys." Zoe looked wary, and like she was afraid of Flicker now. "And their father."

"Right. Three sets of eyes." Flicker got to her feet. "This is pointless. We should go."

"But . . ." Kelsie stared at her mother. There had to be some plea Zoe would listen to, some guilty heartstring Kelsie could pull.

Then a voice came from the darkness.

"Mommy?"

The word drove a knife through Kelsie's chest.

In the hallway, one of Zoe's sons stood, his hair shining in the hall light.

"Theo!" Zoe reached down and the child crossed to her at once. He stood in the circle of his mother's arms, his head on her shoulder. Then he looked up at Kelsie in wonder.

"This is Kelsie, honey," Zoe said.

Another boy had appeared in the hallway, nestled up against a bearded man in pajamas. The two stood there patiently, as if they were used to nighttime visitors looking for another shot of clarity.

"I'm . . . ," Kelsie began, but words failed her. She had to say *something* to convince Zoe to help them. The lives of her friends and everyone in the city might depend on it.

That included her brothers' lives too. For the first time, Kelsie realized that what was left of her family lived right here, in the eye of the storm.

She could imagine what Chizara would say if she were there. Maybe Zoe didn't deserve forgiveness for what she'd done. But she deserved a second chance. And to get that, she had to survive tomorrow.

"Zoe," Kelsie said. "If you can't help us, then please listen to me—you have to leave. New Orleans is going to be destroyed."

Zoe looked at her like she might be crazy.

Kelsie felt crazy too. Torn between getting the help she

needed for her friends and making sure her brothers were safe.

"If you ever loved me," Kelsie pleaded, "put your boys in a car and get them out of here."

As she spoke, the horror she felt reached out and took them all. There were six people awake in the house now, enough to form a feedback loop.

"*This* is your power?" Zoe murmured. "Making people afraid?"

"No," Kelsie said, trying to keep her voice from shaking. "I share my emotions. You're afraid because I am. Because I *know* something bad's happening tomorrow."

"That's what I'm feeling?" Zoe put a hand to her chest, and tears came to her eyes. "What's inside you?"

Kelsie took a step closer. She'd been in a thousand feedback loops—with strangers, with friends, with Zara. But this was something strange and new, being linked to her own mother in this small, intimate loop. Bound this way, if only by the fear of some uncertain nightmare.

But there wasn't time to linger.

"You have to go," she said. "Tonight, while there's still time."

"Zoe?" the man said, holding his son tight. "Maybe we should . . ."

Zoe stood up and grabbed a coat from the rack by the door.

"Get some clothes on the boys! I'll be with you soon." Zoe turned back to Kelsie. "If this city's getting hit again, Oliver needs to know. I'll take you to him."

CHAPTER 57
ANONYMOUS

THIBAULT DUCKED, AND THE GUY'S FIST HIT THE WALL.

"Ahh!" The grunt echoed down the hallway, and that burning lance of focus flew apart into sparks.

Thibault slid to one side. He grabbed the radio from Noah's belt and sent it skidding down the hall.

Noah followed its motion, his focus narrowing again.

Thibault stood in the corner trying to breathe. His shoulder burned where he'd been punched; his heart thudded pain through bruised ribs.

He needed to slip away, to make a different plan. Maybe if he staged a break-in downstairs, Noah would be pulled from his post.

But the guy was still staring at the radio, his knuckles reddening and speckled with blood.

Go over there and pick it up! Give me some room.

Instead the guy spread his arms out, almost wide enough to span the hallway. He began slowly moving toward Thibault.

Thibault stayed where he was, ready to snip away any glimmer of attention that came his way. But Noah's eyes were shut. His other senses coiled in the hallway, like Flicker's when she was alone with Thibault.

"We practiced with one of you," the man hissed.

Thibault froze.

"Put her in a room. To see if we could find her and take her down." The guy smiled. He was getting closer, step by gentle step.

They'd used Rien for *practice*?

The world grew dark around the edges, started closing in.

"It's not that hard," Noah said, almost soothingly. "You just have to *focus*. Like she's not really a person. Like it's all just a video—"

Thibault struck hard and without thought, straight to Noah's face.

The response came too fast to see—a kick that swept Thibault's feet from under him, a punch that drove the breath from his lungs. Then he was on his back, Noah's weight on top of him, a fist pulled back for a finishing blow to the face.

Thibault grabbed that fist. He channeled his anger, his horror at letting himself be driven to violence, into their connection. He pulled both of them into the Nowhere, throwing their bodies off like discarded costumes behind.

The hallway turned black around them. They were deep in, teetering dangerously on the edge of nothingness. All Thibault wanted to do was dive into the darkness ahead. No one fought there. No one was used for combat practice.

"What *is* this?" Noah had gone slack with fear.

"This is where Piper wants to take the world. This is where you'll be living tomorrow—unless you open that door for me."

"The *hell* I will!" Noah said, but his voice quavered. "This is just some superpowered trick!"

"This is reality," Thibault said with utter conviction. "This is how things are when you disconnect from other people. This is what Piper wants—a world like *this*."

Noah took Thibault by his jacket, clinging like a terrified child.

Thibault drew him further in, further down, colder. The Nowhere pulled at the light, at their lives, like a strong tide, tearing away their connections with the world back there. There were only the two of them, and soon even they would start to dissipate.

"What's your name?" Anon asked in a freezing whisper.

"I don't know," Noah whimpered.

"Scary, isn't it? Do you ever want to know it again?"

The guy nodded.

"Then do exactly what I say. Stand up."

Noah's body, way back in the real world, clambered upright.

Distant Thibault stood too, shaky and hurting. "Put the code in."

A faraway hand punched plastic keys.

The iris scanner blinked, and Noah lined up his eye without being told.

The door clicked and eased open.

"Now walk down that hall," Anonymous said. "You need to get out of this building. Away from its evil. Don't try to remember what just happened, but know in your bones that you never want to see this place again."

Noah nodded, as if remembering any of this was the last thing he wanted in the whole world.

As he pulled away, though, the predatory focus flickered in his eyes again. He scanned the hallway, ready to attack. But Anon was a million miles into the darkness.

The big guy gaped, and a shudder went through his body. Then he shoved his fists into his pockets, hunched his shoulders, and staggered away down the hall.

"Who the hell's out there?" came a voice from the open cell door.

Anonymous turned, racing back from the darkness into his hurting body. Verity sat inside the cell, cross-legged on a slab of bedding on the floor.

She was looking off to his left a little, her eyes not quite finding him.

"Are you . . . ," he began, then shook his head. "How can you hear me?"

"You're a Stalker, right?" She stood up. "I heard you shouting when the power shield was closed. Come in and let me see you."

Of course—she'd been inside the cell, his anonymity blocked from her. He saw now that the walls were lined with a hexagonal mesh.

He stepped inside. The cell grew lighter as he pulled back from the edge of the Nowhere, as being seen pulled him into reality.

"He knocked you around pretty good, didn't he, Stalker?" she said.

"My name's Thibault Durant. I'm from Cambria—"

"Ugh. One of *you guys*. You working for Piper yet?"

"No," he said eagerly. "I'm here to rescue you."

Thibault blinked. It was just like Ethan had described—an itch to tell the truth. Even with only two of them in this power-shielded cell.

"Then let's get out of here. Piper wants to use my power to fuck up the world." Verity was already walking past him.

He stood in her way. "Wait. We have to find my friends Nate and Chizara. Piper's got them, too."

"Saldana and Okeke?" Verity shook her head. "Piper

doesn't want another Charismatic, and she's got two dozen Electrokinetics. They're not part of this."

"But she's got them locked up."

"We'll just get caught!" She elbowed him aside and stepped into the hall. "I'm the one she needs. Come *on*."

Thibault grabbed her arm, the cold surging in him again. The hallway darkened around them.

Verity stared down at his hand. She let out a little grunt as the Nowhere claimed the two of them.

"Almost forgot about this trick. Rien used to . . ." She sighed sadly and murmured, "Shit. I'd forgotten her."

"She's still around. I saw her yesterday. But you need to help me find Nate and Chizara, or I won't help you escape."

Verity stood there a moment, teeth against her lower lip.

"Whatever," she finally said. "But if it's them or me, I'm out of here. Piper doesn't care about them."

Thibault stared at her. "Why not?"

"Because you five don't have anything new! Well, except maybe that kid in the bank video. His mind control, or whatever it is, is amazing."

"Um. You think Ethan's amazing?"

"Of course," she said. "I bet Piper wants him bad."

CHAPTER 58

SCAM

"OUCH."

Ethan poked at the bruise on his head. It hurt. He totally blamed Flicker for this. Who the hell crashed a truck *on purpose*?

To be fair, Ethan had done the actual crashing. But he'd just been following orders!

And really, it all came back to Nate and his stupid idea to rescue Verity. Like the Cambria Five didn't have enough problems without getting mixed up in the apocalypse?

He went into the bathroom and flipped on the lights, giving himself instant retina burn. Who needed a bathroom this bright? It made his eyes ache.

Or maybe that was a symptom of his brain swelling up, pushing against the insides of his skull.

Searching "brain injury" had been a bad idea.

He started rummaging around in the bathroom cabinet. There had to be something for his head. He found a small white bottle and squinted at it. The letters danced in front of his eyes.

Yeah, that seemed to say aspirin.

He wrestled with the childproof lid for what felt like forever. Squeezed and pushed until the bottle spun out of his hands. A rain of white pills scattered across the floor.

"Crap!"

He bent to retrieve a couple, washed them down with tap water from his hand. It wasn't only his head that was throbbing. He ached everywhere, and his clothes smelled like flop sweat, but he didn't have the energy to shower.

He lay down on the floor and rested his forehead on the cool tiles. Maybe he really did need a hospital. Or some of his mom's chicken soup. Which was a weird thought, because his mom didn't make soup.

Maybe he just needed his mom.

His phone went off, echoing in his skull. No doubt Flicker with orders for him to crash some new vehicle into a wall.

"What?" Ethan croaked.

"Put me through to Mr. Barrow, please," a voice said.

"Who?"

"This is Mrs. Lavoir," the voice said. "I live next door to the Barrows. I have something important to tell him."

Too late, Ethan realized the Barrows lived *here*, in the

house the Zeroes had squatted. Crap, she must've seen them all staggering home in the dark. Probably thought they'd been drinking, especially the guy in the middle they'd practically had to carry.

But how did she have *this* number?

Right. Every time they all got new burners, Anon went over and wrote Ethan's number by Mrs. Lavoir's phone. That guy had *way* too much time on his hands.

But it had paid off. Maybe if he said the right thing, he could delay her until tomorrow, when the world was going to end anyway.

Too bad the voice didn't work on the phone.

Ethan gathered himself, trying to sound official. "Yes, you have reached the correct establishment. Unfortunately, Mr. Barrow isn't here at this time. May I take a message for him?"

As he spoke, he got up gingerly and crawled out of the bathroom. Aspirins crunched under his knees.

"Tell him there's been some suspicious activity at his home," Mrs. Lavoir said. "I'm going to call the police."

Ethan's heart flipped inside out. "Yes, I see. But I'm sure the police are only interested if there's been damage to the property."

"They've stepped on the flower beds!" Mrs. Lavoir exclaimed.

"No we didn't!" Ethan started—not his smoothest move. But luckily Mrs. Lavoir was still talking.

"There's five of them. Sneaking through the kitchen door right now, like they're about to play some prank! I can see them through the windows."

Ethan sat up straight. "What?"

"They're wearing masks," Mrs. Lavoir said. "They're clearly—"

Ethan spun. A creaking sound came from the staircase.

"I'm sure it's okay!" he squeaked. "But I'll have Mr. Barrow call you back!"

He stabbed at the phone to cut off Mrs. Lavoir and darted toward the nearest open bedroom door. A shadow detached itself from the staircase and hurtled toward him.

Ethan slammed the door shut and locked it, backed away from the thump. He looked down at the phone. Flicker's number was one of the five programmed into it, but he hadn't bothered to label them.

Click.

He looked up in horror. The door was unlocking, right in front of his eyes, just like when . . .

"Chizara?" he asked hopefully.

No answer. The door was easing open now.

Come on, voice, get me out of this! Anything that will scare them away!

But the voice was silent.

Whoever it was, the voice knew that nothing would scare them away.

CHAPTER 59
CRASH

CHIZARA STARED AT THE MESH-COVERED WALLS of her cell.

It didn't make sense.

She was full of Crash power, full of fixing juice, her mind still spinning from everything the black box had hit her with, her body singing, dancing, laughing with it.

And yet everything was quiet. No sound, heartbeats, brain pulses, not even the roar of the city around her.

Total silence.

Her fingertips brushed the wall, feeling the ripple of the hexagonal metal lattice beneath the paint.

Here it was at last: power shielding.

It was like a Faraday cage on steroids. She threw her power at the wall just to feel how it dropped out, how the pattern deadened it. It was like shouting at a soundproof wall.

How strange. This silence was the thing she'd always craved in the middle of a blaring city. To lose her power. To live in a world empty of electronics. But this was getting weird.

She snapped her fingers, just to hear something.

The euphoria from the black-box blast was fading, her mind putting itself back together. And with it came a slow and anxious realization. . . .

Normal people lived in this dead world all day, every day. Was this really what it was like for Mom and Dad, for Ik and Bin? What a freak she must have seemed to them, distracted by every phone, every laptop.

But she didn't feel *normal* in here. She felt neutralized, reduced, ordinary. Unable to sense the world, unable to find anything to grasp, to control. She barely felt alive.

The only tickles she could sense were the bare lightbulb overhead and the hums of her own body. The whir of her nervous system, the spark of her brain, her muscles as loud as revving motorcycles against the backdrop of this deathly *silence*.

She wondered if she could slow her own heart, quiet her own mind, become one with the silence. If they left her in here long enough, it might become a temptation. To crash her own heart, maybe.

Chizara sat up. *Get your head on straight.*

Door, walls, ceiling, floor—every surface was textured with

the power-shielding mesh. There had to be a chink in this armor. Some tiny gap her power could worm its way through.

What had her old boss in the fix-it shop, Bob, always said?

Everything has a favorite way to get broken.

Just the thought of all those busted radios, TVs, laptops, and toasters made her feel better. Like she had a chance. She could break this cage, find its weakness—or at least distract herself from approaching panic.

Bob had always been so calm, so methodical, always making her check her work. The Makers who'd built this cage were geniuses—they had flair, ingenuity, their own glorious leader. But did they have anyone like Bob in their lives?

Maybe one of them, at some crucial juncture, hadn't checked their work.

Was there any leakage in the cell? She strained to hear past her pulse. It might be tiny. The smallest of oversights. Hope could come in a minuscule package.

Look at the seams; check every corner. Get in close and listen hard.

Ten minutes later she hadn't found a single flaw, when a thump came from outside.

Chizara could sense nothing of the lock's workings, but she heard it click. She stepped back, ready to fight.

The door swung open.

Outside was—no one. Just the distant roar of signals from the city.

"Hello?" she said softly.

Two people took shape out of nothingness. A boy and a girl, vague forms that tugged at her memories . . .

The girl's name played on her lips. "Verity?"

Chizara looked past them. Was Nate here? Had all the Zeroes arrived to rescue her?

But the two pushed their way in and shut the door behind them.

"Quiet!" Verity hissed, leaning back against the wall, breathless. "We sent your guard away, but she might come back."

"She won't," the boy said. "Being in the Nowhere scares them too much."

Chizara stared at him, and suddenly she could remember everything:

Thibault Durant—the sixth member of the Cambria Five. The Zen Boy who'd killed Quinton Wallace. He needed to be tracked, because the redwoods still called to him. He belonged with Flicker forever, but he didn't quite know it yet.

Shutting the power-shielded cell had snapped away all of his anonymity. She finally *knew* him.

"Thanks for coming for me," she said.

"Don't thank us yet," he said. "We've still got to find Nate. But at least we've got you to bust him out. The locks around here are seriously high-tech."

"You're telling me?" she said.

Thibault smiled and opened the door again.

Signals piled in on Chizara like a litter of puppies, a noisy but welcome assault. After hours in silence, she felt ready to take this whole building apart.

But as she led the others out the door, the hallway shifted, slanted. The right angles of walls and floor and doors all went wrong—even the roar of the distant city shrieked discordant.

Chizara dropped to one knee, both hands on the floor for support.

Laughter. She looked up.

About twenty people were coming at her, led by a girl all in leather. A girl she should know. A girl she should be afraid of.

"Talk about bad timing!" Glitch said, laughing. "Get them back inside."

Chizara felt herself dragged back into the awful cell, her brain glitched, her hope shattered. But she tried to hold on, to keep thinking and understanding.

She heard Glitch's voice again.

"We don't have time to set up more cells. Throw them all in there. Ethan Cooper, too!"

CHAPTER 60
MOB

"IT'S NEARLY DAYLIGHT," FLICKER SAID. "WE DON'T have much time."

"Zoe said he'd be here." Kelsie looked up and down the path, shivering in the predawn cool. Flicker slumped on a wrought-iron bench under a palm tree, but Kelsie was too nervous to sit still.

Her mother had left them at the entrance of an aquarium, right on the Mississippi River. As far as Kelsie could tell, there was no one around. She couldn't stop looking at the sign above the aquarium entry—a shark caught midtwist, ready to snap up some defenseless fish.

As they waited, the sky grew lighter, but a chill clung to the air.

A small group of joggers moved through the dawn, along

the edge of the water. She could feel their steady, determined energy.

But there was also a disquiet in them. Like soldiers approaching a battle.

"The guy in front," Flicker said. "He's checking us out."

Kelsie squinted in the rosy light. "It's him."

Oliver peeled off, waving the other joggers onward. He headed toward Kelsie and Flicker on his own.

When he got close, he flipped back the hood of his sweatshirt.

Kelsie moved to greet him. "Thanks for meeting us."

He wiped his face with the towel around his neck. Without the crowd around him, Oliver's glow was gone. He suddenly looked young for a Zero.

"You told Zoe the city's in danger?" he began.

"Yes. There's someone with a power. She's planning to take over Mardi Gras."

He considered this. "That sounds like my old friend Piper."

"You know her?" Flicker got to her feet. "Do you know what she's up to?"

"No, but . . . Piper is complicated," Oliver said. "And her bark is worse than her bite."

"Her *bark*?" Kelsie shook her head. "She's stockpiling food and guns."

Oliver put his hands in the air. "Hold up. You ever *met* a Charismatic? They invent crazy projects to keep everyone's attention on them. They don't always follow through."

"This isn't some plea for attention," Flicker said. "She kidnapped a federal agent. Took our friends!"

Oliver hesitated. "That's a little extreme, even for her."

He stared. Trying to assess them.

"If you don't believe us, we'll take you to her headquarters," Kelsie pleaded. "Take a look at what she's up to. With your power you can make her see how dangerous it is."

Oliver shifted his weight awkwardly. "Is that how you think this works? You think I force clarity on people?"

Kelsie shook her head. She hadn't thought of it as using force—his power was recognition, not intimidation.

Flicker spoke up. "All we want is to help Piper see the error of her ways."

"She knows how to find me," Oliver said. "If she wants my counsel, she can come and get it. We don't always agree, but there's one thing we all believe—me, Piper, Verity, Beau, and . . ."

He frowned. Kelsie knew that look. He was trying to place someone who'd gone missing from his mind.

"You had a Stalker," Flicker prompted. "One of us met her."

Oliver's expression cleared. "Right—my girl Rien. There were five of us in those days. We made a pact, to use our powers only for good."

"But Verity joined the Feds," Flicker said. "She *hunts* us now. And Piper's got some plan that involves a private army and a stack of guns! So maybe you guys have different ideas about what *good* means."

He shrugged. "That's the way the world's always worked. All my power does is let people see what they already know—what they already feel in their bones, right or wrong. Clarity won't change the fact that Piper is a Charismatic."

"Not all Charismatics are the same," Flicker said. "We have one too. He made us rehearse rescue missions in malls. That's a little different from blowing up Mardi Gras, don't you think?"

"And you must know that your power changes people," Kelsie said. "Otherwise, why would you bother with the Clarity Circle?"

He looked straight at her. "Did it change the way you feel about Zoe?"

Kelsie felt her heart wrench. For that one moment in the crowded church, forgiveness had been easy. But earlier, facing Zoe without Oliver there, all the pain had welled up again.

"So your power's just a con?"

"No, it's not a con. But it's also not an instant cure. People come back to the Clarity Circle for months. Years."

"We don't have that long," Flicker said.

"But it did change me," Kelsie said quietly. Before yesterday she would never have asked for her mother's help. That moment of forgiveness had started some process inside her. "Maybe Piper just needs a push?"

Oliver didn't answer. He looked across the park to where

his friends were making their slow loop around the track.

Maybe he was dependent on his own power to make decisions. Helpless without the Curve.

So why had he sent them away?

Then Kelsie realized: "You're afraid of me, aren't you?"

He looked at her for a moment. "It's obvious you're a predator. And you show up at my meeting full of fragile people seeking help? You could have lost control."

Kelsie took a step back. "At Clarity? I never would—"

"And now you want to use me to get close to Piper? What if you lose it on her? What if you turn into a Swarm?"

"That's *not* who I am!" Kelsie shouted.

Flicker put a hand on her arm. "That's not helping, Kelsie."

Kelsie took a slow breath, trying to rein in her anger. Oliver was staring at her, his suspicions confirmed. She'd lost her temper.

"I'd never hurt anyone," she said evenly. "I've been in this crazy town for four days, and I haven't even gotten close to turning into a Swarm."

"Impressive," he said. "But do you think you can face clarity on that subject, right now?"

She stared at him, then at the joggers.

This had all been a setup. A test.

"Okay, I'll play your game," she said. "But if I prove to you there's hope for a baby Swarm like me, then will you agree that Piper could change her mind too?"

Oliver nodded. He turned and waved at the joggers. They changed course instantly.

Kelsie felt the Curve build at their approach.

Oliver looked her in the eye. "When you were at the Clarity Circle, you were thinking about your mother. But now I want you to think about yourself. About what might send you down the path that Quinton Wallace took. There's a hunger inside you. I want you to really *think* about being a Swarm."

Kelsie's gaze dropped to the path. It felt shameful even entertaining these thoughts. But she had to make him understand. If she could choose not to be a Swarm, then Piper could make a different decision too.

So could Oliver—he could choose to intervene. To take a stand.

"I'm a good person," she said. "Not a killer."

"Being good or bad," Oliver answered, "that's not a one-time decision. Just like forgiving someone."

She started to answer, but then she felt it—the onset of clarity. That wave of recognition fell on her again, and this time it was awful.

She saw the hunger inside her, where it had always been. Her anger at having been abandoned.

She saw her power reaching out for Oliver's crew, yearning to make them hers. To make them something hungry and dangerous.

And worst of all, she saw her own repressed memories of

the AA meeting—being part of the Swarm, at the righteous center of all that fury, tearing Officer Delgado apart. For those moments she had felt the purest expression of her power, the paragon of her very being.

That was her, too.

Kelsie let out a wail of pain, and her knees gave way. Around her, the others reeled back, caught in the feedback loop.

They all felt it with perfect clarity—what is was to be her, a Swarm. Every ounce of the darkness inside her was laid bare.

This wasn't *fair*. She'd worked so hard, fighting Quinton Wallace. Battling this thing. Hanging on to who and what she really was.

Hanging on to . . .

"Zara," she said.

More clarity—she wasn't alone in this. She had someone to hold on to, which Quinton Wallace had never had.

Even if Chizara didn't need her in the same way, that was okay.

Kelsie became herself again. Around her, the feedback loop settled.

"Did I pass your test?" she asked quietly.

"It wasn't a test. It was a reminder."

"Of what? That I'm evil inside?"

"Not evil." Oliver looked away. "I've also done bad things, Kelsie. My power is just like Ren's. I've stolen recognition and understanding. But I fight it all the time. If we're going to face an ego like Piper's, you have to be ready for that struggle."

Kelsie nodded. "I've got someone to fight for."

"So you're coming with us?" Flicker asked Oliver.

"Yes." He looked at Kelsie. "Between us, maybe we can make her see."

CHAPTER 61
BELLWETHER

THIS WAS A HUNDRED TIMES WORSE THAN PRISON.

During those weeks in Dungeness, there were always slivers of contact. Nate's guards, his fellow inmates, even the janitorial staff formed brief, uncertain alliances. Wisps of Curve that he could latch onto to feed his thirsty power.

But there was *nothing* here.

Nate touched the walls. Some kind of mesh was set into the plaster. It didn't look like much more than a chicken-wire fence, but it somehow blocked the tendrils of his ability. Left him starving and alone.

In prison he'd always wondered if the Feds would go full Guantanamo on him and use waterboarding, beatings, electric shocks. The only thing that had kept that fear from overwhelming him was the hope that they would put too many people in the room, and he would *win* somehow. In Nate's dark fantasies, the pain only made him stronger.

But this absence, this hunger, was torture of another order.

He would pay any price to stop it.

How long had he been here? Hours? Days? The room had robbed him of time as well. All he felt was himself withering, made less than. What if his power turned inward until, like Thibault, he erased himself?

Finally the door opened.

As the seal of mesh broke, the crowd outside came flooding in. Nate's power leaped out hungrily.

A Zero-aged white guy, over six feet tall, stood smiling in the doorway. He wore an outlandish Mardi Gras costume—a tailored suit covered in tiny mirrors. He looked like a person-shaped disco ball.

"I'm Troy," he said.

One of Piper's triumvirate of powers. Did he know what Nate had let happen to Davey, his fellow Coin?

"You're the one who pulled off that Super Bowl stunt." Nate kept his voice steady. "Pretty impressive."

"You bet." Troy was all smiles. "Five hundred thousand people, all with tickets that looked legit! Had a little help from Nexus, though."

"Of course," Nate said. Projecting a power across that big a crowd would require help from the machine. "So messing up the Super Bowl was just a test run?"

That made Troy laugh. "It was diddly-squat compared to what comes next. Come on, Piper wants to see you. It's almost party time!"

On the main floor of the power plant, the parade float was ready to go.

The engine had been closed up. The KREWE DE NEW WORLD ORDER sign was hung straight. A taller chair—a throne, really—was mounted behind the seats for the three powers.

Troy left Nate's side to jump aboard, inspecting the satellite dish full of plastic Mardi Gras beads.

"Not the best quality." He picked up a string of the beads. "But I'll get it done."

The beads changed in his hand, became gems of breathtaking beauty.

"Glad you could join us, Nataniel," came Piper's voice from the float. She was in a recessed seat beneath the satellite dish, half-hidden behind bunting, fiddling with a panel of buttons and switches.

"It's better than that cell," Nate said.

Piper looked up from the controls. "You don't have to go back, you know."

Nate felt a surge of hope—but he knew what she was asking, and what the answer had to be. He changed the subject.

"Let me guess." He gestured at the highest seat on the float. "The throne is for you."

"No, it's for a friend. Someone pretty enough to focus every eye on Nexus. You met him in the graveyard."

"You mean Beau," Nate said—the Zero with the beauty power, who Flicker had run into yesterday.

"It's probably overkill," Piper said. "The whole crowd's gonna want to jump his bones. I have to restrain *myself* sometimes."

Nate stared at her.

Piper smiled. "Too much information? We should get to the question at hand."

"We should," said Nate firmly.

Piper stood up on the float, put two fingers between her lips, and blew a short, sharp whistle. Every gaze in the place swung to her, and she suddenly shone with attention.

"It's time to make your choice, Nataniel," she said. "Do you want to watch the new world order come in? Or go back to your cell?"

The words spilled from him. "I can't go back in there."

"That's not what I asked," Piper said. "What I need to know is, will you help me wrangle the crowds today? Will you *obey* me?"

Nate swallowed his answer. He wanted more than anything to say yes. He couldn't face the dread silence of that room again.

"Are you going to betray me?" Piper asked.

He tried to open his mouth, ready to promise anything, to

convince her of his good faith. But no sound came.

Piper laughed, hooking a thumb over her shoulder.

Then Nate saw her back in the shadows: Verity. She was in costume, draped in long black judge's robes, held between two guards. She looked exhausted but unharmed.

"Tell the truth," Piper said. "Are you on my side?"

There was no fighting Verity's power.

"I don't know," Nate said.

"Then think about it harder," she commanded.

Nate looked around at the dozen Zeroes in the room, all of them staring back at him. Expectant, hopeful for the future, even though they knew the world was terrified of them and would crush anything it feared.

Phan wanted to throw them all in prison, or make them his agents. Headlines screamed murder every time they flexed their powers. The guards at Dungeness had threatened him under their breath—threatened his whole kind with extinction—as they led Nate, hooded and manacled, from wing to wing.

And when he looked up at Piper, at the corona of adulation that surrounded her, he felt something better than hopelessness. She was the focus not only of attention, but of trust.

Of love, even.

And when Nate thought about the sheer scale of what she wanted to pull off today, he too was stirred.

The truth finally pushed up through him, coiling past his

will, seizing the muscles in his throat and mouth and forcing out the words.

"Yes, I'm on your side," he said. "Let's burn their world down."

She didn't even look surprised.

CHAPTER 62
FLICKER

"WE'RE STOPPING?" OLIVER ASKED FROM THE BACK-seat.

"This'll only take a second," Flicker said as the car came to a halt. "We need to make sure our friend's okay."

"He got knocked on the head pretty bad," Kelsie added from the driver's seat.

"Piper *hit* him?" Oliver asked.

"Yeah, sort of," Flicker said. She wouldn't have had the brilliant idea of crashing the car if Piper hadn't sent her Maker in pursuit.

When Kelsie brought the car to a halt, Flicker opened the passenger door and headed across the Barrows' lawn. The grass was soft beneath her feet, changing to the concrete of the path leading around to the kitchen.

Kelsie's footsteps fell lightly behind her. "Do you see him yet?"

Flicker shook her head. There were no eyes inside the house. Hopefully Ethan was asleep.

But when her palm closed around the handle of the outside kitchen door, Flicker froze. It felt too loose, wobbly in her hand.

Her fingers traced the wood around the knob—no scratches. The door hadn't been jimmied, but something had forced its mechanism.

The front doors of the safe houses had all felt the same way—once Chizara had unlocked them with her power.

Flicker went into Kelsie's vision. She was looking at the neighbor's house, where a light was on in the window.

"Kelsie." Flicker kept her voice a whisper. "I think someone broke in."

Kelsie's eyes swept back, peering through the kitchen window. "Are they still in there?"

"If anyone's inside, they're unconscious."

Or dead.

Flicker pushed the door open, strode across the kitchen to the stairs. After four days, the Barrows' home had grown familiar in the aching way that their borrowed houses always did—her body settled into the space just before they had to move on, leaving another ghost house in her memory.

"Everything's like we left it," Kelsie said. "No sign of a struggle."

"Ethan?" Flicker called up the stairs. Then repeated herself, louder.

No answer. No vision coming slowly awake.

Kelsie pushed ahead of her. "Come on."

A minute later they had searched the whole house. Every room, the closets, even under the beds.

They didn't find any dead bodies, at least. Just pills scattered across the bathroom floor and another wobbly handle on one of the bedroom doors. And, lying on the carpet behind it, Ethan's phone.

"They got him," Flicker said. "Piper knew about this place. We never should have left him here!"

Kelsie hand took her shoulder. "We had no choice. In a hospital, the Feds would've gotten him."

"Then we should have found another safe house. Or a hotel. Anyplace that Piper didn't know about!" Flicker pulled herself together. "We should get back to Oliver, in case she left one of her goons behind."

Flicker turned and ran down the stairs, her palm hot with friction against the bannister. Kelsie followed at a run, passing her and reaching the kitchen first, where she skidded to a halt.

Flicker slowed, put her vision in Kelsie's eyes again.

A silhouette loomed at the kitchen door, framed by the bloodred light of dawn.

"I've a mind to call the police!" the figure said sharply.

Flicker sighed with relief. It was only Mrs. Lavoir from next door.

"Pranks all night," the woman went on. "And now you two come stumbling home at seven thirty-six a.m.! Well, I'll have you know that I've left a message for Mr. Barrow!"

Flicker frowned—Thibault had changed the number at Mrs. Lavoir's the last time they'd switched burners. Which meant she'd really called . . . Ethan.

"How *were* the Barrows?" Flicker asked. "Are they okay?"

"Well, we didn't talk directly." Mrs. Lavoir's voice softened a little. "It was a bit strange, I suppose. The young man who answered seemed very flighty. But if there are any more disturbances, I'll be calling right—"

"You won't see us again," Flicker interrupted. "We're leaving now. For good."

She went to the door and pushed it open, heard Mrs. Lavoir stepping backward in surprise.

"And if you see *anyone* around, you should call the police," she added. "Actually, make that the FBI."

"Excuse me, young lady?"

"Trust me. Just ask for Agent Phan," Flicker said. If Mrs. Lavoir was determined to cause trouble, the least she could do was inconvenience Piper's crew.

The Zeroes were done with this house. Another safe place that was no longer safe.

"Let's get out of here," Flicker said to Kelsie, and headed across the lawn.

The parades would be starting soon. They had to intercept Piper and subject her to Oliver's power. They had to *make* her see that her plan was too dangerous. They had to—

Just before she reached the car, Ethan's phone jangled in her pocket.

Damn. Was this a ransom demand? Or Mrs. Lavoir calling the Barrows to report more strange behavior?

Flicker came to a halt, muffling her answer with her hand. "Mm-hm?"

"Hey, Sugar Bear!" came a voice. "You still sleeping? It's the big day!"

"Uh . . . ," Flicker said. The voice was familiar, but she couldn't quite place it.

"We're all headed to the parade route early. To make sure we get good seats!" A laugh. "Everyone's dressing up. I'm a penguin! Weird-hunters are totally into cosplay, turns out."

Weird-hunters. It clicked into place.

"Sonia Sonic?" Flicker asked.

It was Sonia's turn to be confused. "Um, yes? Who is this?"

"Flicker. How did you get this . . . Did you just call Ethan *Sugar Bear*?"

"Oops." A pause, then a sigh. "Let's start over. Why do you have Ethan's phone? Is he okay?"

"No. Someone grabbed him."

"The Feds?" Sonia cried. "Or *Piper?* That evil cow! I'll strangle her!"

Flicker frowned. "Wait. You know about Piper?"

"Ethan said she kidnapped Verity. And now she's got him, too? She is *so* dead."

"Ri-ight," said Flicker. "So you know everything."

If Ethan ever managed to get rescued, she was going to have a long talk with him about boundaries.

"Can I help find him?" Sonia pleaded. "I'm really good at investigating stuff. Just yesterday me and Ethan were looking for—"

"No, you can't help!" Flicker cried, heading toward the car again. "But you should know—something bad's going down today. You guys have to get out of town."

"Are you kidding?"

"Do I *sound* like I'm kidding? Tell everyone at your convention to get as far as they can from New Orleans."

Sonia gave a dry laugh. "Like that'll work. 'Hey, weird-hunters! You should split town because something *weird* is going to happen.' They're all going to the parades today, hoping there'll be some serious crowd psychosis!"

Flicker hesitated, her hand on the passenger-side door handle.

"So they'll be at the parades, no matter what you tell them?"

"Definitely."

Maybe it was Oliver's presence a few feet away, with just

enough neighbors around to nudge clarity into play. Or maybe it was Flicker's certainty that she needed to play every card she could or Piper was going to win this game. But whatever the reason was, Flicker saw perfectly what she had to do.

"Okay, new plan," she said. "Tell as many weird-hunters as you can that you're in touch with the Cambria Five, and that something huge is happening today."

Sonia's voice went low. "Okay, then what?"

"Tell them to go to the parades," Flicker said. "And to look for a float called Krewe de New World Order. . . ."

CHAPTER 63
CRASH

CHIZARA WOKE GASPING.

Her head was muzzy, the air thick with the smell of sweat. And there was something wrong with the world itself—a huge suffocating silence hanging over her.

It took a moment to remember. Power shielding in all directions, packing her brain with cotton balls and wax.

That awful feeling of powerlessness. Of silence.

She hadn't meant to pass out, but being hit with the blackbox blast and glitched in the same night had been too much.

She sat up. Something had changed. . . .

Thibault and Ethan were still here in the cage, both fast asleep.

But Verity was gone.

"Guys?" Chizara said. Her voice came out cracked and

dry. A few bottles of water had been left by the door, and she reached for one. The skin of her palm scraped dry against the plastic top. She drank long and hard.

How long had they been in here? Was it morning yet?

Had the end of the world already happened?

If something went wrong with Piper's plan, they could be trapped in here forever. Deep in this abandoned building, with no one on the outside aware this room existed.

Chizara nudged Thibault.

He stirred, looked around. "Where's . . ."

"Verity's gone," Chizara said. "They took her while we slept."

That woke him up. He drew in a sharp breath at the pain of pulling himself straighter. He had a purpling bruise on his side, like a horse had kicked him.

"That means they've started," he said. "She's part of the plan. They're going to project her power."

Chizara nodded. "Yeah, you said. But I still don't get how everyone telling the truth messes up the world."

"Verity's only part of it," Thibault said, then poked Ethan with his toe. "Wake up, Scam."

"Help!" Ethan cried out, then sputtered awake. He looked frantically in all directions. "Oh, right. They already got me."

"Yeah, they did." Thibault leaned closer, gently turned Ethan's head to look at the wound. "How is it?"

"Hurts," Ethan said with a wince. "But at least I can see

straight now. I don't think I'm going to die. Where are my shoes?"

Thibault pointed at the corner. "You took them off last night, despite our protests."

"Who the hell sleeps with shoes on?" Ethan argued.

Chizara ignored them, scanning the mesh of the ceiling, walls, and floor, enough hexagons to exhaust her eyes. "We need to get out of here. This seems like a bad place to ride out an apocalypse."

"But your power's blocked," Ethan said. "Are we supposed to break the door down?"

"Hmm," Chizara said. "That's not a bad idea."

Last night she had checked every corner, every join in the mesh. She'd gone over it with a fine-toothed comb. It was signal-tight all over.

But what if the mesh was broken?

"Do you have anything to dig at the walls with?" she asked. "Maybe we can cut one of these lines of metal."

Both boys stared at her, reached into their pockets, then shrugged.

Useless.

Chizara scanned the room. Water bottles, their shoes and clothes.

Everything was too soft, except . . .

"Ethan. Give me your belt."

"Um. Why?"

"The buckle." She held out a hand. "I need something hard."

He rolled his eyes, but pulled the belt out of its loops.

"If my pants fall down—"

"Then you will *hold them up*." Chizara squeezed two fingers through the buckle, like it was a tiny set of brass knuckles.

She rapped the wall with them.

Solid.

But beside the door was a spot she'd noticed the night before, where the mesh protruded a little. Whoever had spread it out hadn't pushed it deep into the plaster, just painted it over.

Chizara smiled. Bob would not approve.

She started whacking the spot with the buckle, chipping away paint until the metal itself was exposed. What was this stuff? Reaching her power into it, she didn't recognize the alloy. Probably something that the Makers had whipped up themselves.

She felt a pang of envy—she still had so much to learn.

Whatever the metal was, it was strong. Ten minutes later her knuckles ached and the buckle looked bent. But the mesh showed no signs of fraying.

Thibault stepped up beside her. "Let me try."

He started pounding away.

It was weird, how clear Thibault seemed here in the cage. All their missions, all their interactions, the sign on his door at the Dish—ANON EXISTS HERE—it was all so sharp and detailed in her memory. This must have been what Nate had been seeking when he took Thibault camping: a place where the city noise wouldn't blur the guy into the background. . . .

He was actually kind of handsome, in a brooding-too-hard way. Chizara could understand what Flicker saw in him, like she'd never seen before.

He kept on with the belt buckle. Why didn't anyone come to tell them to stop banging? Was Piper's army all out enacting the final plan?

Maybe it was already too late.

"Got it!" Thibault finally cried.

She pushed him aside and looked close. Two of the little hexagons had been broken, their shared side hacked cleanly in half.

Chizara closed her eyes and pushed all her power at the break.

Nothing.

"Damn it."

"Too small?" Thibault asked.

"Hang on." She threw herself at it again, and saw why. "Right. This mesh is only a part of the shielding. There's another mesh behind it, and *another* behind that."

A triple-decker sandwich between thick layers of plaster and paint. Together the hexagons set up a pattern in the wall itself, a resonance that went beyond any single stretch of wire.

"This is pointless," she said. "We'd have to hack out a chunk of wall the size of a fist!"

She tore the belt from Thibault's hands and tossed it at Ethan.

He let it fall to the floor. He was staring up at the ceiling.

"Hey, do that again," he said.

"Do what?" she snapped.

"Get mad."

Chizara stared at him. She was plenty mad now. Enough to punch someone. Especially an annoying white boy telling her what to do.

"You did it again!" he said, still looking up. "The light, it flickered a little when you got mad."

Chizara let out a sigh. "No kidding, Ethan. The light's on this side of the power shielding. It's the one thing I can use my power on."

The lightbulb was there, in the corner of her awareness. The faintest whine, like a mosquito on the other side of a large room.

"I can crash it if you want," she went on. "Shall we all sit here in the dark?"

"No thanks." Ethan knelt to pick up his belt, then passed it through the loops around his waist, looking thoughtful. "So the electricity comes from *outside* the cage, right? Through a wire?"

Chizara gritted her teeth. "Yes, Ethan. That. Is. How. Lights. Work."

She was about to explain further that water was wet and gravity made things go *down*, and ask whether there was anything else he needed explained, except that suddenly her anger was fading.

Was Ethan actually making sense?

"Remember how we had that landline in the Dish?" he went on. "Because the Faraday cage blocked our phones, but it couldn't block a telephone wire."

Have you checked everything, *Chizara?* Bob's voice said in her head.

Maybe she hadn't.

"Are you asking me," Chizara said slowly, "if I can send my power . . . *down a wire?*"

Ethan started to answer, but she waved him silent.

Of course. Zero powers were like signals, which was why Essence and her crew had figured out how to broadcast them on a satellite dish. So why not transmit them the old-fashioned way?

On a freaking piece of wire.

"Were you using the voice just then?" Thibault asked. "Tricking it into saying something useful?"

"No." He frowned, put a gentle finger to the lump on his forehead. "My head feels funny. But that was me talking."

"Huh." Thibault exchanged a look with Chizara. "You think you know someone. . . ."

Chizara stared up at the light. She reached her power up

to take hold of the almost-inaudible buzz of its little filament. It found the wire there, a slender, simple line of copper— perfect simplicity. The sort of thing she hadn't ever noticed before she'd become strong enough to sense nerves and muscle twitches.

She pushed upward, her awareness sliding through the copper tendril like a snake up a drainpipe, coursing alongside the sizzle of electricity flowing to the lightbulb. She felt that sizzle in her spine. She felt the deadening hexagons surrounding the wire, but there was still that hair's-breadth path through.

The hexagons fought her, pressing her power inward, squeezing it down into the minuscule wire.

And there she was on the other side, in the blare of the city, in the roar of the world. Her power flashed from circuit to circuit, finding its way to the lock on their cell door. To the keypad—pfft, no problem. To the iris scanner, which was only a little trickier.

"Get your shoes on, Ethan," she said. "We might have to run."

CHAPTER 64
BELLWETHER

THE CROWDS WERE GLORIOUS.

People were packed onto every sidewalk, every balcony, every rooftop. They leaned out of the windows of bars and restaurants. Stood on parked cars and hung from lampposts. Thousands of them, tens of thousands, all beaming with drunkenness and glee.

And this was just a side street—the Krewe de New World Order float hadn't reached the main parade route yet. It was pushing slowly through the Mardi Gras throng, forcing its way toward ever-larger crowds.

Parade marshals had stopped them a few times, looking annoyed and asking for permits. But sweeping aside these functionaries was the easiest of Nate's tasks. Sitting up here on the front of the float, he had the authority of multitudes flowing through him.

His main job was sculpting the attention of the crowd. Guiding it into the satellite dish. It acted as a receiver as well as a projector, sucking in all that raw power and storing it in the guts of Nexus—ready to be used.

The float was a gaudy, unlikely engine of apocalypse.

Beau sat on his high throne, wearing a mask that hid his face. Piper had told him to wait till she was ready before revealing himself.

Troy sat in the center of the triumvirate, behind the satellite dish full of beads. He sparkled in his mirrored suit as he flung beads into the crowds, who fought wildly for the false gems even after the float had passed.

His power wasn't fleeting, like Davey's had been. He'd learned to create lasting illusions of value into people's minds. It was Coins like him who would mint the currencies of the new world.

Verity sat on Troy's right, in judge's robes. Her anger was obvious, but the handcuffs that kept her in the chair were hidden by her costume.

On Troy's left was Essence, in a stockbroker's power suit and red tie. She had the biggest job—crashing the machinery of power itself. The military and surveillance hardware of the world's governments, the banking and trading systems, the databases of wealth and debt and ownership. She was going to wipe the slate clean.

Piper wanted to replace all of it with her own rules. Her own systems, with Zeroes at the center of everything.

Whenever a flicker of doubt went through Nate, he looked back at her in the control seat. In this vast crowd, Piper was incandescent, filling him with certainty that her plan was the best way forward.

At the very least, her upending the world meant that Nataniel Saldana would never go to prison again. No Zero ever would.

The float came to a jolting halt.

Nate stood up for a look. A crowd of costumed people was in the road, all of them holding up their phones. They were ignoring the gemstones raining from Troy's hands. Instead they were shooting video, their phones scanning every face on the float.

And they were blocking the way, keeping the Krewe de New World Order from the main parade route three streets over.

What the hell?

Then Nate saw a bolt of bright magenta hair sticking out of a penguin costume, and he realized who they were.

"Sonia Sonic," he said. "And her fucking weird-hunters."

CHAPTER 65
FLICKER

SHE COULD SEE ANYTHING. EVERYTHING.

She had a thousand eyes. More.

Flicker was everywhere at once, shooting down the alleys and sidewalks, perching up on terraces. Staring at the bottoms of empty glasses and lingering on bare skin.

Dizzily, omnipresently, wildly searching for the words KREWE DE—

"Got her," she said. "Turn right up here."

"Can't do that," Oliver said. He'd taken over driving when Kelsie had started to feel the crowds.

Flicker brought her vision closer, swung around to look at the car from all directions.

They were hemmed in, half a mile from Bourbon Street.

And a policeman a block away had just noticed the vehicle intruding into the pedestrian-only zone.

"Time to bail," she said.

"Here?" Oliver asked. "And just leave your car?"

"Who said it was ours?" Flicker said with a laugh. This was the most serious situation she had ever been in, but she kept giggling. She could see so *much*.

Kelsie, in the backseat, was quiet, the sheer multitudes overwhelming her. But at least they were a happy crowd—so far.

"I wanted to catch Piper before now," Oliver said. "Wild crowds like this aren't good for clarity. I'll have to get right up next to her."

"We'll get you there," Kelsie said, but her voice sounded shaky.

As they emerged into the throng, Flicker sent her vision searching again—found the float, a purple, green, and gold island in a sea of humanity. It was trapped there, held hostage by a hundred weird-hunters.

"Good job, Sonia," Flicker murmured.

But was that . . . Nate?

He stood on the front of the float, trying to charm the weird-hunters to one side. He was *helping* Piper.

No. It had to be a trick he was playing on her, a ruse to gain her trust.

But there was Verity as well, looking miserable beside a boy in a glittering suit. If she was there, then how was Nate hiding his intentions?

Flicker almost stumbled.

"What is it?" Kelsie asked. "Are we too late?"

"No. But I think Nate's gone over to the dark side."

"Piper can be very persuasive," Oliver said.

Flicker swore, pushing them both forward faster. In an unwelcome flash of clarity by the aquarium, she'd known that one day it would come down to a struggle between them, her versus her old friend. Her big brother, like Ethan used to say.

What broke her heart was that it had happened so soon. And with him in the service of someone else.

She jumped into Piper's head—her eyes were focused on a control panel. A throttle, switches, a big button in the middle. Some kind of gauge with a needle edging its way up to maximum.

Flicker had no intention of seeing what happened when it got there.

She scanned the streets ahead. "We're only a block away. The alley to our left goes through!"

She shot back into Piper's vision. Her eyes were on the gauge. On that big red button. *Shit.*

"Run!" she cried.

Piper was turning around, looking up—someone was perched on a high throne, lording over the rest of the float, wearing a garish mask.

When Piper waved at him, he pulled it off.

It was Beau. But only for a moment.

As the eyes of the crowd swung to him in their thousands, he transformed. His complexion cleared, glowed. His hair thickened and grew so glossy that her fingers tingled, wanting to run through it. His jawline firmed, his cheekbones were higher. His glory drew more regard, showering him with more attention, redoubling his glamour.

Flicker sagged to the ground, overwhelmed, for a moment unable to retreat inside her own head. Unable to escape the numberless eyes gazing upon him.

"What's wrong?" Kelsie shouted.

Flicker tried to stand again, failed. "It's Beau. That pretty boy. He's pulling all the crowd's energy into Piper's machine!"

"What do we—"

"Go *stop her*. She's about to push the button!"

CHAPTER 66
MOB

"LEAVE YOU?" KELSIE CRIED. "BUT WE'RE ALMOST—"

Then it hit her, too.

A moment ago the celebration had been a fractured mix of crowds—Sonia's weird-hunters, Piper's crew on the float, gaggles of drunken frat boys hanging from terraces, countless other friend mobs in clumps along the sidewalks. . . .

But Beau's power had changed all that. When his radiance was unleashed, all the groups connected and focused. On him.

They all wanted him. Straight, queer, bi, none of the above—it didn't matter. Kelsie felt it in her bones, desire sweeping across the crowd. A brushfire of lust lit her up from head to toe.

For a moment, the wanting made her think of Chizara.

Of bodies and hearts mingling, hot and certain. But this was sharper, grasping, almost the opposite of love.

It was *greed*. . . .

Exactly what she'd felt in the Desert Springs Mall. Hunger. Need. Being overwhelmed by something bigger than herself—something *starving*.

She fought it, gritting her teeth, pressing her palms to her eyes.

Someone took her arm, and clarity flowed into her, displacing some of the desperation.

Kelsie remembered who she was.

"Thanks, Oliver," she said.

"I've got you," he said. "But we need to get closer."

As he steered her through the crowd, Kelsie was bumped and jostled. She stumbled and was pulled upright. Every affront nudged her closer to anger, but she was Kelsie Laszlo. Not Swarm.

She had Zara. She had friends.

"Will Flicker be okay back there?" she asked.

"Seems like she can take of herself. And we have to get to Piper."

"But it's getting worse as we get closer!"

He squeezed her arm, and another rush of his power came. Kelsie felt that sense of relief again—seeing herself, like reaching air after a long time underwater.

But the same clarity also showed Kelsie the future, that

every day would be like this. Making the choice not to lose herself, over and over and *over* again. Every minute for the rest of her life.

She would always have Swarm inside her. Waiting.

Unless she surrendered. It would be so easy to take the path of greed and violence. The crowd wanted to possess, to destroy, to *have*.

She wanted that too.

Sometimes clarity was a bitch.

"Maybe the safest thing would be to knock me out," she said. "I could swarm this whole crowd!"

"They need you, Kelsie," Oliver said. "If we shake Piper's confidence in her plan, they could turn into a mob."

"But I—"

"We're almost there."

Kelsie took a breath. This close to the float, there were gems strewn on the street, strings of emeralds and rubies and gold. Shiny enough to distract people from Beau, to make them fight.

Their greed flowed into her, their anger. Maybe they *deserved* to be swarmed, to cut each other into pieces. . . .

The float loomed, the achingly beautiful boy shining overhead.

"I'm going up to talk to Piper," Oliver said. "Keep them from losing it!"

"Wait—"

He let go of her arm, placed one foot against the side of the float. Hauled himself up by the rails, and then he was gone, along with his power.

Recognition was gone. Certainty was gone.

A moment later, Kelsie was gone.

CHAPTER 67
BELLWETHER

"WHAT THE HELL ARE YOU DOING HERE?" CAME Piper's cry.

Nate spun around—a dark-skinned kid with a peach-fuzz beard was climbing onto the float. He somehow ignored Beau's radiance, heading straight for Piper. Nate moved to intercept.

Piper waved him off.

"An old friend." She turned to the boy and laughed. "A little late to join me, isn't it, Oliver?"

"I'm not here to join you," the guy said. "I'm here to show you what this really means."

"Better late than never, I suppose," Piper said. "I've missed this."

She held out her hand. Oliver took it.

Nate felt the change right away. Something shifted in

Piper's hold over the crowd around the float, a moment of uncomfortable self-awareness.

What were they all *doing* here? It was like being at a masquerade and the masks had all come off too soon—the lights too bright, the guests too sober.

This new Zero was shaking Piper's certainty.

Nate stepped forward, reaching to pull the two apart. But when his hand grasped the boy's arm . . . something awful happened.

Nate saw it—the truth of Piper's plan.

The economy foundering as money became worthless paper. The finely tuned machinery of exchange and production breaking down. Cities crumbling, their food supplies choked off in midwinter. Millions dying in the February cold.

It was agony to see it all so clearly, and to realize that he was playing a vital part.

Worse, Nate saw how he'd fooled himself into going along, into thinking all those people were expendable. Because from the earliest days of his power, since he'd first realized how completely he could charm and influence and beguile, other people had always been expendable to him.

His friends at school. His family. Even the Zeroes. Nate had played them all, and now he was being played himself.

He pulled away and stared at Piper. She stood there, still grasping Oliver's arm, looking awed.

"You saw it too," Nate said. "You know what this plan of yours will do!"

"With gorgeous clarity." She gathered herself, smiled, and shoved Oliver backward, hard. He tumbled from the float and into the crowd. "Hit him, Troy."

Troy laughed and threw two handfuls of beads where the boy had fallen. As the crowd fell on him, Nate felt something ripple through them, a familiar hunger that set his teeth on edge. But the noise in his head was too great to recognize it.

"Get Glitch up here," Piper called, "in case he comes back."

Nate turned to her. "But you can't still . . . All those people are going to *die*!"

She focused all her radiant attention on him. "Don't go soft on me, Nate. Today we fix this stupid planet!"

For a moment he felt it again. The comforting belief that her new world, built for people like him, *had* to be better than the old one. That all those ancient arrangements of power and money and law were meaningless in this age of Zeroes.

But then he remembered Davey, torn to pieces. . . .

No one was expendable.

"I have to stop you," Nate said.

He raised his hands high, trying to find some purchase among the confused and tangled skeins of attention flowing from the crowd. He could convince her. Charm her. Bellwether her.

Piper sighed, shook her head sadly.

And from the first seconds of the battle, Nate knew that he would lose.

CHAPTER 68
FLICKER

"AT LEAST YOU TRIED, BELLWETHER," FLICKER SAID.

Nate went down, his vision fading to blackness in her head.

Flicker made another attempt to stand, using the brick wall against her back for leverage. But her legs were weak, her mind still overwhelmed from seeing Beau's beauty through so many eyes.

The crowd around her rumbled with confusion, their emotions tossed and twisted by the Zeroes battling on the float. Oliver and Kelsie had left her a block away from the action, trapped by the human mass against the wall of an old building. How the hell was she supposed to help from here?

Flicker spread her vision across the crowd—eyes were swinging toward Beau again. In this chaos, his beauty gave people something to focus on.

And once Piper had the crowd unified and connected to her machine again, she would push the button.

"Here, let me help," someone said—a girl's voice. A hand helped Flicker to her feet.

"Thanks."

"You were with him, weren't you?" the girl asked, still holding her hand. "Thibault Durant. When he went to Piper's lair last night."

Flicker spent a moment looking, but none of the nearby eyes saw anyone around her.

Then—a glimmer of dirty black hair, gone a second later.

"You're . . . her."

"Rien." The voice came from right next to Flicker, along with an unwashed smell.

The Anonymous girl that Thibault had found.

"I wanted to help you guys last night," Rien said. "But then Piper and her crew came out, and I ran."

"You can help us now," Flicker said. "She's going to—"

"I know. But in this crowd, it's hard not to fade." Rien drew nearer, her breath rasping with every word. "*You* have to stop her."

"I can barely stand." As more eyes gathered on Beau, Flicker retreated inside her own head. "And I can't even use my power with that guy being so fucking pretty."

"Yes, you can," Rien said. "You can be as pretty as him. Steal all that attention!"

Flicker didn't answer. Beau had made it sound so easy. But the idea that she, Riley Phillips, could make herself into some kind of retina-scalding beauty . . .

"That's not my style," she said.

"Girl, this isn't about your self-image," Rien snapped, squeezing Flicker's hand too tight. "This is about stopping Piper. Turn your power inside out. Now!"

"I don't know how!" But Flicker remembered Beau's words: *Stop throwing your vision into other people. Instead, draw their vision toward* you.

And what had Thibault said about avenging angels?

"Just do it," Rien said. "That boy's getting awfully fine."

"Well, shit." Flicker stood straighter. "Guess I don't have any choice but to be awesome."

She flexed the muscles of her power—the stations of her will that sent her vision outward—and gathered the dregs of her resolve.

And began to turn herself inside out.

CHAPTER 69
ANONYMOUS

"ALMOST THERE!" THIBAULT CRIED.

He'd seen it from blocks away, all that attention focused in a single direction. The crowd surging—wanting, *needing* to get closer to something around the corner.

"Can you crash it yet, Chizara?" Ethan shouted above the noise.

"No!" she yelped. Since they'd entered the thronged streets of Mardi Gras, Chizara had been wincing like her brain was being crushed.

"This way." Thibault pushed forward.

The others probably couldn't hear him. In this multitude, the Curve was strong enough to wipe him from their awareness. Enough to erase him completely if he wasn't careful, wasn't mindful about keeping himself present.

The massive crowd fizzed and roared ahead. Whatever was grabbing everyone's attention had a brutal pull. It made Nate's greedy power look like gentle persuasion.

The moment they rounded the corner, Thibault's gaze was snared like everyone else's, bent around and lifted, hopelessly stuck—

The boy seemed to hover above the crowd. His beauty was a spear through Thibault's chest. Perfectly self-assured, without swagger or ego. Visibly, transcendently good. Entirely at peace with himself.

And beautiful.

It took Thibault a moment to realize that the boy was on a parade float. Purple, green, and gold. Krewe de New World Order.

"That's Piper's machine!" he cried, pointing. "Shut it down!"

Chizara squeezed her eyes shut, shook her head. "I can't feel it. There's too much noise! Too many phones!"

"Damn," Ethan said. "Maybe we should just go punch Piper!"

"Keep trying, Crash," Thibault yelled. "I'll run ahead and see what I can do!"

He dove into the crowd, wriggling through, always at the edge of erasure. Their attention, their focus on the beautiful boy, grew thicker, stronger, with every second.

Surely Piper was about to start up her device.

The crush grew worse as he neared the float. He'd never get through. These people couldn't see him—they kept digging their elbows into his already bruised ribs.

But then something shifted in the air above him. The focus of the crowd swung around.

Thibault turned. He looked up and followed the sheaf of attention that was falling the other way. They were all looking at someone *else*. . . .

A girl was being lifted up on people's shoulders. A girl full of glamour, and fearsomeness, and authority. He'd never seen anyone like her, never wanted so badly to be near someone. His whole body ached with it, and he pressed forward with the rest. He needed to be near her, needed to see the eyes hidden behind those dark glasses. . . .

"She's mine!" he cried out from his very depths.

Because it was *Flicker* up there.

Shock threw him from the vision. And for a moment, before her power grabbed hold of his brain again, he saw the reality behind the transformation: his girlfriend superimposed on this inhuman beauty.

Then she was an angel again, and two agonies warred inside him—jealous rage, now that everyone saw a truth that had been his alone, and loss, because like a titanic fool he had walked away from her.

He let out a moan of pain, covetous and unworthy.

Just faintly Thibault registered how absurd it all was. This was just Flicker twisting her power around, fueled by the massive crowd. All this glamour was for one simple reason—to create a distraction.

She didn't want his worship. She wanted him to stop Piper.

He reached up and sliced his own attention away, breaking her spell. Then he turned and fought against the crowd. It surged away from the float now, relieving the press of bodies, making way for him. He was nearly there.

But a familiar black-clad figure was scrambling to a vantage point halfway up the throne.

"Glitch," he whispered.

She turned, and flung out an arm—

Power arced out of her on a wave of confusion. Thibault's world whipped sideways in meaning, and a thousand bewildered cries rose around him.

But he knew the target. He turned and saw Flicker's glory wrench and sputter. She fell to the street as the crowd that had lifted her melted, addled, crying out in fear.

Thibault turned back toward the float, his rage lighting it in hyperreal detail:

Glitch smirking, like she expected applause.

Verity on the float, straining in her seat, desperation on her face.

Piper in a triumphant stance, with *Nate* sprawled at her feet!

The crowd's attention began to coalesce again. Drawn back

toward the beautiful boy, high up on the float, his face awe-inspiring perfection again.

Thibault pushed forward again, his teeth set in anger.

He didn't have much time. And he was ready to hurt some-one.

CHAPTER 70
CRASH

"CRASH THAT THING!" ETHAN CRIED. "QUICK!"

Chizara growled, eyes shut in concentration as they forced through the melee toward the float.

She couldn't let her gaze glom on to that angel boy and his wondrous face, or she wouldn't be able to think of anything else. Like the fact that Flicker had been a goddess about ten seconds ago, a phoenix of brain-rattling beauty, only to be struck down by Glitch.

Chizara sought out a space inside herself, trying to ignore the madness of everything happening, the shrieking galaxy of phones. The desperate wondering: *Where's Kelsie? What's this crowd doing to her?*

What will she *do to this crowd?*

Crash reached out through the phone pain, through the

roar of the city, grasping at the workings of that transmitter.

But the machine felt dead, like an abandoned car with the barest trickle of juice in its battery. She forced her Crash power hard at the thing and felt a familiar dullness, that barrier of mesh inside the swags of glittery bunting.

Damn. The device inside the float was power-shielded.

Her eyes flew open, and there was Piper, lifting her hands above the control panel, a smug smile on her face.

"I can't crash it!" Chizara cried.

"Keep trying!" Ethan yelled. "Maybe I can help Thibault!"

He ran off, leaving her wondering . . . *Teebo?*

The name slipped away into the noise around her, because everyone was calling up to the beautiful boy on his throne. No one was watching Piper. No one cared that she was about to blow their world apart.

And Chizara realized . . .

There was only one way to stop this.

Resisting the beautiful boy's enchantment with an effort that made her eyes ache, Chizara riveted her gaze on Piper. And reached out toward *her*.

There was no choice.

It took all the finesse, every scrap of precision Chizara possessed, to slide her power through the incoming barrage of signal. She slipped past everyone's phones and cameras, past the scream of hotel wifi and storefront tech nagging her from all around.

She focused, and it was like being deep underwater, all the street noise gone silent, with only glimmers of phosphorescent fish pulsing in the darkness.

A cloud of heart fish. Brain fish.

She had to do this. She had to become everything her mother had warned her against.

Piper reached out for the controls.

Chizara made her move.

It was a small move, the smallest she knew how to make. Across the twenty yards that separated them, Chizara singled out Piper's heart and brain where they hovered.

Pulse-pulse.

Flash-flash.

She pinched them out. It took no more energy than blinking. She snuffed that brain and heart out into the oceanic darkness.

It was so ordinary, watching Piper fall. Her head went limp and rolled backward, her body slumping next to Nate's.

A moment ago, Flicker's collapse had lit a wild anger in Chizara. But this tumble made horror blossom. What she'd done was evil, wrong, and there was no way back from it. No way to uncrash hearts and brains.

Just like Ethan's voice had predicted two summers ago . . .

She was a demon now.

CHAPTER 71
ANONYMOUS

THIBAULT SAW PIPER DIE IN FRONT OF HIM.

Her hand fell limp and bounced from the edge of the control panel. The smug expression went from her face, the glitter of focus from her eyes. She slumped sideways, rolling onto Nate's unconscious form.

But she wasn't just unconscious. He knew at once.

Just like Craig's lifeless body outside the Dish, but this time Thibault had *seen* it happen. Had watched Piper disconnect from the lacework of humanity.

A girl in a suit and tie clambered down from the rightmost seat of the float. She knelt beside the empty husk. "Piper? Ren! Something's wrong!"

Thibault turned, and his anger rushed back.

Ren—Glitch—who'd tossed Flicker aside like a piece

of trash, was making her way down from halfway up the throne.

Thibault didn't even think. He threw himself forward, scrambling across the float. As Ren reached the controls, where the other girl was still cradling Piper's head, he reached out and grabbed them both.

They looked up, startled as he appeared from nowhere, but Thibault didn't give Ren time to use her power.

He flung himself, flung all three of them away from this disaster, far out into the void, where they could do nothing, harm no one.

Farther away than he'd ever gone.

CHAPTER 72
SWARM

AS KELSIE FELT PIPER DIE, THE LEASH SLIPPED
from the swarm.

It was a small thing at first, that loss of one Charismatic,
with so much going on. Priceless gems underfoot. The dueling
angels at opposite ends of the street. The waves of clarity and
charisma and glitchiness and honesty that billowed out from
the float in turn. And underneath it, the hunger that threatened
to break out and consume them all.

Kelsie—what was left of her—was stretched so thin, her
will at the breaking point. And as Piper snuffed out, it was clear
that only her hold on the crowd had been keeping it together.

Swarm was rising now.

Then someone yelled, "It's the cops!"

"Perfect timing," Swarm murmured to herself.

Black flak jackets with white letters across the front and back surged into the crowd, heading for the float. Their training kept them distinct from the throng, so far.

But Swarm could easily make them part of her.

Agent Phan was shouting through a bullhorn, telling everyone to clear the way. His tenor of authority stilled the crowd for a moment, steadied them with some distant memory of civilization.

But Swarm reached out and took her followers back, blended these newcomers into the mass.

The buzz was building, her body extending up and down the street. But even at the edges of the swarm, there wasn't room for running. Not enough space for the trick of furious motion that Quinton Wallace had taught her at the Desert Springs Mall.

So much struggle, compressed into such a small area. But maybe this packed parade route was just the core of her swarm, and she could spread out to take the whole city . . . even more.

"Kelsie," came a voice.

Swarm looked down at a bloodied face. A guy the crowd had fallen upon a moment ago. Gems sparkled on the ground around him.

"Take my hand," he pleaded. "You don't want this."

Meaningless words, but some human reflex made her reach out, and his fingers brushed hers.

And Swarm understood with perfect clarity—she *did* want this.

She didn't want to be on the run anymore. Or held in some prison, alone forever in a cell. Her fear of that arced and spat, sending anger through the crowd. She wanted multitudes around her, always, forever.

The crowd vibrated beneath her. The bloody-faced guy clung to her, pumping certainty into her veins.

This was what she'd always been . . . love at its most terrible and pure.

Swarm looked out across the horde—her new body, her destiny—and smiled.

Then her heart skipped a beat, and she gasped.

It happened again, something twisting sideways. The faintest wrong flutter in her chest, as if two fingers had pinched her heart.

"Zara?" she whispered.

Zara was going to stop this. By killing her.

Swarm drew back in incomprehension, but Kelsie shut her eyes. Thankful.

Do it. Don't let me take them all.

Then Oliver—she knew his name again—squeezed her hand harder. Something pushed into her, a new sliver of understanding.

What if Swarm could be bargained with? Satisfied and then put aside, as long as she took a Zero into herself? She could save all these people.

And she only had to sacrifice one.

Kelsie looked up at the beautiful boy, the center of everyone's attention. Of course it had to be him. Just one life to save the rest.

Her hunger guided them.

And she was lifted up.

CHAPTER 73
SCAM

ETHAN'S EYES WERE VIBRATING.

He knew this feeling. He'd been like this before, at Officer Delgado's funeral, when he and his mom and every cop in Cambria had been . . .

Swarmed.

He swept up onto the float, carried along in the press of jittering bodies, a buzzing darkness crowding out every thought. Ahead of him the crowd was already climbing the spire in the middle, up to that throne, reaching for the figure who vibrated and shuddered, blinding bright and beautiful up there.

They reached him, a maelstrom of hands and screams and teeth. To Ethan's swarmed ears, it sounded beautiful. Blood rained down across the float, pieces of costume and bits of flesh.

A mask was flung, spinning away.

In a few ravenous moments they consumed the angel boy.

A moment later Ethan's eyes stilled in his head. People stood all over the float, released again. They were staring at their hands, looking at all the blood, stunned for the moment.

A familiar figure lay in front of Ethan.

"Nate?" he asked.

He knelt, checked for a pulse. But it was impossible to feel anything over the thudding of his own heart. The crowd was panicking now, starting to stream down from the float. A guy in a sparkly mirror suit pushed past Ethan and jumped into the throng.

"Turn off the machine!" came a ragged voice.

Ethan turned. It was Verity, still handcuffed to her chair. Some kid with a bloody face was lowering Kelsie into the middle seat. She looked dazed, her eyes rolled back in her head.

Was another dose of Swarm coming?

"Nexus is still full of power!" Verity cried. "Shut it down!"

"Okay, okay!" Ethan replied, and turned to face the controls.

Another body was slumped beside the panel—Piper.

And that was when he knew that Nate had to be alive. Because Piper looked completely different from him. She was just . . . gone. Her face too pale, her body too still.

There was a big red button in the middle of that panel. Clearly *not* the right one to push. Around it was a constellation of switches and gauges, but nothing was marked.

The sound of the crowd around him was changing again.

"What now?" he looked up.

But he knew that buzz sweeping across the throng. An army of bees. And out in the crowd, freaky rattling eyeballs and chattering teeth. He hated that look.

"It's happening again!" Verity cried.

"I can *see that*!" Ethan yelled.

Beside her, Kelsie was waking up, getting that evil look on her face again. The guy on the chair beside her was holding her hand, as if he could argue her out of becoming a Swarm and tearing them all to pieces.

Verity strained in her seat, trying to free her wrists. Ethan felt sick. It was the exact way Davey had died. But this time Beau was only the first of many.

"Nate!" Ethan cried. "Wake up! Help me figure out these controls!"

He slapped Nate's face—no response.

Ethan felt the vibration filling his bones, spreading into his mind.

Happy thoughts! Happy thoughts!

He wasn't sad. He wasn't angry. No reason to join a swarm!

Yesterday had been the best day of his whole freakin' life. Sonia Sonic had kissed him! She was the coolest girl he knew.

And she had *kissed* him.

Happy sunshine thoughts!

But the however many thousands of people around the

float didn't seem to feel that way. The buzzing spread in all directions, the crowd lifting up like a tsunami again, climbing on top of one another.

Beneath him, the float rocked and shuddered. People were mounting the sides, hauling themselves up by the metal rails. The surface tipped, like a ship in a storm. Verity was screaming.

They all should have gone to Mexico. Whatever Piper's plan had been, it probably wouldn't have worked out *this* badly.

But that wasn't a happy thought! He had to keep thinking—

"Sonia," he gasped.

She was climbing the railing at the front of the float. Her teeth chattered and her eyes rolled sightlessly.

Typical. He was going to be killed by the first girl he'd ever really kissed. Who was dressed like a penguin.

Ethan struggled to stand. To run . . . somewhere.

The float heaved again, tipping Ethan forward. He threw out his hands to stop his fall—the control panel came up at him.

"Uh-oh," Ethan said.

He watched his outstretched hands fall upon the big red button, and then his brain exploded across the universe.

CHAPTER 74
NEXUS

KELSIE LASZLO

All at once, an overwhelming tsunami of noise hit Swarm's body.

It vibrated up her spine, echoing in her ears, shuddering in her temples. It squeezed her lungs until she was gasping for air. The relentless force of it rolled on and on, flattening her, turning her bones to paste. So vast and loud that she was lost in the noise of it.

This was her chance to make them all into a single swarm. One body. One beast.

All of humanity. Forever.

But in that murderous ecstasy she felt something else.

A small voice inside her—Beau. She remembered the crowd of lost souls inside Quinton Wallace, all the Zeroes he'd killed. All those lives consumed.

And now a small glittering particle of Beau was inside her, too. Also forever.

A sadness swept over Kelsie. She'd done what she had sworn never to do, and there was no escaping that.

But that sadness formed the kernel of her fight to remember herself. To remember that she had friends, had Zara. Had a mother and two little brothers.

She could deny the Swarm inside her and make her own choice. She could forgive herself, and keep the struggle going for another minute, another day.

Kelsie chose to fight.

CHIZARA OKEKE

They all felt it happen. But only Chizara knew what it meant.

She'd been so close to doing the unthinkable, with her power wrapped around Kelsie's heart, ready to prevent a slaughter, to make up for being a demon. . . .

But then the shielding around the guts of Nexus split apart. A glorious maelstrom of complexity erupted, blazed with the force of a celebration a million strong, crashing against the exosphere, flashing down again. With the suddenness of a big bang, the transmitter flung three powers out across the world, from the Zeroes sitting on the float's three chairs.

Verity. Clarity. Mob.

A lightning storm of signal encased the globe, struck everywhere, changed everything.

It was massive, the speed of it, the force.

All Chizara could see, all she could *feel*, was the lightning storm. How had Essence and her crew *made* this thing? It was so powerful it should have blasted itself apart with its own strength. What gigantic, monstrously subtle genius!

Chizara saw what it had been designed to do, and the supervillain part of her could only laugh. It was meant to pull the world apart, impoverishing billions, creating chaos. Crashing banking systems, blowing apart a thousand police stations. Melting the very concept of money. Shredding even the memory of lies.

The scale of it was beautiful. As was the fact that the geyser of energy carried her mind along, so she could *see* the world wrapped in powers.

But a different set of powers than intended.

Instead of Verity, Coin, and Crash . . .

. . . Verity, Clarity, and Mob rained down.

They came out of the sky in a lacework of lightning, connecting separately, multitudinously, to everything, to everyone. Divided into electric mist to touch everyone in the crowd around her, activating who-knew-what in everyone's bodies and brains. Across the city, the continent, the world, the whole of humanity lit up and changed before her mind's eye.

Chizara herself changed—she felt the zap and rattle of the transformation, the pains and pleasures of being crashed and rebooted.

Soon enough, when this eon passed, she'd know what was happening to her, to the world. But for now, this front-row seat at the change itself, the god fingers reaching down from the fire-splashed heavens, the angel touch lighting up parts and paths too tiny for humans to yet have the means to see—that was all that existed, all she cared about, all she ever wanted.

THIBAULT DURANT

The three of them floated there, nameless, knowledgeless. Any farther and they'd melt away into the darkness. No way back—no need, no desire.

Good-bye, Flicker.

That last twitch of her name kept the boy's eyes open. Staring through the scrim of stars, across the distance between him and the broken world. And a nagging thought kept him from slipping away: He'd stolen these two people, taken them without consent into the Nowhere.

They deserved it! he roared at himself, but rage sounded puny and petty out here. He had to take them back.

And as he pushed closer to reality, he could see that it was busy falling apart.

Some vast force was spreading from this machine, shaking everything down to its foundations. The bones of the old world were crumbling.

Everything was different now.

Piper had won. Or maybe, against all logic, the Cambria

Five had thwarted her. But whatever had happened, there would be new battles to fight now.

The boy murmured a proverb:

"Let go over a cliff, die completely, and then come back to life."

And he steeled himself for more.

He had no choice but to take up his earthly existence again. Running away didn't fix anything, and there were always, always, always things that needed fixing. So all he could do was revel in any human connection that came his way—*Flicker,* he said again—and be ready to accept a world whose gaze might never meet his, from now until the end of his days.

And hey, what if this new world was one worth returning to?

NATANIEL SALDANA

Something jolted him awake, like an earthquake in the middle of the night.

For a moment Nate didn't understand. Then his eyes opened, and he saw Nexus spewing a glorious fountain of crowd stuff into the sky. The energies of a million people stored and compressed and then sent heavenward . . .

Earthward, really. The fountain arced against the dome of the sky, spreading out in all directions.

Piper had humbled him again.

From the first moment, she'd shown him how small he was. A boy from a small city, with small plans. A small crew who barely tolerated each other.

But this new humbling was something else entirely. A world-changing event. Piper bending reality to her will.

Until Nate realized—

Piper's plan had come undone. She lay beside him, unmoving, and all around was chaos. Blood and bodies and tumult. Even the triumvirate wasn't the one she'd planned.

Verity was still in her seat, but some new boy with a bloodied face was to her left . . . and in the third seat?

Kelsie. One of his Zeroes.

A third of the Krewe de New World Order was *his*.

Nate smiled, deciding to call that a victory.

RILEY PHILLIPS

The world had fifteen billion eyes, and Flicker could see through all of them.

Every.

Single.

One.

And it was pretty fucking awesome.

She was done being a sidekick, stuck in Nate's shadow. Done worrying about stepping on toes. Done with using only one side of her power.

Terrorist or avenging angel, good or evil twin, love of Thibault's life or the chain that kept him bound to this heartless, broken world—she could be everything at once.

Because she was pretty fucking awesome too.

CHAPTER 75
ETHAN THOMAS COOPER

"ETHAN, CAN YOU HEAR ME?"

It was Sonia's voice. It sounded very far away. Like he was underwater.

He rolled onto his back. Why did he always end up face-down on the ground? And what the hell had happened?

It felt like an explosion had gone off in his brain.

"Ethan!"

Sonia kept saying his name over and over. He tried to signal that he was okay, that if she would just let him rest here for a minute, everything would be fine. He'd get up and walk away. Before Phan found them. Before Piper zapped them all with juiced-up superpowers.

Wait, had that already happened?

He sat up gingerly. He seemed to be in one piece.

"You're alive," Sonia said.

He nodded—he *was* alive. Especially his brain, which was on fire.

Sonia looked great in her penguin costume. She always looked great. Smartest, most switched-on girl he'd ever meet. He knew that for sure.

He knew a lot of things for sure. It was the weirdest feeling, knowing everything and being certain about it.

He knew that all over the world, thousands of bankers, fund managers, and financiers were having the same revelation right now. A need to tell the truth had shaken them hard, and all at once they were deciding to spill the beans about their companies' crooked schemes.

Ethan also knew that, starting today, countless tech heads would focus less on making clever gadgets and more on creating decent communities. Suddenly people could *feel* the feedback loops online, in that gut-level way Kelsie felt crowds, so taking hatred and bullying out of those loops would be a priority from here on out.

He also knew that blasts of clarity were hitting people the world over, making billions of small repairs in families and workplaces and sports teams and marching bands and class-rooms and small towns and political parties and big cities that would, over the next few decades, bubble up into real change.

Best of all, he knew the Feds would never lock him up.

Crap. That was a lot to know. Maybe his brain really *had*

exploded. What the hell did Ethan Thomas Cooper know about banking or tech or politics?

He tried to open his mouth to ask Sonia, but his mouth still wasn't working.

"What happened?" she asked.

The world had changed. Nexus had spat out truth, clarity, and a big loving dose of Kelsie Laszlo.

But here around them, all was silent.

He looked around. Nobody was moving.

"Are they all dead?" Sonia whispered.

Ethan shook his head. Only Piper and Beau were dead. This street might look like the end of a very long slasher film, but all those people were just resting. Pretty much everyone in the world was going to sleep well tonight.

"Okay, good," she said. "I was worried. I think I love you."

Sonia's eyes went wide with horror.

"Oops, I didn't mean . . ."

Ethan could only chuckle. He knew that too—that he and Sonia loved each other.

He pointed at Verity, but Sonia didn't understand. Not yet.

With Verity's power projected around the world, nobody was going to lie for . . . three months, ten days, and sixteen hours. At that moment, Ethan somehow knew, a kid named Guo Huateng was going to tell his mom that he'd done his homework, when he hadn't. Inside eight months, lying would make a comeback worldwide. But those months of the unvarnished truth would make everyone think a little harder before they rained bullshit on the world again.

Damn, Ethan thought. He really *did* know a lot.

Too bad Piper would never get to see the new world she'd helped make. That new world was pretty awesome.

With enough clarity, the truth wasn't such a bad thing to hear. Especially when everyone had a Kelsie Laszlo–DJed dance party in their head, all day long.

"Let's get you out of here," Sonia said.

She dragged him up by an elbow until he was standing—unsteadily—on his feet. She pulled him down from the float and through the crowd. Sleeping people were everywhere.

It was so peaceful.

Even when they all woke up, the world wasn't going back to the shitshow it had been. A lot would change in those long months of honesty and clarity and Kelsieness. Corruption disrupted. Governments overturned. Laws changed.

But much more important were the small groups that would form during those months of truth and clarity. Crews of five to seven people that would last long after the other echoes of Nexus had faded, and would help to build a world where no one was excluded or misunderstood. Where no one reacted out of brain-clouded fear.

Ethan recalled—or maybe just *knew*, because he knew everything now—a Martin Luther King quote, that all evil needed to succeed was for good people to do nothing. And he realized that it also worked the other way around:

All that good needed to succeed was for evil to take a few months off.

The problem was, that had never happened before.

Around the corner from the float, he and Sonia found people who were awake. Not just awake—they were slow dancing.

Ethan grinned. All these people, hanging on to each other, holding each other, a big happy crowd beast. Not what Piper had planned, exactly. But the best outcome Ethan could imagine, and suddenly he could imagine a lot.

He turned to Sonia. She was grinning too.

He kissed her lightly, and Sonia squeezed his arm. She pushed him further along the street. When he realize that she was guiding him toward a diner, he gave her a questioning look.

"Seriously?" she said. "You, not talking? You must need food."

Did he?

Ethan knew a lot now, with the barrier between his omniscient voice and his brain blown away by Piper's machine (huh, so *that* was what had happened), but until the smell of hash browns hit him, he hadn't realized how hungry he was.

Like Sonia knew him better than he knew himself.

The staff ignored them as they entered the diner. They were all pressed up against the windows, staring out at the change in the crowd. From the boisterous chaos of Mardi Gras to people slow dancing.

Nothing to worry about. The party would be back on by sundown, more rambunctious than ever.

Ethan found a booth with red vinyl seats and a table fixed to the wall. Perfect. He sat down and spread his hands on the freshly cleaned Formica.

"You think your friends are okay?" Sonia asked.

Ethan nodded. He could see what the Zeroes had in store. Every choice that would lead them toward their destinies.

Nate was going into politics, but not the elected kind. From now on, prison reform was his jam. No stopping that guy. He and Phan would work on the Powers Amnesty Act together. For everyone, even the kids who hadn't been born yet, so people could explore their powers, unafraid. Ethan's mom would wind up on the nondiscrimination task force. And years down the line his sister, Jess, as a federal marshal, would enforce the ever-living shit out of it.

Eventually there would be backlash, as there always was when a new group of people had their humanity recognized, but Flicker would protect the Amnesty Act from the bench. Seeing from other people's points of view was a pretty useful move when you were a federal judge.

As was turning into an avenging angel of retina-burning beauty.

Chizara was going to become a surgeon. Her work would be cutting-edge, which was a nifty trick for someone who never used a knife. She was going to give "Do no harm" a whole new meaning. A vast wave of Makers would follow her example, fine-tuning human bodies into healthier machines.

Thibault's future was harder to see. For a while, he'd move around. Town to town, country to country. Working with people one on one. Taking care of loners. People who got ignored, who needed a friend. As for him and Flicker . . . well, that was private.

But they would always be there to help each other see.

And then there was Kelsie. Ethan had to laugh. No one even had a word yet for what she would become. DJ ambassador? Negotiator-at-large? Planetary music therapist? People would love her, always, because no one would ever forget that microsecond after she defeated Swarm, when they were all in her head, feeling what she felt.

Which was love. For everyone.

Even her own mom.

There was a lot she could do for a world in which everyone trusted her. In fact, everyone would go on trusting her, no matter what, even if she turned evil one day and really did bring down that endless, global swarm.

Lucky for humanity, Chizara would always be there to keep her honest.

A waitress finally noticed them sitting at the back and came to take their order.

"You guys see what went down on Bourbon Street?" she asked.

"Front-row seat," Sonia said. "It was kind of like . . . an explosion."

The waitress's eyes widened. "Is everyone okay?"

Sonia nodded. "Mostly. Coffee?"

"Sure thing, Penguin Girl." The waitress looked at Ethan. "And for you?"

Ethan opened his mouth to order something—anything—but he was overwhelmed by another omniscient kick to the brain. He could see the waitress going home tonight, ready to tell her boyfriend she wanted to get pregnant. But when she got there, he was gone. Packed up while she was working and fled to another town.

Ethan tried to talk. He wanted to tell her it was all going to be okay. She was better off without him anyhow. So was her kid, who would come in three years. And that kid was going to be amazing. Smart and capable and talented and extra-freaking-superpowered.

One of the next generation, the Ones, with way better abilities than the—let's all face it—generally crappy Zero powers.

But Ethan couldn't tell her any of that, because his voice was gone. His Zeroes voice and his real voice. They existed only inside his skull.

He knew everything, but he couldn't say any of it.

"Ethan?" Sonia asked again.

No big deal. He didn't need a voice to communicate. And anyhow, Nexus had caused this. It was only temporary. Maybe?

His own future was one thing he couldn't see.

Ethan gently wrested the waitress's order pad from her hand and gestured for her pencil. She handed it over, not hiding her pity.

He positioned the pencil over the pad, ready to scribble down everything he'd just realized, about everyone. The waitress, the Zeroes, *everyone*. He rubbed his eyes and wondered how to begin. It was such a giant, intricate jigsaw that he didn't want to skip any details.

Fitting it all down on one notepad would be impossible. He'd need months. He'd need help from Sonia to make his writing sing. But it would be his contribution to the new world order. His and Sonia's.

He hoped so, anyhow.

After a minute he leaned back and gave up with a sigh—he'd only managed to scrawl two words in his spidery handwriting.

Sonia took the pad and read it, her eyebrows raised.

"Poor kid," the waitress said. "What's he want?"

Sonia looked at Ethan, and grinned.

"It says, 'More coffee.'"